# EMISSARY

E.B. BROOKS

Second Edition: September 2023

ISBN 978-1-7347398-8-6 (ebook)

ISBN 978-1-7347398-6-2 (Paperback)

ISBN 978-1-7347398-7-9 (Hardcover)


First Edition: April 2020

ISBN 978-1-7347398-2-4 (ebook)

ISBN 978-1-7347398-0-0 (Paperback)

ISBN 978-1-7347398-1-7 (Hardcover)


Cover art by Julisa Basak, based on concept by Kirk DouPonce

Maps by Soraya Corcoran

Sheet music written with MuseScore v3.4.2

❀ Created with Vellum

*To my children, and all the dreamers*

# CONTENTS

To provide and maintain a secure arena for the nurturing and refinement of the essential qualities of humankind.

To guard and shelter what remains, holding it in trust for our descendants.

To endure and survive, until we earn the Mother's forgiveness.

— MISSION STATEMENT OF THE CENTRE
FOR THE PRESERVATION OF THE HUMAN
LEGACY

# PROLOGUE

Treanna thought the day would never end.

Not that it was a particularly hard day, or unusual. If anything, the perfect usualness, the dreary precision of it all, beat at her skull. As she had every day since becoming full-time with Caretaking, she'd reported in at the administration desk at the nexus above the game floors. Chief Pell handed her a task list, with routes optimized by the Centre's LOGOS operating system to keep her in one of the six assemblages whenever possible. That was a small kindness; the assemblages had no connections except for the nexus, and each was nearly a mile across. Multiply that by the hundreds of tubes she'd inspected today, and…

Caretakers had the best legs in the Centre. That was the most common line from the people who propositioned her.

Treanna sighed and leaned against the glass, massaging her calves as the elevator took her back up. Innumerable small lights, mostly green with the occasional red and blue scattered throughout, drifted past her as the elevator climbed, like motes of the fairy fire she'd read about but never seen. The lights weren't her problem anymore. Not until tomorrow's shift, at least.

Not until Grandfather formally announced her candidacy as Chief Pell's successor, any month now. Then they would all be her responsibility, for the rest of her life.

As she ascended in silence, Treanna indulged in a moment of despondency as she reviewed her day's work, thumbing the names and statuses across her duty tablet. Four hundred thirty-eight egg extractions, two hundred ninety-six sperm collections. All clinically done, and not a word exchanged with any of the donors. No one would know; no one would care. And her own descendants, such as they were, would have more of the same. Nothing to aspire to, beyond a chief's insignia or the Director's seat.

*We're nothing but midwives for the Mother,* she thought sadly. *But she's as good as dead, and her children might as well be, for all we've accomplished in her absence.*

At least she hadn't been on red-light duty this time. All the hot water in the Centre couldn't wash away the stench of hydrobiotic catalysts and disinfectants.

The elevator drew to its apex, and the glass doors released her onto the moving walkway from Assemblage Five to the nexus proper. As Treanna let it take her forward, her eyes adjusted to the brightening light, a welcome transition before the inevitable glares in the residential level above.

She turned over her duty tablet to Chief Pell with a practiced smile. "All finished, ma'am."

"Thank you, dear." Maura Pell took the device with a wrinkled but steady russet hand, sharp in contrast to Treanna's pink ivory. Her fingers closed carefully around the tablet, as though the names it contained were the same as the lives registered to them. "Oh, and Annie, will you let your grandfather know I'll be late to tomorrow's staff meeting? I've got an appointment with Angela in Medical."

Treanna suppressed a scowl. *I asked people to stop calling me that when I came of age. It's already been four months!* "Can't you reschedule it?" she asked.

"Not at my age," the chief replied mildly.

When no further explanation followed, Treanna suppressed a sigh as well. Grandfather didn't like being surprised, and she'd learned over the years to agree with him. The days were crushing in their sameness, true, but if history had taught her anything, it was that change was rarely for the better.

"I'll inform him," Treanna said. "Is my relief here yet?"

Chief Pell smiled kindly at her. "Michael will be along shortly; you needn't wait." Her eyes unfocused, and her smile became wistful. "I remember how valuable nights were, at your age. Do you have any plans?"

Treanna stiffened. "Nothing out of the ordinary."

"That's lovely, dear. Have a nice time."

She ran into Michael at the main elevator. He smiled and dipped his head, avoiding eye contact the way he typically did. "Hello, Treanna."

"Michael," she replied, finding she didn't have to force warmth into her voice for a change. The young man's face was blistered over in the worst case of acne she'd ever heard of, the red spots making his face appear even paler by comparison. That alone made him ostracized by the more superficial, hedonistic staff. *It's their loss,* she thought. Under that face lay an empathetic mind and a generous spirit. "How are you?"

"I'm well," he said, his voice the soft near-whisper that most caretakers adopted on the game floors. "I hope I haven't kept you."

Treanna smiled. "Not at all."

She didn't have anything more to say, but she also didn't have anywhere to go. No one else to speak with, not that she was speaking now. The silence between them lengthened into awkwardness.

"So…is there anything new to report?" Michael asked.

Treanna shook her head, mentally slapping herself. *What am I doing?* "No. Nothing ever changes."

She let him pass, then rode the elevator up to the residential level, where she stepped out and squinted down the arterial corridor. Other staff members moved quietly along its walls, keeping clear of the middle to maintain good traffic flow. One or two of them glanced up at her, but when they recognized her, they averted their eyes. Unlike Michael, they looked elsewhere on her body—until they saw her hands curling into fists.

*I don't know why I expect anything different*, she thought with an inner snarl. *I'm fresh meat, for now at least.*

Not wanting to deal with more of the same, she ignored her own hunger as she made her way past the crowded dining hall to her quarters. Her quarters. The idea was still strange, even after months of residency. Grandfather was still nearby, of course, but now that she was seventeen years old, it was expected that she would want to have a private space, for entertainment purposes if nothing else.

*One day*, she mused as she stripped out of her uniform and made for the shower. *Just…not because of everyone's expectations, and not until I choose.*

When she'd finished drying and changed into pajamas, she flung herself into her bed, taking pleasure in both the creak of the springs and the absence of Grandfather to scold her for abusing the equipment. The pleasure was as short-lived as the sound, though, and in moments she was doing the same thing she did every night: lying on her back to stare up at the moss covering the ceiling, wishing it would give her a fresh opportunity along with the oxygen it provided.

What else was there to look forward to? Tomorrow's shift?

Treanna lay there, letting the day's names and numbers trickle away from her mind. Such variety in those names. She'd asked Gabriel once if they were assigned, but he'd laughed, given her that sympathetic, commiserating smile, and explained that such choices weren't left to the staff.

He did have a nice smile. And those intelligent blue eyes had a quiet desperation in them, as if he was as bored and lonely as she was and they both knew it. As if they were the only people in the Centre who truly saw things as they were.

Hopeless, and so dull it wasn't even worth crying about.

Treanna sighed again and reached for her personal tablet on the nightstand. A short query later, and she was reading from her favorite ancient tales about valiant knights and formidable ladies, of the politics of the court and the occasional audacity that upended them. There were friends in those stories, people who had more to offer than a leer and a spiritless embrace. People who also shared her desperation, but didn't have to be quiet about it. People who knew how to change the world, for better or worse.

That brought a pang of bitterness. *Mother of all...why couldn't it have been for better?*

She allowed herself the fleeting amusement of picturing Grandfather as a stern king, and Michael and Gabriel as radiant knights jousting for the honor of doing her bidding, but such fantasies were only that: fantasies. Her world had no room for them, not anymore. All that was left was an endless, thankless slog with no vision of how or when it would ever end, much less a guarantee.

Treanna sighed and returned the tablet to its place. The darkness closed in around her, the silence. She might as well have been at work again. She might as well be logged in on the game floors, lying there in a tube instead of here, like she would have...

She violently pushed that thought away. Grandfather was

right: no matter how bleak things were in the Centre, it was the only place where anyone could accomplish something. Leave the dreams tucked into the Mother's womb, he would tell her; the Centre needed to act to preserve those dreams, not emulate them. They needed to survive, because without that, they truly would have nothing.

It was no wonder the staff sought comfort with one another. Any comfort, no matter how fleeting or meaningless.

Ten minutes later, Treanna walked through the door to Grandfather's apartment. He'd left the lock keyed to her voiceprint, and she'd used it when the loneliness got to her, sleeping in her old room while he worked through the night. She admired that about him. Loved it, even: that constant, unspoken consideration throughout a life of care. Grandfather always put the Centre first, no matter the personal cost, because to do so was to put humanity first.

But tonight, the apartment was as empty as Treanna's had been. She considered going back; then she walked to her old room and lay on the bed. It was closer at this point, and it wasn't as if anyone would notice the difference.

She'd almost gotten to sleep when she heard the voices.

"Please, come in." Grandfather's voice. A deep voice, firm but not unkind, though Treanna immediately sensed an undercurrent of tension. *That's odd; why would he be tense? It could only be Alice he's inviting home, at this hour.*

But the voice that responded was male; she recognized it as Chief Root's. "Thank you, sir. I'm sorry for the inconvenience, but for this, I feel safer underground."

"I completely understand, Ben," Grandfather said.

Treanna stepped silently to her closed door, almost without realizing it. An uneasiness began to form in her belly. What would make the chief of Scouting prefer the residential level? And what did he mean about safety?

She cracked the door an inch.

The two men in the next room sat: Grandfather with care, Chief Root with a violent exhaustion. The chief let out a long, shuddering sigh.

"When you're ready," Grandfather prompted, his face grave. In the room's low light, his almond skin looked ashen.

Ben sighed again and buried his face in his weathered sandstone hands. "All these years with nothing but sand and rubble...now we've got ten dead."

"Accidents have happened before," Grandfather said. "The Wastes claim the unwary."

Ben looked up with a glare that startled Treanna not least because it was Grandfather he dared to use it on. "My people are sharper than that. I've got Karl's report; his crews went over the wreck. Carmine, the blast originated in the control room."

He passed Grandfather a tablet, and as the older man reviewed it, frown deepening, Treanna's breath caught. Scouting crews kept explosives on board the harvester transports to facilitate accessing materials, but those wouldn't be stored in the control room. *They certainly wouldn't be detonated there.*

At length, Grandfather put the tablet in his lap and cleared his throat. "What do you believe happened?"

Ben lowered his voice, as if he somehow realized Treanna was eavesdropping. "Karl ran the ballistics report by Gabe's team—"

"Without my permission?" This time, it was Grandfather who glared. "How many people know about this incident?"

Ben looked at him in disbelief. "We can't sit on this! You don't think the victims' families will talk about it?"

"Not if they are sufficiently diverted."

Treanna rolled her eyes in the darkness.

Ben wasn't diverted at all. "Gabe thinks the charges were planted."

Grandfather's voice became even harder. "By whom, Chief Root?"

"I don't know! But it wasn't my team. They wouldn't damage our own equipment. Not unless..." He watched the other man's face, testing his limits. "Not unless it wasn't our equipment, anymore."

The uneasiness in Treanna's belly pressed into her lungs, diminishing her breath. All the staff knew the Wastes were harsh; that was why so few became scouts. Equipment malfunctioned, and salvage teams might be stranded, even suffer injuries or starvation. But nothing like this had ever happened. And what Ben was suggesting...surely that wasn't possible.

*Dear Mother, are we not your only children after all?*

Grandfather blew through his white beard and mustache, then leaned back in his chair. His voice went back to calming, reassuring. "Chief Root, I see nothing beyond a tragic accident."

"But sir—"

"You are to treat the contents of this report as classified. I will distribute it to the other chiefs, and I will ensure Chief Reid knows the sensitivity of this information."

Ben sighed, eyes lowering in submission. "Yes, sir."

"In the meantime, direct your teams to avoid the northern reaches for now. If nothing else, it will put them at ease." Grandfather's voice relaxed further, regaining its usual paternal warmth. "It will be all right, Ben. We'll survive."

A few moments later, the chief was back in the corridors, and Grandfather settled into his chair with a long sigh. "Mother help me or not," he murmured, "but we'll survive."

Treanna didn't move until she heard his snoring. Hardly daring to breathe, she crept into the main room and looked at the tablet in his hands. A video was playing on loop on the small screen: black smoke billowed from the twisted wreck of one of the Centre's largest transports. As Ben had said, the damage was mostly in the front, not in the cargo bay.

*That was no accident,* she thought. *But who would do such a thing?*

More importantly, what could the Centre do about it? Grandfather's plan was clearly to avoid further confrontation, but if the transport had been attacked—the thought made her stomach twist—then they must be prepared to defend the Centre against further attacks, at any cost. But who would be defending it? Scouting was clearly unable to, and Security was hardly combat-trained. The staff were carefully selected, ensuring that no more people than necessary were required to fulfill the Centre's mission.

No, the staff had their duty, already busy protecting the Centre's most valuable resource on the game floors. It would be fitting for the denizens of those floors to provide the defense of their caretakers. It would also be unprecedented, and Grandfather clearly wouldn't be willing to commit support staff.

But Grandfather wasn't the only one who knew.

*Something has to change, however much that frightens us. I'll simply have to keep the surprises to a minimum.*

Treanna had a week of leave accrued. She wasn't a chief—not yet—and could move independently of them. She could risk a visit to Programming, obtain some additional credentials. Then it would be a matter of selecting the right people to approach and offering them the chance to act in everyone's best interest.

When she finally got to sleep, she dreamed of knights.

# PART I

# VERIDOR

ENCIRCLING OCEAN
World's Edge
Argentine R.
Dunbriar
THE ARGENON
Veridor
200 mi
Arctus
Anthar
60°
Whitehaven
40°
World's Edge
20°
Greatfield
Portent
0°
Torpal Isles
Rio
Arborough
20°
High Cliff
80°
40°
20°
0°
20°
40°

Northwestern Veridor
2063 CR
As revealed by the Logos's Grace
ONE MOUNTAINS
The Spine
Helm R.
The O'mearas' House
Whilehaven
Shield R.

## 1

## THE CAVE

Ewan O'Meara checked the map again, automatically bending a branch away from his face as he went. An owl's hoot drifted down from above, filtered through the budding canopy and a sky that had already taken on the darkening tinge that warned of dusk.

He wouldn't go home empty-handed, but he hadn't planned on them being out quite this late.

As though answering his thought, a smug voice behind him called, "You don't have a frapping clue where you're going, do you?"

He winced. "Kate, language!"

"Mom's not around. Besides, you're the one who ought to worry about her right now, keeping your little sister out after dark looking for some Gems-forsaken cave. That goes double, after burning an hour stalking that random boar."

Ewan ground his teeth and rounded on her as she crunched the twigs underfoot with her usual finesse—the kind of stealth that had blown his shot at the frapping boar. "You're the one who wants to go mining. You're the one who read up on where to look. This whole trip was your idea!"

"Getting lost wasn't."

Kate's face was the picture of innocence: hazel eyes twinkling through freckles and skin forge-tanned to a darker shade of oak than Ewan's own, all framed by frizzy red hair. But her solid build and the pair of wicked hand axes dangling from the sides of her oversized backpack shattered the illusion.

That, and the smirk.

Ewan opened his mouth, then broke into a grin of his own at the sight of a broad, sloping hole at the far side of a small glade, not twenty yards over her shoulder. "What about walking right past it, then? That part of your plan?"

Her face colored, redder than her hair, as she turned. "I'll be nerfed. Good job, E."

His grin broadened as they backtracked to the cave's mouth. "My name's more than a letter."

"Yeah, well, I don't like saying you-win."

"You didn't mind when you were little." Ewan scrubbed his fingers through his black curls, fighting down a familiar frustration. "Besides, at this point, I'll take all the wins I can."

Kate chuckled and drew out her crooked dowsing rod. "That, I believe. You ready?"

Ewan reached back to loosen his swords in their scabbards behind his shoulders, pretending that his green eyes were gleaming like a cat's as he peered into the hole. "Always."

Kate lit her lantern and hooked it onto the pack, then followed him through the mouth into a comfortable tunnel, ten feet around and sloping gently downward. The air inside felt damp and cool the way only a cave's air could, and as they left the fading daylight behind, a sprinkling of phosphorescent mosses retained a lingering glow from the lantern's halo as they passed by.

For a while their footsteps were the only sounds, whispering in the corridors. Ewan closed his eyes, using the faint echoes to guess at myriad side passages as they went. He liked the darkness of caves. Granted, it could be a little creepy, and he was a lot more likely to get jumped underground than he was on the surface, but to his mind, that was a good thing. Cave-diving was challenging, and he needed to be where the challenge was.

*How else am I ever going to be the best?* he thought in frustration as they rounded a bend. *There's got to be something worth hunting in here.*

As if on cue, his senses suddenly warned him he and Kate weren't alone anymore. He froze and strained his ears, hand thrust back to stop Kate before her clomping got them in trouble again.

As the silence deepened, faint breathing became audible in a passage ahead, to the left.

Ewan slowly drew his swords, their steel gently scraping against the leather as they slid out, then crept toward the sound.

The breathing stilled.

*Now that's more like it.* Grinning, Ewan retrieved a pebble and tossed it against the opening.

A monstrous form sprang into being, landing gracefully in front of him on four padded paws. It squinted in the lantern's light, its lupine face ringed with vicious spikes as it bared its teeth.

That squint was all Ewan needed. Whirling his blades, he rushed the beast. It swiped at him, but he sliced the clawed foot off cleanly, turning in and driving his other blade up between the spikes into the creature's throat. He pressed in close, too close for the thing to land a decent hit, and after a moment's deadly embrace, it slid to the ground.

"Nice!" Kate clapped his back as she moved to take a closer look. "But what's a graptor doing underground?"

Ewan winced in sympathy for the beast's corpse as she wrenched a spike free. "They like to overwinter in woodland caves. Dad and I cleared out a den last year, that time he took the cartographers north of the Helm. I stumbled right into the middle of them," he admitted, smiling at the memory, "but he hauled me out before it got too rough."

Kate scowled as she tucked the spike away. "Gloat a little more, why don't you?"

Ewan shrugged. "It's not my fault Mom thinks you're too young to tag along."

"Oh yes it is. She thinks that because you always come back wrecked!" Kate snapped off another spike and jammed it in her pack. "I'd be a lot more careful. We all know it."

Ewan chose to ignore the jab. "She probably just wants to have more time with you. You know she can't hear well over your forge."

"Whatever."

After Kate finished dismembering the carcass to her satisfaction, they moved on, settling into their usual rhythm. Kate witched for her mystery ore, holding her dowsing stick out in front of her, and Ewan filled out his map to help them find their way back out later. When they encountered the occasional aggressive creature, she gave him the bulk of the kills, stepping in only now and then to help dispatch a few for good measure. Between skirmishes, she checked over their gear and patched up what minor injuries they took with the first aid kit in her pack, while Ewan kept an eye out for his next target.

The arrangement worked well for them. It always had, ever since Kate declared her professional intent three years ago. She got her materials, and Ewan got some exercise and combat practice. Not nearly enough, these days, but it was better than nothing. Plus, their mom was more tolerant about his cave diving when he framed it as helping Kate.

Finally, toward the end of an especially long corridor, Kate pointed at something that seemed more like a hole to Ewan's eyes than any kind of material. She put her rod away and jogged over to it, doffing her pack and jacket to free up her shoulders.

"Sweet!" she said, hauling a pickaxe from the pack. "There must be half a ton, at least."

And then she tuned him out, totally focused on whacking away huge flakes of the stuff, eyes sparkling and sweat dampening her sleeveless shirt.

Ewan shook his head and smiled, taking a breather while his sister did her thing. With all the smithing she did and the way it built her up, Kate had started getting attention from the local boys in the past year. But she never seemed to notice, much less care, instead sending the hopeful little goobers packing with their flowers and telling them to come back with big chunks of rock and metal. She was bound and determined to become the greatest crafter in all Veridor, and at the rate she was going, she was on track to make it.

Ewan's smile slipped into an annoyed frown. *She also doesn't get everyone telling her to quit trying.*

"You're about due for an upgrade," she commented after a while, her voice muffled by the pickaxe's steady ring. "Using those overgrown knives of yours for the better part of a year now. How about I make you something new?"

Ewan inspected his blades, his mood lifting again as he remembered the story for each nick in their edges. "We'll see when we get home. You don't make swords often, and I need quality. And no, for the thousandth time, I'm not switching to axes," he added with a grin when she whirled around. "You want to be a great smith? You should be more flexible."

She glowered at him. "You and your swords. What is it with boys and swords, anyway?"

"They're the weapon of choice; the Church's soldiers aren't called Axes. Besides, all the legendary adventurers of old—"

"Okay, okay. I get it," she grumbled, before smirking. "Your man crush used two swords, so you've got to."

Ewan choked. "Man cr—Old Max was an inspiration for plenty of us!"

Kate drew herself up and cleared her throat in a perfect imitation of their village pastor. "Maximilian the Great represents the pinnacle of the Veridian Hero, as befits the last great adventurer in history. It's a pity you insist on emulating the less reputable parts of his career, young O'Meara."

"Oh, shut up."

She laughed and went back to work.

After another good hour of making him wait—and miss out on bonus hunting—she stood and stretched, cracking her knuckles. And elbows. "All right. That's enough for now, but there's plenty more here."

Ewan dutifully marked the vein's location on his map, then sketched in the shortest route from the entrance. "There. You ready?"

Kate crammed the rest of her stuff in the poor pack before hauling it up like it was feather-light. "Yup. Lead on, Hero," she teased, punching him on the shoulder.

Ewan smarted as he led her back out, and from more than the punch. *If she can go for greatest crafter ever, why can't I do the same with adventuring? It's not like there's any competition out there. All I need is a big break, something to help me off this frapping plateau!*

Then he saw it. Right in the center of the passage, as if the Logos had simply been waiting for him to demand a bigger challenge.

He whistled softly and knelt, pressing his hand into a paw print almost as wide as he was. "Look at that."

Kate groaned. "Are you for real? We're already late, we've got a good hour back to home, and you want to go attack a— whatever that is?"

He glared back at her. "What? You already got your loot. I need to take on the big game if I'm ever going to get to the top."

"Not in the middle of the frapping night!" She tried to roll her eyes, but they didn't quite pull away from the massive print. "Just leave it, E. We can come back tomorrow."

"It might not be here tomorrow; it's here now. I want to at least try it."

"Do you even know what made that crater?"

He stood and grinned. "Nope. That's half the fun."

She smacked her forehead. "You're going to get yourself killed! We're tired, and I don't know about you, but I don't have a lot left in me for fighting." She narrowed her eyes, assessing him. "Screw that. You don't have a lot left, either."

"But think of the materials!" Ewan tapped his foot in the print's toe. "It's got to have some serious claws or something."

Kate stood there with crossed arms, rooted and unmovable and looking ready to try and haul him off on top of all that ore. "I'm so telling Mom."

"Once she's done scrubbing your mouth." She didn't budge, though, so Ewan swallowed his pride and pulled out the big eyes, willing to lose a little face for a shot a something that huge. "Look, if it goes south, we'll bail. Okay? Please?"

Kate's stony frown cracked, and she barked a laugh before glancing down the tunnel to where the print pointed. "Some mature example you are. Fine, but it's your corpse."

"Thanks." Ewan chuckled as he peered into the darkness, trying to guess how far away the creature was, and whether it could already hear them. "You'd better nix the lamp. We might need the jump."

"Might?" she said incredulously.

He tapped his nose, then drew his swords again and slipped into the tunnel.

It led downward, deeper than they'd gone so far. Kate kept grumbling as they went, but Ewan paid her no mind. He walked softly and swiftly, putting enough distance between them that he could listen for early signs of his quarry—and to help it focus on her stomping instead of his own approach.

The passage opened abruptly into a wide, circular chamber, about fifty feet across and at least as high. Soft moonbeams trickled through cracks in the ceiling past roots dangling from above, warning him how late it really was.

He paused, then crept in.

The creature was on him in a flash. Out of nowhere, a monstrous, hand-like paw sent him flying across the room, slapping his head against the wall and blurring his vision. Ewan pushed through the blindness and pain, listening instead as the thundering footfalls drew close. He ducked away from the next strike, getting only sprinkles of shattered rock in his hair as he rolled to the side.

His vision cleared a few seconds later, and his nerve failed him as he finally got a good look at the thing.

*A behemoth...oh, frap!*

Even on all fours, the beast was easily ten feet tall at the shoulder, its fiery breath glinting evilly off its long, curved horns as it wrenched them from the wall and moved to block the exit.

Then its head turned down the corridor, sniffing.

"Kate, don't come in here!" Ewan shouted. He was in for it now, he knew that, but he couldn't let her die. *Not after all the work to get her that ore!*

Shouting like the lunatic he apparently was, he charged the behemoth. It glanced back and for a fleeting second looked surprised, but then it bellowed and belched fire at him.

His leather armor ignited, forcing him to the floor in another desperate roll to put it out, a roll he only just finished before that enormous paw slammed down where his head had been.

He sprang up between the beast's shoulders, slashing and driving his blades into its underside up to the hilts, but all he accomplished was enraging it further. The behemoth spun, taking his swords with it as it launched him again across the room and into the wall.

Ewan thought he heard Kate calling, but between his ringing head and the blood pounding through his ears he couldn't make it out. "Go!" he shouted again. "Don't let it get you too!"

He had no way to know if she'd heard, much less obeyed, over the roars and stomping as the beast charged him. He crouched back against his wall, then put everything he had into a leap at the last moment. The behemoth aimed low, bashing into the rock again to deal itself a lot more damage than Ewan had inflicted so far. He landed awkwardly on its shoulders, blinking down at the broad neck as wide across as his arm was long. He laughed giddily, wished for a fleeting moment he'd been carrying an axe after all, and swung under the creature's chest to lunge for his swords.

By some miracle, he caught them.

He held on for dear life, alternately pulling them out and driving them in deeper, again and again, as the monster reared up and beat at him with its paws, smashing his body into its own. Pushing through the pain, he gave one last desperate stab, heard the wonderfully satisfying shriek of the monster's death cry, and whooped in triumph as the beast fell onto him with crushing force.

As the world around him faded out, a pair of sentences flashed up, blood red, in his mind's eye.

*You have died. Time to respawn: 1:00.*

2

———

# THE O'MEARAS

Darkness, utter and complete.

Ewan let himself drift along in the still blackness, at peace and fully relaxed while soaking in every detail of being a spirit. As usual, it inexplicably felt like a light breeze was wafting over him, slow and patient. As usual, he tried to determine its source. Without a body to get his bearings, though, he didn't have much luck.

After a while, he heard a soft chime in the back of his mind, its familiar tone a reassurance that the void would take a break again soon.

*Menu,* he thought, and it immediately filled with a collection of tables and icons, dazzling in their bright simplicity.

It never ceased to astonish him how easily the menus responded to his will, even without the rest of him. How tangible the glowing symbols seemed when he wasn't caught up being embodied, as though here in the darkness they were somehow more real than anything else.

He grinned in his mind. *They ought to be, as much time as I spend out here.*

Like anyone, he'd died before. Like the more reckless types, he'd died more often than usual. In truth, he didn't know anyone who died as often as he did. Not that he was a poor fighter. He'd already earned a reputation as a daring swordsman among his old classmates and the merchants who welcomed his steady supply of loot, and his strength and agility were well ahead of the curve. He just needed to keep pushing his abilities to stay at the cutting edge, and that meant a certain amount of risk.

The breeze stirred again. He used the menus' location in front of him to try getting a bead on it. *Behind me, maybe?*

The Church insisted that limbo was a place of meditation, that the time spent out of body was meant to cool rash tempers and allow the deceased a chance to reflect on the choices that had gotten them killed. This was supposed to give the respawned a better perspective on life for some reason, or at least make them behave better the next go around.

Ewan preferred using limbo to think about how close he'd been to a clean victory, then work out the ways he could have pulled it off.

He reviewed his recent jaunt through the cave, his nonexistent chest swelling with pride as he imagined how he'd looked taking the behemoth down. It had killed him too, sure, but it died first: that meant the experience points would stick, and for something that big, there would be enough points to make it worth the death-lock release.

Ewan scowled in his mind. For all the priests extolled personal growth, they were perfectly happy to freeze a respawned guy's stats until he paid for the blessing to apply his hard-won points. It wasn't even the money he resented; gold was easy enough to come by. It was more the priests' attitudes, their uncharitable remarks about his prospects and barely-concealed disdain for his chosen profession.

*I'll show them,* he thought, after deciding the breeze was

coming from above. *I'll figure out how to release the lock on my own. Then I can get on with living and dying more comfortably.*

Eventually a second chime sounded in his mind, and with a slight tingling sensation his body reformed in his bedroom, fully healed and equipped exactly as it had been in the cave. He chuckled, guessing by the moon's long shadows through the window that he'd beaten Kate home with his shortcut. He tucked his gear into inventory and stretched out on his bed, idly wondered why his fresh body needed to sleep, and eventually drifted off, still grinning about the successes of the night.

When he woke, the sun's rays were poking his face. He blinked them away, then blinked again when the Logos informed him it was already half past nine. Yawning, he swapped out his clothes for a fresh set, then lumbered out to the kitchen to see how much loot he could offload onto Kate.

His mom was clearing dishes from the table. Her hair, dark as Ewan's but wavy instead of curly, was tucked back in a neat ponytail, and her expression was neutral. A little too neutral.

"Hi, Mom," Ewan said brightly. "Dad already head out?"

Tricia O'Meara rounded on him. "Don't you 'hi, Mom' me! Kate came in after midnight, worn out and worried about you. She said you picked a fight with something well above your level."

Ewan winced. "Um, yeah, kind of. But I killed it; it was worth a ton of experience! And Kate got the ores she was after too, so I don't see why she's complaining," he added loudly over the stomps approaching from the hall.

Kate entered and raised her hand to thump him, but after seeing their mom's glower, she settled for making a face instead. "It's because you weren't there to help me carry all of the ore back. Do you know how long it took me to haul that stuff home?"

"Not that long, between your stats and that enchanted

pack," Ewan countered, grinning when she dropped into her chair as heavily as if she was still wearing it.

Tricia resolutely moved back into his field of view. "Sweetheart, you die an awful lot, even for someone your age."

Ewan started to roll his eyes, but he caught himself when she folded her arms. "You know I've got my bind here. It's not like I'm going anywhere."

"You might have been logged out," she said bluntly. "Accidents happen; even the Logos can err." Softening her voice, she added, "Every time you die, I stay up waiting for you to respawn. Just to be sure."

Ewan suddenly noticed the dark circles under her eyes. He lowered his own, discovering he didn't have to fake looking properly chastised this time. "Sorry, Mom. I'll try to be more careful."

Satisfied, Tricia squeezed his shoulder and moved back to the stove. "And don't take your sister into such dangerous places anymore."

"I wasn't in danger!" Kate protested.

"And I'll have it stay that way, thank you."

Kate shot Ewan a death glare, then scowled out the window.

"Come on, K. Don't be like that." He called up his inventory, his grin respawning. "Check out what that brute dropped."

A pair of massive horns materialized on the table with a heavy thud, way too big to fit in his hands. Way bigger than he remembered, actually. Even with their curve, they reached over both ends of the table, each one thicker than his leg at the base.

Tricia tsked. "Ewan, no loot on the table! What would your father say?"

"Good job," Kate muttered, but she turned to see. Her eyes widened as she gasped, and in an instant she was tucking her hair behind her ears, leaning forward to peer at the horns with a focus that told Ewan she was using her appraisal skillset.

After a minute she whistled, her face coloring slightly. "No frapping way—"

"Katrina O'Meara, mind your tongue!"

"*Golly Gems*, E," Kate amended quickly, shooting Tricia a sheepishly defiant glance. "These are high-quality materials. Class S, and flawless condition at that! Even the Swords don't use better than Class A, not unless they're way up the food chain."

She traced her fingertips over one of them, giving it a longing, regretful look. "You could make a fortune selling these guys off," she said.

"Maybe," he conceded. "But I think I'll just give them to you."

Her head whipped up. "For real?"

"Call it my way of saying thanks for humoring me. Besides, they're bound to give you a boost. That only seems fair, after all the points I got."

"I'll bet," she said, already pressing her nose to the horns again. "I'll have to burn mine just to start working with these. Then I'll need to research known properties and buffing alloys and dig up historical precedents...I've never seen anyone with behemoth-horn gear before!"

Tricia harrumphed from right behind them, startling them both. "Your breakfast is reheated, if you can find room for it," she said wryly.

Kate mumbled what might have been an apology and touched the horns to claim possession. A second later they vanished into her own inventory, neatly tucked out of the way until she was ready to have another look.

They spent the next few minutes divvying up the rest of the loot, making line-of-sight transfers to keep it off the table. Ewan gave Kate as much as he could, only keeping the gold and a few lightweight trophies to cover his costs.

"I don't suppose you could find any plant monsters next

time?" Tricia asked as he transferred various meats to the cupboard. "You don't eat enough greens."

Ewan chuckled. "Next time a celery raids the village, I'll be right on it."

She laughed too, but her brown eyes took on a wicked gleam. "In that case, I'll give you your next quest, adventurer. A horde of weeds has invaded my garden, harassing the local produce. Will you be my hero and vanquish them for me?"

Ewan groaned. "But I was going to head into town to get unlocked!"

The gleam intensified. "If mobs and Church won't slow you down, then I will. Consider yourself grounded for the day, young man."

"Busted," Kate whispered as Tricia turned to go down the hall.

"Oh, and Kate?" she called over her shoulder. "Hurry up and change into something presentable. I volunteered us to do Widow McCarthy's laundry, and I won't have you wearing those filthy rags in public."

With that, she vanished into her room, leaving her children to glare impotently after her.

All told, Ewan decided he had the better of it: at least he got to cut something down. It was tedious work, sifting through the rampant weeds to ensure he didn't whack a prized turnip, but he knew better than to risk another day's penance for being sloppy.

When Tricia returned with Kate later that afternoon and pronounced them both free, Ewan escaped with his sister to her workshop out back. The whole building, forge and all, had been a gift from their parents when she'd declared her profession as a craftswoman. Unlike her room, it looked as neat now as it had then—though Ewan couldn't avoid gagging as he passed the tanning rack.

Once inside, Kate walked to the bellows, gave them a few good pumps, and went over to one of the many storage chests she'd built over the years.

Ewan lounged by the wall, avoiding the worst of the heat as she hauled out some steel ingots. "I thought you'd be on those horns, first thing."

"Business before pleasure," she replied, passing the ingots into the forge before returning to the bellows. "We passed by the stable on the way home. They're short some stirrups, but those are easy enough."

Ewan smiled. For Kate, business was a pleasure. It always amazed him how she could take random drops and make treasures from them, one step at a time. It was the only case he could think of where she was more patient than he was.

"By the way," she said quietly as she dipped a form into water for cooling. "Thanks for drawing that behemoth's aggro last night. I was sure it was going to trample me."

Ewan nodded. "You're welcome. Truth be told, I was kind of spooked by that one."

"Me too. For a moment, I thought you'd finally gotten yourself logged." She closed her eyes. "I'm going to have to make you some seriously great gear if you start taking on mobs like that."

She looked at him expectantly, and he called up his roasted armor and handed it over with an embarrassed smile. "Well, at least you've got the materials for it," he said. "Just keep my stuff light, okay?"

She grimaced as she put a hand through a hole in the shoulder. "It's a wonder you don't die even more often, wearing as little as you do."

"Not a wonder. That's what agility's all about."

"If you say so," she said dubiously as she turned back to her work.

Jack O'Meara returned home that evening, with a tired smile on his lips and a grizzled shadow on his chin that blended the chestnut of his skin with the gray in his wiry red hair. Not long after, the family of four sat down to roast graptor and steamed vegetables, trading news of the past day and night.

Jack's gray-green eyes lit up as Ewan told him every last detail about his fight with the behemoth. "Well done, Son! But you shouldn't stay out so late, especially if Kate's involved," he added quickly, after catching his wife's expression.

"I know, sorry," Ewan said equally quickly. "I'll be going into town tomorrow, to get unlocked again. Can I come with you?"

"At least part of the way, if you can drag yourself out of bed before sunrise. Sebastian decided to go a week early," Jack explained to Tricia with an apologetic shrug. "He wants his party in the foothills by tomorrow evening, the mountains proper the night after that."

Ewan frowned. "That's a rough place for a bunch of scholars."

"That's why they hire me," Jack replied with a grin. "Someone's got to bash those mobs' heads while the scholars use theirs. But you know," he added, trading another look with Tricia, "I could use a pair of young legs to help me out. How'd you like to come along, Son?"

"But I need to get unlocked."

Jack grinned. "I'm sure a behemoth killer like you could make do for a hike."

"I can go," Kate said.

"Oh no, you can't," Tricia answered. "You're too young."

"But E was going at my age!" Kate argued.

"And he died every time," Tricia countered flatly.

"Not *every* time," Ewan muttered, trying to ignore Kate's glower.

"Nearly enough," Tricia corrected. She regarded him with narrowed eyes as she read his aura. "Your skillset is almost identical to your father's. You really should consider apprenticing for the college."

"Mom!"

Jack rubbed his chin. "Thomas mentioned just the other day that he had a vacancy in his squad. You'd like it, Son. Academic escorts get fair wages, and our discounted lock fees might come in handy."

"Especially for a frap—for a crazy suicide runner," Kate grumbled.

"Whose side are you on?" Ewan snapped. "I just helped get you a bunch of rocks!"

"But that's pretty much what I do," Jack offered mildly. "If you're going to do the job anyway, you might as well get paid for it."

Ewan glared down at his graptor chunk, wishing he could kill it again. "I'll think about it, okay?"

"That's all I ask," Jack said easily.

They ate in silence for a while, letting things rest. Eventually, Kate spoke up. "So, what's in the mountains, anyway?"

"Oh, some crafter wants to observe the eagles in flight." Jack chuckled. "Thinks he can fashion a winged contraption for people to use. Could you imagine that?"

"Yes, I could," Kate said defensively. "People can craft anything, with the right skills and supplies. Imagine how great flying would be, sailing over the fields and mountains—even the clouds!"

Jack scratched his head as she closed her eyes, arms lifting of their own accord. "I'm sure it would be wonderful, but we'd have wings if we were meant to fly."

Ewan sighed and tuned the conversation out before it could

turn on him again, but soon a message appeared, overlaid across his vision.

[Help me with the dishes?]

He glanced up to see his mom watching him, a little smile playing at the edge of her mouth. He nodded, and the two of them silently cleared the table, politely not interrupting Kate while she told Jack exactly how she thought wood and leather could be made to soar.

"I'm sorry," Tricia said quietly, once they'd gotten into a pattern with her scrubbing and Ewan drying. "I didn't mean to upset you."

Ewan frowned. "Then why do you keep pushing me?"

"Call it an old career habit," she said after a moment. "Antagonizing the priests isn't a viable profession, you know."

"I know...but working for them? Being at their beck and call, stuck on guard duty instead of chasing whatever amazing thing I come across? It's not for me."

"Maybe not," she said patiently as she scoured the last bowl. "But is adventuring?"

Ewan tried not to hear the doubt in her voice, the unspoken tally of sleepless nights matching his abundant death count. "Adventuring's freedom, Mom. I can explore the world on my own terms. You know?"

"It seems to me that you find yourself in the cathedral as often now as you would be, working as an escort. Except now, you're the one paying them—I'm sorry, I'm doing it again. I just want you to be happy, dear."

Ewan sighed as he added the bowl to the stack. "I know. I don't mean to disappoint you."

She sighed as well, but she also smiled as she squeezed his shoulder. "You don't."

Ewan woke half an hour before dawn, when the Logos pinged him to let him know his parents were heading toward the kitchen. Kate's hammer was already ringing from the workshop.

*Now who's rubbing it in?* he thought, scowling as he grabbed a new outfit from his dresser. *You get a whole frapping building instead of lectures.*

After a light, quiet breakfast with his parents, Ewan stepped out to give them the privacy for one more goodbye. Once in the yard, he equipped his swords and let them wake him up as he moved. Half his stances were made up, since tutors for dual-wielding adventurers were in short supply, but he was proud of them anyway. All the greats had their signature moves, and things like that just had to be worked out on their own.

He took a few good swings in the general direction of Whitehaven and its cathedral, then tucked his swords away and stretched up toward the stars, their twinkling lights also not quite ready to yield to the coming day.

*What's it like up there, in a sky as black and still as limbo? Could Kate's flying thingy go that high?*

"Pretty, aren't they?" Jack said, breathing in the cool air as he came out.

"Yeah," Ewan replied as he lowered his arms. "It's too bad they're not around during the day."

"Maybe they are. The scholars think the sun's a star, too, just one that's much closer." Giving Ewan a little smile, he added, "Some of them even figure there might be other worlds up there, if you could believe that."

Ewan pondered this. "Well, if there are, I hope their adventurers are having better luck."

Jack chuckled. "Ready to go?"

"You're the one who was taking forever."

"That long, was it?" Jack replied lightly. He equipped his walking hat and led the way through the little gate to the path up the hill. "I'll admit, it gets harder each time. I find myself pacing around, checking a thousand times to make sure your mom will have whatever she needs while I'm out. You and Kate, too."

"Dad, we've been out of school for ages."

"So that's forever too, is it?" Jack smiled. "Sometimes I wonder where all the time went. It still seems like yesterday that you were ten, just declared and boasting you'd be the best adventurer ever."

"Maybe to you," Ewan admitted. "But that was six years ago —and I am on my way to being the best."

"To be sure," Jack agreed. "I'm proud of you, Son, but not for your skills in combat, however impressive they may be. I'm proud of you for your good heart."

"Come on, Dad."

"I'm serious. Any fool can pick a fight, but not everyone would be so willing to take a death for a loved one."

Ewan's face heated. "It's just dying. The lock release isn't even that expensive."

Jack kept walking, slowing slightly as they started climbing. "I don't recall thinking so when I was your age. And it certainly seemed expensive enough when I covered you that first year."

Ewan winced. "I paid you back as soon as I could."

"I know," Jack replied, still smiling.

When they reached the top of the hill and the road that connected Whitehaven to their village half a mile the other way, they both turned to look back. Years ago, Jack had told Ewan how he liked to fix the image of the little thatched cottage in his mind, to help speed him safely home in case of a deadly accident. It was his own small way to keep the Logos from glitching on him.

Ewan had been quick to make the ritual a habit of his own.

He looked down as the growing light gave the first blushes of color to the buildings below. Smoke was billowing from the forge out back now, almost in time to the hammer as it rang through the calm, crisp air.

*This is my home*, he thought. *My place of return. I'll see it again, no matter what.*

They eventually stepped onto the road, the colors slowly blooming out from the landscape around it as the sun cleared the horizon. To the southeast, its fire silhouetted Whitehaven's skyline, with the cathedral's great spire easily visible even from five miles away. To their right, the peaks of the Argenone Mountains stretched from south to north in a great chain, some fifty miles distant at the closest approach across the fields and forests in the outlying areas.

"Quite the sight, isn't it?" Jack commented, following Ewan's gaze. "We get so used to the beauty around us that we tend to forget, but it's still there. Just waiting for us to notice again."

"Yeah," Ewan replied, enjoying the view with the person who'd taught him to appreciate it. "The mountains seem so far away."

"They're closer than you think. You see those streams? They're fed by melting snow from the mountains. The springs and summers in this part of the world are green because of it, and just when the snowpack begins to run out, the autumn comes to replenish it. Every time you take a drink in Whitehaven, you're sipping a little of the stuff of the Argenones. It's all quite neat, when you stop and consider it. Another one of those little things in life, so important that we take them for granted."

Ewan smiled, letting the words paint a picture of a seamless world where everything fit perfectly. His dad made it all seem so simple, so obvious, that it was hard to argue with how things were. *No wonder he never feels the need to change anything. Why change what works just fine as it is?*

But his smile faltered as he considered what that meant for

an adventurer. *Why live in a world that doesn't need for anything? What's the point?*

"Hey, Dad? Why do you think we're here? What are we supposed to do with our lives?"

Jack said nothing for a few moments, still watching the morning as they walked. "Well...I like to think we all have our own reasons for being here, waiting for us to figure them out. Reasons no one else can hand us, in the end," he added with sympathy.

"Yeah." Ewan looked up at the brightening sky. The stars he'd seen so clearly earlier were gone now, pushed aside by the sun as it told everyone to quit dreaming and get on with the day. "But how am I supposed to find them?"

"I used to think about things like that in limbo. It always seemed like a good time for it. But I haven't been there for, well, over ten years now. Not since Kate was knee-high."

"Ten years? I can barely make it a week."

Jack chuckled. "It's just part of getting older. Being a husband makes a man more careful; becoming a father makes him doubly so."

"But you can afford the fees!"

"Glitches can still happen," Jack replied, shrugging. "I don't see the need to risk it anymore, though of course helping the rest of you would still be worth a death in my book. I suppose that would be my answer to your question, too."

"What answer?"

"I used to wonder about my purpose, too. You'd be hard pressed to find someone who never did. But I guess at some point, I realized that I was happier when I didn't worry about it." Jack gave his hat a little twist to face it forward, then grinned at Ewan. "So, I chose to be happy."

Ewan sighed. "I don't see why you can't be happy and understand things, too."

"Well, maybe you'll find the way," Jack said. "I hope you do."

They walked on, eventually stopping when they reached a pair of cart tracks branching west to cut through a field. A carriage approached up the road ahead, no doubt filled with eager scholars.

Jack's eyes twinkled as he raised his hand into a wave, returned by the driver. "Last chance to come along? Should be fun."

"No," Ewan said, trying to ignore just how tempting the offer was. "But...thanks."

Jack nodded, then pulled him around into a hug as the carriage creaked to a stop nearby. "Any time, Son. I love you. Have a safe trip."

"Yeah. You too."

Ewan watched him climb on board next to the driver, then kept watching until his waving hand vanished into the distance. *See you later.*

## 3

## WHITEHAVEN

A LIGHT BREEZE RUFFLED EWAN'S HAIR AS HE CONTINUED ALONG the main road to the city, but other than that, the morning was calm. The Swords kept the roads mob-free with their routine patrols, and this early, there wasn't even another person out and about.

Ewan stowed his blades, swapping them for his guitar so he could strum and say hello to the day as he walked. Kate teased him for hauling it around, but the space it ate in his inventory was a small price to pay for the ability to make a little music when he was out overnight.

He'd traveled this path more times than he could remember, and not just for unlocking. Whitehaven was the cultural capital of the region and the unofficial capital of all Veridor, ever since the war. It was easily the greatest city Ewan had ever seen.

It was the only city he'd ever seen. So far.

For years, he'd dreamed of visiting the rest of Veridor, trying his hand at the different challenges the wider world had to offer. But a trip like that cost gold he hadn't saved up yet, especially for getting the Church to transfer his bind spot around with him in case he died. It was simpler to stick close to home and make use of the bind he already had.

That, or somehow figure out how to shift it on his own.

As the morning wore on, Ewan met the occasional party coming up the road, but they never exchanged more than a friendly nod as he played. It was about as exciting an encounter as he could hope for. The texts from school told about how a traveler could get waylaid easily enough long ago, even on the main roads. But the Church had put an end to the bandits and highwaymen, using one arm to make things easy for people to get without stealing, and using the other—the Sword arm—to cut down anyone who tried.

Toward noon, Whitehaven's alabaster walls faded into view in front of the high towers, looking like a miniature version of the snowy Argenones. Ewan's path widened into a road as it merged with more from the other nearby communities, and farther on, there was a steady stream of traffic going both ways on foot, horse, and cart through the satellite town which crowded around the gates.

When it became too much to hear himself think, much less play, Ewan sighed and unequipped his guitar.

A group of armored guards stood at the main gates, watching the traffic with an alert but slightly bored air while the aura readers among them made random scans through the crowd, checking menus for contraband or active bounties. Like all Swords, they had white tabards over their mail, each emblazoned with a large black sword on the breast, point-down, the grip and pommel in the likeness of a yew tree. Ewan gave them a friendly wave, but he didn't linger. The Swords were usually polite enough, but they didn't hesitate to kill first and apologize later.

And unlike for some professions Ewan could name, the Church waived their lock fees for mishaps in the line of duty.

Inside the city proper it was even louder, as though all the pent-up noise was struggling to break through the walls and spill out into the countryside beyond. *Would a forest would seem as loud if I could hear the trees speaking?* Ewan wondered as he drifted toward the shopping district. The merchants were happy to see him as always, and once he'd haggled them up by adding the thrilling tale of his duel with the behemoth, he left with a lighter inventory and enough coin to cover the fee and be done with it.

Bracing himself, Ewan turned toward the city's center. He walked past the brightly cobbed shops and apartments, then all the tourist traps and marbled upper-class inns as the avenue widened into a broad square. Two hundred yards to a side, it easily held all but the most festive crowds, but it still looked small compared to the cathedral's glinting central spire beyond: a giant needle, made of one piece, that scratched the sky while the Church's banner stretched out from it to ripple in the winds, high over the city.

In the square's center stood a statue, much smaller than the spire but considerably larger than the behemoth that had sent Ewan into town this time. The man it depicted raised his arms triumphantly, each hand gripping a greatsword and crossing them over his head. His tunic bore the Swords' emblem, partially concealing his segmented heavy armor and a chain draped around his broad neck. A party of school kids blocked the base and its inscription, but Ewan had read it so many times he could see it anyway.

*Maximilian the Great, Hero of Whitehaven.*

Ever since Ewan could remember, he'd wanted to earn a monument like that. To do something so amazing that the Church would set it in stone, for everyone to see.

He looked up at the stoic, bearded face and sighed. *You were too good at it, Max. There's nothing amazing left to do.*

Ewan moved on, working his way to the far side of the square and the broad steps that led to the cathedral's elevated entrance. A pair of great yew trees flanked the steps' base, standing a safe distance away from each other. Planted after the war to celebrate Veridian resiliency and the respawning of the world, they were as ancient as the statue and easily Ewan's favorite part of the whole complex. He walked over to each and pressed his hand against their scaly bark, greeting his namesakes with a rueful smile. *I bet you're put out too, stuck in the Church's shadow all the time.*

Not that they were the only ones, not by a long shot. The Church of Veridor oversaw virtually every aspect of life, managing more than ruling. It enforced its laws with the Swords. It funded and promoted the public schools and centers of higher learning, like the city's college, always with an eye to helping each citizen reach his or her highest potential.

And when people got logged out, as everyone eventually did, the Church provided comfort to their families. The priests created funeral effigies of the logged ones and buried them, ensuring the dearly departed couldn't become ghosts. Instead, their spirits respawned in a new life, blessed with the chance to start over and try out the skills and experiences they didn't get around to in their last go.

It was a neat solution, self-contained like the rest of Veridian society. Why bother believing in some made-up afterlife, when Veridor had so much to offer? Why waste a prayer on the ancient Gems, when the Logos and the Church had already proven their might in the war?

*But no one knows for sure,* Ewan thought, frowning up at the cathedral. *Why can we die all we want, but we never respawn from logging? Why don't you let people study that in your colleges?*

Having decided on exactly how he'd annoy the priests today, Ewan sprinted up the steps—but he'd barely cleared the top and started across the courtyard beyond when someone grabbed his arm, spinning him about and tripping him with a yell. He caught his balance and found himself face to face with a brown-haired boy his age with light skin, wearing an obnoxiously stern expression over the cadet's armor and the broad shield strapped across his back.

"Oh," Ewan said. "Hi, Paul."

Paul Castel—no doubt Gate Guard in Training, Paul Castel, by now—released his arm. "How many times must you be told not to run in the cathedral, Ewan? We're not children anymore."

Ewan pulled his arm free. "What are you, the courtyard police?"

The young paladin's scowl flipped to a grin as he touched the black sword on his tunic.

"Oh, right," Ewan muttered. "Well, I was watching where I was going."

"Aside from running into me."

Ewan scoffed. "Besides, I need to stay in shape. Keep up my agility, you know?"

"Tell me honestly. Did you run at all on the road to town?"

"Okay, you got me," Ewan said, clasping hands with his old classmate. "I'll slow down—this time."

Paul shook his head, watching about him like he really was a gate guard in training. "We should catch up. It's been at least a season since I spoke with you."

*Ugh.* "Aren't you on duty?"

"Not officially. Just doing my part."

"Making the world a better place, one stopped jogger at a time?" Ewan glanced around for an excuse. "Well, it was nice seeing you again, but I really ought to get unlocked."

Paul's eyebrows rose. "Again? Then I insist on lunch. Don't worry, it'll be my treat," he added, gripping Ewan's arm again when he tried to slip away. "I wouldn't want to deprive you of what little gold you manage to keep after paying the fee."

Ewan opened his mouth, but his stomach gave a treacherous vote for a meal. "Oh, all right."

In fairness, he hadn't spoken with Paul for a while. Or anyone from his school days, for that matter. Adventuring didn't lend itself to much of a social life, between the hours and the smell. Kate was the exception, not caring much about either, so they had remained close, forming their happy-go-lucky family party as they each chased their dreams. But most people, especially self-righteous tools like Paul Castel, tended to drop off Ewan's contact list.

Ewan sighed as he followed the paladin down the steps. *Maybe the smells from our professions drift both ways.*

They turned right from the square and headed a block and a half to a tavern. Its brightly painted sign sported a dragon pointing and laughing at the flaming silhouette of some poor fool, his sword and shield flying through the air behind him as he ran away with arms flailing.

Ewan winced at the all-too-familiar image. "Can't we go somewhere else?"

"The Toasted Tank has the best atmosphere in town," Paul said, opening the door to herd Ewan in.

*Atmosphere indeed*, Ewan thought incredulously as his senses adjusted to the noisy interior. Even at midday, the place was packed full. Buxom waitresses bustled about the tables in their ruffled uniforms, alternately teasing and dodging the patrons. On the little side stage, a trio of bards played an off-key tune about the cities of Veridor, with each verse ending in a raucous cheer about the girls therein that made Ewan blush.

"I still don't understand why you come here," he grumbled as they were seated at a small table.

Paul looked appreciatively at the scene, its raunchy chaos making him look even more clean-pressed by contrast. "I think it's because I really get to see the people. It reminds me of why I serve in the Swords: protecting them, so they can be carefree like this."

Ewan rolled his eyes as a pretty blond waitress with cloud-white skin glided toward them with a smile. "I think it's because the girls in here like your uniform."

"That doesn't hurt," Paul agreed with a grin. "They offer a discount to military personnel too, not to mention the Church's sanction for ale on signing up."

"Hey there! I brought your usual," the waitress said as she materialized an ale and a steak for Paul. "Who's your cute friend?"

Paul returned her smile, though his eyes flicked to Ewan. "This noob? Ewan O'Meara, we went to school together. He's tried and died more than anyone I know. Ewan, this is Tina Mayberry. She helps me out from time to time."

"Ah," Ewan said noncommittally. "Well, it's nice to meet you, Tina. Can I get a malt, please?"

"You got it." Tina's smile became salacious as she produced the drink and leaned forward to set it on the table, her eyes playfully watching his as she lingered. "Anything more you'd like, hon?"

Half expecting to see her inventory emblazoned across her chest, or that so much as a grunt would commit him to a full meal, Ewan quickly glanced away. "Um, no, thanks."

"If you're sure," she said, sounding disappointed. "Let me know if you change your mind."

She swished off, and Paul—pompous, straight-laced Paul—unabashedly watched her go, which only made Ewan's face heat even more.

"Scarier than mobs?" Paul asked lightly.

"No! I just, um...not many want to go dungeon-diving for a date."

Paul turned to his meal. "You might be surprised. Tina's got a sharp eye."

"I'm sure," Ewan grumbled. *Why am I explaining myself to frapping Paul? What am I even doing here?* "So. How are you, these days?"

"I'm well, thanks. Training keeps me busy. Commander Martin drives us hard, but I'm gaining tons of experience under his instruction. He takes us on raids now and then with the full battalion, as part of our studies." Paul took a bite of steak, neatly cut, and shot Ewan a challenging grin. "I don't think I've died but a dozen times since I joined up, and I'm sure I've fought bigger mobs than anything you find in those caves of yours."

Ewan returned the grin, relieved to get back to more comfortable ground. "Want to bet?"

Pausing to take an occasional drink, he gave a perhaps slightly embellished blow-by-blow account, savoring the way Paul's face went from impressed to incredulous to annoyed. Before long, everyone at the neighboring tables had turned around in their seats to listen. Even Tina was lurking nearby with an intrigued gleam in her eyes.

Paul noticed, too. When Ewan finally finished, he held up his hand and declared, "Well, that's quite an impressive kill. Good enough, even, to join the Swords." He lowered his voice as the crowd returned to their own conversations. "Don't scowl like that. I'm serious."

"That's why I'm scowling!"

"You'd have much more support than you do now. I'll put in a word for you to the commander; they could even let you re-spec. It would be like old times."

"I am not running fetch quests for the frapping Church!" Ewan snapped, straining to keep his own voice down.

Paul took a slow breath. "They're not fetch quests, Ewan. You could do some real good for the world, if you'd stop thinking only of yourself."

Ewan snorted. "How can I think of myself, with everyone always thinking for me? You fight the good fight, Paul. I just want to be the best adventurer there ever was."

"Like Old Max, I know." Paul tapped a finger to his white

tabard. "But he saw the light in the end. Remember that." Lowering his voice even more, he added, "But Ewan? Be careful around the priests, okay? You're not just a kid pulling pranks anymore, not if you can kill a behemoth solo. They won't take kindly to a powerful heretic."

Ewan shoved his chair back and stood, shaking the table. "Yeah. Thanks for the meal."

"Any time," Paul replied calmly in his normal voice as Ewan made his escape, dodging around Tina as she returned. "Say hello to Kate for me."

Ewan stalked back to the cathedral, muttering under his breath and avoiding eye contact with everyone in case he saw any more old classmates. The lobby was full enough, but the lines for unlocking weren't long, what with other people apparently having sold out to the Swords. Less than half an hour later, he'd taken a seat in a small wooden booth, one of many in the large room. An intricately carved screen divided the interior in half; on the other side sat a robed and hooded priest, his face barely visible.

"Young O'Meara...we are blessed to see you again so soon. Shall we begin, my son?"

*I'm not your son,* Ewan thought, but he took a deep breath and counted to ten before playing his part.

"Father, I ask your forgiveness and blessing." The words fell from his mouth like dropped clutter, heavy and useless. "I faced my death and was found wanting. I offer you this tribute, that I may more fully resume my life in the world and apply it better after my rebirth."

In response, a small menu appeared in his field of vision. He linked with it, winced at the figure, and transferred a good thousand gold pieces.

The priest took a moment to confirm the transfer before continuing magnanimously. "Then be reborn, my son, and learn well from your deadly mistakes."

Ewan tried, like he did every time, to see precisely how the priest's hands moved next, but somehow the screen always seemed to obscure it just enough. A tone sounded in his mind, telling him the lock had been released—but the door stayed closed so he could get browbeaten again before they let him go.

"So." The priest's voice was genial, but Ewan could feel the smirk behind it. "What was it this time, only one short week since you last graced our chapel?"

Ewan gritted his teeth and counted again. "I died after killing a behemoth to protect my sister."

"Is that so?" The priest seemed taken aback, but only for a moment. "I wonder, why were you near such a dangerous beast in the first place?"

This time, Ewan only made it to five. "You know, Father, I've got a question too. In limbo, I'm sure I felt a cool breeze. Why?"

The priest's indulgent tone vanished even more quickly than Ewan's gold had. "Come now, you and I both know that isn't possible."

"I'm telling you, I could feel it. A breeze, in limbo."

"No one else speaks of such nonsense."

"Maybe that's because no one else spends as much time in there as I do," Ewan retorted, remembering his mom's advice with a fey grin. "You people should be paying me for exploring the gap between life and death all the time!"

"Mind your tongue, young man. The mysteries are not to be discussed so lightly. Our faith—"

"Can't replace experience. The one thing we all do is get logged, so why not try and figure out what that really means? Wouldn't that help people more? And where is limbo, anyway? It can't be part of this world, since a corpse vanishes way before its owner respawns, so where does the spirit go? What else is there, besides Veridor?"

"The body is absorbed into the Logos," the priest answered, his voice increasingly vexed. "It ceases to be, and by the grace of the Logos, it is reborn. It is one of the great miracles: to be praised, not studied."

"And that's another thing! Why isn't there a school for the mysteries at the college? Gems of old, I would have signed on for that in a heartbeat!"

"Do not invoke the ancient powers, foolish boy!" the priest snapped. "It should be enough for you to be thankful you were reborn at all. If you pick at the fabric of existence to learn how it is made, then you risk unraveling it!"

He sighed, leaning back onto his own bench. "For your blasphemy and incendiary words, I must censure you again. Expect a one hundred percent increase for your next unlocking fee—"

"Oh, come on!"

"—the cost of ideas as dangerous and unrepentant as your behavior. I would begin saving up if I were you, young O'Meara," the priest said as the door slid open. "You'll doubtless need it soon enough."

*I'll show you,* Ewan thought with a growl. He stalked from the booth, swearing under his breath enough to earn him another censure if someone heard. He stormed out into the main lobby, so lost in his own thoughts that he didn't notice the crowd shuffling, parting to make a space in the center of the room.

Didn't see the girl, until her yell made him look up.

Startled, he watched as she tore down the aisle, a pink-robed blur hurtling right toward him in the middle of the gap. Fifty yards behind her, two Swords were in hot pursuit.

He swerved out of her way, but for an instant he saw her pale face—and everything else seemed to slow, dimming in contrast. Her brown eyes held an entire world of terror, her open mouth calling wordlessly, pleading for someone to deliver her from danger.

She was looking right at him.

Ewan didn't know why he did it. He had plenty of reasons. He was angry about getting censured, annoyed with Paul's warning to keep his head down, and embarrassed by how quickly he'd ignored it. No one took him seriously as an adventurer, much less understood when he asked the big questions.

But, more than anything, looking into those eyes, he simply knew this girl was in trouble, and that he wanted to help her.

She flew past as time resumed its normal flow; Ewan shouted and leaped in front of the Swords to draw their aggro. He called up his menu, winced when he remembered he'd given Kate his armor, then equipped his blades anyway.

An ominous tone sounded in his mind, and a warning flashed across his vision that he now had a bounty, along with a reminder that only Swords were permitted to equip weapons in the cathedral. As if to prove the point, the soldiers slowed as they saw the blades flash into being on his back, but with grim smiles they equipped their own and changed targets.

Ewan spared a quick glance behind him to see the girl vanish down the steps, then turned to face his opponents.

The crowd was whispering excitedly now, but he focused on the Swords, quickly calling on his own basic aura-reading skills to scan them. They were stronger than him, and bigger too, but neither had bothered to bolster their defense beyond their armor, clearly seeing him as an easy mark.

*Time to see what agility's all about*, he thought with a nervous chuckle.

They rushed him, but he stood there, waiting. They closed, lowering their weapons at his heart, but at the last possible moment he fell back onto the floor, stabbing his blades across his body and into their legs. The steel found the joints in the armor, piercing cleanly through to the knees, and both men toppled forward with shouts as they grasped their legs.

Ewan leaped back to standing, then ran up and slapped

them across the face with the flats of his blades, hard enough to knock them out. Breathing heavily and senses buzzing, he looked up to see the crowd's excitement turn to shock as everyone realized the outlaw had actually won.

He shot them a wan smile as he realized it too, then quickly hid his blades in his inventory and sprinted down the steps before any more Swords could come.

## 4

---

# ON THE RUN

EWAN RAN FOR HIS LIFE, SWEARING AT HIMSELF FOR HIS
recklessness, but even as he slowed to shoulder his way
through the confused masses in the square, he couldn't shake
the image of those brown eyes. As the bells rang out behind
him, he couldn't be sure whether the ringing was for him, or
for her.

*What in Veridor could she have done to draw so much aggro?* he
thought.

He forced himself to move normally, to act appropriately
nervous and clear the area with everyone else as a torrent of
white-clad Swords poured down the steps. The Logos helpfully
added a collection of matching red dots to his map, indicating
them as being hostile to his apparent newfound cause, but
instead of coming straight for him, they fanned out in a search
pattern. Taking this as a hopeful sign that the Logos hadn't
similarly tattled on him, Ewan slipped away before any gawkers
in the crowd could.

He walked with forced casualness into the streets, making
for the back alleys while trying to keep from running outright.
The Swords would be as capable of sensing his fear as any mob,

aura readers and red dots or not, and he dared not give them an easier target.

After a few harrowing minutes of cat and mouse, Ewan ducked into a cramped little dead end and collapsed behind a half-broken crate, out of sight from the main thoroughfares. Catching his breath, he checked the quest boards for his own name.

It was there, along with a picture of him taken by the Logos the moment he'd equipped his swords in the courtyard. He smiled to himself at how heroic and rakish he'd looked, but then a stream of location updates scrolled across it as the public realized a bounty hunt was on. Out in the street beyond, the usual city chatter began taking on a deadly, focused undertone.

Ewan scrubbed his face to rub some sense back into his head. "Gems of old."

A thump and a gasp sounded from right next to him, making him jump half out of his skin.

Cursing at himself for not thinking to do it sooner, Ewan called up his detection filter to check for life signs in the alley. The crate instantly lit up, and he stumbled back in shock as a pair of eyes watched him from within: dark brown, terrified, and familiar.

He scrambled up to the broken wood, and the eyes retreated. "Shh," he whispered, placing his finger over his lips. "Do you remember me?"

The eyes blinked, and a soft, trembling alto voice answered. "Yes. You were the one who intervened?"

"That's right. My name's Ewan O'Meara."

The girl remained silent, hesitating, so he gave her a reassuring grin. "Don't worry, I'm on your side."

"My side?" she said blankly. "How could you possibly know what side that is?"

"Well, you're not a red dot."

"A what?"

Ewan checked his map again, but her dot's color stayed reassuringly neutral. "Look, can we at least agree that we'd rather not get arrested right now?"

"Definitely," she replied, her voice becoming slightly more confident. "You may call me Treanna."

"Okay, Treanna, the first thing we need to do is get out of the city—starting with that crate." He went to open it, but the boards were still nailed shut. "Huh."

"What is it?"

"You're nailed in. How'd you get in there?"

The eyes looked away. "I wasn't—I'm not entirely certain."

Puzzled, Ewan gave her aura a quick scan, then did a double take when the Logos listed her as being at level one. "Fair enough," he said, turning back to their immediate problem. "Hang on."

Keeping a sharp eye on his map and ducking as the occasional Sword raced past, he equipped one of his blades and got to work, prying the boards open on his side. After a minute or two, he got them free enough to give the girl a hand and help her out, finally getting a good look at the rest of her.

She was pretty. Very pretty, actually. A couple inches shorter than him, not nearly as buff as Kate but clearly in decent shape, judging from the way she pulled herself up. Her hand felt warm and smooth, despite the tension of her grip. She had fair skin, almost rose: not as pale as it had been earlier, now that she'd escaped immediate danger. Her long hair spilled into her robe's hood behind her shoulders, looking like a pool of honey. Her jaw held a proud, determined set, though her full lips were drawn tight under high cheekbones and narrowed eyes—

"Enjoying the view?" she asked irritably.

"Yeah...I mean no! Or yes? Frap. I, um, sorry," he stammered as blood rushed to his face. "You look great, but you're going to need a disguise so we can sneak out of here. Do you have any spare clothing?"

Treanna's eyes narrowed further as she opened her hands. "Do I look like I have any spares?"

"Well, I don't know. I can't see in your inventory," Ewan said. "But I can lend you some of mine. Hang on." He hastily equipped his clothes from yesterday, glad now he'd been too lazy to put them away in the morning, then sent her an invite to join his party.

He didn't know whether she jumped more from the sight of his gear swapping out or from the invitation, but between the two, she toppled back into the crate with an undignified crash.

"Dear Mother!" she exclaimed. "How did you do that?"

"Look, we don't have much time." Ewan hauled out the clothing he'd been wearing and tossed it to her. His map showed a red dot approaching down the main street, a Sword coming to investigate the cause of the racket. "Did you get my invitation?"

"Yes," she said uncertainly. "What does that mean?"

"Just think yes!"

A moment later, he heard the chime in his mind, indicating that one Treanna Rothchild had joined his party.

"Thanks. Now I can track you in case we get separated. Not that I plan to," he added quickly when she stiffened. "You'd better put those on."

Treanna looked at him like he'd lost his mind, but then those narrowed eyes respawned. "Aren't you going to turn around?"

"Huh? Just use the menu—frap, hang on!"

He ducked as the red dot came to the end of the street, then held his breath, praying to the Logos or Gems or whoever would listen that the soldier wouldn't come all the way down.

The clinking of heavy footfalls came nearer still.

Taking a last glance at the map, Ewan grabbed a piece of crate with one hand and took an apple out of inventory with the other. He lobbed the fruit high, waited a split second for the soldier to hopefully look up, then sprang out and smacked him across the head to knock him senseless.

"Gems, that was close," he muttered as he dragged the body as quickly as he could, behind the rest of the crate.

Treanna looked at him, wide-eyed. "Did you just...kill that man?"

Ewan huffed. "Of course not, but I had to do something. If he'd found us, he'd have called his buddies over. But if he'd seen me attack him outright, I'd get ID'ed as a hostile. Then we'd be on their maps as surely as we see them." He shot her a grin. "Good thing you're in my party; the Logos treats bystanders as valid witnesses."

If anything, she looked more baffled, but she stood up. "So, are we in immediate danger now?"

"Not anymore, but we need to move before this guy comes to."

"Then would you *please* turn around?"

"Oh, right." Ewan obeyed, wondering again why she didn't just equip her clothing like a normal person, but his face burned when he heard the rustle of cloth dropping to the cobblestones.

"There," she said a moment later. She placed a hand on his shoulder to turn him back, then gave him her old clothes. "Would you mind holding these for me, or whatever it is you did?"

"Yeah, sure," he mumbled, unable to stop glancing at her as he tucked her gear into inventory. He passed a hand through his hair, hoping it was properly rakish, but then he realized she wasn't the only one who needed to change her style. With a sigh, he called up his appearance submenus and hacked away, and the curls dropped off and disappeared into the Logos.

"You're hardly catching me at my best either, for what it's worth," Treanna said, giving him a brief smile—the first he'd seen—that made his sacrifice totally worth it. "Please accept my thanks...and my apologies as well. I never meant for you to get involved."

"It's okay," Ewan said. "I was on the Church's list, as it was." Offering her his hand again, he added, "Come on. If we're lucky, we'll get to the gates before the Swords lock them down."

She gave him a long, guarded look, but she took it.

The gates were still open as the fugitives approached a few minutes later, but now two dozen Swords were there, herding the traffic into narrow lanes.

"This isn't good," Ewan muttered. "They're scanning everyone."

Treanna's hand tensed. "Won't our disguises be enough?"

"Not against aura readers. I'd hoped they'd still be doing passive scans, but they're going to ID us."

He started to tug her away to come up with a better plan, but she didn't budge. "You mean they'll be looking at our names?"

"Yeah. The stealthiest people alive would give up their names to a skilled aura reader, even if they could mask the bounties."

Treanna smiled to herself, then plunged her hand into her belt pouch. "Keep walking, then."

"Didn't you hear what I just said? They're going to nail us the moment they see our names!"

"Trust me," she insisted, looking down at something inside the pouch. "Keep walking."

Sweat beaded down Ewan's neck as they joined the lines and inched forward. The guards looked anything but bored now, a predatory eagerness burning in their eyes as they waited for Whitehaven's brashest to show himself. Archers watched from the turrets above, searching for signs of distress that Ewan only just managed to rein in. His hands twitched, aching to reach back for the blades that were only a menu away, but he knew full well it would mean instant death.

He sighed inwardly and kept his eyes caged forward. *Wouldn't it figure if I die less than an hour after getting unlocked?*

And then they were through, without a word of protest from the scanners, or any sign that they were anything other than a couple of normal, law-abiding teenagers leaving the city.

Ewan turned in astonishment to Treanna as they slipped into the open, but she placed a finger to her grinning lips.

"See?" she whispered. "I told you that you could trust me."

"I'll never doubt you again." He risked a glance back to the Swords, but they weren't paying him the slightest attention. "Thanks for bailing me out, too."

They continued as quickly as they dared, but as Whitehaven's walls faded into the distance behind them, Treanna slowed, each step getting shorter. Less sure.

"So," Ewan asked gently, "what will you do now?"

"I'm not certain." She shivered at a gust of wind from the west. "I feel terrible that you're in danger as well. Otherwise, I'd...I don't know."

He reached over and gave her hand a reassuring squeeze. "Don't worry about it. I wanted to help."

Treanna froze, looking down at his hand on hers. "And why is that, precisely?"

Ewan scratched his head with his free hand; his fingers searched for his missing curls. "It just seemed like the right thing to do."

"That's all?"

"Sure. I don't take kindly to the high and mighty running roughshod over helpless people. No offense," he added quickly when she looked up at him, her brown eyes now hardening as she searched his for something.

"And you desire nothing from me in return?" she asked.

Suddenly, Ewan realized what she was getting at.

"Nothing untoward!" he yelped, blushing furiously as he jerked his hand away. "I'd have done the same, even if you were some ugly guy—not that you're ugly—you're very pretty! And you're obviously not a guy!"

Her lips twitched. "Obviously."

"I mean I'm glad you're pretty—and a girl." He groaned and scrubbed his lame hair. "Sorry. Let me try that again?"

"Please do."

"I just...I'm glad I could help. I'd like to keep on helping you, and get to know you better. If that's okay? We're in this together, now."

"I suppose we are." She sighed, but she took his hand again. "As such, what do you suggest we do next?"

"Well, for starters, we've got to move," Ewan said, exhaling slowly as the tension eased. "The Swords are bound to start searching outside the walls before long. I don't suppose you can tell me why they're after you?" he asked, giving her a sideways glance as he led her up the road again.

Her face darkened. "I must have said something offensive."

"That's easy enough," Ewan replied with a grin. "But you must have really ticked them off to get the Swords called on you like that."

Treanna frowned. "Swords? What are those?"

Ewan blinked. "You don't know the Swords? They're the Church's military—and they're coming," he growled as a bunch of red dots came flying from the gates on his map, far too fast to be on foot. "They're mounted; we'd better hide."

"How could you know that?"

"Trust me, this time!" He grabbed her and took off at a sprint, diving off the road at the first convenient hedge.

Moments later, a party of eight Swords charged past at full gallop.

"Oh Gems, they're headed for home," Ewan whispered. "I've got to warn them!"

"Warn who?"

"My family. Hang on a moment, okay?"

Ewan called up his menus again and selected the one other person in his party. A messaging window opened in his mind's eye as the map flew over to the forge beside his house.

[Kate!]

Her soundless reply scrolled across the window in his vision. [E, what's going on with you? And why are you adding people to our party before checking with me?]

[I don't have time to explain. There are eight Swords headed for home, right now!]

He could almost hear his sister's palm slap her forehead. [What did you do, pick a fight at the unlocking booths? Or does it have to do with that plus-one you're cowering with in a hedge?]

Ewan spared a glance at Treanna; she was staring at him in complete bemusement. [Yeah. She's on the run from the Church and I, um, kind of beat up a few Swords to help her get away.]

[Are you out of your frapping mind?]

[Kate, language!]

[Don't scold me; you just went outlaw for some girl!] After a moment, she added, [So, what do you want to do?]

[You've got to bail from the party.] He winced, picturing her response to that. [It's the only way to make sure the Swords can't use you to get to me.]

[And where, exactly, are you going?]

Ewan flipped the map around, to scan the places they'd recently been. [I'll take her to the forest cave. It should be safe enough, now that we cleared it. Can you go now, with some camping supplies?]

Another long pause. [Mom is going to kill you.]

Ewan sighed as he watched the dust floating up in the horses' wake. [Yeah, well, she'll have to get in line.]

[No kidding. I'm on my way; see you in a few hours.]

A moment later, Katrina O'Meara's name vanished from Ewan's party list, prompting another gasp from Treanna.

"Well, that's done," Ewan said regretfully, trying without success to remember a time when he and Kate hadn't been partied up. "Come on, we'd better get moving."

The Swords' patrols forced Ewan to take Treanna cross-country, cutting across the fields and taking whatever cover was around any time the Logos warned him that mobs—or Swords—were nearby. To her credit, the strange girl didn't complain once about the miles-long hike.

She didn't say much of anything, actually, even though it wasn't until evening that they finally made it to the forest glade.

Kate was there, waiting for them with arms crossed over her armor as she sat on a pack by the cave's entrance. "Took you long enough," she muttered.

"Sorry," Ewan said. "Thanks for coming."

"I wouldn't just leave you to freeze out here. You going to introduce me to your girlfriend?"

"She's not my girlfriend! Treanna, this is Kate O'Meara, my kid sister. Kate, this is Treanna Rothchild, my, um—?"

"Accomplice," Kate supplied. She shot Treanna a scowl. "Look here, Tree-elf. I don't know who you are or what you're up to, but let's get one thing straight right now. E's a good guy, but he's got a real thing about playing the reckless hero. I won't blame you for getting him in trouble with the Swords, but you'd better keep him from dying out here."

"Of course!" Treanna said, face paling in the waning light.

Kate rolled her eyes. "I said dying, not logging. Just help him work off his bounty, okay? How big is it?" she asked Ewan.

He called up the figure, then stared at it in horror. "Three hundred thousand gold? All I did was assault a few Swords. I didn't even murder any of them!"

"But you helped me," Treanna said quietly. "Ewan, I'm—"

"What did you *do*?"

She flinched under his glare. "I had no idea your Church would become so angry," she whispered.

"Our Church?" Kate asked. "What, they're not yours too?"

Treanna stared fixedly at her feet. "I didn't—I'm sorry."

"Kate, lay off her," Ewan growled. He took a long, sort-of calming breath. "Hey, Treanna, can you give us a moment?"

"I—yes. Where should I go?" she asked, looking around as if Swords climbed trees.

"You can stay here. We'll just pop into the cave for a minute. Shout if you need me, okay?"

As soon as they were out of earshot, Kate thumped him on the head.

"Ow!"

"What were you thinking?" she snapped. "She's pretty and all, but getting into a fight with the frapping Swords? You are so dead."

Ewan groaned. "Actually, I'm thinking I can't afford to die now."

"You got that right." Kate chuckled darkly. "It's going to take you at least a year to work that bounty off." Glancing back toward the cave's mouth, she added, "I bet the Church would cut you some slack if you turned her in."

"Kate, I can't."

She shrugged, then gripped the haft of one of her axes. "Pansy. Want me to whack her for you?"

"No! I don't regret helping her, okay? She needs it. I don't know if you noticed, but she's only at level one."

Kate frowned at him. "No frapping way. She's got to be older than you; how could she have no experience?"

"I don't know," Ewan said, keeping his voice low. "But she'll die without any help, and I can't stand the thought of her trapped in the Church's dungeons if they nab her on the respawn. It's not just that, though. There's something odd about her. She doesn't seem to know how to use the menus, but somehow she got us past the aura readers earlier, and she obviously knows something the Church doesn't like. I, um, want to know more about her."

Kate rolled her eyes. "You are so predictable: totally throwing for some girl, just because she aggroed the Church. She's going to have you wrapped around her finger."

Ewan huffed, but he also grinned. "I'll admit, I couldn't have picked a better partner in crime. Seriously, though, tell Mom and Dad I'm sorry for all the trouble. Are you all going to be okay?"

"We'll be fine." Kate said, as she tucked her hair into a frizzy ponytail. "I bet it won't be long before the Swords decide it's easier to wait for you to die like usual and come crawling back in for a lock release. They'll leave us alone after a few days, a week, tops."

"I hope you're right," Ewan said, offended but not enough to argue. "Make sure you take a roundabout way home, just in case."

"I've already got an alibi," Kate replied. "I was in the village all day, helping out at the school."

"Thanks, Sis. I owe you one."

"You're frapping right, you do." She pulled him into a back-popping hug. "Come on. Your Tree's going to think you ditched her."

They found Treanna near the cave's entrance, lost in thought and looking as exhausted as Ewan felt, but she straightened as she saw them approach. After one last warning to keep Ewan alive, Kate trotted off, vanishing into the night.

"You both seem so generous," Treanna murmured. "So

willing to help." She nodded to herself, then looked right at him. "I thank you."

There was something about her gaze, something hopeful yet calculating, that raised the hairs on Ewan's neck. He turned away and hoisted the pack, grunting in surprise under its weight. "Come on," he said as he pulled a lantern out. "Let's get inside and set up camp."

They spent the next half hour cleaning out one of the side rooms—not the behemoth's chamber—and arranging their gifted supplies along the wall. For some reason, Treanna locked onto the moss hanging from the ceiling, glancing at it frequently as they shared a late meal of jerky and bread.

She gave Ewan another hard look when he pulled out a pair of bedrolls, but she said nothing as he took his a respectful distance away. But when they finally lay down, she looked even stiffer than the rock floor, and her eyes kept darting about the room, chasing the lantern's flickering light.

Smiling as he remembered his own early nights out, Ewan equipped his guitar and started playing one of the songs he'd made up to help him keep his courage. Letting his fingers roll over the strings in a gentle series of chords, he closed his eyes and sang softly into the dim room.

*Shadows fall as the sun slips away*
*A gentle quiet steals across the land.*
*Evening's call at the end of the day*
*Will turn your thoughts homeward again.*

*The world settles down as the light fades and dies*
*And weariness begins to bow your head.*
*Drifting from the town, you can hear the muffled cries*
*Of children being herded to their beds.*

*But when the light of day is gone the stars can truly shine*

*Their flickering light made of the stuff of dreams.*
*A hidden world reveals itself to those who make the time*
*It teaches us the universe runs deeper than it seems.*

*Insects sing in the air cool and clear*
*Their music echoes through the darkened sky.*
*Bats take wing as the birds disappear*
*To ride the winds above the branches high.*

*But as more creatures stir, quiet phantoms in the night*
*You realize that the familiar world is long since dead and*
> *gone.*
*Your heart is gripped by fear, and it beats with all its might*
*Reminding you how far you are from home.*

*But when the darkness seeps into your soul, do not cry*
*Don't give it power to rob you of your mirth.*
*Allow the night to teach you that the reason we all die*
*Is so we can experience the wonder of rebirth.*

*So when the shadows fall and the sun slips away*
*Remember in your heart its light will never truly end,*
*And answer evening's call with the courage to stay*
*And greet the unfamiliar as a friend.*

He played through the chords one more time, then opened his eyes to find her staring at him again. But this time, her mouth was parted and her eyes were wide, as she propped up on one elbow.

Ewan grinned, self-consciously. "Sorry. I'm not very good."

"I've never heard anything like it," Treanna whispered. Her lips lifted into a warm smile, the first he'd seen from her since Whitehaven, as a tear rolled down her cheek. "Thank you, Ewan, for sharing it with me."

"You're welcome," he replied, suddenly lightheaded. *I'd play every night if it makes you smile like that.* "Feeling better?"

"Yes, much."

"In that case, how about we call it a night?"

He put the guitar away, then turned out the lantern and soon fell asleep.

## 5

## FIRST STEPS

WHEN DAWN CAME, EWAN SHIFTED ON THE CAVE'S FLOOR, rubbing a crick from his neck. The room felt dim, like he'd drawn the curtains last night.

Then he opened his eyes and remembered where he was, how he'd gotten there.

Wincing, he called up his bounty again. The absurd sum flashed up and blinked at him a couple times, then settled in the lower right corner as a reminder of his recklessness.

*Whatever,* he thought as it faded along with the rest of his menus. *It was worth it.*

He grinned and turned to Treanna—and realized she wasn't there.

Ewan looked around the cave room, but all he could find of her was her bedroll. "Hey," he called, softly at first, then again with more volume.

There was no reply.

"Treanna? Where are you?"

*Maybe she went for a walk, to think things over?*

Ewan checked his map. The Logos didn't see her. He pressed, and it informed him she'd left his party.

Wide awake now, Ewan raced out of the cave's mouth into the cool, misty air of the forest. The leaves were heavy with dew, glistening in the morning light, and the open ground around him seemed to be coated in strings of diamonds as the moisture hung from spiders' webs in the grass.

"Treanna!" he called again, a knot rising in his throat as his voice was absorbed into the woods.

There was still no reply.

Ewan swore. *She won't last five minutes out here, not at her level! Surely she knows that much?*

He spent the next hour roaming through the forest, shouting with increasing alarm, disrupting the birdsong as he called out for his own partner.

There was no sign of her. No bent blades or broken branches, no path cut through the dew.

*At least there isn't a corpse*, he told himself, but it was a vain hope. He didn't know when she'd left, and her body could have long since been absorbed by the Logos if she'd died quickly. Without a party link, he'd have no way of finding her again.

The thought left him hollow.

But by the time the sunlight began to cut through the branches, Ewan was steaming as much as the fading dew. Why had she left? He would've protected her, and she must have known after yesterday she had nothing to fear from him. Did she seriously believe ditching him would help him smooth things over with the Church, get his life back on track?

He kicked a branch as he made his way back to the cave. *Gems of old, she should have told me!*

The Logos chirped in his mind, different from the offended birds around him. He called up the menus again—and to his utter bewilderment, saw Treanna Rothchild right there in his party.

*How is that even possible?* he thought. *She couldn't rejoin, not unless I accepted her invitation!* But there she was on the map, back in the cave where he'd last seen her.

He banished the graphic and charged full sprint into the darkness before she could disappear again. He heard her before he saw her, a soft sob that made his heart twist as he realized that she was the one who thought she'd been ditched.

"Treanna!" he called.

The sobbing cut off, but her tense voice replied a moment later. "Ewan?"

He raced around the corner and found her there, standing up as if she was about to draw a weapon. "Easy," he said, raising his open hands. "I've been looking everywhere for you! What happened?"

She glanced past him, eyes haunted. "Looking? For me?"

In answer, he threw his arms around her, half to keep her from vanishing again. Her shoulders tightened, but her own shaking arms wrapped around his back. Once, she began to speak but instead sighed, leaning her head into his shoulder.

Eventually, she released him and sat down. Ewan sat with her, making a point of pressing his ankle to hers, just in case.

She smiled at him and pressed back in understanding.

"What happened?" he asked.

Treanna hesitated. "I'm sorry. I didn't mean to worry you. I went to sleep last night...but when I woke, you were gone. I thought you'd abandoned me."

"Not a chance," Ewan said firmly, peering at her until she looked at him. "But you did more than just go to sleep. You vanished."

"I vanished?" She frowned, then put a hand to her mouth. "But surely I was still here, even when I—are you certain?"

She said no more, leaving Ewan to wonder what had really happened. Had the Logos glitched somehow and put her in limbo? But party members still showed up on the menus, even after they died. He knew that perfectly well.

"Trust me," he said after a while. "You weren't here. Even the Logos couldn't find you. It was like you were logged or something."

She said nothing.

He shrugged. "No offense, but I figured you'd ditched me and struck out on your own."

"Why would I do that?" she said, eyes widening. "I don't know anything about this place!"

Ewan laughed at that. Treanna laughed with him, which made him laugh even more, and before long the two of them were letting out the rest of their anxiety in a giddy fit on the cold stone floor until they were both leaning back on their hands.

"I guess it's time we talked a little about what you do know. If you don't mind," Ewan said, sighing when she dropped the smile and reequipped the guarded expression. "I mean, you don't have to, but I think it's only fair for me to learn more about who you are, and why you came to Whitehaven."

Treanna took a deep breath and sighed as well, staring into the space between her knees. "You're right, of course. You've already assisted me twice and shown me nothing but kindness, while all I've done is placed you and your family in danger. But...Ewan, what I'm going to say will frankly sound insane. You'll have to trust me when I cannot explain further, but I promise to tell you everything I can, when I can. Will you accept those terms?"

*I don't exactly have much choice, do I?* he thought. *But I'll be nerfed if I don't follow through now.* "Sure," he said aloud.

"Thank you." She thought a moment, opened her mouth, closed it, thought a moment more, and finally shrugged. "Perhaps it would be easier if you asked me what you want to know."

*Like everything?* Ewan gave her a halfhearted grin to cover his growing frustration. "For starters, I'm guessing you're not from around here. Are you from one of the other cities?"

"No." She turned her eyes inward. "To put it in terms you could relate to, let's say I'm from a secluded place, far from here. My people have long maintained a strict policy of not interacting with…" She paused, searching for a word in the moss hanging above them. "With any of this."

"What, the world around you?" he asked flippantly.

"That will do, yes."

Ewan blinked, startled by the simple honesty in her voice. "That must get boring."

She gave him a little smile. "You couldn't begin to imagine."

He scratched his head. *What kind of place could be at arm's length from the Church? More importantly, would they let me in, with my crazy bounty?* "Well, you sure interacted with us yesterday. How come?"

A shadow crossed her face. "I've been asking myself that since I spoke with your Church's leader. I failed to anticipate what it would be like when I arrived from…I'm sorry, Ewan. I can't tell you more. Not yet."

Treanna looked away, leaving him to stew again. If anything, the little she'd told him made him more curious. Could anyone be so sheltered that they'd be level one, at her age?

*Well, I'll never learn more unless I help her out,* he thought with a sigh. "I'd be happy to show you the ropes around here, but before we get started, how about you come outside with me?" He stood and offered her a hand up. "It's a nice morning, and for once I don't want to spend it cooped up in a cave."

"I completely understand," she replied as she took his hand.

She followed him cautiously, but the moment they stepped into the glade she gasped in wonder. "I had no idea that a forest could be so beautiful!"

"Yeah, I really like them," Ewan replied, glancing crosswise at her. "I guess you don't have any near this secluded place of yours?"

She shook her head, still looking all around. "No. I've read about places like this, but I've never seen one until now. It seems too fantastic to be true."

"It's the real deal," he assured her, overriding his growing unease. *No forests?* "Let me give you the tour."

He took a few minutes, pointing out the different trees and grasses in the area, as well as the spiders in their webs and the birds still singing in the aging morning. He was no scholar, but he'd learned the basics well enough over the years.

She seemed especially interested in the trees. "Your sister. She called me a tree last night?"

"Um, yeah." Ewan passed a hand through his stubbly hair. "She's got a thing about making up nicknames for people. Sorry."

"Don't be." Treanna smiled, turning dark eyes on him as she rested her hand against a yellow poplar. "I'd be honored to be named after something so magnificent."

"Okay," Ewan replied, coloring when his voice cracked. Clearing his throat, he added, "I'm named after a tree as well, actually."

"Really?" The smile got stronger. "Which one?"

"The yew," he said dizzily, gesturing her over to a downed log nearby before dusting it off with his hands. "It's a tough old tree. Yews live practically forever and they're deadly to anything that intrudes on them, so they symbolize life, death, and respawning. That's why they're the Church's symbol."

Treanna—Tree—frowned. "Respawning?"

"Yeah, you know, what happens after you die."

"What?"

The look on her face warned him she knew even less than he'd thought. "Okay...let's start with the basics of the basics. We're alive now, right?"

She nodded, slowly, as though not quite sure about that, either.

"But sometimes we die, be it from combat with a mob—that's a monster or beast—or maybe a bad status takes us down. When you die, you go into limbo, kind of a waiting space, for a little while, usually a few minutes. Then you respawn."

Tree stared at him blankly.

"Respawn," Ewan repeated. "You know, where your body reforms at your bind spot, the place you tell the Logos to put you when you respawn."

He sighed, realizing he was going in circles. It was like trying to explain how you breathed or looked at menus; even little kids knew how to do that instinctively.

"Let me try that again. I died killing a mob the other night," he said, deciding not to mention exactly where that had happened. "After I died, my corpse got absorbed by the Logos, into limbo. An hour later, my body respawned: that is, it reappeared with full health and all in my bedroom, which is where I have my bind. My soul went back into it from limbo, and I woke up right there, good as new. Does that make sense?"

"So you can die, again and again?" Tree asked. "And the Logos keeps putting you back? That is, it respawns you?"

"That's right. Getting logged is a different story, of course."

She glanced away. "Suppose I don't understand that, either."

*What in blazes do they teach people where you're from?* he thought. "Getting logged is what happens when the Logos takes you but you don't respawn. It happens to us all in the end, but the weird thing about it is that people, usually elders, get logged even if they haven't died. Then, once in a blue moon, it happens to others. My family worries about me because of that since I die, um, sometimes."

"I see. That would match with what I know in my home,"

Tree said carefully, offering him a weak smile in place of a real answer. "But tell me about your Logos. What is it?"

Ewan gaped at her. "Gems of old, they don't even have the Logos where you're from? I didn't think there was anywhere it couldn't reach!"

She shifted uncomfortably, but said nothing.

"Okay," he said, easing off again. "The Logos is everywhere, around us and within us. It's the ultimate power in the world, and it coordinates everything, from our stats and skills to the schedules that mobs spawn at. I guess you wouldn't have realized it, but you used the Logos yesterday when you joined my party."

"You make it sound like a divine being," Tree mused. "Like the Mother."

Ewan waited, hoping she'd elaborate, but she merely watched him. "I guess," he said with an inward sigh. "Anyway, whenever you use your menus or equip gear, or when you check your status or your maps, or allocate points, you're working with the Logos."

Tree raised her hands. "Slow down, please! One thing at a time. What is a menu? Is that what you wanted me to use yesterday?"

"Yeah. You can do it anytime, though. Try it now; just think *menu* with that little voice in your head that everyone has."

Tree jumped and gasped.

Ewan suppressed a chuckle. "Good! Okay, now take a look around in there."

"How do I? I see a cluster of boxes and words."

"Put a little thought pressure on the one you want. Try opening your party menu by focusing on that line."

She beamed. "This is incredible! And to back out?"

"Just will it," Ewan replied, heartened to see she was having fun—and glad for the chance to watch her without getting the stare of doom. "The Logos is very responsive, but it understands when you're speaking to it. Idle mental chatter won't affect it, not usually at least. Try checking your status by focusing on that submenu."

"It says I'm at level one, but that I have new experience points? What does that mean?"

Ewan couldn't help but grin at her, though his mind was burning to know how she could still be such a noob at her age. "Levels are how the Logos rates our general ability. We all start out at level one, with base stats good enough to get around and take care of ourselves. But as we do things, we gain experience points related to the skills required to do those things."

"Like what?"

"Pretty much anything. For example, when you walked with me last night, you probably gained some experience in endurance, and maybe navigation. If I pick a flower, like this," he said, reaching out to pluck a little windflower from the ground, "then I gain a slight experience boost to my alchemy skill, because I could use this plant to make potions for healing or buffing—that is, boosting my status—or poisons for inflicting damage or nerfs."

"How many skills are there?" Tree asked. Her eyes flicked back and forth as she scanned her menus.

"For that, you'd have to see the skill tree," Ewan said. "It's on the main menu, but it cross-links to your status. Just focus on a particular skill, and you'll get there."

"Amazing," she whispered. "And every pl—person in Veridor can do this?"

He hesitated, wondering what she'd almost said. "Yeah, as easily as we're talking now. Until I met you, I thought everyone could."

Tree didn't hear the slight edge in his voice. "All right, I see the skill tree...dear Mother, it's enormous! How can you possibly learn everything?"

"I don't think you can," Ewan replied. "That's why the

Church says when we get logged, we really respawn with a blank tree and no memories. So we can try out whole new branches the next time."

"How do you choose?"

"Well, most people pick professions. Those are collections of related skillsets that the Logos bundles together. Or maybe the Church does…I'm not sure which, come to think of it. When you choose one, you get a bonus to experience for its skills, to help you learn quickly in the areas you're focused on."

"I see the list," Tree murmured. "There are hundreds of them as well. Which one are you?"

"I'm an adventurer," Ewan said proudly. "Hardly anyone chooses it these days, but it suits me just fine." He paused, hoping to hear her impressed reply, but she was too busy to notice. "So, I get bonuses to my strength and endurance, agility too, since adventurers go out into rough terrain, exploring old caves and fighting mobs. Kate's a craftswoman, so she gets boosts to her intelligence and endurance. She can carry more than I can without movement penalties."

"Penalties?"

"Yeah. Every item out here has a weight associated with it." Ewan handed her the flower, then blushed when she took it with another one of those smiles. "The weight gets offset by your carry stat, which is based on strength and endurance, but it also gets modified by conditions in the environment. On a hot day, for example, your carry drops and it's harder to walk around quickly. If you get over-encumbered, you'll move slower and slower, until you're practically standing still."

"But why would you do that?" Tree asked, idly twirling the flower in her fingers.

Ewan shrugged. "Maybe you're carrying some really good loot: that is, stuff you found or got from mobs. I try not to carry too much since I need to be light on my feet to fight well, but Kate's a mule. She can haul tons, almost literally, and not get slowed down by it. Of course, she's got enchanted gear."

"Gear?"

"Weapons, armor, clothing. Whatever we're carrying and using. You can see your gear in your personal storage or inventory. Here," he said, handing her the pink robe she'd been wearing yesterday. "Try putting this in there. You just hold it in your hands to show the Logos you have it in your possession, then access your inventory and tell it to transfer the robe in."

The pink garment shimmered away, making her jump. "Where did it go?"

"Check your inventory."

"Okay...I see it on the list now, but where is it?"

"In your inventory," Ewan repeated. He grinned. "You can reequip it in the menu. If you do, then your current clothing will go into storage and your new stuff will appear on you. It's a fairly instant process, so you usually don't need to worry about privacy, but glitches can happen," he added, blushing again.

Luckily, she didn't notice. "But where does the material *go*?"

"The Logos keeps track of it, takes it into itself, so you don't have to actually carry stuff by hand. You can, but that's unwieldy, not to mention dangerous for fragile things. Here, let me show you."

Ewan called up his own menu and equipped his steel swords, feeling their reassuring weight as they shimmered into existence on his back. He drew them out and held them up, catching the light.

"There, you see? Up to spec. Mostly."

He returned his blades to their sheaths and unequipped them; Tree gasped yet again, prompting another grin from him. *She's like Kate was, when Kate was little.* "We'll need to get you some weapons of your own, down the road. It's dangerous to go out and about unarmed, but you've got me to escort you."

Tree smiled at him, then tucked the flower into inventory

with increased confidence. "This is all so much. Thank you, Ewan, for helping me."

"Hey, I'm happy to," he said sincerely, running his hand through his hacked-off hair again. "I like to explain things, anyway. Besides, we were all noobs at some point. The least I can do is get you up to speed. Speaking of which, go ahead and apply your points from last night; that'll take you to level two."

Tree narrowed her eyes, checking her options. "I don't know where to put them."

"You can always put them into the skills they came from; that's usually easiest. You can also burn them on something totally unrelated, like aura reading or strength, but if you do, you'll only get a fraction of the points' value, since you didn't really earn experience with those skills. You can also hold onto the points, save them for a rainy day and all that. I try to keep a good number back, in case I need to bump a skill up in an emergency, but for you, I'd suggest putting them into their parent skills."

"This is all so confusing," she muttered, but she was beaming.

Ewan's grin turned into a full smile as her level rose to two on his party status. "I know it can seem that way, but in no time you'll be leveling as easily as I do. And once you've got the hang of it, then we'll see about paying off that bounty and making the priests listen to you properly."

Tree's smile took on a stronger, determined cast, and her eyes came into sharp focus as she closed the menus and looked at him. "Right."

*Time to see what you've got.* Standing up and equipping his swords as she stood beside him, he said, "Then let's get started."

## 6

## THE QUEST

A soft wind pressed against the cliff and wove through the canopy above, causing the rising moon's light to dance across the ground.

Ewan lay on his back, staring up in bemusement at the rock he'd been standing on a moment ago.

Footsteps approached, and Tree's faces appeared over his.

*Faces?* he thought. *When did she get two of those?*

"Ewan?" she whispered. "Ewan!"

He sat up, though it felt like half of him stayed right there on the ground. Wincing, he ran his fingers through his hair. It was well on its way back to rogue curls, but the bloody gash he found on his scalp wasn't going to help it grow. There'd been plenty of those, after over two months of living out.

Were they scarring over? He'd never survived long enough before to have one.

"Hold still," Tree warned. The world went sideways as she tilted his head, probing the wound with one hand while her other drew a salve from inventory.

Ewan sneaked another glance at the ledge they'd been on.

*Funny. It seems higher from below.* "I guess we should have gone swimming, after all."

"You nearly did," she told him. "The water's only a dozen yards away."

"Too bad I missed," he said with a grin. "It would've hurt less. Still, the view was worth it. Right?"

"I don't know yet." She finished matting his hair with goop and helped him up. "Now that I know you're still with me, let's go back up and find out."

They crept around the hill's side, sticking to the underbrush. Tree kept her eyes on the nearby farmhouse, but the lights were out.

After a moment, she shook her head and muttered, "For all the gold you owe, your Church doesn't seem to care about finding us."

Ewan shrugged, conceding to himself that Kate had been dead right. After an intense fortnight of constant patrols near his family's house, the Swords apparently decided it really was easier to wait for him to come to them. Which meant the outlaws got to make their forest camp a permanent hideout. "I'm not complaining."

In fairness, that was only half true. To make sure he didn't get stat-locked, Ewan had kept his party away from the most dangerous—and, sadly, lucrative—mobs. Two long months of farming slimes was making him stir-crazy, but he didn't see a better option.

At least the company was good.

He followed Tree as she picked her way up the slope, turning her feet sideways just like he'd shown her. Her leather armor was nicely broken in now, pliable enough to give her good movement. *Better than that steel cage Kate tried to stick her in,* he thought with a grimace. *And she called it a frapping wedding present!*

Not that he'd admit it to Kate, but Ewan had only become

more taken with his mysterious partner. She'd seemed so alone at first, like she didn't have a friend in the world. He'd done his best to be one for her, and she'd quickly returned the sentiment.

He blinked, then blushed and glanced away when he realized he'd been watching her climb a little too closely. He'd done his best to be a gentleman too, much preferring her smile to that soul-drilling glare.

Her knee-jerk suspicion had thawed over the weeks, allowing their friendship to blossom into a warm companionship. Every day, she listened to his songs and stories so intently that he felt no need to embellish them, knowing she was truly impressed by his accounts of the wonders and dangers he'd faced—and sometimes survived—out and about. Every night, she went to sleep behind the little screen he'd rigged for her privacy, but without fail her hand would reach around the edge and find his before her breathing slowed. It was a constant comfort, after her disappearing act that first morning.

He smiled as she grabbed a red oak's trunk and swung herself up to the path above.

Sure, Tree was beautiful. She had a mind as sharp as her wit, too, but Ewan was most impressed by her determination. Once she'd gotten the hang of the menus, she'd thrown herself into leveling with a ferocity that Ewan had only ever seen in himself, and maybe Kate. When he'd suggested she wait to choose a profession until she'd gotten a feel for the various skillsets, she'd given him a wry smile and immediately chosen *healer*, noting that she'd get more of a point bonus—and that his reputation warranted the precaution.

His hand automatically combed through his hair again, searching out the wound, but it didn't hurt anymore. *She's pretty good at it, too.*

Not that Ewan believed for a second that she'd come to

Whitehaven to learn about salves and potions. Or aura reading, despite the way she overloaded the skill. Even after months outlawing together, she'd avoided telling him about her quest in any useful detail, but he'd managed to tease out bits here and there.

Just enough information to whet his appetite for more.

Treanna Rothchild was from a foreign land, one that had escaped the Church's unification by virtue of its isolation. She and her people were the guardians of a priceless treasure, but something had happened recently to threaten it, something her people couldn't handle on their own. So, she had come for help, only to learn the Church didn't take kindly to never-before-known foreigners wandering in.

After her disastrous introduction to the priests, she'd accepted Ewan's advice to build herself up before trying again. But the anxiety and frustration, hanging off her like a bad status whenever she thought he wasn't looking, told him plainly that while she seemed happy to be out here with him as a person, she was also taking every night they spent in the field as a professional failure.

They rounded the bend, returning to the hilltop clearing. Tree sat on the edge and glanced back, her dark eyes laughing as she offered her hand. "So you don't fall off again. I'm out of herbs."

Ewan blushed again, but he took it and joined her. "It was worth it. That branch was blocking the view. See? On a clear night like this, we should be able to see Whitehaven from up here."

He pointed with his free hand, trusting his map until his eyes adjusted. Sure enough, after a few minutes he spotted the alabaster spires, some twenty miles distant.

"It's beautiful," Tree murmured. "Not just the city. All these forests and farms and streams...they're all fantastic."

Ewan privately declared another successful stealth date, but his smile faded when he saw her grim expression.

"Worrying about the priests?" he asked gently.

She nodded after a moment. "In a manner of speaking. I didn't expect we would still be in hiding by now."

He leaned into her a little, bumping her with his shoulder. "Most kids would take a year gaining the points you have. You should be proud of all you've accomplished."

"I am," she said distantly. "It's just...frustrating. I was gaining experience so easily at first, but now it feels like I'm stalling."

Ewan shrugged. "You're plateauing. You still level when you play it safe, just nowhere near as quickly."

"Unfortunately, I need 'quickly,' or this may all be for nothing." Tree pursed her lips, sparing a glower at the distant city. "It's ridiculous that stabbing beasts and making potions should help me negotiate."

Ewan leaned back on his hands. "Yeah, well, every little bit helps, right?"

She sighed. "You've introduced me to places unlike anything I'd dreamed possible, and that does count for something. But I'll need real support in order to complete my mission."

Ewan winced. "I've been giving you real support. The best I can."

Tree smiled sadly at him. "Yes, I suppose you have. I'm sorry; I didn't mean to belittle you."

A muffled thump shook the hill, jostling the trees and sending the nearby birds squawking.

Ewan jumped to his feet. Tree was right beside him, her hand reaching toward her dagger as it materialized on her belt.

"What was that?" she asked warily.

"I'm not sure," he replied. He checked his maps as he equipped his swords. "I don't see anything coming, but—Gems of old, what is *that*?" he exclaimed as a pillar of orange erupted from Whitehaven, twisting and rising into the night sky even higher than the cathedral's spire.

"Could it be a fire?" Tree asked.

Ewan narrowed his eyes, but the city was far outside his filter's range. "It definitely looks like one, but I don't know what it could be eating. Most of the buildings in town are made of stone, at least on the outsides, so there shouldn't be anything that could that run that hot." He scratched his head, accidentally tearing his cut open. "Ow. I mean, it's possible an epic mob's attacking the city, I guess, but the odds of that are crazy small. Even then, I'd expect the fires to be on the walls, not in the center."

The light vanished as suddenly as it had come, and Whitehaven disappeared back into the night, its previous faint glow invisible against the burning afterimage in his eyes. Ewan shivered a moment later as an unseasonably chill wind blew in —from the direction of the city.

"That was no ordinary fire," he muttered.

"Agreed," Tree said. "But what could it mean?"

"I wish I knew. I've never seen anything like it." He called up his menus to scan Whitehaven's quest boards. "There's nothing coming in from the Logos about a battle or disaster, but it looks like someone bumped our own hunt back up."

Tree huffed. "Do you think it had to do with us?"

"I don't see how," he said, trying to ignore the cold sweat forming on his neck. "We'd probably better get back to camp, though. Just in case."

She took his hand, and they retreated down the darkened hill as briskly as his pride would allow.

They made it back without incident, but Ewan slept poorly that night, troubled by dreams of fire and wind. When the morning light eventually filtered down through the cave's mouth, he sat up and gave Tree's hand a gentle squeeze.

She didn't react at all.

Ewan smiled to himself. *At least that's the same.* Ever since that first night, she'd slept like a rock, and later than anyone he'd ever heard of. After weeks of trying to wake her and getting only slow, steady breathing in reply, he'd privately made plans to haul her out and apologize later if trouble came looking for them.

He slipped his hand out from under hers and made his way to the glade, brushing his fingers against the now-polished stone of their makeshift hallway. The air was still crisp, so he warmed himself up with a few stretches.

He'd only just finished when he heard heavy footfalls.

Taking cover behind the log, he equipped his swords and drew them...then laughed in relief when Kate stomped into the clearing with a huge pack on her shoulders.

"Don't point those things at me," she growled.

Ewan grinned. "I thought you were a mob, crashing around like that."

"Funny. Keep 'em out," she ordered when he started to sheathe his blades.

"What for?"

Kate slung the pack onto the ground with a thud. "Didn't you hear?"

"Hear what?"

"About the fire, you aurochs!"

The cold sweat from last night returned. "We saw it, but then it went back out. There wasn't anything on the quest boards."

"Well, it was all over town this morning," Kate grumbled as

she dropped onto the pack. "The frapping Diamond Lord appeared, right in the middle of the cathedral."

Ewan blinked, but the sweat became icy. "The Diamond Lord? You mean the Gem, from the old days?"

"Yeah, that one." She let out a dark laugh. "Like there are others. And you'll never guess what he wanted."

"What who wanted?" Tree asked, stepping softly into the glade to join them.

"The Diamond Lord," Kate repeated.

"Who?"

Kate scowled at her. "Don't act like you don't know what the Gems are!"

Ewan shot his sister a warning glare. Turning to Tree, he said, "The Gems ruled Veridor in ancient times, in the days before the Church. There was one for each of the major cities, nine in all. They all died in the great war, killed by Old Max, but Kate's saying the Diamond Lord of Whitehaven came back last night." He glanced at Kate. "No frapping way."

Kate crossed her arms. "Why would the Church make it up?"

"Why not? They make up plenty."

"E, this isn't like your crazy ideas!"

"I don't understand," Tree interrupted. "If these things lived so long ago, how can one be here now?"

"How, indeed?" came a male voice from the trees; a second later, Paul stepped into the glade in full armor.

"You," Ewan growled as he leveled a sword at the cadet's throat. "How did you find us?"

Paul froze, hands raised. "Take it easy, Ewan. After what happened last night, I expected Kate would go warn you if she had any idea where you were hiding. I followed her out here."

Kate snorted.

Paul offered her a wan smile. "You really should work on your stealth. You leave a trail so obvious, a blind man could follow you. No offense intended, of course. And you must be the fugitive," he continued, regarding Tree cautiously.

Tree gave him a scathing glare in return as she moved behind Ewan to a support position. "Ewan, do you know this boy?"

"He's an old friend," Ewan grumbled. "Paul, I won't let you take her in."

"I didn't expect you to, but that's all right. I'm not here to arrest anyone."

Ewan scanned the area on his maps, then checked with his eyes. The only people he saw were the four of them, but that didn't count for much against the weak line of sight in the woods. "In that case, what do you want?" he asked, still holding his blade high.

"I have a favor to ask of you," Paul replied. "But I'll come to that. As a sign of good faith, let me tell you what I know." Keeping his hands out where Ewan could see them, he sat on the log. "I was on duty in the main chapel last night. I saw everything; it was straight out of a nightmare. The roof exploded as a column of fire descended, and the Diamond Lord himself stepped out of it, right into the middle of the room, with silver fire in his eyes and massive white wings." He closed his own eyes, shuddering at the memory. "Two of my comrades attacked him. He raised a hand, and they burned right there."

"Gems," Ewan muttered, stomach curdling at the oath as he lowered his sword. "What did you do?"

"I took cover behind the pews," Paul admitted, still pale-faced. "When the Patriarch came to speak with him, the Gem said he was pursuing a fugitive. From his realm."

Ewan blinked. "A fugitive?"

Paul nodded, then looked right at Tree.

"Me?" she gasped.

"Her?" Ewan shouted. He flicked his swords back up.

"I told you." Kate huffed.

Paul nodded, eyes locked on Tree. "I'm afraid so. A girl, he said, here without authorization. One who would bring ruin to us all, if she was allowed to inflict her will upon the world. He ordered the Church to hunt her down, promising rewards beyond belief to the party that managed it."

"And the Patriarch said yes?" Ewan snapped, trying hard not to think about the rest. "After the Diamond Lord just stormed in there and killed a bunch of people?"

"Especially after that!" Paul shot back. "Ewan, you weren't there; you don't understand! I'm no aura reader, but even I could tell you he was overpowered, beyond any epic mob." He took a long breath. "We wouldn't have stood a chance, fighting him head-on. And since the Church was already looking for the two of you, it made sense to ally with him."

"I'm sure it did," Ewan growled. He glanced back at Tree, but her face was as blank as limbo. *First the Church, and now a Gem of old? What does she know?*

Paul sighed. "Once he'd gotten the Patriarch's cooperation, the Diamond Lord said he would be checking in on us, as a test of our faith. Then he vanished."

For a second, everyone stood there. Then Kate turned on Tree, axes drawn. "You frapping Gem. What are you playing at?"

Tree flinched back. "I didn't even know what a Gem was until this morning!"

"The Diamond Lord didn't say she was!" Ewan protested, sheathing his swords and stepping between the two girls. "He only said she was from his world. Right, Paul?"

"That's an awfully fine hair to split, Ewan," Paul warned.

"She's spent two months with me, and she hasn't burned anyone. Nerf it all, she didn't even know how to use the menus when she got here! That's right," Ewan said, glaring at Paul as the cadet's eyes widened. "Not at all like the guy who one-shotted the Church's capital last night, is it?"

Paul's eyes narrowed. "Even so, what are you going to do? Are you suggesting that you'd fight a Gem to keep her safe?"

"Absolutely," Ewan answered without hesitation. "It seems to me that he's no better than the rest of you, hunting someone who needs our help."

"I'm relieved to hear you say that," Paul said. "Because I'm really here to ask for your help in taking the Diamond Lord down again."

"You—what do you mean?"

Paul regarded him levelly. "Right after the Gem left, I received a quest from the Logos. Epic level. Every Sword got it, as far as I can tell, which would make sense, given that Maximilian founded our order to rid Veridor of the Gems."

The blood started to pound in Ewan's ears, shattering the icy grip on his neck. "But there hasn't been an Epic-level quest since the war."

Paul nodded, smiling wolfishly. "Exactly. The quest directs me to retrieve an artifact from the heart of the Argenones."

"The Argenones?" Kate said. "What's there?"

"A fighting chance, I hope," Paul replied. "It's not public knowledge, but the Swords believe Maximilian possessed a secret weapon, an artifact of great power."

Ewan frowned. "And that's how he beat the Gems?"

"We believe so. Unfortunately, Maximilian took his secret to the Logos."

"Then how do you know about it?" Ewan asked.

"We don't know; we guess. He was the only person who could inflict damage on the Gems, so it seems reasonable that he possessed an item which made it possible. If the Logos is pointing us toward that item, then we need to find it as soon as we can."

"But why are you telling me all this?" Ewan grumbled, fists clenching his swords' hilts. "I'm an outlaw, in case you forgot. If the Swords come looking for this weapon or whatever, then the last place I want to be is in their way."

"They're not going to look for it," Paul said quietly.

Ewan gaped at him. "What? Why not? Gems of old, it's an Epic quest!"

Paul's face darkened. "In the interest of compliance with the Patriarch's agreement, our Grandmaster ordered every Sword to decline the quest. Moreover, a good number of them decided they'd rather hunt the two of you down and claim the Gem's reward instead." He narrowed his eyes, checking his menus. "Several of them are on their way, as we speak."

Ewan snarled. "You son of a—"

"It was going to happen anyway!" Paul snapped. "Given their prompt arrival, I'm sure I wasn't the only one who thought to watch Kate's movement."

"Don't blame me," Kate shot back. "They probably just tracked you!"

Paul held up a hand, and a quest invitation appeared in Ewan's vision. "We don't have time. Ewan, I'm giving you the chance to stop the Diamond Lord. He's a threat to everything; already he's got half the Swords following him. If we don't do something soon, all of Veridor could fall back into the chaos of the old days."

Ewan opened his mouth to argue, but he couldn't. He'd wanted a taste of the old days ever since he was a kid, but not like this. Not with the Church and a Gem—a frapping Gem!—hunting for him and Tree, maybe even his family.

But how could he turn down an Epic quest?

"Fine," he said, accepting the invite. "But I'm not doing this for the Church. I'm doing it because it's right."

"As long as you do it, I don't see the problem," Paul replied, shoulders straightening as the menu vanished. "Be careful, Ewan. There's more going on here than we've been told, and what we don't know is now actively trying to kill us."

*Tell me about it*, Ewan thought, glancing at Tree again.

Her face colored, and she looked away.

"Now," Paul said as he stood, "all that remains are the loose ends."

"Yeah." Ewan readied his swords again. "Kate, if anyone other than Mom and Dad asks, I dragged you out here as a hostage, got it?"

She snorted. "Right. And I got away when Mr. Pompous Do-Gooder over here came in the nick of time to attack you."

"And died in action," Paul finished wryly as he drew his own sword. "Anything else you need, Ewan?"

"When I get this secret weapon of yours, where should I meet you?"

"Look for me in the Toasted Tank. If I'm not there, my contact will be. I'll tell her to keep an eye out for you. Not that anyone in Veridor won't be, once the Diamond Lord's quest makes the boards."

With that, the Sword cadet rushed Ewan, swinging at his head to claim aggressor status. Ewan deflected the strike and lunged, but Paul threw up his shield to block.

"Couldn't you drop the armor?" Ewan grumbled.

Paul grunted. "Not if I want it to look convincing. You'd better hurry. The others are only a few minutes away."

Ewan knocked Paul's shield aside, then stabbed him through the seam in his mail. "You have got to be the worst helper ever."

"All for the cause," Paul replied, coughing blood from a weak grin. "Don't loot me, okay?"

Ewan couldn't help grinning back. "You don't have anything I'd want, anyway. But Paul? Thanks for trusting me."

The cadet nodded as his health bled out; then he slumped to the ground. "Prove me right."

Ewan sighed as he nudged his friend's corpse into a slightly more dignified position before turning to Kate. "You'd better run, or they'll be onto you next."

"Don't worry about me, aurochs," she muttered, handing him the pack and scoffing when he stumbled under its weight. "I put some upgrades in there. There's a new dagger for you," she added, glaring at Tree. "In case your secret Gem powers don't cut it. Mind who you use it on."

"Of course," Tree murmured. Her eyes were locked onto Paul's corpse. "Thank you."

Kate ignored her. "I expect you to tell me how the new gear held up when you get home," she said to Ewan. "And bring back any good ores you find. The Argenones are rich in coresilver, and there's plenty of room in the pack."

"I'll do what I can," Ewan said. "Tell Mom and Dad I'm sorry."

"They know." She gave him a quick hug as the first red dots appeared on the edge of his local map. "They send their love, and said to just keep following your heart."

"Thanks," Ewan said, increasingly convinced his heart had led him off a cliff. "Now go, please!"

Kate sprinted off, faster than he'd ever seen her run before.

Ewan grabbed the pack and hoisted it onto his shoulders, then turned to Tree. "We've got to go too," he grunted, wondering more than ever just who—and what—she really was. "We'll talk about all this, once we get somewhere safer."

She nodded, still avoiding his eyes.

For once too stressed to be excited about learning more, Ewan led her from the glade at a run, before the Gem's Swords could find them.

**7**

---

# TO THE HILLS

EWAN AND TREE HURTLED THROUGH THE UNDERBRUSH, LEAPING the stream well above the falls that fed their former swimming pool.

Tree hurtled, at least. The frapping pack encumbered Ewan like nothing he'd ever carried, making it a struggle to keep up with her. Grudgingly, he called up his menus and dumped some emergency points into endurance, and his stride lengthened slightly.

As he ran, he split his attention between the tangled way forward and his map, overlaid across his vision. Three red dots ghosted over its eastern side despite the rough terrain, vengeful spirits come to claim the fugitives at long last. The wood's edge lay to the west, with some forty miles past that to the Argenones.

"This is no good," Ewan panted, slowing as his stamina tanked out. "I've got to ditch the pack."

"If you do, we won't have any food," Tree argued. She looked back and passed him a potion, via line of sight. "Here, drink this."

He took it, then sighed in relief as the second wind hit. "Thanks. How many more of these do we have?"

"Not enough to sprint all the way to the mountains," she replied. She stopped, glancing back to the east as Ewan caught her up. "We should stand and fight."

"Tree, we've been over this. If we make the first aggressive move, we'll get ID'ed as hostiles to every Sword in Veridor. They'll find us in no time!"

"But we can still act in self-defense...or in the defense of the party."

"Yeah, but—no."

Her expression hardened. "I'm the one they want."

"You'll get yourself killed! Tree, these aren't wood rats; they're real people!"

She flashed him a grim smile. "Then it's a good thing I have real support, isn't it?"

Ewan watched her eyes, but they didn't waver.

"Okay. But if things go south, you run as hard as you can."

"I'll be fine. Trust me."

They ran on, making it to the open fields a minute later. Ewan took position in the cover of a dense thicket on the fringe, dropping the pack with a grateful sigh. Tree transferred a few stamina potions to him just in case, then raced out about fifty yards into the tall grass.

And screamed.

"Please, wait! My leg's broken!"

Ewan watched in horrified wonder as she limped about, putting on such a convincing, guilt-tripping show between her cries and halting steps that he would have raced over to help, had her status not been right there in his menus.

The red dots on his map shifted course and picked up their pace, converging with deadly precision on her location.

*Here we go.* To take his mind off the soldiers' approach— and Tree's accusations that he'd abandoned her—Ewan dug into the pack, searching for their new gear in the huge inventory list that came up. There was a dagger and a set of enchanted earrings, which he transferred to Tree via line of sight, and after more searching, he grabbed a pair of swords and armor for himself.

He equipped them, and even Tree's anguished cries faded out as he looked, awestruck, at Kate's latest creations.

The armor was clearly made from the ore they'd gotten months ago. Blacker than a moonless night, she'd worked the hardened material into carefully mosaicked plates, affixed to a durable mesh fabric by precise stitching. Ewan flexed his limbs, and the plates seemed to realign over his muscles, matching his movements and poses perfectly. It made him feel as unencumbered as a newborn babe, while providing him with a skin as tough as steel. Tougher, if all Kate's ranting about night ore had been even half true.

But the swords...the swords were a masterpiece. Like the behemoth's horns from which they'd been crafted, they had a slight backward curve to them, with dark spines that faded to a pale tan at the razor edges, somehow filed from the horns' inner layers. Their full tangs were set into solid grips, made from the same mesh that underlaid the armor. They were incredibly light, with tips that glided effortlessly and seemed to sigh as he drew them across the grass, neatly trimming the stems.

*Sis, you really outdid yourself this time,* Ewan thought, humbled by her love and faith in him, as armored footfalls joined Tree's cries. *I swear I'll put them to the best use.*

Three white-clad soldiers broke from the woods, weapons drawn and moving straight for Tree.

The moment the Logos informed him she was under direct attack, Ewan flew from the thicket. Upgraded and without the pack, he easily overtook the first Sword. He stabbed for the armor's shoulder seam, but the horn blade was so light, he misjudged and hit the woman square in the back—and punched straight through the steel armor as though it were wool.

She fell with a cry that mirrored Ewan's own shock, but her comrades turned, took one look, and forgot about Tree. They both came at him: one with a massive greatsword, the other with a halberd.

Ewan rushed the spearman first, trusting now to Kate's gear. The night-plate turned the halberd's blade, giving Ewan only a firm bump. Amazed but still running, he plowed into the man and staggered him back before bringing his blades around to take the guy's head clean off.

He spun to face the greatsword, just in time to see the man's eyes bulge as he stopped short.

"You can't run forever," he gasped before toppling forward, leaving Ewan with a stark view of Tree and her bloody new weapon.

She glared down at the man, holding the dagger high as though expecting him to respawn right there. Hoping, even.

"We got them," Ewan said, warily moving toward her. "Check your map. No more red dots."

Tree nodded, then slowly crouched and wiped her blade across the corpse's chest, the way he'd shown her with mobs.

It looked a lot different on a human.

"He'll be back, won't he?" she asked, her voice as distant and unknowable as the Gems' realm. "They'll keep coming."

Ewan swallowed, pushing his dread down. "Maybe. Though I doubt they'll be so bold next time. You okay?"

"I'm fine," Tree said, still watching the body. "I just...I've never killed another person."

"Me neither."

She looked up at him. "What about your friend?"

"Not in anger, anyway," he corrected, hesitating. "Veridor's got enough challenges in it without people needing to hurt each other, you know?"

Her expression hardened. "It seems we no longer have that luxury."

Ewan sighed, trying to think of something encouraging to say. "I guess not. But if these guys are determined to attack us, that's on them. I'll protect the people I care about, with deadly force if need be."

Tree considered this and smiled, grimly. "I was prepared to do whatever I had to as well, to complete my mission. At least, I thought I was. I suppose I still am." Her eyes clouded as she looked down again. "It's just...I'm supposed to be taking care of people like this, not killing them."

Ewan shrugged. "The Church waives the lock fees for Swords. He'll get over it."

He knelt by the man's body, more to give Tree a moment than to loot the corpse. She'd been rattled the first time she'd killed a mob, but just as her fear had given way to determination then, there was something else there now. Something calculating. Something that gnawed at the corners of his heart, making him listen for any sign she might use that dagger on him next.

*What did she mean, that she was supposed to take care of the Swords?*

He looked at the man she'd killed, then realized he'd seen the face before. Slapped it, in fact, in the cathedral's courtyard. He searched the corpse's inventory, then blinked at the name that came up. "Caleb Martin."

"What?" Tree asked, still at a safe distance.

"That's his name. Why does that sound so familiar? Martin...Martin." He frowned. "Come on; we need to loot these guys before they dissolve."

"For the disguise?"

Ewan shook his head. "The Swords know their own; we wouldn't read as part of their guild."

"Then why bother?" she asked.

"The more we take off them now, the less they'll have when they respawn." He shot her a little grin. "Might as well try to make it a little harder for them, right?"

They took a moment to pull everything out of the Swords' inventories—though Ewan left more on the woman, for modesty's sake—just making it before the Logos reclaimed the bodies. Ewan kept the gold and a few potions, but he dumped the rest of it in the grass. The pack was already heavy enough as it was.

They made it another eighteen miles that day, walking as quickly as they could to conserve Ewan's stamina. They spoke little, ostensibly for the same reason, but Ewan's mind burned with questions every time he caught Tree's eye.

She was quick to look away whenever he did.

The combat was disappointingly light: a couple of boars near a stream, and later a scrum of elves, more obnoxious than dangerous thanks to the little poisoned arrows they liked to fire from ambush. They evaded him almost as adeptly as his companion, but he got at least a few of them.

When the sun faded behind the mountains proper, Ewan called a halt for the night. He picked out a bramble-ringed campsite just inside a small copse, then dropped the pack and plopped down beside it with a huff, scratching his cheek at the boils made by the elves' arrows.

Tree came over, to offer him a salve without meeting his eyes. "We made good distance."

"Yeah." He idly panned the map to their quest marker, a little arrow out in the middle of nowhere. "But we've still got a long way to go."

She said nothing.

Ewan sighed and checked the pack. Kate had stuffed it with

gear for just about any terrain short of swimming the ocean, along with mining equipment for him to bring back some loot for her. Thankfully, his mom had managed to also tuck in enough home-cooked rations to last several weeks.

"So," he said, pulling out an apple and handing it to Tree. "We need to talk."

She sat down carefully before looking at him. "I know. But first...Ewan, thank you. You didn't hesitate to say you'd fight this powerful Gem and protect me, despite how worried you must feel."

"Well," he said, not trying to cover the doubt in his voice. "It seemed like the right thing to do."

Tree stiffened, then sighed. "It is. I'm sure of it. I want to tell you more about my mission, at least as much as I can. I'm sorry to keep asking this from you, but please be patient a little longer for the rest?"

"Yeah, sure. We're in this together now, right?"

"Right." She hesitated, then took a deep breath. "I'm not actually from this world."

Ewan's heart sank. "So you really are from the Gems' realm."

"No. I don't understand why your Diamond Lord would say that. Perhaps it's trying to distract attention from itself?"

*He wouldn't be the only one,* Ewan thought irritably. "Then where are you from? What are you?"

"I'm human, just like you," Tree said as though not convinced, herself, "but I wasn't born here. In fact, I'd never been to Veridor until the day we met."

*Never? That explains her low level, I guess.* "So," Ewan said, as casually as he could, "if there's some other world out there with people just like me—us—then where is it?"

She turned the apple in her fingers. "It's difficult to explain. You might say our worlds run alongside each other, but strictly speaking, my world is more like the parent to yours. Without it, yours couldn't exist."

Ewan's heart sank even more, but his hackles rose. "That sounds like what the Gems used to say."

Tree shook her head. "I told you, there aren't any Gems in my world. We have enough problems, as it is."

"So you weren't lying about the danger, at least?"

She gave him a pained look. "I've never lied to you. I promise you that I never will. It's just...you saw what happened with the Church. I don't want to anger you, too."

Ewan rubbed his face to hide his impatience. His mind sifted through her words for clues or hidden meanings, but she was choosing too carefully. Speaking slowly, as though assembling a glass puzzle.

Or a trap.

He tried to keep his voice level. "Tell me what's going on. Please."

"I'm trying." She took another deep breath, before squaring her shoulders. "My home, the Centre, is tasked with monitoring your world, among other things. We've done so for a very long time."

"Wait. You mean we're your priceless treasure? The one you're protecting?"

She nodded.

*Gems of old*, Ewan thought, suddenly remembering the priest's warning about invoking the ancient powers. *Help from another world? No wonder the Church didn't want to deal with you!* "But something's threatening it—us? What is it?"

"I'm not sure. No one is, not yet." She shook her head in frustration. "It's still so hard to explain. The best evidence we have suggests a hostile force from outside the Centre."

"What, like an invasion?"

She nodded again, her dark eyes deadly serious.

Ewan's blood chilled, despite the lingering warmth in the

air. An army, just...appearing out of nowhere to destroy Veridor? The thought made him feel exposed, even more so than the Diamond Lord's sudden return.

The Diamond Lord. Could the Gem have come back to protect his old domain from this invasion? But why would he be after Tree, if she was the one with the warning? It all had to be related, no matter what she thought. If the bad guys were in her world, maybe he simply thought she was with them and couldn't tell the difference?

How many other worlds could there be?

"And you told the priests all this?" he asked.

"Yes." Tree sighed. "And more. Their reaction is the reason I've been so hesitant to tell you everything."

*Everything? You've only just now told me anything!* Ewan gave her hand a little squeeze anyway and said, "Well, I'm not the Church. I won't claim to understand half of what you're telling me, but that just makes me all the more fired up to learn about it."

Her voice faltered as she glanced at him. "Then you believe me?"

"I trust you," he corrected, that voice suddenly making him struggle for words as well. "You're, um, a dear friend, and I still want to help you, and get to know you better. Nothing you've said changes any of that."

She held his gaze, searching for something as though he was the one keeping secrets, but then she reached out and stroked his cheek.

"You're dear to me too," she whispered as her fingers traced his chin and floated away.

It took Ewan a moment or ten to remember where he was, but eventually he smiled back. "Um, yeah...now that that's settled, what can we do?"

Tree's eyes hardened, all business again. "We've got to convince the Church to help us. Their soldiers, if based in the

Centre, could prevent danger to Veridor."

"But even if the Church agrees, how are we supposed to get there?" Then it dawned on him, a sudden thought that made his heart leap. "Wait! Does it have to do with logging out?"

Tree hesitated, telling him in an instant he was right. "Ewan, I'm—"

"It does! Gems of old! Your world's where we go when we get logged?"

"It's not as simple as you're thinking! It isn't what we call it… but yes, I suppose people who are logged out do pass through my world."

"I knew it!" He let out a whoop. "Just wait till I tell the priests—oh, I guess we already know what they thought."

Her face darkened. "All too well."

But Ewan laughed in reply, feeling more lighthearted than he had in weeks. Here he was, on Veridor's first Epic-level quest in centuries, with a pretty girl who knew more about limbo than the frapping Church did! "They'll have to listen, once we get Max's secret thingy," he promised. "And we won't back down until they do."

Tree seemed to take his cheer as a good stopping point, and he didn't press for more details. After dinner, he sang her to sleep as usual, but he stayed up for a while, in case of trouble.

In truth, he spent most of it watching her, his fingers idly tracing his cheek where she'd touched him.

It was intimate, and fascinating, to see Tree sleep. Without the privacy screen, he could see now that her breathing was slow and automatic, too much so to be natural.

*Has she been logging out to her world, this whole time?* The thought unnerved him, stoking a sudden guilty sympathy for how he'd made his family feel over the years.

She returned around three in the morning, insisting he get a few hours of sleep, but they set out again shortly after sunrise. Ewan kept a close eye on his map as they went, searching for a convenient pass in the Argenones' eastern crest, but he also watched for signs of the Swords. By now, Paul could have gotten busted for transferring the quest, but the only thing Ewan could do to help at this point was to complete it.

The ground became rockier as they went, with noticeably more steps up than down, and by late morning the great peaks loomed high above them, still snow-covered even this close to midsummer. New mobs came out to challenge them, with fewer elves and wolves and more in the way of goblins and the occasional bear. The fighting was definitely tougher than their forest battles, but Ewan startled himself with just how cautiously he was taking things, adopting one defensive position after another to keep Tree—and himself—from danger.

He told himself it was because his encumbrance was a lot higher than he was used to, and he spent every point he earned to boost his agility in an attempt to compensate.

When the sun sank behind the peaks that afternoon, it seemed to take the heat of summer with it, leaving the outlaws in a numbing chill that further slowed them down. They paused to rummage through the pack, finding two fur-lined parkas Kate had stuffed in there to deal with the cold.

"It's getting dark," Tree said, watching the mountainous silhouettes as she equipped her parka. "We should look for a defensible place to make camp."

"Yeah, you're—gah!"

Something punched into Ewan's armor from behind, knocking him onto his face and taking a chunk off his health. Tree yelled a warning, and he rolled over just in time to dodge the next arrow as it glanced off the rock.

"Nerfed elves!" He stood, but when he looked back he saw a figure, a good three hundred yards distant but easily visible in its white tunic and polished armor, glinting in the waning light.

"Gems," he gasped as a third arrow narrowly missed his head. "A Sword. We're dead if we stay in the open."

Tree helped him to the cover of a boulder, then began tending to his wound once he'd unequipped his cuirass. The arrow had somehow found its way through a narrow gap in the armored plates, piercing deep into his left shoulder.

"Can you fix it?" he asked, clenching his teeth as she worked the arrow out.

"I'm trying." She rubbed a stinging ointment onto the raw wound, to stem the bleeding. "But I'll need time to make it heal properly."

"We don't have it." Already the red dot was coming up the hill, a frapping sight faster than they'd done. "Just close it up the best you can, and I'll take care of it."

She gave him a dubious, worried look, but she obeyed.

Ewan reequipped his armor, then peeked his head over the boulder to see the Sword, a hulking, ruddy-faced man who apparently preferred kicking rocks aside to stepping around them. "Who do you think you are, shooting at travelers like that?" Ewan called.

"Don't patronize me," the man growled. "You and that girl have already humiliated me twice!"

Ewan called up his aura reading and winced at the man's overpowered strength, but then he groaned in recognition as he saw the name: Commander Caleb Martin. Paul's hardcore squad leader.

*That's just perfect. But how did he get so strong, all of a sudden? He wasn't like that outside the woods.*

Caleb loosed another arrow without slowing, forcing Ewan to dive back behind his rock. "This time I will bring you both to the Diamond Lord, dead or alive."

Ewan sighed and glanced at Tree, crouched beside him with dagger out. "Stay back. He could one-shot us."

Taking her silence as agreement, he ditched the pack and

hauled himself up to fight, wondering how in Veridor he was going to survive this time. "Yeah, well, unless he's offering me a discount on lock releases, I think I'd prefer to skip that. You're one sorry excuse for a Sword, though. Aren't you supposed to kill Gems?"

Caleb laughed as he closed to a dozen yards. "Times change, boy. Under the Church's thumb, there's only so much glory for a soldier to have, dragging raw noobs out on the same old trails to fight the same tired mobs. Only so much sanctioned ale and tail to sate his ambition." His eyes flashed as he looked in Tree's direction, through the boulder. "But the Diamond Lord? He's given me the strength and stamina of three men to hunt you down, and promised me a hundredfold more, on delivery."

Ewan blinked. "More? To do what?"

Caleb chuckled, watching him with murderous eyes. "Anything I please. A Sword could never rule over the priests, but with my new lord's boon, I could overthrow the Church and claim Veridor for myself." He smiled wolfishly as the bow vanished from his gauntleted hands, replaced by a greatsword even bigger than the last one. "All I've got to do is bring the girl to him, and you're half-dead already."

"Even all-dead, I wouldn't let the likes of you have their way," Ewan retorted, drawing his own blades and hoping against hope that Kate's crafting could stand up to a Gem's buffs. "And I think you'll find I'm still too much for you to handle."

Caleb gave an indignant roar and charged.

Ewan waited, letting the man's heavy gear and the run uphill do their work, but when he deflected the Sword's first strike, his shoulder screamed in such pain that he dropped his left blade. He staggered away as Caleb spun around and lopped off the top of the boulder beside him. Ewan lunged for the man's feet with his remaining blade, but Caleb kicked it aside, forcing Ewan to roll out of the way as he brought the greatsword down into the rock where his head had been.

"If you give her up now, I'll vouch for your cooperation." Caleb grunted, slipping on the loose terrain as he leaped back from Ewan's counterstrike. "Maybe even keep that little family of yours safe and sound. The Church may not forgive your sins, but a Gem could wipe them away."

"Not going to happen," Ewan panted. He chugged a potion to give himself a lift, but he was in trouble. That first blow had torn his shoulder open again, and he was bleeding out health.

Caleb laughed softly, reading Ewan's status with a sadistic gleam in his narrowed eyes. "You're dying, boy. And when you respawn, I'll be there."

"You wouldn't get to my bind in time," Ewan countered. "I'll be long gone."

Caleb's next laugh was incredulous. "We've impounded your bind! You'll respawn in the Church's darkest pit, the one for irredeemable heretics."

Ewan barely had time to register his new panic before Caleb swung again, knocking him down like a ragdoll as he tried to stay between the Sword and Tree. He sprang up only to get beaten back again, and again, before the world began to swim around him in the dizzy haze of imminent death. A death he wouldn't be returning from, not in any way that mattered.

Why would a man this strong want more strength?

*I won't let him have it*, Ewan thought, bracing himself for the inevitable but refusing to go to limbo alone. *I'm sorry, Tree.*

He gathered the last of his strength as Caleb came forward. The Sword spun the blade high for a finishing strike, but Ewan leaped up and drove his own straight through the man's throat, praying for an instant kill.

Caleb stood there with his mouth open, but all that came out were gurgles. After a moment, he fell, crushing Ewan as surely as a behemoth.

Ewan strained against the corpse, trying to tell Tree to keep going as panic gnawed at his heart. But then he felt an odd, soft sensation, like water gently flowing through him.

He blinked, then gasped as his health rose.

As soon as he could, he shoved Caleb's body away and pushed himself to kneeling. Tree was running to him, her hands reaching out as the cool sensation swept through again. The pain in his shoulder receded enough that when she flung her arms around him, he didn't cry out.

"How?" he asked, baffled but elated.

"I used a healing spell," she said, half giggling with wild eyes.

"A—what?"

"A spell. I only just unlocked it with points I'd saved back like you suggested, for an emergency!"

His elation stumbled, overtaken by a new swell of worries. "You mean...magic?"

"I suppose so. Why?" She was shaking wildly now, making him wobble.

Ewan looked up at her, almost afraid to say it. "Because there hasn't been a mage since the time of the Gems."

"Then it's lucky for you that I learned how," she said, before smacking him on his newly mended shoulder. "Don't risk your life that carelessly again!"

*I can't afford to anymore,* he agreed silently, picturing the Church's dungeon. But as he looked past her to the Argenones, waiting for them with mobs and hazards tougher than anything he'd ever faced, he said, "I can't promise, but if you've learned to use magic, I think our chances of getting through this just went up a ton."

**8**

———

# FIRE AND ICE

A STORM WAS BLOWING IN FROM THE EAST, FLASHES OF LIGHTNING illuminating the darkened spaces over the distant fields below.

Ewan shivered and wrapped his parka tight as a gust of icy wind whipped around his perch on the rock face. Turning back, he climbed down and made his way among the jagged boulders toward the cave he and Tree had used as their camp for the night.

It was dangerous up here, between the cold and the mobs. In the week and a half since they'd begun climbing from the foothills, they'd had plentiful opportunities to work in their new gear on the intimidating creatures that roamed the area. Above the tree line, fire-eyed golems patrolled the peaks, undeterred by the oversized eagles that occasionally swooped down and knocked them off.

Ewan shuddered, reliving a particularly nasty fight yesterday afternoon that had only ended well for him because Kate's pack had proven too heavy for the eagle to carry off. His hands automatically reached for his swords, relaxing when they found the mesh grips just over his shoulders. His old steel blades would have broken a dozen times over in the past week from the golems alone, but the behemoth's horn hadn't even chipped.

Yet.

Even so, if they'd only had Kate's gifts to rely on, they wouldn't have made it beyond the foothills. Ever since Tree had saved him from death by Caleb, Ewan kept trying—and failing—to wrap his head around the power she now wielded. Somehow, she'd opened a completely new branch on the skill tree, one that, if it existed, hadn't been used for hundreds of years. Enchanted gear was common enough, at least for someone with a smith in the family, but casting spells? Buffing with a thought? That was something from the histories, making Tree's new skillset just one more relic of the Gems' time to come roaring to life again.

When she'd first shown him her skill tree, its labyrinthine arcane paths branching off of a high aura-reading base, he'd stared at it blankly, trying to reconcile how different it looked from his own. She claimed up and down that she'd simply followed his advice to pick useful skills, acting as though she'd known all along where she was headed but never realizing it might be important.

*Why should she?* Ewan thought as he picked his way around a fallen rock. She'd been just as flummoxed by his own skill tree, the first day he'd shown it to her. How was she to know what was normal or not?

But surely her path wasn't normal. Even if he didn't know the other professions well, if magic was available enough for a girl with a few months' heavy experience to obtain, then someone else should have noticed!

That no one had really worried him.

Not that he was complaining. Magic had made their insane trek into the mountains much more survivable. Almost comfortable, even. Thanks to Kate's earrings, Tree's boosted experience was unlocking new spells each day, from how to make fire—a Gem's gift in their current situation—to every buff he knew.

Then there were spells for which he couldn't even think of a nonmagical counterpart.

He rounded the mountain's shoulder to find their camp, easily visible by the odd film of snow and pebbles that had blown up against the shield she'd cast. She'd tried to explain it to him, something about the air being coaxed into a crystalline form by rearrangement of the subordinate elements in it, but having only just learned it herself two days ago, she'd admitted she didn't understand what the Logos meant by the description.

Whatever the theory, though, she'd quickly grasped its practical applications. Rigged up as it was, her shield provided a nice barrier from the biting wind, but when cast on the move, it absorbed some damage in combat, although it took a lot out of her to do it. She was determined to make a weapon of it, something to use at range, but so far, she hadn't worked out how.

The barrier shimmered as Ewan walked through it, somehow keyed to his life force to admit him into her private sanctuary from the harsh environment. Tree was seated on the pack by the cave's wall with cupped hands, making shadows dance across the stone as a chain of sparks bounced from one finger to the next. The effect was eerie, but mesmerizing.

*All part of being sure she can get the priests to listen,* he thought uneasily. He moved to dust the snow off his shoulders, before remembering that her shield already had. "Hey."

She looked up, banishing the sparks with a smile. "Hey. Do we have time for breakfast?"

"Not much. There's a storm coming in from behind, and I don't want to get caught on this side of the Spine. Did you have any luck mapping out a route to that pass we saw last night?"

"It depends on how much risk we're willing to take," Tree

said, narrowing her eyes to share her map. "The mountain we're on has a spur alongside the one holding our pass, here... but there's a gap of some thirty feet, over a chasm quite deeper than that."

"I'm pretty sure I can't jump that far, even without extra weight." Ewan frowned, glancing at the pack. There was a good bit of climbing gear in there, but between the ice, the eagles, and their need to stay alive, he wasn't keen to try it.

"You probably could if I buff your strength well enough, but it's not a guarantee."

"And if we play it safe for a change?" he asked.

She panned the map a few miles to the north. "We'd have to work our way down here. By the time we crossed and regained our current elevation, it would be dark. Do you think the storm will hold off that long?"

"Not a chance." He sighed. "It'll be on us by mid-afternoon, if not sooner."

"Then we'll have to try the crossing."

Ewan started to protest as she banished the map, but his words caught when he looked at her. The confident determination in her dark eyes was like a spell in its own right; the voice of authority and its simple finality somehow seemed natural, coming from her.

"Okay," he said, willing to follow her renewed sense of direction. After all, he was the one who was helping her.

He shivered when she dropped the shield, letting the wind back in. *At least, I think I am.*

They moved on, racing the storm as quickly as they could in their hiking gear while the morning sky turned from faint gray to a milky blue. As part of Kate's attempt to prepare for every last possible contingency, she'd provided them with some snowshoes. The broad, net-like soles gave excellent grip in the wintry terrain, a good trade for the minor penalty to Ewan's agility—next to nothing, really, on top of everything else.

Refusing to be outdone on the precaution front, Ewan tied a few yards' worth of rope between Tree and himself. Not only did it mean they wouldn't get separated by a slip down the side of the hill, it also reassured him that a marauding bird couldn't snatch her from behind without faceplanting into the snow under their combined weight.

He needn't have worried. When they got jumped—dived—by another eagle, Tree found yet another use for her shields. After leaping nimbly out of the bird's attack and lighting its tail feathers on fire, she cast the barrier right over it, pinning it down to give Ewan an easy kill.

*And just like that, yesterday's terrors are today's lunch,* he thought as he spent the new points to keep his agility on track.

By the time they reached the crevice, the storm clouds were sweeping over the eastern peaks, racing up the mountainsides far more effectively than any human could. Watching its approach, Ewan hoped it would deter the likes of Caleb, although he suspected the Sword was simply waiting in the foothills, bench pressing logs or something to while away the days.

Shaking his head at the image, he turned to face the more immediate threat to his safety. "Last chance to back out and take the slow route?"

"I think the weather's outvoted us already," Tree replied. "Only a fool would ignore his environment."

"Yeah, really."

Ewan grinned over at her, but she was glaring at the clouds, fists sparking as though she wanted to blast the incoming storm right out of the sky.

He squeezed her shoulder, getting zapped for the gesture. "Hey, don't worry. We won't let it get us."

She nodded, but her smoldering eyes screamed that she couldn't have agreed less.

When they got within a few yards of the edge, Ewan took a

couple picks from the pack, then transferred everything else to Tree. He dug out an anchor in the snow: a nice, broad loop two yards in diameter and several feet deep. Under the additional weight of their gear, Tree slowly moved to stand in the center and threaded her end of the rope around the anchor. She traced her hand over the loop, and the snow around it melted; she touched it again, and the water refroze, locking the rope into place.

She nodded, satisfied with the failsafe, but her face fell as she glanced up again at the gathering clouds.

Ewan forced a chuckle, hoping it would catch. "Don't take this the wrong way, but I'm glad you're a heavy girl."

She made an over-encumbered slap that he easily dodged, but she did smile. "Go jump off a cliff."

Ewan flipped her a salute and checked the rope's other end around his belt as he stomped his way up to the edge. Making one last scan for mobs, he hopped lightly into the gap and rappelled down as Tree fed him rope, a bit at a time.

He went about forty feet down before settling on a small foothold and pulling out the picks. "Okay, I'm ready!"

A moment later, his muscles were filled with a warming strength to supplement his own. Coiling his legs and trying not to look down, he sprang with all his might up and across the gap, letting the tightening rope guide his ascent. When he got close enough, he struck out with one pick; it bit into the icy cliff face, and he pulled hard on it, hooking the second pick in, a few feet higher as the ice cracked. Keeping the momentum, he swung the first pick up and drove it in even higher, scrambling up the face using the pits he'd made as footholds.

Eventually, Ewan met snow instead of ice, and he hauled himself up onto it as the buff faded. He dug in a second anchor, then stabbed his feet inside it as deeply as he could before waving to Tree.

She thawed her end of the rope and checked the knot

around her waist, then walked to the edge. "Here's the pack," she called as she made the line-of-sight transfer, causing the snow to crunch under his boots even more. "And here I come!"

Ewan's heart fluttered as he watched her plummet. This was easily his least favorite part of the plan, but neither of them had felt confident about the prospect of leaving one end of the rope untended while he came back across. His end jerked against his hands but didn't slip, his armored grip and augmented weight enough to hold onto it.

He looped it around his anchor, then cautiously let go. It stayed put, so he re-equipped his special shoes and hurried to the edge to haul her up a hand at a time. *At least she's not wearing the pack*, he told his arms when they yelled in protest.

Even so, he flopped back into the snow, panting, once he'd finally gotten her to the top.

"That wasn't so bad," Tree remarked, her eyes sparkling down from within the hood of her parka. She offered him a hand, but when he pulled, she fell beside him with a yelp.

"Sorry!" Ewan panted, belatedly remembering to drop the pack before getting to his feet and helping her up. Across the gap the clouds were still building, but they looked a lot farther away now. "Great job."

Tree dusted the snow off herself, then reached around to get his shoulders. "You too."

Once he'd caught his breath and hauled the pack out of its crater, they continued westward, working their way up to the ridgeline of their new spur while staying to the warm side. It connected to an ominous peak, stark and jagged against the afternoon sun, but not far down its southern face was their pass: a deep notch that looked as though some epic mob had clawed the mountain itself.

By mid-afternoon, the icy wind had begun to howl around them, but they made good progress, veering toward the pass wherever the going seemed stable. They encountered a golem as they reached the main slopes, but it was no match for Ewan's speed—at least, once he'd passed the pack to Tree. He tripped it and finished it off with a stab through its glowing eyes, then reluctantly harvested the coresilver ore it dropped, to add to his rock collection for paying Kate back.

As they began climbing again, the wind picked up even more, bringing flurries now.

"We need to hurry," Tree called over the noise.

Ewan glanced back; the mountain they'd camped on last night was now veiled in swirling gray. "I've never heard of a storm that crossed the Spine. If we can just get through, we should be okay."

"It's like it's chasing us," she said, her voice tense. "Is it possible that the Diamond Lord sent it?"

Ewan shrugged. "I guess he could have, but I doubt it. The Gems were infamous for sending adventurers out to do their work for them, for better and worse. That's how Old Max earned his name before the war. Questing for the Diamond Lord most of all, if you can believe that." He blinked as the wind threw ice in his eyes. "Come on; we'd better get through before things get rough."

They only got another few miles before the pursuing clouds swapped the flurries for heavier, wetter flakes, then swallowed the afternoon sun as they surged past. The wind continued to get stronger, until it was whipping the snow around them in such a frenzy that any mob insane enough to be out and about could have taken them by surprise, if it could have seen them to do it.

It got so bad that Ewan only knew they'd reached the pass by looking at the map, the two towering walls resolutely firm as his nerfed line of sight updated the image with snowbanks. He reached back and took Tree's hand, bringing her close, and they began their final climb.

"You know," he said as they entered the gap, "we'd be talking about how hot it was right about now in the forest."

"And I wouldn't even have the magic to cool us off," she replied with a wry smile, half covered by her hood. "I'm so glad we took a vacation."

Then a thundering crash, louder by far than the Gem's visit to Whitehaven, seemed to shake the very ground. Ewan stumbled, then looked up in horror as the rock face on the northern side of the pass gave way, surging down right at them.

"Run!" he yelled, but she was already jerking his arm, sprinting back to the southern wall's outer edge in a mad rush to relative safety. She flung out a shield as soon as they cleared it, just before the first of the debris could catch them up.

It was the most terrifying spectacle Ewan had ever witnessed. The solid mountain shifted and flowed, a raging flood that emptied through the gap and swept away everything before it as it poured through the path they'd only just taken. He watched in awe as rocks bigger than his house bounded past, careening off each other and hurling deadly shards in all directions. The noise was deafening, and more than once he nearly fell as his legs lost track of which part of the ground they were dug into. Behind him, Tree's hands clenched his arm through the parka, squeezing hard enough to make him gasp every time a rock bounced off her shield.

When the torrent finally subsided and the blizzard settled back to a simple whiteout, Ewan looked at the pass on his map. It was gone, only recognizable by virtue of the southern wall's peak, still rising like an island above the re-frozen sea.

To the east, the path they'd come along had vanished without a trace.

"We need to get through, now," he said nervously. "There's no telling how much snow will come down, and we can't afford to get caught under it."

Tree nodded wearily as she checked their rope. Ewan

pulled out his picks, hoping they'd be able to get purchase in the newly settled rocks, and they began climbing up the rubble.

It was extremely tough going, and their progress was alarmingly slow. Tree gave them both repeated warming buffs, but she was worn out from the shielding, losing her grip on whatever force she drew on for her magic. Before long, the cold was burning through Ewan's gloves, forcing him to clench and unclench his hands to keep them from freezing around the picks.

Then, just when he thought things couldn't get worse, the rope tightened around his waist.

He stumbled and fell with a shout, landing hard and barely catching himself with the picks to avoid tumbling back into the darkened white below.

"Tree!" he called as he pulled himself back to standing.

There was no answer.

Ewan followed the rope and found her prone on her side, already half-covered in snow.

"Tree! Treanna!"

She didn't respond. Her health seemed okay: penalized from the cold, but stable. Then Ewan saw a faint trace of vapor misting away from her parted lips. Another breath came and went, then another, in a regular, automatic rhythm that made his stomach churn in recognition.

"Nerf it all, don't log out now! We can't stay here!"

It was no good: wherever Tree was, she couldn't respond to him. Panic tore at his throat as he fumbled through his inventory, searching uselessly for a way to call her back to the world, his world, but he had nothing. He cursed his own ignorance, not even knowing if she was simply in her other world or if she'd truly been logged.

*I never thought to ask what would happen to her!*

With hands shaking from more than the bitter cold, Ewan lay down beside Tree, wrapped her rope around his torso, and heaved himself back to standing. Between the blizzard and her weight on top of the pack's, he could hardly move—even after ditching the coresilver—but he knew full well he didn't have any choice. It was either clear the pass or lose consciousness to die under yards of snow, and he wasn't about to let that happen without a fight.

Feeling truly solo for the first time in months, Ewan resumed the climb up the clogged pass. He slung his picks ahead, one after the other, burying them into the loose rocks and pulling himself up.

In moments, he was dragging himself instead. Already the whirling snows were covering the spill, making it look as if the pass had never been, while flinging icy needles into his face and lungs to cut him down from without and within. He kept to the southern side for what shelter it provided, fearing with every passing second it would fall in too.

Without Tree's warming magic, the health and stamina penalties from the harsh environment mounted up. Before he'd even gotten two-thirds of the way, his health bar appeared in his vision and began shrinking steadily as the chill ate through his parka, then his armor, then his skin and muscles. He forced himself forward, clawed hands be nerfed, locked in a deadly race against time, laughing wildly in his mind that a bout of bad weather was about to accomplish what countless mobs and dozens of Swords hadn't managed for months.

As he continued to climb at an increasingly glacial pace, the world closed in around him, reducing life to a struggle to stay alive, to move while he still could. More than once he nearly gave it up, ready to accept the comfort of death to wake up an hour later in his bedroom, but then he remembered what Caleb had said about the Church hijacking his bind. That was enough to move his body another few feet, but when death's call grew stronger and a heretic's cell sounded pretty warm, he thought about getting separated from Tree for good.

He kept climbing.

Then, after what might as easily have been hours as minutes from the pain of it all, he swung his pick through open space instead of snow. It fell, clattering away in front of him, and he lay there, staring at his empty hand in confusion before the meaning registered in some back corner of his mind that hadn't yet succumbed to the cold.

*Down.*

With one final burst of energy, he crawled over the top of the debris, slipping and rolling down the far side in the pick's wake. He collapsed for a moment, panting in surprise at how much warmer it felt. Above and behind—blessedly behind him—the remains of the pass stood guard against the storm, sheltering him.

And Tree, still alive.

In the wind's sudden absence, Ewan's heartbeat seemed to ring off the stone and ice around him, insisting that he had enough left in him to make her a shelter before he died.

Hands cracking, he fumbled with the ropes until he managed to free her from his back again. He scooped her up and took her from the storm, trudging and slipping down the frozen landslide until his legs finally gave out and he fell to his knees. Holding the pain off just a little longer, he hacked out a small bowl in the snow beside the southern wall and wrapped her up with him in their blankets, gifting her his remaining warmth to give her a chance.

Too exhausted to speak, Ewan held her close and let the silent words flow from his heart to hers: how glad he was to have met her, how important she'd become to him, and—finally—how sorry he was that he'd failed her after all they'd accomplished. He promised to find her again and, as satisfied as he could be with his efforts, he relaxed, letting the darkness take him at last.

**9**

---

# BEHIND THE CURTAIN

When Ewan woke again, he thought he was still dead.

The sunlight beat against his eyelids, a lot brighter than he'd expected for a Church dungeon, and the rest of him burned. He tried to take a breath, but it was like inhaling shattered glass. Cold glass, at that. He coughed and shuddered, hurting even more as the air fled his body again.

"Mmm," came a sleepy voice, muffled but familiar and right in front of him—and all his thoughts of pain vanished. He opened his eyes, slowly, trying to hold onto his sense of balance, then saw with an elated jolt that Tree was snuggled up against him, her back pressed into his chest.

He tried to move, but she grabbed his arms and pulled them tighter around her body. She felt strong, strong enough to keep him there even if he'd wanted to leave. He tried to hug her in return but found that he couldn't manage more than a vague pressure. His hands burned and throbbed and itched, as though they were too small for the blood moving through them.

How badly had he torn himself up? And how in Veridor was he still alive?

Thanking the Logos, Ewan closed his eyes and just breathed: as slowly and deeply as he could, feeling the cool air trickle into his battered body, catching a faint flowery scent from Treanna's hair that made no sense in their current situation but helped him relax enough to return to sleep.

When he woke, the light was fading again. Tree was now sitting a couple feet away with her back to him, checking the pack. He managed to turn his head this time, looking up blearily to see the snow dusted over the shield that defined their shelter.

She must have heard his movement, because she turned and smiled at him, warmly enough to thaw the mountains for miles around them.

"My hero awakens."

Ewan smiled weakly in reply, cracking his frostbitten lips.

Tree saw his wince and scooted closer to place her hands on his face. Her cool healing spell flowed through him, making the pain in his body relent a little. Gently, she tilted his head and peered into his eyes as though somehow identifying his every injury through them.

Given her crazy high aura reading, she probably was.

"Where are we?" Ewan croaked. His mouth tasted of blood.

She put a finger to his lips and opened a message box in his mind's eye. [Don't speak yet. Your throat is still mending. It'll take several passes for me to repair the damage.]

Then, she pulled a small bottle from inventory and leaned over him. [Drink this; it will help you sleep. I'll keep watch,] she added, seeing the worry in his eyes. [I'm not logging out anymore.]

She tipped the potion into his mouth, something like a mix of cherries and honey. In seconds his eyelids got heavy again, but as the world returned to darkness once more, he heard her whisper, "Get some rest...I'll be here."

The next time he came to, his throat was much better.

Breathing no longer felt nearly so painful, and he even managed a few deep gulps of air without coughing.

The snow had blown off the shield to reveal the night sky above, the familiar stars glittering with surreal clarity through the cold mountain air and the ethereal wisps of snow riding the wind. The mountain beyond remained reassuringly unmoved, steadfast in giving them its own protection.

Tree was snuggled up against him again, but this time he managed to give her a proper hug. She arched her back into him in her sleep, making him stiffen in shock at the proof she hadn't logged out, that for the first time she was really sleeping beside him. He held her a while, reveling in how every irregular, natural breath she drew made her press slightly against his arms—and smiling when she snored—but eventually he drifted back to sleep.

The following morning, Tree gave him another dose of the healing spell, then helped him sit upright. Ewan's muscles groaned in protest, but he overrode them, happy to claim any minor victory.

"How long?" he asked. The words still scraped his voice.

"It's been three days since you escorted me across the pass," she answered, smiling when his eyes popped. "Don't act so surprised. Surely even you understand how serious your injuries were."

He tried to reply, but his throat seized up.

Tree wrapped her fingers around his neck to apply another dose of healing, but she also gave him a playful shake. "It's a wonder your mother never strangled you, with all the risks you take."

Ewan grinned back, cracking his lips again, but the light it evoked in her eyes made it totally worth the pain.

"Stay there," she ordered, before releasing him to return to the pack. "If you're strong enough to sit, then you should eat."

She produced a bowl and filled it with a mix of meat,

vegetables, and cheese. Glancing up at him, she scooped some clean snow off the shield and added it as well, then gripped the bowl with both hands. A moment later, the snow fell in, melting from the magical heat she was producing. A moment after that, little trails of steam danced away from the surface, filling their bubble with an aroma that made Ewan's stomach roar.

Tree laughed and added a little more snow to keep the broth up, then sprinkled a few herbs onto the finished product before handing it to him with a sly smile.

"I thought we were rationing?" Ewan asked, impressed yet again by how she could cook with her hands.

"We are rationing," she countered. "You've had nothing but potions for the past three days, so consider this a back payment. If it makes you feel better, we can share," she added, scooting beside him to offer a spoon.

He tried to take it, but pain lanced up his arm and he dropped it.

Tree's lips tightened, but she took his hands in hers and supplied them with another healing boost. Recovering the offending utensil, she scooped out a chunk of stew and blew across it, her eyes never leaving his. "I could feed you myself."

Face burning from both her own assertiveness and how tempting her threat was, Ewan took the spoon.

They ate in happy silence, interrupted only by the occasional ping of something bouncing against the shield. They passed the spoon back and forth—although he could have sworn she gave him extra turns—then mopped up the last bits with some bread. When they'd finished, Tree put another handful of snow into the bowl and scoured it clean before tucking it away.

"Thanks," Ewan said gratefully as the meal bolstered his stats. "And, um, sorry."

"Sorry? For what?"

"For putting you to all this trouble. Delaying your mission."

Tree pressed a finger to his lips and gave him her forbidding look. "Don't be absurd. I'm the one who owes you an apology, and my thanks...and an explanation." Her eyes clouded, and she sighed. "I'm sorry about my disappearance during the storm. I'm sure you guessed it wasn't planned, and I did everything I could to get back as soon as possible, but it still took hours to...settle things. When I returned, I found myself safely on the other side, with your unconscious body covering me like a shield." She poked him in the chest. "You were in critical condition. I thought at first you'd died, forgetting for a moment that you wouldn't be here if you had."

Ewan nodded. "Yeah...I was pretty worried when you got logged, too."

Tree looked at her hands. "I healed you enough to keep you from slipping away altogether. I've been shielding us, maintaining the shelter, ever since."

"Thanks," he said, leaning into her. "That had to be a pain."

"It's what I do," she said softly. Automatically. "Ewan...you still don't understand who I am or why I'm here, but you continue to give me your very best." Still looking down, she took his hand. "And your best is impressive, no matter what anyone else may argue. I can see from here how difficult that climb must have been, even without a storm or so much weight. You did the impossible, and you did it for me. You are by far the bravest and kindest person I've ever known, in my world or yours. Thank you."

Somehow, she sounded more bitter than grateful, but Ewan squeezed her hand in return. "Well, I'm saying thank you anyway. I thought I was dead, and I would have been, if you weren't so resourceful and determined. And as for courage, I'm not the one diving between worlds to protect people who'd rather get rid of me to avoid thinking about a real problem."

Her eyes flashed as she looked up. "You're welcome, then.

As for my explanation, there was an urgent matter in my world, and I was summoned by the people there."

"Urgent? The invading army?"

Tree shook her head and scowled. "No. Nothing important enough to drag me out of the...no, it wasn't the threat I mentioned. I should caution you, though: not everyone in my world approves of my coming here."

Ewan blinked. "But didn't they send you here? Aren't you on a mission?"

"I am—that is, I mean..." She flushed and stiffened, avoiding his eyes again. "But most people in the Centre don't know that. They didn't, at any rate," she added irritably.

A grin cracked Ewan's face, despite his good sense. She looked just like a normal teenager, caught out of bounds. Had she actually come to Veridor without getting permission?

*That's what the Diamond Lord claimed*, he realized with an ominous jolt that wiped the grin back off.

Tree didn't notice. "Anyway, I do have some support now, which is why I've been able to stay here overnight."

"No more surprises, then?" he asked hopefully.

"Right. I'll receive a message if I'm needed, but they won't force me out again."

"Well, that's something," Ewan said. He stretched, cracking his knuckles. "I'm feeling a lot better now. When do you want to start moving again?"

Tree looked at him, wide-eyed. "Can you even stand?"

He gave it his best shot, but after she'd hauled him off his face, he conceded that he needed a little more rest.

The afternoon's meal and a fourth night of solid sleep did wonders. After successfully getting up and walking around outside the camp the next morning, Ewan insisted that moving on would help him work out the remaining kinks in his body. Tree protested, but only halfheartedly, seeming to agree that they dared not rest overlong.

They made good progress the next few days, putting the Spine a dozen miles behind them. Ewan warmed back up to his usual self battling the local mobs, but as the eagles started actively avoiding them, he realized he was starting to plateau again, incredible as that seemed. Had other adventurers had made thrill-seeking passes through the Argenones, with similar benefits?

One adventurer apparently had, or they wouldn't be there now.

Four evenings after they'd left the pass, Ewan and Tree reached the mountain guarding their quest target: a random peak, one of hundreds in the area. As tempting as it was to simply rush the slope and get inside, they agreed they'd be better equipped to deal with whatever was waiting after a good rest. They made camp by a small crevasse near the mountain's base and shared a light dinner under the stars, back to their usual rations now that the eagles had stopped doling out free lunches.

When they finished, Ewan pulled out the blankets and climbed in, then held them open for Tree to join him. He hardly needed the extra warmth anymore, but somehow they'd kind of just continued to sleep close. He didn't know what to make of the new situation, choosing to err on the side of caution and not make anything of it at all, but he felt a thrill every time she cuddled up against him.

"Hey," he said as she brushed her ear against his cheek. "I just wanted to say, um, that whatever happens tomorrow, with the quest and all…I'm really glad I was in Whitehaven that day." He swallowed, then cleared his throat. "I also want you to know that even if getting this weapon doesn't help you convince the Church of anything, I'm still with you. All the way."

Tree took his hand and wrapped hers around it, pressing it to her heart through her parka and armor. "Likewise. I can't imagine what my life here would have been like without you, aside from short and fruitless. It's difficult to believe that I've only known you for a few months. There's so much about you I still don't know."

*That makes two of us,* Ewan thought, but his usual frustration didn't stick, not when he was this close to her. "I know, right? We were so focused on getting you up to spec at first, and then it's all been questing time." He stretched his legs under the blankets, against hers. "Maybe we can do something about that now? It's a nice night to just talk."

"I'd like that." She turned to face him, with her head draped across his arm. "Let me see...when is your birthday?"

Ewan blinked, not expecting such a factual question. "I'll be seventeen this December, on the tenth. Um, how about you?"

"I'll be eighteen on the sixteenth of November."

"I thought you might be older than me," he said, pleased. "What else you got?"

She smiled, her breath warm as her lips parted. "Your favorite color?"

"Blue. That rich kind you get on a clear afternoon, when you look up and it seems like the night sky is reaching through into the day. You?"

She put her hand to his cheek, looking into his eyes as she whispered. "Green."

Ewan's face burned, doubly so because he was sure she could tell. "Now I wish I'd said brown!"

Tree giggled, confirming his worst fear. "Tell me about your childhood. Were you always this sweet?"

"I don't know," he said honestly. "I think you're the only person who would call me that."

"Your mother and sister don't think so?"

"Okay, maybe Mom. But Kate?" He grimaced. "She'd only say that to get under my skin."

"If you say so. I'm certain they miss you." Tree frowned, tensing in his arms as less-than-playful sparks danced in her eyes. "You're lucky to have such a caring family."

"Yeah...when you put it that way," Ewan said slowly. He wished the Logos could give him a map of her feelings. "I grew up in a cottage, near our forest. My parents bought it before I was born. We've got a little garden; Mom used to say it was the only way we'd eat anything other than monster meat, the way my dad is."

Tree's frown faded. "Is he an adventurer, too?"

"No, he's more respectable than me. He escorts scholars from the college whenever they do field work. That lets him do some traveling, and if you travel the wilderness, you get combat. So, he gets his fair share of loot. I loved the days when I got to skip school and go out with him."

"I never enjoyed the Centre's school, either," Tree said. "I preferred to read on my own. My favorite stories were of knights and heroes, people brave and strong enough to save the world from any danger." She pulled slightly closer. "Did you always want to be an adventurer?"

Ewan smiled, picturing his school and the mock battles he used to fight with Paul and the others. Wondering what the heroes in Tree's stories, heroes from another world, were like. "Yeah, for as long as I can remember. Everyone looked up to Old Max, but I guess I was the only one who liked hearing about his solo days, before he got all tangled up with the Church. He was fearless. He loved exploring, and he could handle any trouble that came his way. I wanted to be like him, living in the days where an adventurer could go questing all over the world." He chuckled. "I just didn't know what that meant."

"Do you regret it now?"

"Not at all." He risked a hug, then released a breath he hadn't realized he was holding when she returned it. "But I do worry about Mom and Dad, and Kate. Even Paul. They're all at risk, helping me help you."

Tree sighed and pushed away, her eyes looking past him to something only she could see. "I'm sorry."

"Hey," he said, mentally kicking himself for breaking the mood. "We've been through this, remember? I trust you, and you let me know when you're ready to tell me more."

"Then perhaps I can do that now," she said slowly. "Perhaps you can ask me about it, like I've been doing to you?"

A hundred questions scrambled for Ewan's voice, but he reined them in for fear of screwing up even more. "Sure. Um... are you a healer, in your world?"

"Not precisely. I'm a caretaker, tasked with ensuring that people like you can live their lives."

"Like the Church claims to?"

She shook her head. "More literally than that. It's the duty of caretakers to maintain the...people. To keep them alive."

A chill seemed to slip past her shield and cut through him. "Alive?"

"Yes. Without the Centre's help, Veridian civilization would collapse within a generation."

"Gems," Ewan muttered, pulling his arms closer. "That's not exactly a comfort, is it? Why are we so dependent on your world—really?"

Tree hesitated, the shadow of old fears slipping back into her eyes as she watched his own take root. "The truth is, your ancestors were from my world. They...I suppose you could say they colonized Veridor."

The chill turned into a whispering dread. "Colonized? But no one's ever heard of that!"

"I know," she said, bitterly. "It was a long time ago, thousands of years. But some people, my people, stayed behind. To this day, we keep the supply lines open between the worlds."

Ewan took a minute, trying to process this. What had happened to the good feelings about favorite colors and birthdays? "But no one here knows about your world. How can there be a trade route between them? Unless...unless the Church is dealing with your Centre in secret!"

She gave him a pitying look. "If that were the case, then I wouldn't have needed to come here, would I?"

"Oh, right. What do you mean, then?"

Tree took a slow breath, eyes studying him carefully now. "The Centre provides the energy necessary to maintain this world. Everything here, even the Logos, depends on us. If something were to happen to break those connections, then everyone here would die within the day."

Ewan's heart was racing now, but not at all the way he'd hoped for five minutes ago. Her every word, each frightening detail she revealed, stirred an anger inside him. A primal anger, wounded but proud and not at all patient to have secret Gems helping him around when he didn't need them.

*But if she's right...we may have never really gotten rid of them.* His fists clenched. *Can't ever get rid of them.*

"I must look really helpless to you," he grumbled.

Tree smiled sadly, cupping his face before he could turn away. "Not to me, Ewan, not at all. But yes, life here hangs by a very fine thread. That's why my people work so hard to protect it. It's why I came, to do something about the danger that threatens everything."

Ewan huffed, shivering despite her warmth. "So, this army of yours. I guess it never needs to set foot in Veridor?"

"No," she admitted. Slowly, she withdrew her hand. "I'm sorry. This is all too much to take in."

"Yeah, maybe. For now," Ewan added, with a touch of defiance. He had even more questions now. Why was it so important for her people to keep Veridor alive? Wasn't it a ton of trouble? What did the Veridians give back in payment for all this secret, unwanted help? But between her worried tone and his own rising unease, he knew he had to keep being patient if he wanted to hear the answer another day.

And he wanted to hear it—needed to, now—because apparently the connection between the worlds ran a lot deeper than he'd realized. Than anyone had known.

*Anyone in Veridor, anyway.*

Trying not to grind his teeth, he said, "Thank you. For telling me what you can."

"You're welcome," she murmured. "I'll find a way to explain it all to you soon, I promise. Until then, please remember how dear you are to me."

"You too," he said automatically. "Sleep well, Tree."

She pulled in close, pressing her face against his shoulder before turning around to snuggle against him, the way he'd so quickly gotten used to. Eventually she fell asleep, like a normal person might, but Ewan didn't follow. He lay back to take his watch and try to make sense of it all, but as the stars crept over the valley, he couldn't escape the feeling that the more Tree told him, the less he knew.

10

---

# THE AMULET OF BALANCE

Thoughts of enemies hiding in plain sight lingered in Ewan's mind after Tree relieved him, but eventually he got to sleep. When he woke, she was still curled up tight against him, as if drawing more warmth from him than from the blankets, or any kind of magical spell she'd yet learned.

Using him, for her own purposes.

He banished the thought and sighed, then stretched hard enough to wake her.

She flinched, knocking him back so she could sit up. "Morning? When did that happen?" Her cheeks flushed. "I'm sorry, I must have fallen asleep again."

"Well, we seem to be in one piece," Ewan answered. The mobs were avoiding them outright now, anyway.

*Maybe they know better than I do.*

Tree finger-combed her rumpled hair, still blushing. "So... how far are we from the marker?"

"As the eagle flies, about a mile north." Ewan flipped the map on its side and grimaced. "But as the goat climbs, I'd say it's more like two."

"At least we'll be nicely warmed up for whatever's in there," she said with a faint smile. "What do you think we'll find?"

"Not a clue." His mood lifted slightly as he imagined how much experience they'd get, clearing out a deep mountain dungeon. "But we'll take it easy, and we'll be patient. It's not like that weapon's going anywhere after—what?" he asked, when Tree stifled a laugh.

"Nothing," she said, but her eyes were sparkling. "I just think that's the first time I've ever heard you suggest patience."

Ewan stared at her, then laughed as well. "I blame you."

She shot him a wicked grin. "Then I'm honored to not be an entirely bad influence."

She broke camp by waving her hand to disperse their bubble in a poof of snow, and they began the long climb up the mountain. It was slow going, but between Tree's buffs and Ewan's increasing skills with the ice picks, they managed to go more or less straight toward the marker.

By late morning Ewan had hauled himself, then Tree, up to the ledge that housed their target. It was nothing special, not even remotely. Had the Logos not put a maker on the place, Ewan would have gone right past it. He sat there, working snow through his hair to cool off and spending his hard-earned points on additional strength and agility, then looked into the maw carved into the rock face with a winded sigh.

"Is something wrong?" Tree asked.

"Not really. I'd just figured Max would've chosen somewhere with more, well, oomph than a random cave."

She peered in, expressionless. "Keeping something hidden is the first and best step to keeping it safe."

"I guess. You ready?"

"I'm fine," she replied, offering him another smile as she dusted off her parka. "You did all the work."

Ewan chuckled. "How about you fight the mobs in here, then?"

She smacked him on the shoulder but helped him to standing, and they went inside.

Ewan's first impression of the cave's interior was that it was absurdly dark, especially after the morning-lit snow a few yards back. But after lighting their lamp, he could see that the small mouth was a clever disguise for something much larger. He whistled as he held the light aloft, revealing a broad passageway that descended into a spiral stair, cut seamlessly into the silver stone.

"Okay," he said, dropping his voice as he handed Tree the lamp, then calling up his detection filter. "I'll take point."

The stair took them down, and down...and down some more, eventually taking Ewan's mood with it. After a while, he lost count of the turns; after a while more, he got the feeling they'd have done better to drill straight into the mountain from the camp and meet the frapping stairs halfway. No mob showed itself, no side passages appeared, but the whole time the Logos insistently placed his quest marker just around the stairs' curve, taunting him as it tested his newfound patience.

Then Tree gasped.

Ewan whipped his swords out, but when he whirled about, she was kneeling down, tracing her fingers along a step.

"What is it?" he asked, reluctantly sheathing the blades.

"There are names." She frowned in the lamplight. "Inscribed into the stone. Look."

He squatted beside her, seeing that there were indeed names. A lot of names. Six rows running from wall to wall, with letters chiseled at precise angles and even intervals.

"What in Veridor?" he muttered.

Tree lifted the lantern, revealing more names on the other steps around them. "I think they're on every one," she whispered. "But whose names are they?"

Ewan looked down again, unease prickling his neck.

"Matthew Buckner, Sarah Greenhart, Sydney Kennedy, Jessica Reed, Julian Klimov..." He shook his head. "I don't know."

"Could they be the people who built this place?"

"Maybe...but why would anyone carve a big stairway in the middle of nowhere?"

"Perhaps they were helping Old Max."

"I guess," Ewan said dubiously. As many steps as they'd come down already, there had to be tens of thousands of names, maybe more. He'd never heard of anyone coming out to the mountains for something like this, and even if they had, why hide it in a cave?

He stood again, the prickling sensation reaching his legs as he realized he'd been treading on graves. "Come on."

They kept going, stepping as gingerly as they could between the names, but the stair continued on for what seemed like forever. When it finally straightened out, Ewan checked his map and saw they'd come well below their morning camp.

He dismissed it, then looked down at the final few steps. These were carved from colored stone, and each held only one name, but Ewan's heart started to hammer as he realized that he knew these names. Names any tried-and-died Veridian would know.

"The Sapphire Prince," he whispered, pointing to a step as blue as the ocean before turning to the next one, a faded lilac. "The Amethyst Oracle...the Opal Corsair." His voice trailed off as he silently read the names of the most powerful beings to ever trouble the world. The Citrine Mistress of Greatfield. The Ruby Tyrant of Anthar. The Emerald Lady of Arborough.

The Diamond Lord of Whitehaven.

And, carved into the obsidian floor of the chamber that opened beyond, was one final name.

Maximilian, the Fool.

Ewan jumped with a yell when a hand touched his shoulder, but it was only Tree. He looked ahead, but the air seemed to swallow her lamplight, as though it was made of black fog.

He took a shaky breath, sweating freely now. "It's a memorial."

"What?"

"The steps. The names…a roster, of everyone who fought in the Gems' war."

"Everyone who perished, in truth," came a deep, raspy voice from everywhere around them, a voice that made Ewan's bones buzz.

He yanked his swords free, sweeping at the fog, but the voice continued, unmoved. "It was the least I could do, considering that I killed them."

At once, light seared out from torches that lit themselves along the room's perimeter. The dark fog rushed past, knocking Ewan off balance as it caught him in the back, but then it coalesced, swirling over a black throne at the far wall. Ewan gave chase but slowed, muscles freezing, as the form took on a likeness he knew well: a large, walnut-skinned man of powerful build, with a full black-gray beard and long hair above heavy segmented armor and a pair of greatswords strapped over his broad shoulders.

"Max," he whispered.

The dark warrior regarded him and frowned. "Max…yes. I was called that, long ago."

[Ewan, what is that?] Tree messaged from behind him.

[It's him! Tree, it's old Max!]

[But you said he died centuries ago!]

[I mean, he disappeared after the war, but—]

"I removed myself to this place," the ancient hero rumbled, cutting him short. "To fulfill my final obligation: in body then, in spirit now."

Ewan watched his hero—his hero's ghost—and his mind unfroze a little. "Your secret weapon. You're still guarding it!"

Maximilian nodded, dark eyes locked on Ewan. "I did not suffer the Amulet of Balance to be looted by thieves in my life, and I maintain that oath, even today. Who are you, if not a brigand or thief?"

Ewan suddenly remembered his swords were out. Sheathing them quickly, he said, "My name is Ewan O'Meara. I live near Whitehaven, actually. I'm here on a quest to retrieve that amulet."

"Is that so?" The ghost stroked his beard. "You don't look like one of my Swords."

It was all Ewan could do to keep his voice level. "I'm not. I'm an adventurer, like you."

"Ewan, this doesn't make any sense!" Tree whispered in his ear. "How can someone who's been dead—logged—just suddenly appear?"

He started to answer, but Maximilian spoke first.

"You look like you may yet grow to be an adventurer," the ghost said with a slight smile. "Out of professional respect, then, I will give you fair warning. In my day, I used the Amulet to drive the Gems from this world, but its power came at a cost. Only one of noble heart may use it, for the power it represents, that of the Logos itself, is too great a temptation. If such power were to fall into the hands of one who nurtured hate for the world and its people, the consequences would be cataclysmic."

"That's why you hid it out here?" Tree asked, still staring at him like her own world didn't have ghosts. "But surely you could have found a worthy successor."

"Girl, you assume that I was worthy to wear it," the ghost rasped. "As I said, the consequences were cataclysmic."

"But you won the war," Ewan protested. "You wiped out the Gems."

"And half of Veridor's people in the process!" Maximilian thundered, pointing at the stair. "No...I have had centuries to reflect on my rise, and my fall. Such power as the Amulet contains is only meant to be tasted, never held. But hold it I did, for five long years. With it, I committed acts as cruel as any Gem, in the name of my fellow people. People who cursed my name—my name!—as they stood against me for their overlords. Such power must not be loosed upon the world again."

The ghost stood, seeming not so much to move but simply reform a yard closer. "I know not what quest you are on, children, but I will not allow you to leave with the Amulet."

Ewan swallowed, trying to push his panic back down. Maximilian the Great, as terrible as a Gem? He'd clearly proven more powerful than they were. Had the Church's histories glossed over his own dark deeds?

Mustering his courage, he said, "We need that amulet. The Diamond Lord has returned."

The ghost blinked. "He has? Impossible. I annihilated him myself; I remember it well."

"Well, he's found a way back," Ewan said, his panic turning to impatience as he gestured to Tree. "He burned Whitehaven's cathedral overnight, nearly a month ago. He's after my friend, and he's already got the Swords rushing to do his bidding! They're the ones who got the quest, but they can't come for it themselves, not with the Church insisting they follow the Gem's orders."

But Maximilian seemed not to hear. "This Gem...what aspect did he have? What form did he take?"

Ewan's fists clenched. "I didn't see it myself, but my contact in the Swords said he came down in a column of fire, right through the cathedral's roof. He was tall, with huge wings and dressed in white and silver."

"My old, erstwhile friend," the ghost murmured, narrowing his eyes as though he still had menus. "Have you truly found a way to survive, after all these centuries?"

His eyes came into sudden focus, black and keen and hard. "Very well, adventurer, I believe you. What is your will?"

Ewan sighed in relief. "We need to get that amulet to my friend in the Swords."

"No. What will you do? Will you strike at the heart of every Gem, and restore Veridor's sanctity?"

"If I have to, then yes. I won't let them hurt Tree."

A cold smile lifted Maximilian's lips, seeming to darken the room as he regarded her. "Even if this girl numbers among them?"

Tree drew a sharp breath, but Ewan's heart froze.

The ghost's lips pulled back, the smile becoming a snarl. "Tell me, young adventurer: what do you know of her?"

Tree was waiting, waiting for Ewan to step up in her defense again, but hearing his hero's anger stirred his own in sympathy, bringing with it all the frustration and fear of the past months. "I know she's not from Veridor."

"That, she most certainly is not," the dark warrior agreed, his voice a clear accusation.

*Max understands,* Ewan thought as his gut churned. *He of all people knew the Gems! He'd know one by looking at it. Her. But... would she have lied to me?*

He didn't feel a need to answer that.

Fists tightening, he turned to Tree. "Why is the Diamond Lord after you?"

Her voice shook. "I don't know."

"Is it because you're a Gem? Did you cut into his territory?"

"No! There's no such thing in my world!"

"But you've got their powers! You got us past the Swords that first day; you use magic—frapping magic, Tree! And last night, you told me that everyone in Veridor could be logged if your kind wanted it!"

She stepped back, eyes widening. "We don't want—"

"Someone does!" Ewan snapped, closing the gap again.

"That's why you're here, isn't it? Getting my people to help, passing out quests? Just like the Gems did."

She flinched. "Ewan, I've never lied."

"But you haven't told me everything either, not even close!" He swung his hand across the space between them. "You keep stringing me along with half-truths, throwing my world into chaos and dragging me off on this quest like it's all just a game for you!"

"The Gems of my time felt so," Maximilian growled as he moved beside Ewan in a miasma of black fog. "They took great pleasure in reminding us that our lives were nothing without them, and nothing to them."

Ewan glared at her, smelling blood as he breathed the fog in. "She's done that well enough. But why...why, Tree? What gives you the right to jerk me around?"

"Nothing," she whispered, shaking as though she scented it too. "I'm not trying to. I swear to you, I'll tell you everything one day, but right now we need to clear you and keep your family safe, and for that we need the Amulet."

"We?" Ewan took another step toward her, driving her back. "It's all been about you. You and your frapping mission!"

"She uses you for her own ends, just as all Gems do," Maximilian intoned.

Tree shook her head. "Ewan, we're—"

And she went silent. Her lips still moved and her eyes bulged, but no sound came out.

"Behold, your proof!" Maximilian thundered in the sudden silence. He raised a hand, fog swirling in lethal intent, to point at her, but it was a glint of gold in the fog's center that caught Ewan's attention.

An amulet, hanging from the man's neck. An amulet that crippled Gems.

Tree raised her hands to cast a spell, but nothing happened.

Maximilian laughed, harsh and triumphant. "Your quest is

before you, young adventurer. Accept it! Take the Amulet, drive her and her kind from Veridor, and you shall have all the reward that I did!"

Fury surged from the dark warrior, resonating with Ewan's own, threatening to sweep him away. A yard in front of him, Tree was tensing, preparing to run. She wouldn't make it to the door if she tried. She looked so powerless, so helpless, watching him with white-rimmed eyes. A sprint and a thrust of his swords, and it would be over.

But even as the image formed, his heart screamed at him, shouting over the rancor in his mind and soul.

It was madness to believe he held any power over her. Even if he killed the body in front of him, her soul was in the other world. The world he so desperately wanted to understand, despite his fear. The world his own depended on. The world on whose grace he lived at all.

And he was still alive, even now, even when he threatened her.

Ewan closed his eyes on the hateful scene. He took a deep breath and let the rage blow away with it, then turned to face Maximilian. "No."

The warrior glared at him. "She is a Gem! You would risk everything to help her?"

"I would," Ewan answered, heart flipping in his chest as he drew blades against his old hero. "Gem or not, she's my best friend. We'd have died a hundred times over just trying to get here, without each other." He glanced over his shoulder at Tree, still watching. Still there, despite her terror. "What little I know about her mission scares me out of my wits, but I don't have to know everything to know that she's trying to help. I believe— no. More than that, I trust her."

Her words were still silent, but her relieved smile said everything.

Turning back to Maximilian, Ewan said, "It doesn't matter

what world she's from. It doesn't even matter what she is. What matters is whether her heart's in the right place, and I'll stake my life on the notion that it is."

Maximilian gave him a long, hard look; then he raised his hand. At once, the darkness lifted and flowed back into the vengeful ghost's armor, leaving a man whose eyes looked every bit two thousand years old.

Tree's breath returned, a series of quick huffs as she glared murder at the ancient warrior.

"Well spoken, adventurer," the ghost said, smiling wearily through the beard. "You have passed my first and most important test. One I myself failed in life, to my everlasting regret. In the end, consumed by righteous wrath, I turned on my best friend and ally, so caught up in my hatred of his kind that I blinded myself to everything he'd done for me and my people. Perhaps his return was thus doomed to be."

Ewan lowered his swords, hardly daring to breathe. *Old Max and the Diamond Lord, best friends? What would everyone say? What would the Church say?*

"I swear that I'll uphold your faith in me," he murmured, starting a little when Tree's hand slipped over his. He looked at her, with lifted chin and a grim tautness of her lips—and something else, something that warned him she was done with denying her powers.

He squeezed her fingers and turned back to Maximilian. "Will you be giving us the Amulet, then?"

"Not so easily as that," the old ghost replied. He smiled wolfishly, eyes lighting up, as he reached back to unsheathe the massive swords from his back, each nearly as long as Ewan was tall, black as his armor.

The warrior chuckled, following Ewan's gaze. "The Diamond Lord of old made these for me, as a gift of friendship. He claimed to have forged them from fallen stars. They lasted me through a decade of peril and war."

He turned one, letting it drink in the torchlight, then looked at Ewan. "I said you passed my first test, and while it was the most difficult, the second is by no means a simple task. I expect that so bold an adventurer as yourself must have been disappointed to find so little to do in this ancient tomb?"

"You could say that," Ewan replied, grinning as he lifted his own blades again. "Are you ready?"

"Ewan O'Meara, for two thousand long years I have waited here. I am more than ready."

"Wait!" Tree looked between them. "You mean that after everything you've just said, you're going to try to kill each other?"

Ewan gave the ancient hero a sympathetic look and tossed his pack to the wall. "Well, yeah. I need to prove I'm as strong as the guy who destroyed the Gems, or I know I won't stand a chance, right?"

"It is good to see another adventurer again," Maximilian said. He let out a boisterous laugh as Tree facepalmed and muttered something. "Paladins just weren't quite the same."

Ewan laughed too, picturing Paul's scandalized face. "Any rules?"

"Only that you do all within your power to survive. *En garde!*"

With a speed that surely no living man could have managed, the warrior lunged at Ewan, forcing him to dodge to the right—straight at the second sword arcing through the darkened air toward his head. As the blood rush took over, seeming to slow time, Ewan brought up his right blade to meet the celestial steel, even as his left blade swung up inside Maximilian's guard.

With a deafening clang, the hero's sword smashed down with such force that Ewan's knees buckled. He tried to roll away from the juggernaut, but Maximilian's second sword slapped him on the back, hard enough to chip his night armor. Time resumed its normal flow, and Ewan went stumbling across the chamber into the wall.

"Gems of old," he panted, wincing as he watched his health drop.

"The Gems of old could not stand against me," the hero said proudly. "But you are not using all of your strength, young adventurer."

Ewan coughed in reply. Not that he'd have admitted it aloud, but he'd used everything he had—everything he'd gained in the mountains—and it was still only just enough to keep his head attached to his shoulders.

He swung his blades forward, noting with pride that the behemoth horn looked as keen as ever, and raced back into the fray. Another rapid exchange followed, and Ewan found himself against the other wall, swaying dizzily with another tenth of his health down.

"You'll never defeat me like that!" the ghost taunted. "Do you not have any more resources?"

"Ewan, you're wounded," Tree warned unnecessarily from the doorway. "Let me heal you!"

"No." He grunted, feeling blood soak his shirt under the armor. "It wouldn't be fair."

"Fair?" Maximilian laughed. "The Gem has the right of it, boy. You should listen to her."

"But," Ewan stammered, as Tree's healing spell restored him to full health. "But you defeated the Gems singlehandedly!"

The ghost smiled. "Is that what they say? Yes, I delivered the final blow, but surely you understand I had an army of followers? The Diamond Lord will not give quarter for your chivalrous pride!"

Ewan braced for the warrior's lunge, but this time Tree hit him with a strengthening buff. His muscles caught fire, and he was able to deflect the massive sword and deliver his own cut at the ghost's shoulder.

"Yes!" Maximilian roared as he leaped back. "Use everything at your command!"

Tree boosted Ewan's agility as well, and he charged the spirit, now strong and quick enough to hold his own. As he parried and slashed, deflected and thrust, Ewan watched his old hero with awe. Even as a ghost, he was incredible! He wielded the star-metal greatswords as easily as Ewan's ultra-light blades, and he moved as fluidly as if he wasn't wearing any armor at all. Buffing magics or no, Ewan was hard pressed to land a blow without getting run through or decapitated.

But then Tree began using her magic more directly, casting fire and lightning with increasing confidence when Maximilian didn't use the Amulet on her. The deadly rivers of flame and force mercifully passed through Ewan, but they struck home at the ghost, knocking him back.

Maximilian grunted, flinging up his own energy shield—*the histories never mentioned that he was a mage, too!*—but Ewan pressed his own attack, bringing the behemoth-horn blades to bear on the great warrior and dividing his attention, while Tree unloaded her fury on him.

"Enough!" he called out after a minute, knocking Ewan back and bending forward to rest his hands on his knees as Tree gave him one more good blast. "That will do, young adventurers. You have passed my second test. Do you understand its purpose?"

Ewan sheathed his own blades, sagging a little as the buffs wore off. "That we can win if we work together?"

The ghost nodded. His gaze slid to the pale white step, just above his own epitaph. "Precisely. Without the Diamond Lord's help, my rebellion would have faltered and died, just as you would have. Remember that like you, your worlds can only fulfill their potential when they work in concert."

He pressed himself up to standing, sheathed his greatswords, and bowed formally to his opponents. "I will entrust you with the Amulet of Balance. However, I must warn you that as one final protection against the treachery of thieves, I have cursed the Amulet, so that its power may not yet be unleashed."

"What?" Ewan groaned. "How do we break the curse?"

"In my day, when I destroyed the Gems, I took from each one a trophy of sorts. In order to unlock the Amulet's potential, you will need to visit each of the great cities of my time, there to find these trophies. Upon their discovery, the Amulet will resonate with them and be restored, one piece after the next."

"You mean we have to cross this entire world?" Tree asked in disbelief.

"If you wish to wield the Amulet, then yes," the ghost said simply. "In this way, you will understand the path I took, and perhaps you will learn to find a better one."

He lifted the Amulet over his head and held it out, looking at it. "I never did claim my friend's feather," he said wistfully, closing his eyes. "But that is for the best. My spirit can fill the void in his place. Take it with my blessing, and remember where your own strength comes from."

Ewan nodded and reached forward to clasp the Amulet. Up close, he could see it resembled a map of ancient Veridor, chipped and scratched, with small indentations marking the locations of the oldest Veridian cities.

"Thank you, Max," he said, looking back up into the ghostly eyes. "We'll use it well."

"Then I gratefully leave this world, in the knowledge that it is in better hands than my own," Maximilian said, dissolving into the black smoke as he released the Amulet. "May the Logos guide you."

The smoke dispersed and the torches flickered out, the source of their flame gone at long last.

"You too," Ewan whispered. Then he smiled, making the dim light of their lamp flicker as he shook with laughter.

"What is it?" Tree asked.

He wiped tears from his eyes, gasping. "Paul's going to be so ticked off. I'll never let him live this down, passing up the chance to meet Old Max himself!"

He looked at the Amulet, now with a diamond affixed to the place marking Whitehaven. His throat tightened at the reminder of Max and his broken friendship with the Gem, and of his own murderous temptation.

"Tree," he said, tucking the artifact away. "I'm sorry about earlier. I won't lie and say I'm not fed up, but I want you to know I trust you. I meant what I said about you being my best friend...and I want you to know I'm still with you, all the way."

Tree smiled, a tear forming in her eye as well. "Likewise, and I forgive you for being upset with me. I can't blame you."

"I'm not in trouble, then?"

"I didn't say that," she said dryly as she took his hand. "Oh, and Ewan?"

"Hmm?"

She reached up on her toes and gave him a kiss on the cheek. "Thank you."

Ewan gaped at her, flushing as the room spun yet again, but then he saw how crimson her own face was, even in the lamp's light. She was biting the edge of her lower lip, but her eyes sparkled, catching the flame and seeming to fling it back at him, as though asking whether he could really handle everything she held behind them.

His lips broke into a slow, goofy grin as he decided he'd gladly live with whatever trouble she brought him. He squeezed her hand in return, not daring to treat her kiss as anything more than the best quest reward ever, and together they began the long hike up the memorial stairs, back to the light of day.

**11**

───────

# OUT OF THE MOUNTAINS

THE MOMENT EWAN STEPPED OUT INTO THE SUMMER SNOW, THE Logos pinged him with a quest update.

Tree sighed beside him, eyes narrowing to scan her copy. "It seems we have some decisions to make. Where should we go?"

Ewan stumbled with a shout when a map of all Veridor leapt across his vision—in front of their landing's edge.

Tree caught his arm to keep him from falling. "Sorry."

He blindly patted her hand, though his fluttering heart still seemed to think he was on the long way down. "No worries. Gems...Max wasn't kidding about going all over the world, was he?"

"Evidently not," she said irritably. "We've already spent so much time. How long will this new quest take?"

"I don't know. Even with horses, it would take a few weeks to get from one city to the next. And that's not accounting for the Church giving us any trouble." He gave her a sidelong glance through the world's outline. "The Gems of old could go from one city to another in the blink of an eye."

Her eyes hardened as she stared right back. "How wonderful for them."

"Yeah," he said, sighing inwardly. "Failing that, I don't think we've got much for it but to keep on going."

"Fine," she said in a tone that made it plain it was anything but. "What's the nearest city?"

Ewan queried the Logos, getting a table of distances in return. "Technically, Whitehaven's the closest, but since Max gave us that piece already, we probably shouldn't go there until last." He smiled despite himself, at the prospect of a world tour. "Apart from that, the next closest city is World's Edge." He angled the map, placing their position on the right and the coastal city on the left, some two hundred sixty miles distant. "It's actually a perfect place to start."

"How so?" Tree asked.

"World's Edge was where the war began. It's about as far away as you can get from Whitehaven, aside from the Torpal Isles off the southwest coast." He cast his mind about, dredging up his history lessons, then laughed out loud. "And there's magic."

"Magic?" Her voice turned suspicious. "What kind?"

"Not anything bad for us, now, but back in the Gems' time, a lot of the citizens were powerful mages. They put up quite a fight, too: during the war, World's Edge was one of the last cities to surrender." He dismissed the map and grinned at her. "Not a bad place to go for a couple of heretics."

"This is going to take us months," she said, sighing.

Ewan shrugged. "We didn't know the Amulet would be cursed. But it worked, didn't it? On you—I mean, um—"

Sparks flew from her hands. "For the last time, I am not a Gem!"

"Okay, okay!" He gave her his best rakish grin and tried to ignore her glare. "But who knows? Maybe we'll find something at World's Edge to help you learn some new magic. Maybe even a way to teleport us to the other cities! At least the company's not bad?" he tried.

She scoffed, but she did squeeze his arm. "Definitely not. I... I just hope nothing happens to the Centre in the meantime."

"Yeah. Me too," he said, losing what little good feeling he'd had.

The map reappeared, guided by Tree's mind now. "I see no passes for at least fifty miles, north or south."

"Me neither. It looks like the mountains just kind of drop off past the last crest, straight into the plains."

"That won't do," she muttered. "Unless we can shoot the eagles down, we aren't likely to find food to last us a detour that long."

"We could always learn to eat rocks," Ewan joked as he panned the map. "Wait, here's something: the Argentine River. Its mouth is only a dozen miles from World's Edge, and it's got tributary streams that merge here," he said, marking a point a few days' hike to the northwest. "And one of those has its source not too far from us. What if we followed it down to the river proper and went out where it does? I'm sure we could find a ledge or something when we get there."

"That could work," Tree said, taking control to glide the map out over the plains. "There are a few villages along the river. Will they be a problem?"

"I doubt it, but we can avoid them to be on the safe side. Or, we could use them as practice for sneaking into the city."

A little smile played at the edge of her lips. "It would be nice to sleep in a bed again."

They spent the next three days finding and tracking along the stream, through increasingly rough terrain as it grew wider and swifter. Before long they were hemmed onto a narrow ledge, with all of a yard between stone wall and rushing water. Now and then a golem would spot them from above, but Tree would simply whack it with a shield, not even slowing as she sent it tumbling to join the other jagged rocks now dotting the young river.

Ewan's last hopes for easier going vanished when they turned the final corner around a jutting rocky outcrop and found themselves at the intersection of their own noisy stream with its northern companion. The rushing water cut a deep, sharp groove in the rocks, not yielding even a hand's width on its bank. On the opposite side, the sun-warmed cliff shot almost straight up, a black rock wall that reached a good fifty feet before it offered purchase. It looked like it wouldn't take a pick easily, and it was far higher than Ewan could jump, buffs or no —to say nothing of the thought of hauling Tree up behind him even if he did somehow make it.

He shouted over the rivers' din. "I think we've got a problem."

"I don't suppose Kate put a boat in our pack?" Tree shouted back.

Ewan grinned ruefully. "No, actually. We may have to backtrack."

"We've only got enough food to last us a few more days, not nearly enough to go fifty miles on the hope we find something better. There's an opening here."

"Yeah, but there's an angry river using it at the moment!"

*Why can't one of these mountains fall over?* Ewan sighed as he scanned the map for miracle passes. "What about magic? Is there something you can do to get us across?"

She pursed her lips in thought. "I might be able to use a shield to carry us over...care to let me test the idea?"

Ewan checked their rope around his waist as he pictured airborne golems in the miles ahead. "Yeah, okay."

Tree closed her eyes and lifted her hands toward him, and a moment later he lifted off the ground, exactly like how his boots pushed him up with he equipped them.

"This is amazing!" he shouted, but Tree cried out and grabbed her head. The shield vanished, leaving Ewan to slip and stumble on the wet rocks before landing with a thump.

"There's too much noise; I can't hold it!"

"It was worth a shot," Ewan said, rubbing his backside as he stood again. "Any other ideas?"

"If it were only me," she muttered, scowling like she was ready to order the river to get out of her way. "The only thing I can think to try is making a boat out of ice."

Ewan looked at the water, churning and frothing around the rocks. "I don't know."

"I can reinforce the hull as needed once we're underway. What alternative do we have?"

"None, I guess. What can I do to help?"

"Keep a close eye on me while I work," Tree said, offering him a smile that would've turned any bad idea into a good one.

She thrust her hands out over the bank, leaning against the rope, and a thin wall of ice crystallized, curving out about ten feet into the river. Water pooled up in the little harbor, raising the level enough for her to begin crafting.

Ewan watched her work, reminded strongly of Kate in her forge. But where his sister used fire and steel to beat the metal into place, Tree coaxed her medium, shaping it with nothing more than her will. As she worked, her face relaxed, as though the act of creation mattered more than putting it to use—if only for a moment. In almost no time she'd fashioned a vessel roughly seven feet long and about half as wide, with a pair of benches and a reinforced prow that tapered up into a slender curve. A diamond tendril, graceful and elegant, that seemed downright unfair to the poor boat, given its one and only voyage.

When she'd finished, she sat back on her heels and closed her eyes, resting as the boat bobbed up and down in the harbor to patiently await their departure. Ewan scooped up a cupful of the frigid water and handed it to her.

"Nice work," he called over the rivers' roar, slightly dulled by the ice wall. Trying to remember anything about boats, he added, "I guess she ought to have a name."

Tree looked at the boat, tracing a finger over its curve as though faintly surprised that she'd crafted such a thing. "*Esperanza.*"

"What?"

"It means 'hope.'"

"I like it." Grinning, Ewan took the cup back and splashed the remaining water across its bow. *That's what people do with boats, isn't it?* "May she guide us safely to the other side, and I don't mean limbo." He glanced at Tree. "By the way, I've never actually ridden in a boat. Have you?"

Tree shook her head. "There aren't any rivers near the Centre. But I've seen images of them, in my reading."

*Images?* he thought, secretly relieved that ice would float whether it was pretty or not. "In that case, double nice work."

They had a bite to eat, and when Tree climbed into the front seat—and when he couldn't think of any more excuses to delay—Ewan clambered into the rear.

"Well, one way or another, we'll be out of the mountains soon!" he said in what he hoped was an encouraging voice, as he pulled their shovel from the pack and rested its blade on the water. "Shall we?"

Tree raised her hand to acknowledge, then confidently reached forward to melt the harbor wall.

The *Esperanza* spilled out, whisked into the current. Almost instantly, she lurched toward a rock spire jutting up on their right, but Tree quickly cast a shield so they felt only a light jostle instead of a bone-snapping crunch.

"Try to guide us around the rocks!" she shouted over her shoulder.

"Right!" Ewan answered, more convinced than ever that this was reckless, even by his standards. He dug the shovel into the flow, feeling the boat turn as he angled the blade in his hands, but it took a surprising amount of force just to keep a grip on it. He put all his effort into making it behave while Tree called out directions and warnings from her forward vantage.

They swept into the Argentine proper, spinning unnervingly as the current from the northern stream tangled with that of their own. Ewan switched the shovel to the other side to compensate, keeping them facing roughly forward but unable to prevent them from thumping into a rock and scraping the ice.

They picked up speed as the river collected itself, so much so that before long, Tree couldn't give him even split-second warnings about the incoming hazards as they surged blindly ahead. Swearing under his breath, Ewan called up his map, using the Logos and Tree's line of sight to see for himself. It helped, but his nerves rattled with every sickening crunch and thud from below as the *Esperanza* skimmed rocks hidden under the surface.

"I need to reinforce the body!" Tree shouted. "Can you keep us from hitting anything large?"

*What do you think I've been doing?* "Yes, I've got it!" He craned his head around the side as Tree turned and began scooping water into the boat to make frozen patches.

They held, well enough at least. With a flourish, the *Esperanza* rose on a swell as the final crest whipped past and opened onto a broad, cloudless sky. The wind, now unhindered by the mountains, blew Ewan's hood back, and he squinted in the bright afternoon light to see the western prairie stretch out before them—disconcertingly far below.

"Can you scout farther ahead?" he asked, afraid he already knew what was coming.

Tree paused for a moment, then grabbed his leg, her eyes widening in confirmation. "There's a waterfall, half a mile!"

Ewan swore and steered hard, trying to make for the banks that had tauntingly broadened on this side of the crest, but the current was too strong for him. He made a desperate stab into the water at a sharp angle, but all he accomplished was getting the shovel wrenched out of his hands altogether.

A moment later, the *Esperanza* slammed into a particularly large rock, spraying ice shards and turning broadside as her delicate prow caught and shattered across the stone. Mere yards ahead now, Ewan could see the river vanish, plummeting over the cliff just like the map had warned.

"We'll jump, okay?" It was pointless and he knew it—they'd only fall that much farther—but he had to do something. Shouldering the pack and wondering if he even could jump with it equipped, he slipped on what was left of the icy deck as he stood and grabbed Tree's arm.

After one last buff from her for good measure, Ewan leaped with all his might as the *Esperanza* pitched, her battered body tipping in farewell as she dove over the edge. The Argentine River was below them, some two hundred feet beneath and almost as wide in a pool at the base of the falls, waiting patiently to claim them.

For an exhilarating moment, with the wind whipping about his face and arms as he flung them out, Ewan imagined that he was soaring through the air. *Kate should've packed us that flying machine,* he thought, laughing hysterically. *Hell, I'd even take an eagle dumb enough to try and snatch us!*

But then his weight returned, replacing his wishful delusions with rushing dread.

Face burning for letting them die by misadventure after everything they'd been through, he pulled Tree close, wrapped his arms tightly around her, and turned to keep himself between her and the waters below.

His back tingled as she shielded him in turn.

He looked into her eyes, seeing her fierce determination to protect him. A determination to mirror his own...and an affection, one that went beyond friendship or shared circumstances, beyond quests or Gems or even worlds.

With the clarity death's approach always brought, he knew he had to tell her before he lost the chance.

"Tree, I—"

The impact nearly knocked him unconscious; he was certain he'd have been obliterated without Tree's shields in place. His feet felt as though they were being ripped from his legs, and his head was likewise trying to race away from his shoulders, as if only the force of his will held his body intact while his health bar flared up in his vision, a good chunk of it torn away by the blow.

The water prickled like a thousand stabbing needles as Ewan and Tree tore into it; then it slammed down, pummeling them to chastise their foolish disregard for its power. As they sank, sucked down by the current and their own momentum, the cold bit through Ewan's clothing, even more than the blizzard at the Spine had.

Pushing through the tearing pain in his head, he checked on Tree.

She wasn't moving.

Ewan tilted her head back, but her eyes were closed, and air bubbled out from her parted lips. Her status in the menu read as okay, but there was an ominous, unfamiliar icon beside it.

Feeling a surge of panic, he tried to swim her up to the surface, but between the shock of the landing and the weight of their gear, it wasn't happening. He tried again to rouse Tree, but she didn't respond. Then the icon by her health bar sprouted a little gray bar of its own, already shrinking.

Swearing furiously in his mind, Ewan ditched the pack.

The movement penalties lifted instantly. Kicking hard, he swam up with Tree's limp form in his arms. He looked back once, just in time to see their supplies vanish into the depths.

*Kate's going to kill me*, he thought as he put everything he had into breaching the surface before he passed out as well.

The first screaming breath of air felt like fire in his lungs. He sucked it in desperately, spluttering and hacking as he released it again. He held Tree's head up, but she showed no signs of waking. Fighting to keep focused, Ewan turned and pulled her arms over his shoulders, grateful now for all the time they'd spent swimming in their little forest pool.

Sidestroking as best he could with a person on his back, he made for the southern bank and a small shelf of flat, dark rocks. Their sharp edges sliced his palms open as he climbed, but he pulled himself up and hauled Tree beside him. Half falling and half setting her down, he fumbled with her parka, released the clasp at the neck, and watched in vain for signs of breathing.

Her lips remained slightly parted, as though she was only logged out, but now her chest was utterly still.

"Not like this," Ewan whispered, unable to believe that now, after Swords and Gems and blizzards and frapping ghosts, she was about to die. And then the Church would have her. She'd respawn, probably in Whitehaven, where at best she'd take out a few Swords with her magic before they brought her down and the priests—or worse, the Diamond Lord—came to collect her.

*And if I suicide to get back quickly, I'd respawn in a cell!*

Something in him snapped, unleashing a fury that boiled away his own cold and fear. He yelled, then did the only thing he could think to do. Tree wasn't breathing, so he would do it for her.

Ewan sucked in a lungful of air and pressed his lips to hers, exhaling hard. It rushed back out her nose, so he pinched that shut and tried again.

This time, her chest swelled up under his arm, with a faint bubbling sound trickling past the pounding in his own head.

As he released the breath, a mix of water and metallic blood rose into his mouth. He sat up quickly and spat it out, then took another breath to give her, becoming her lungs again and again.

Just as his fury began to cool into a numb dread that he was too late after all, Tree's body convulsed, lurching up as she gasped on her own power.

Ewan helped her sit, gagging and retching as she expelled the rest of the fluid from her body. The moment she stopped, he hauled her into a tight, squashing hug that he only released when it occurred to him that he might be cutting off her air all over.

"Don't you ever leave me again," he whispered fiercely, gripping her shoulders instead. "Don't you ever!"

After a few moments of coughing and shaking as though the mountain was moving underneath them, Tree managed to slow her breathing. Looking down at his bloody hands in surprise, she took them and mended them, putting an end to the stinging sensation he'd been ignoring.

"I thought I was the healer," she said at last. "How did you know to give artificial respiration?"

"Artificial what?" Ewan asked, shivering his fear away. "You needed air. I didn't know what else to do. I just put my mouth to yours." He froze, an entirely new panic rushing up his throat. "I'm sorry! I wasn't trying to, um, I mean—"

Tree grabbed him around the head and kissed him full on the lips, pushing him onto his back and crushing him to the stone with startling strength for someone who'd been on the verge of dying just moments before.

The world went all wobbly around him. He flailed about, half expecting to see the ominous icon appear on his own health, but after a moment he decided that dying from lack of air could be a good thing, if done properly. He kissed her back, then broke away in laughter when the Logos informed him that the experience had just unlocked a new branch on his skill tree.

Ewan wasn't sure how long they lay there on the sun-warmed rocks, sharing their joy at being alive and being together, but he would gladly have stayed there all day. Eventually, Tree rolled over to lie beside him, panting with a giddy smile to match his own.

"Well," he said, still breathing hard. "That was something."

Tree sat up on an elbow, grinning wickedly. "Oh, it was?"

"Yeah. I, um, well, I never did that before," he admitted, suddenly feeling like a noob again. "Was that okay?"

Her laugh was clear and joyful and not at all at him. "Yes, you were perfect." She tilted her head, watching him with shining eyes. "Your kiss was the breath of life. You are so precious, Ewan."

"You too. I thought we were dead for sure this time. All I could think about as we fell was how I wanted to stay with you." His resolve returned with the memory, and he mustered his courage again, certain that of all the foolish, risky things he'd done today, his next words would beat them all.

"Treanna, I love you."

Tree's eyes flashed with something, an odd mix of surprise and hesitation that dried his mouth. But then she smiled. "I love you, too," she whispered, shaking her head as if in disbelief. "I truly do, despite everything! You're not from my world, but I'm bound to you. And I wouldn't have it any other way."

Ewan's heart did a lap around his ribs, but the tension of months fell away—most of it. "So we're from different worlds," he said with a tired grin. "We'll figure it out."

She snuggled against him, then turned to watch the sun sink toward the broad western plains beyond. "We will."

## 12

## DOWN TO BUSINESS

THEY SLEPT OUT UNDER THE STARS THAT NIGHT, TWO TEENAGERS in love enjoying the lingering warmth in the rocks. Ewan kept leaning over to kiss Tree, but she smiled and kissed him back each time: proof he wasn't dreaming.

When morning came, though, the first feeling Ewan had was hunger. He extracted his arm from under Tree's head and sat up to check the pack—then groaned.

"What is it?" Tree asked, yawning.

He shivered in the cool air as he looked around, in the hope a spare might spawn as easily as mobs. "I don't think we've got much for breakfast."

She sat up beside him, still moving sluggishly. "What do we still have?"

"Aside from each other?" Ewan scanned his inventory. "I've got my combat gear, a spare set of clothing, and...about four thousand gold. Oh, and the Amulet." He grimaced, picturing how much trouble they'd be in if their secret weapon had been in the pack. "How about you?"

Tree shrugged. "Just what I'm wearing."

"Plus your magic," Ewan said. Then his stomach growled. "I'll go get our stuff."

Tree looked across the pool to the falls, still going strong. "I don't know."

"Well, this time you don't have to go in."

"But what if you get hurt? Or killed?"

He stood, giving her his best rakish grin. "Me? Die?"

She smacked him on the leg, but she took his hand to pull herself up, too. "Very well. I've got a new spell...here." She put her hands on his chest, making his lungs tingle. "That should help you hold your breath longer."

"I expect that would come in handy," Ewan said, grinning even more now. "When exactly did you learn it?"

She blushed but didn't elaborate. "I'll augment your strength as well, in case you find it."

Once the usual warming sensation had taken hold, Ewan sucked in the equivalent of several lungfuls of air and dove in. The water was even colder in the mountains' long shadow, freezing his chest and taking his breath even more effectively than Tree had yesterday. He saw no sign of the pool's bottom, though, and far too quickly the little gray bar appeared in his vision, warning him not to overdo it. Exhaling slowly in frustration, he sped back up to the surface.

"It's no good," he called, gasping. "I couldn't even see it."

Tree frowned down at him. "You don't remember where you left it?"

"I was a little busy at the time! Sorry," he added quickly, startled at himself. "Let me take another look."

Ewan ended up burning the next hour in a fruitless search before finally giving the pack up as a loss. As he hauled himself up beside Tree, his stomach, skin, and pride were all locked in battle over who was suffering most, and all his brain could come up with was a numb reassurance that he hadn't had a smarter alternative.

He kicked a pebble at his watery adversary. "Stupid frapping pond!"

It rippled smugly in reply, daring him to waste even more time, swimming around like a fool instead of hunting like he should have been.

"It's okay. Really," Tree said. She produced a flame over one hand, then sent a light wind through it from her other to help dry him off. "We've got the most critical items in our inventories."

"Aside from food."

"I'm sure there's game out here," Tree said firmly. She gripped his chin, locking onto his eyes with a mischievous gleam. "And I expect it will be easier to catch, now that you're not carrying hundreds of pounds of rocks."

His scowl broke. "Fair enough."

Ewan quickly discovered that without the pack's weight to bog him down, he'd leveled his speed enough to keep pace with a good number of animals, which made hunting them with a pair of swords comically straightforward. They began to replenish their inventories over the next few days with the plentiful game and forage in the lower prairie, settling into a comfortably frugal rhythm of keeping well-fed by day, keeping close by night, and saying nothing about quests or missions for a change.

The good times ended for Ewan when they came across their first village, about three dozen miles west of the mountains and a few miles to the south of the river. The map labeled it as Dunbriar. To Ewan's eyes, the cluster of tilting buildings and weedy lawns looked more like a dump.

"Let's go around," he said, watching from where they lay behind the crest of a nearby hill as a shepherd opened his sheep's pen—*at three in the afternoon, no less!*—and wandered to a nearby building, leaving them to their own devices.

"I want to go in," Tree said. "It's perfect."

"You're kidding."

She smiled at him, reading his thoughts, and shook her head. "No. It'll have a shop, so we can get a pack and some fresh clothing, and perhaps even some food other than meat on a stick. And if there's an inn, we can finally sleep in a bed."

"Yeah, but—"

"Besides, I'm not seeing any Swords," she added, narrowing her eyes to check her map. "It's our first opportunity to practice blending in...and my first chance to see a village."

Ewan sighed. How was it that in almost four months, he'd never managed to show her around a civilized place? "All right. Let's just be casual, and hope no one recognizes our names from a quest board."

"That won't be a problem," Tree said. She laughed softly as she turned away and pulled a...something from her inventory. It resembled a sheet of paper, but it was metal on one side and glass on the other.

Ewan inched closer to peer over her shoulder. "What is that?"

She flinched, automatically moving to cover it, but her fingers reluctantly slid to the edge of the glass, revealing what looked like nothing so much as the Logos's menus.

"This is my tablet," she answered slowly, still looking away. "Or at least, a virtual copy."

"Virtual?"

"My real one doesn't travel here quite as easily as I do."

"Oh," he said, thinking that didn't explain anything. "What does it do?"

"In this case, I'm using it to edit our registrations. To change our names."

"Change our—but I like my name!"

"It won't be permanent," Tree chided, resuming her work and dragging her fingers across the thing—tablet. "I can toggle the edit, like I did in Whitehaven."

"Whitehaven?"

She nodded, finally glancing at him. "You asked me how I'd gotten us past the Swords...I'm showing you, now."

Ewan heard the tension in her voice and scolded himself to relax. *You knew she had secrets. Don't get squeamish just because they're weird.*

Tree took his silence as consent. "I can interact with the Logos using the touchscreen."

"Why not use a menu? Wouldn't that be faster?"

She stiffened, but continued. "This allows me access in ways your menu won't. Look. Here's the field with your registration... I simply select it and open the editor, then replace it with the name I created in Whitehaven."

"Cormac Mullen?" Ewan made a face as his own perfectly good, if outlawed, name vanished to be replaced by the other. "What kind of a name is that?"

"A safe one," Tree said, sounding less patient by the second. "I'm changing mine as well."

A moment later, *Treanna Rothchild* also vanished, replaced by *Alicia Mullen*.

Ewan stared at the name. Turned it over in his mind, compared it with his own. Both Mullens.

"You said you made these that first day, right?"

"Yes."

"What are we supposed to be, brother and sister?"

Her neck and cheek turned crimson.

Ewan thought of all the piercing stares, all the glowers she'd given him that first day. "You mean, even then—"

"I—it seemed the most reasonable thing to do!" she snapped, doggedly staring at the screen.

"I'm not complaining, mind you! It works for us—for now, anyway, as long as you can get our old ones back." He smiled to himself and looked at their names again, swapped out. *Gems of old. If I had an item like that, I'd have pranked the priests all day long!*

"So...do all the people from your world get tablets?" he asked.

"Yes, they're standard issue."

"And you all get to change your names?"

"Not of our own volition," she said irritably.

Ewan hesitated, but he was determined to prove he could handle her secrets for a change. "How come you can do it, then?"

She stiffened again, grip tightening on the tablet. "I got...it was a favor."

"You mean like a gift? From a friend?"

If anything, she got even redder.

Ewan watched her rigid back for clues, but then he had a sudden thought—a really lousy one, at that. "You have a boyfriend."

Tree slammed the tablet back into inventory, then rounded on him with a scorching glare that said plenty. "He was no boyfriend!"

*He was obviously something*, Ewan thought, suppressing a jealous surge even as he fixated on the past tense. "What, do they not have couples in your world?"

For a second she looked ready to slap him, but then she turned away, hugging her knees to her chest as she stared out at the village. "Not as you would understand, no. My people enter into living arrangements to coordinate raising children, but where companionship and sexuality are concerned, they treat their bodies as nothing more than vehicles of distraction. Or bargaining tools. I assumed...I thought I could do so as well. It was a small price to pay for what I needed." Her fist clenched as she glared at the horizon. "He tried to take more than I was willing to give; one kiss was all he got."

Ewan hesitated, throat tightening as he tried to square her

words with a typical Veridian courtship. *What kind of people are they?* He thought again of all those first-day stares. All of Tree's suspicion, all those months. Now he had a good idea of why.

The thought heated his blood.

"Hey," he said, pulling her into a rigid hug. "I'm sorry. I didn't mean to pry."

She thawed slowly as she hugged him back. "I know. I'm just tired of keeping secrets."

"I don't want you to," Ewan said, half to convince himself. Every time he learned more about her world, it felt like he'd been kicked in the gut. "And Tree? If anyone tries to take advantage of you again, I'll wreck them. I don't care who they are, or what world they're from."

She sighed as she pressed away, giving him a pitying look through reddened eyes. "I know you'd try. It's...well, nothing there is as simple as it is here."

"I don't see how that matters. I may not be a Gem or whatever you people are, but I can still do what's right."

Tree watched him silently, but her eyes hardened again, as if she'd made yet another decision he wasn't going to hear about anytime soon. She stood, dusting off her armor as she regarded Dunbriar with an obviously forced smile. "Let's go have a look."

"Yeah, sure." Ewan got to his feet too, more determined than ever to show her a good time in her first village.

He totally failed.

The moment they entered, the people sitting out on their porches turned dull, curious eyes toward them. Tracking, as they walked past.

"We're way too obvious as outsiders," Ewan muttered to Tree.

"We're visitors, here on our honeymoon," she replied.

Ewan snorted. "Who in their right minds would come here for a honeymoon?"

"Whoever said we were in our right minds?"

The first place they went was the sundry shop, as it looked to be in the most urgent danger of falling over. Once inside, Ewan could see that the walls seemed to be propped up by the shelves, leaving him reluctant to pull any items for fear of a cave-in.

The shopkeeper, a rotund, maple-skinned woman somewhere in her forties, fairly squealed as "Alicia" told her the sad tale of how she and her new husband had tragically been ambushed by wolves and forced to abandon their camp, along with their supplies.

The woman gave a disparaging huff and leaned on the counter with an unnerving creak. "Those no-good Swords can't be bothered to patrol this far out."

"Are there none around?" Alicia asked.

"Only when Greasy Tom's got a special on ale." The woman sniffed. "You'll be wanting a room there, of course. Now tell me, what brings you lovebirds out to Dunbriar?"

Cormac scowled, unable to take his eyes off the swaying walls. "It wasn't my first choice."

"It was off the beaten path," Alicia said quickly, stamping on his toe and messaging him to let her handle things if that was the best he could do. "The privacy appealed to us, ma'am."

The woman sighed. "Oh, to be young again! Well, if you're out this far, you really ought to go and see the Argenone Mountains up close. There's a lovely pool at the base of the Argentine Falls. The view is breathtaking."

"We'll be sure to see it!" Alicia replied, shooting Cormac a wicked grin that almost matched her eyes.

Ewan's patience died a little more with every bubbly squeal the shopkeeper emitted as she watched them poke around the shelves, but Tree's mood actually improved when she found a potted plant that resembled a cluster of scruffy, vaguely spade-shaped leaves. She rubbed one and sniffed, then gave a startled, pleased gasp.

"What?" Ewan asked, coming over.

Tree sniffed again, smiling as she pressed her fingers to his nose. "It smells just like breakfast."

Ewan glanced at the plant—it wasn't like anything he'd want to eat—but he humored her and inhaled. And blinked. "What in Veridor? It smells like oranges!"

"Yes, exactly!"

"But that's not an orange tree!"

Her smile faltered, but it came back twice as strong as she accessed her menus. "It's an orange geranium. Alice must keep a stock of them in the Centre...yes, I'm sure she does! The Logos says they can be kept in pots in harsh climates, then used for flavoring. This is wonderful!"

"Why?" Ewan gave the fake orange a suspicious glare. "We can't walk around with a potted plant."

Tree scoffed at him, but she was beaming now. "I know that. It's just that our worlds have more in common than I thought."

"Great," he muttered.

She turned his face to hers. "If an orange geranium can cross the worlds, then so can...others."

It took him a moment, but he blushed. "Well, I guess it's not all bad, then."

In the end, they picked one of everything from the shop's meager inventory of food and clothing, including a pack in which to put their new items. Ewan swore under his breath when the shopkeeper charged him enough to be her weight in gold, but he ground his teeth and made the transfer.

"So," he said as they stepped back outside into the late afternoon. "Where to, next?"

Tree took his hand. "Let's go to the inn."

"But—Greasy Tom?"

"I want a bed," she insisted, still smiling as she glanced at him.

*Someone's feeling better*, Ewan thought, but he wasn't about to argue.

Dunbriar's finest was easily ID'ed by the sign hanging drunkenly off one chain, proclaiming as it wobbled that the establishment within was called the Sprouted Seed. Inside, the main room's air had a smoky, oily cast to it, as if there was already so much grime on all the surfaces that the latest batch had to wait its turn. From the pile of buckets on the performing stage, Ewan guessed that no music had graced this building for a long time.

The portly innkeeper—Greasy Tom, Ewan presumed—lumbered around the place, attending to three men seated by the empty hearth. Two of them looked up curiously at the travelers as the door closed behind them.

Tom came over to the newcomers, smearing his broad oil-coated hands across his apron to give it a fresh coat. "Good afternoon and welcome to the Seed, young friends!" he said, vigorously bobbing his balding head as he opened a transfer menu. "Would you be liking a room?"

Sighing inwardly at the outrageous sum, Cormac paid for one. "And make it as private as possible, will you? We're, um, just married, and we're a little tired from traveling all day."

"This early?" The older man's eyes widened slightly, but then he gave them both a toothy grin. "Say no more!"

The other patrons peered at Tree as they followed the proprietor, but Ewan's glare and blades, just happening to be equipped, had them examining their dented flagons quickly enough.

Greasy Tom led them up the stairs and through to a small door at the end of the hall. "Our best room," he announced, spitting on his sleeve and hastily polishing the doorknob to cover the one part of the surface that actually resembled metal.

"I must say, young master, those weapons of yours look quite impressive."

"Thanks," Cormac replied, still looking at the doorknob with revulsion.

"They don't look like steel. Some kind of mob-horn, perhaps?"

"That's right, they're behemoth's horn. Now, if you don't mind, can we get some rest?"

"Yes, of course! Forgive me for going on, but we don't get a lot of visitors these days. If you like, I can deliver your dinner up to you and leave it by the door?" he added with a knowing wink.

"That would be perfect," Alicia said smoothly, passing the man a large enough tip to make him leave. She waited for Cormac to open the door, then made an exasperated sound and grabbed the filthy doorknob without flinching.

Once inside their room, Ewan closed the door with his foot. It locked with a cheerful, useless click. He exhaled softly, then instantly regretted it the moment he took another breath. Heavy with the odor of something that was definitely not geraniums, the room was so filled with objects and knickknacks it was a wonder anyone could even reach the bed, much less clean the place. Not that they'd bothered, by the look of it.

Tree picked her way around the clutter and beckoned him over to the large down bed lurking in the middle. He joined her and flopped across it, causing a cloud of something to explode from the mattress.

Tree covered her mouth and giggled, then sat down to rub his shoulders and neck. "Well, this is...nice."

"Are you serious? This place is a—"

He moaned, forgetting the filth for a moment as she found a knot.

"I know it seems unsanitary," she conceded. "But it's not as if it's really dust."

"Don't say that!"

"I didn't mean it that—anyway, thank you for humoring me." More softly, she added, "I'm sorry, for being upset with you earlier."

Ewan turned his head around to speak without getting another mouthful of feathers and mold. "Me too. I, um, well… I'm still with you, no matter what. No matter where."

Tree hesitated. "Even in a place worse than this?"

"Sure." He sighed, trying and failing to picture such a place at the moment. "I can't believe this is where we go on our fake honeymoon. Some boyfriend I am."

"*I* invited *you*," she said firmly. "But, if you like, I'll take your complaining as a promise to get me a nicer room next time."

The next thing he knew, she'd pinned him to the mattress with a shield and was tickling him mercilessly.

That night, Ewan lay in bed, looking out the window at the pitch-black sky while Tree snuggled up on his shoulder. He'd decided to keep watch just in case, not trusting for a moment that their room's thin door would block trouble. She'd agreed to split the watch with him as though they were still in the mountains, but she was obviously glad to have a mattress, no matter what horrors it was stuffed with.

As he lay there, trying to breathe without inhaling anything, Ewan stewed over the long day. A feeling that something was off nagged at him, something about what Tree had said. While he could keep his body still for her sake, his mind was a seething storm of half-built, half-banished thoughts as he tried once again to stitch together what he knew about the girl he loved.

That she was a Gem, or at least Gem-like, was clear. It was equally clear that she was still keeping secrets from him: the dark, nerve-wracking kind. Every time he learned about her world, he liked it less.

He sighed, banishing the suspicion—and jealousy—that stirred in response.

He'd said he would trust her, and she continued to hold up to that trust. Even though she had the power to log out and ditch him like she had that first night in the forest, she'd stuck with him, secretly protecting him the way her people apparently did. She truly seemed to love him, and despite everything, he loved her back.

What would happen when they arrived at World's Edge? Her mission didn't require the Amulet, if the Church would only listen to her. It was possible they'd find a sympathetic priest in the coastal city, solve her problem then and there.

If that happened, would she return to her world again, just like that?

Of course, the priests were too savvy to do anything as foolhardy as allying with a new Gem when the Diamond Lord had commanded them to bring her in, which meant he and Tree needed the Amulet and a frap-ton of strength to persuade the Church that fighting the Gem of old was a serious option.

*She needs me,* Ewan thought. *But for how much longer? What am I going to do, log out and go with her? Could I, even? Like a virtual tablet, or some glitchy plant?*

His heart didn't have anything to say to that.

Looking for something more productive to do, Ewan called up his map to get the distance to their quest marker. The Seed's walls formed in his vision as a set of lines, as well as a dot marking Greasy Tom, easily identified by Ewan's detection filter. Ewan watched the man's dot idly, wondering why he was up and about this late, but then it moved to the main door.

Five red dots swept in.

They paused, apparently conferring with the innkeeper. Then one of them started toward the stairs.

Ewan swore as he finally realized it wasn't anything Tree had said that had been bothering him.

Beside him, she stirred. "Mmm?"

"Wake up; we've got trouble."

She heard the tension in his voice, or maybe the heavy footfalls. "What kind?" she asked, forcing herself up and rubbing her eyes.

"Our host just let five Swords in; he must have ID'ed us by my blades." Ewan leaped out of bed, swearing again as he crashed into the junk on the floor. "Come on, we've got to go!"

"No." She stood up beside him and equipped her combat gear; even in the darkened room, Ewan could see the fey gleam in her eyes. The one that he'd seen after their battle with Old Max. "I'm tired of wasting time."

*Oh, frap.* "Tree, you're just plain tired. We can't go brawling with the Swords in here!"

"Why not?" she snapped. She jabbed a finger into his chest, hard enough to make him equip his own armor reflexively. "They're the intruders, coming here to ruin our peaceful night, our first night together in anything like a real bed, and I won't stand for it! What is the point of all the leveling we've done if we can't defend ourselves?"

"Um," was all he got out before the door exploded, kicked in by a mailed foot.

Tree was ready. Her hands flew up, and blinding arcs of lightning erupted from her fingertips, tearing straight through the steel and blowing the Sword back into the hall.

"I will not play your game any longer!" she snarled, before racing out the door to finish the man with her dagger as the red dots downstairs scrambled.

Hackles fully up but not clear anymore about for whom, Ewan followed her with weapons drawn, leaping over the stairs' rail to dispatch the next two Swords before they could counterattack.

They fell, a lot more easily than he'd expected—as easily as soldiers might fall, after a month of taking on golems and giant eagles. Ewan easily parried the next soldier's attack, taking him apart with a cross-cut as the fifth one fell, smoking, from the stairs above.

Then the door opened and another half-dozen paladins rushed in, looking like raw recruits as they tumbled over each other in their eagerness to get some action. One equipped a bow and drew it, knocking Ewan back with her first shot, but before Ewan could counterattack, a fireball flew through him and turned the soldier into a torch, blowing her into a pile of oily rags.

Very aware now that Tree was more dangerous than the Swords, Ewan charged into the new wave—but she beat him to it. The room seemed to ignite from all directions as she flung fire and lightning, looking nothing at all like a healer, and before long only one Sword remained. Ewan smacked him back into the wall, knocking his helmet off to reveal a young man, no older than himself.

Tree strode up to the poor noob and slammed her dagger into his shoulder, making Ewan flinch in sympathy as she pinned him to the wall.

"You," she commanded, her voice brimming with hard fury. "Report back to your masters that we're coming to World's Edge, and that we have a way to stop the Diamond Lord. If they have any backbone at all, they'll help us do it."

"Yes, ma'am!" the boy squeaked, shaking like a leaf.

Tree zapped him with more lightning to speed him along to limbo, then yanked her dagger free and rounded on Greasy Tom, wringing his hands as he cowered in a corner.

"And as for you," she growled, "this inn should be condemned!"

*Oh, it has been*, Ewan thought as the ceiling gave way and their bed dove gleefully into the conflagration, exploded in a cloud of dust and feathers, and narrowly missed the innkeeper as he tried to beat out the flames with his soiled rag.

"Come on; we're leaving," Tree ordered. She swept past Ewan through the flaming doorway.

He gave Tom a commiserating shrug, then followed his raging Gem of a girlfriend out, resolving never to wake her with bad news again. She stalked off into the night, and he chased after her, avoiding the villagers' stares as they came out to watch her flames consume the Sprouted Seed.

## 13

# FOOD FOR THOUGHT

"What in blazes did you do that for?" Ewan yelled at Tree as they jogged west. "We could have just slipped out and avoided the whole problem, but you had to go and burn the frapping inn down!"

"I felt it was necessary."

"Necessary?" He grabbed her arm and hauled her to a stop, then flinched back from the fire in her eyes. "We had a plan, remember? Unlock the Amulet and kick the Diamond Lord's butt, so the Church will listen to you. Right?"

"That will take months," Tree countered. "I don't think we have that kind of time anymore, even discounting the threat to the Centre. If people in a village like that are searching for us, we're clearly under more pressure than we realized."

"But—"

"It's not as if slipping away would have helped, either," she continued. "The innkeeper knew about your blades; he wasted no time in messaging the Church. We were going to be hunted anyway, so I decided to give them a display to make them hesitate."

"Or send a whole frapping battalion next time!"

"At least we can see those from a distance," she said dismissively. "They'll be easy to avoid."

"And if we can't?"

Her voice was dangerously calm. "Then we're not helpless."

*No kidding.* Ewan sighed and glanced back to where her fire had converted the Sprouted Seed into a beacon of overpowered vexation. It looked unnervingly like Whitehaven's cathedral, after the Diamond Lord. "Just when did you decide all this?"

"Shortly after they interrupted our sleep."

With that, Tree turned and resumed her brisk trot, before Ewan could argue more.

Amazingly enough, the Church didn't send any additional Swords their way over the next few days. In fact, the road was empty, aside from a small party of thugs on a long stone bridge over the river. They apparently hadn't gotten the update about Tree's newfound predilection for blasting anything that crossed her, but Ewan was sure they would be quick to tell their friends after respawning.

He didn't even try taking her to any other villages, and she didn't press. Instead, they kept close to the river, continuing west, beginning to relax again in the privacy of the wilderness. The hunting and fishing stayed good enough to keep them fed and perked, and Ewan indulged in the opportunity to discover plants and creatures he'd never heard of as the land continued to flatten into a broad coastal plain.

The weather turned sour on the fifth day after the bridge. A low band of dark clouds swept in from the west, heralded by a rushing wind that had Ewan missing Kate's monster pack more than ever. The new air smelled salty and moist, clearly carried in from the ocean a hundred miles away, but right on its heels came the rain, heavy and hard enough to stagger him as it blew in sideways.

"We've got to get out of this!" he shouted as Tree threw up a shield to take the edge off.

She nodded, clenching her jaw when a gust tried to send them rolling. "There's a farm about two miles southwest."

Ewan pulled up his map to look around, searching for an excuse to keep Tree a safe distance away, but there weren't any options. The local terrain was flat, with nothing so much as a boulder to hide behind. "Fine."

They ran for it, tripping through the lashing grasses as they plowed toward the storm's heart. Without an enemy to engage, there was nothing Ewan could do but hide in Tree's bubble, but she...she was amazing. Hands outstretched as she pushed the raging torrent aside, her eyes flashed with a fierce, desperate fury that told him plainly she was drawing a line not only against the Church, but against the very elements of the world. He watched her, awestruck, as she protected them by sheer force of will, refusing to let the swirling clouds in.

When they finally ducked into a barn near the main house, she dropped the shield and sagged into his arms. Even then, she glared through tussled hair into the darkness, trying to raise her arms as if to shore up the rough wall.

"It's okay," Ewan told her, holding her up. "We're okay. You did great."

She gave a noncommittal grunt and passed out.

"I'll take it from here," Ewan murmured, glad to be useful again. He kissed her brow, hoisted her over his shoulder, and clambered up a ladder into the barn's loft.

He kept watch as Tree slept, listening to the raging storm, shuddering along with the barn every time the winds gusted. On the ground floor, a hodgepodge of animals murmured, their forms illuminated by the flashes of lightning through the gaps in the plank wall. Sympathetic, Ewan scrounged around for some hay and tossed it down to them, then sang to help calm everyone's nerves before leaning back and waiting for the dawn.

It came a lot faster than he'd expected. He closed his eyes for a second, but when he looked again, the morning sun streamed in through the walls, casting thin panes of light that made the barn's dust sparkle. The air remained humid and salty, but now the world outside was utterly still.

Chiding himself for falling asleep on watch, he glanced over at Tree. She was still out, curled up on his side and snoring softly, peacefully.

*It's about time you really rested*, Ewan thought with a pang of sadness. *And it's about time I found you a decent bedroom.*

He moved to rouse her, but he was interrupted by slow, steady footfalls nearing the building.

Ewan whipped his map up, but no red dots appeared. A moment later, he heard a man's voice, wheezy and cheerful, murmuring to the animals below.

"Now, Lottie, what a mess you've made. Were you eating a midnight snack, you naughty girl?"

Ewan cringed as an aurochs lowed happily. He held his breath, but then Tree stirred in his arms.

"Who's there?" she murmured before Ewan could shush her.

The man below gave a creaky laugh. "Don't you worry, young'uns. Thank you for caring for the animals last night; you saved me the trouble. How about you both come down and have breakfast with me and the missus?"

Ewan glanced at Tree. [We should leave,] he messaged.

She narrowed her eyes, looking down through the floorboards. [He's not hostile.]

[Only because he hasn't seen us yet!]

She gave him a sly smile. [I'll be on my best behavior. You

needn't worry about him.] Before Ewan could protest further, she called out, "Breakfast sounds wonderful. Thank you!"

Ewan sighed and followed her down the ladder.

The man waiting for them looked ancient: in his seventies, at least. He had a wiry build under his sun-darkened hazel skin, and he was short the way older people always seemed to end up, but he moved with a sureness that belied his age as he extended a sinewy, spotted hand to them. "The name's Freddy."

"Ewan," Ewan replied carefully, extending his own.

"Not Cormac?" Freddy asked. His blue eyes twinkled merrily.

Ewan blinked, then whirled around to Tree. "Cormac? Still?"

Freddy turned to walk toward the white farmhouse, its exterior glistening wet in the dawn's light. "Ruby's already got breakfast half on the table, and she doesn't like it going cold."

Ewan snatched at Tree's hand to haul her away, but she was already following the old man inside.

The room through the door immediately reminded Ewan of his mom's kitchen, despite looking nothing like it. The walls were yellow, with fat pink-petaled flowers covering it in a regular pattern where they weren't covered up by green cupboards. A tantalizing aroma of pancakes drifted across the air, carried by the sizzling of eggs and bacon from the small range to the right.

Beside it at the cutting board stood a stout elderly woman wearing a plain brown dress, with umber skin and graying hair in short curls. She turned and beamed at the travelers, her knife dematerializing as she held her arms out wide in greeting. "Well, if it isn't our young stowaways. Did my Freddy wake you?"

Freddy chuckled as he closed the door behind them. "They were already up. As still as mice, waiting to see if the cat would notice them."

"We're sorry for the trouble," Ewan said. "We can pay you for the lodgings."

"Nonsense." Ruby tsked, then turned back to cut a pepper into cubes and add it to the potatoes in the pan. "You hold onto your money, dear. You'll be needing it to pay off your bounty eventually, won't you?"

Ewan made little squeaking sounds.

Freddy grinned at him, eyes twinkling even more. "Rubes, I don't think these two are used to company anymore."

"Certainly not company with such high aura reading," Tree said, assessing Ruby.

"Or the type who's not interested in turning us in to the Church," Ewan added hopefully.

"You needn't worry yourselves about that here," Ruby said seriously as she set out a water pitcher and glasses. "We've no want for gold, or boons from the likes of the Diamond Lord."

Ewan winced. "You know about that?"

"Son," Freddy laughed, "there's not a soul in all of Veridor that doesn't know about that. Flashy magic and rare weapons have a way of getting attention."

"Yeah...I know."

"Even so, I think introductions are called for," Ruby said, holding her pan over the outlaws' plates to wait for proper manners.

Ewan flushed and quickly traded his combat gear for regular clothing. "My name's Ewan O'Meara," he said, double-checking that Tree had corrected his registration or whatever. "I'm from the Whitehaven region. And this is my, um, companion, Treanna."

"Companion?" Ruby asked. "Don't you mean wife?"

Ewan choked on his water.

"Not really," Tree said quickly, though her cheeks reddened. "That was just our cover."

"Well you make a fine couple, if you ask me," Ruby said as she heaped eggs and potatoes onto their plates.

"They didn't ask you, Rubes," Freddy wheezed.

She rounded on him, waving her spatula with a smile. "Well, they should! I never understood why people want aura readers around if they aren't willing to listen to us." She turned to Tree and fixed her with a firm stare. "When you find the right person, you hold onto him, no matter what!"

Tree nodded, turning even more crimson when her eyes met Ewan's.

Dead certain there wasn't any safe way to join in the conversation now, Ewan focused on his breakfast, eating as if Kate was there to loom over his plate—or remind him to send out the wedding invites.

When the meal was over, Tree offered to help Ruby clear the table. Ewan stood with her, but Freddy gave him a tap on the shoulder.

"They'll be having things to talk about," the old man said cryptically as he grabbed a wide-brimmed straw hat from a peg by the door.

Ewan hesitated as he glanced back at the women, but he followed Freddy outside—then blinked in the bright sunlight, until his eyes adjusted and he could see just how much of the farm had gotten blown around the night before.

"Would you like a hand?"

"I thought you'd never ask."

The two of them spent the rest of the morning restoring the yard, turning feed troughs upright and gathering fallen branches to cut and stack with the firewood. Ewan offered to split some, and in no time he'd built up a good sweat.

Freddy chuckled, leaning on the fence as Ewan added the last pieces to the stack. "Now, that's a fair sight more helpful than some quest reward."

"You're welcome," Ewan replied as he joined the elder. "It's nice to level my strength peaceably for a change. Thanks...for being the first people we've met who didn't want to turn us in, and all."

Freddy tipped his hat's brim, reminding Ewan sharply of his dad. "You both seem like good people. Ruby would know if you weren't," he added as the house door opened and his wife went out to deliver scraps to the pigs, with Tree following along and watching curiously. "You needed help, so we decided to help you."

"But don't you worry the Swords might come after you for it?"

Freddy grinned over at him. "Did you worry about that when you helped your friend?"

"Of course not! I just did the right thing—even though it made me the bad guy to everyone else."

"Not necessarily," Freddy said gently, tilting his face up to the sun. "Things are rarely as cut and dry as good and evil. We just like to pretend they are, so that we don't have to bother with looking deeper. More's the pity, too, as it's only by looking carefully that we can see the best and worst for ourselves."

"I think I know what you mean," Ewan said after a minute. "I used to aggravate the priests all the time, trusting my experience in limbo more than their teachings. Not because they're right or wrong, I mean. I just needed to see it for myself, come to my own conclusions."

Freddy nodded. "The same is true of people. You have to take each one as they come, sometimes more than once. Almost always more than once, if you want to be fair," he added with a faint smile. "We all have a touch of kindness and cruelty in us. At some point or another, we end up revealing it to each other. To ourselves, too."

"I hear that," Ewan murmured, watching Tree as she talked with Ruby on the other side of the yard. "How can we tell which is the stronger part?"

Freddy followed his gaze. "By getting to know them through and through, and by nurturing the best in them."

"Maybe." Ewan pictured Tree healing him in the mountains, then tried to square the image with the way she'd wiped out the Swords at Dunbriar. How he'd found her locked in an old crate, alongside the Sprouted Seed's fiery demise. "I... I'm just starting to wonder if some mobs are best left asleep."

"All things wake, eventually," the old man replied. "In their own time. The wise person feels out when that is and stands ready to face them with clear eyes."

"And if we don't like what we see?"

Freddy patted him on the shoulder. "Don't refuse the good in people, simply because you've gotten a taste of their darkness. If you do, you'll undercut the best parts of life, skirting around them in the name of staying out of trouble."

Ewan sighed, closing his eyes as he turned his face to the sun. Just last night, he'd been hoping to slip away from this farm without so much as a word to its owners, but he'd have missed a good breakfast. And some of the best philosophizing he'd gotten to do since he'd last seen his dad.

*Is it really so hard, learning the truth while still being happy?*

He looked again at the ladies, now talking animatedly on the other side of the yard, while the pigs did their part to clean up breakfast. "Did your wife have trouble too, being an aura reader?"

"You could say that. Telling people what they need to know instead of what they want to hear isn't exactly a recipe for making life easy on yourself. Ruby used to work for the Church as a soothsayer, but it didn't really suit her."

Ewan did a double take as Tree, arms outstretched and wobbling, floated up and balanced on her shield a good foot above the ground while Ruby clapped.

But Freddy continued talking, unmoved by the sight. "Still, it's hard for a mage to get work anywhere else."

Ewan whipped his head around so fast, it was a wonder his neck didn't snap. "The Church uses magic?"

"'Course they do. Why wouldn't they?"

"It's not on the skill tree! I've never heard of anyone but the Gems who could grant that kind of power!"

"And who handled things before the Church?" the old man asked shrewdly. "Think about it, young'un. The very Diamond Lord you're resisting gave the Church the authority to manage the world, and that includes the professions. Oh, magic's still a viable skill, but only if you play nicely with the priests to get access. I'll guess that your young willow didn't exactly do that?"

"No...I don't think so."

"Maybe that's why they're all up in arms about her," Freddy mused. "The Church has its own take on the world and its workings, and they're dead set about keeping it that way. If someone got around their system, they'd surely want to keep her from sharing the knowledge. Might cause a revolution, otherwise."

Ewan nodded, but his stomach clenched. Was magic just another thing Tree could edit in her tablet, toggling supernatural powers like changing out gear? What would happen if she used it to make her own army, here and now?

*But if she could, why is she here? With me?*

He shook his head. "She's got a quest of some sort, some mission she has to finish. We're still working on it, actually," he said, idly checking on the Amulet in his inventory. "To that point, would you mind telling me what the Church had to say about us?"

"Not at all," Freddy replied. "Let's see...about three weeks ago, the regional quest boards lit up with a Heroic-level bounty hunt, sponsored by a Commander Caleb Martin from Whitehaven."

Ewan swore.

"You know him, I reckon?" Freddy said, chuckling. "The

listing had descriptions of a young couple, a boy with wild dark hair and a unique pair of swords, who'd interfered with the arrest of a girl mage wanted for capital heresy."

Ewan blinked. "They called her a mage? How long ago did that notice go up, exactly?"

Freddy checked his menus. "Twenty-two days,"

"But we were only in Dunbriar nine days ago," Ewan said, doing the math. Twenty-two days ago, he'd been frozen half to death at the Spine—after Tree got force-logged. "How could the Swords have known she was a mage?"

"Oh, they have their ways, no doubt. And no one alive remembers what a Gem might be capable of."

"Yeah," Ewan growled, mind racing now. They'd been totally isolated in the Argenones, but the timing was too perfect for it to be a coincidence. Could the Diamond Lord have learned about Tree's skillset in her world, then told Caleb? But how could that be, when Tree swore up and down that there weren't any Gems in her Centre?

"This quest of hers may be harder than I thought," he muttered.

Freddy smiled, sympathetically. "I'm sure the less I know, the better, but I can't help my curiosity. What might your willow's business be?"

"I wish I knew. Every time she gives me some of the details, I get spooked. Even so, I trust her," he added, almost automatically. "I'll do whatever I can to help."

"If you don't understand what she's working toward, then how can you help her succeed?"

A bird's song rang out across the yard from a nearby tree, reminding Ewan of the night he and Kate had cleared out the forest cave. The night everything had started, for better or worse.

*I'm running blind.*

"I don't know," he admitted out loud. "I need to ask her

about it before we face the Church again. I'm just worried I'm not going to like the answer."

"Maybe not," Freddy replied, patting him on the hand. "But I doubt that would stop a young man like yourself, would it?"

"I hope you're right."

"I have faith. A good heart supporting a head that listens; that'll win out in the end."

A few minutes later, the women went back inside. Freddy levered himself up to go in as well, but Ewan tried one last question for the older man.

"Freddy...where do you think we go when we get logged?"

The elder whistled softly. "Well now, that's the great mystery, isn't it? I don't know. Maybe the Church is right, and we respawn with a fresh start. Or maybe we simply stop existing, absorbed back into the Logos once and for all. When you get to be my age, that doesn't sound so bad. It would be a chance to rest, after all this time." Turning back to Ewan with sharp eyes, he asked, "What do you think, young'un?"

"I've come to believe we go to another world," Ewan whispered, his heart aching at the thought of leaving Veridor for the depressing place Tree had hinted at, filled with dark secrets and jerky people and tablets instead of menus. "But I don't know what kind of a world it would be."

"So, it's still a mystery," Freddy replied gently. After a moment, he added, "Maybe life in this other world of yours would depend on what you make of it? If so, then it's not so different from this one."

*You're right*, Ewan thought, bracing as he pushed himself up to go back in. *I'll just have to make the best of whatever world I'm dealing with.*

# 14

## THE TRUTH

Ewan and Tree left the old farmhouse later that afternoon, equipped with gifted local clothing and Ruby's home cooking. The new garb felt funny: Ewan's white doublet had long sleeves that kept tickling his wrists, and the leather pants were way too tight and short in the leg—although Tree said the outfit made him look dashing. She certainly looked fine herself, with a matching white bodice and a burgundy skirt that flowed around her ankles, giving her the appearance of gliding as she walked.

Freddy had offered to give them a lift, but Ewan had declined. Part of him still worried about the old couple running into trouble on their account, but more than that, he was proud. Even when taking the roads, the journey from Whitehaven to World's Edge was no small thing, and he wanted to revel in the sense of accomplishment that he and Tree had gone directly from spire to coast on their own legs.

"Did you have a good talk?" Tree asked, taking his hand and swinging it.

Ewan smiled and gave hers a squeeze. "Yeah, we did. Freddy

reminded me of my dad, only even older and wiser. How about you and Ruby, though?"

"Oh yes. It was a welcome change to speak to someone without fighting."

"Um…right."

She colored. "I suppose I have been letting myself get a little carried away. It's probably just as well that you shielded the rest of the villages from me," she added wryly, glancing at him. "At least until I could be reminded that I came here for help. If I want it, then I'll need to keep playing by this world's rules."

"I'd say that's fair enough," he said diplomatically. "So, it looked like you were learning some new spells?"

"Yes, I was!" Tree's face brightened again. "According to Ruby, the Church unlocks the magic skills for anyone who passes their application process, but they keep that information closely guarded. She didn't know much about the kinds of spells I prefer, unfortunately, but she showed me how to improve my concentration."

Ewan decided not to ask if she'd meant healing or setting things on fire. "How do you mean?"

"When I cast a spell, it takes a certain amount of focus." She searched the menus. "What the Logos calls 'mana.' I need it to hold the spell before releasing, but the effort leaves me mentally drained, making subsequent spells harder to reach. If I run out of mana, then I can't cast any more magic until I have a chance to recover."

"So it's like a magical stamina?" Ewan asked.

"Precisely. What Ruby did was show me a spell that helps to quiet the mind, removing distractions to improve my focus."

Ewan scratched his head. "But if you're tuning things out, won't that make you less effective?"

"No. I'm talking about an inner stillness, one that sharpens the things I focus on."

"Kind of like how the menus look brighter in limbo?"

"I wouldn't know," she replied with a little less humor. "But on the topic of reckless violence, I don't like the casual attitude your people have about death. It won't serve them well in the Centre."

"Why? Are the fees even worse there?"

"There aren't any."

Ewan grinned. "Well, that's a relief."

In reply, she shot him a glare that wiped the smile right off his face. "Because there would be no use for them."

"Wait—you mean that your people don't respawn?"

"Of course they don't!"

She stalked ahead, but Ewan couldn't bring himself to ask her more just then.

They said little for the rest of the day, even less the morning after that. Despite keeping away from the main roads they made good time, and three days later, World's Edge appeared on the horizon: a blurred smudge at first that slowly resolved into a series of rounded domes, squat and solid behind their walls. They looked nothing like Whitehaven's spires, but they doubtless offered better protection against storms blowing in from the ocean beyond.

The countryside was quite flat now, as though the hot, humid air had compressed all the interesting features right into the ground. The fields they passed through were populated with some sort of scrabbling monsters the Logos called minicores, like yard-long centipedes with crabs' claws. The mobs were quick but low-level, and a lot more easily dispatched than Ewan's mounting sense of foreboding or the continued silence between himself and Tree.

When he could hear the dull, not-so-distant throb of the ocean, he steered Tree slightly north, telling her he wanted to see the coast before they confronted the Church. She didn't protest, if anything looking as troubled as he felt.

Toward mid-afternoon, a thin line of dark blue became

apparent over the horizon, incredibly flat and broad, as though the land and sky had been neatly pressed into a seam. A ceiling of thick white clouds drifted overhead, heavy with rain but content to haul their loot further inland for the moment.

Tree looked up at them, shuddering as they swallowed the sun.

They pressed on; by the time they crossed the last field on the map, the dull throbbing was a long roar, muffled only by a forlorn ridge of sand as low and weather-beaten as the nearby city. It was a gloomy contrast with Whitehaven and the proud Argenones that Ewan was used to, and he sighed as he helped Tree over the last fence at its base.

She looked wistfully at the little clumps of grasses anchored into the dune's lee side, their roots sprawled out as though hanging on for dear life. Stepping around them, she climbed with a reluctance that slowed to a stop at the crest. There she turned, looking back the way they'd come. Ewan turned with her, retracing the long miles from cottage to coast with his memory. It reminded him of the way he'd learned to look back at his home, before leaving.

"They try so hard, don't they?" Tree said, her soft voice surprisingly loud after their long silence.

"Who?"

"These plants. So few, but they work ceaselessly to build up this dune, creating shelter for the green land behind us. Without them, the endless winds would scour those fields beyond bleak and lifeless."

Ewan glanced at her, but her eyes were distant, gazing through welling tears at something only she could see.

"I'm sure the fields are grateful," he offered.

"They're blissfully unaware of their situation." She gave a bitter laugh, then turned to the sands ahead.

Ewan followed her down to the shore, trying to enjoy the stiff wind as it blew his curls back. Not long ago, he'd have been thrilled just to get to see the ocean for the first time. Now, all he could think of was how the waves seemed to stretch out across the ground, wearing it down before patiently dragging it into the depths, one piece at a time.

He shook his head, then unequipped his boots and stepped into the surf. The high pants made a lot more sense with his toes in the warm water, gripping into the wet sand to keep the waves from taking his spot. It felt good, and he took a moment to stretch and look around. To his right, the beach curved gently around a bend, allowing the sea to reach in and embrace it while a group of sandpipers hopped about, pecking at the wet sand. The low walls of World's Edge loomed to the left, capped by a bristling fence of ballistae alternating with the Church's flags, the black yew on white outstretched in the wind.

And before him was the ocean, a vast deep blue fading to gray under the cloudy skies. It stretched off beyond sight, driving home the nearby city's namesake.

Ewan shivered, imagining what it would be like to swim out and leave it all behind. *Like logging. Or just dying, apparently, in Tree's world.*

Turning from the view, he angled Tree to the right with him, scattering the sandpipers as they went. The birds scolded him for interrupting their meal, then flitted back down to resume digging for the little shelled creatures that washed up into the shallow water.

For a while they walked in silence, but the pressure that had been building in Ewan's mind with every step since Whitehaven was reaching a breaking point, the need to ask her pounding in his skull as loudly as the waves. Chiding himself for his cowardice, he dredged up his courage and spoke at last.

"I need to know more about your world, Tree."

At the same time she blurted, "Ewan, I need to tell you the whole truth."

They both laughed, each not quite looking at the other. "In that case, I think you should go first," he said.

Tree nodded, gazing out across the water. The wind blew her long skirt back around her legs, revealing her ankles and feet rooted into the sand, as if she was also keeping it in place.

"I'm sorry it's taken me this long," she said, barely audible over the wind and waves. "I've been so afraid. And ever since the mountains, since you told me you loved me...I don't deserve your love, not unless you understand who I really am, why I'm really here. I've been selfish, but now we can't go any farther. Not until I explain everything to you."

Ewan sighed. *If this is you trying to make me feel better, then I'm in for a rough time.* "It's not just you. I've been avoiding it too, but I have to know." He took a slow breath, drawing on all his hours in limbo, in the cathedral's booths, in the open under the stars. All the joy and thrill of asking questions, so he could hunt down the answers. "I want to know. All of it."

She nodded again, but the motion drew his attention to a single tear rolling down her cheek. He reached up to brush it off, but she turned away. "Ewan, no matter what, I'll always cherish the past months."

"Don't say it like that." He took her hand and braced himself. "I'm still with you, and I plan to stay right here. All the way, remember?"

"Right," she whispered, sniffing as she took another look at the overcast sky. "When you were young, did you ever play games of pretend, maybe with Kate?"

"What, like paladins and mobs?"

"Perhaps," she said uncertainly. "When you played those games, did you ever imagine them in such detail that they seemed real, even for a moment?"

Ewan thought about it, then shrugged. "Yeah, sure, I guess. Kind of like the feeling I get when I enter combat. Only the critical details matter, and I'm so focused on them I don't notice anything else. Hey, isn't that like what Ruby taught you to do?"

Tree's face brightened. "Yes, exactly! You focus only on the things that are relevant, and the rest of the world's noise fades to nothing, as if it wasn't there. Only your perception matters, because that's what makes something real. It's so simple!" She nodded to herself, then turned and locked her eyes onto his. "I can do this. Ewan, do you feel my hand?"

He blinked. "Yeah, of course."

"How do you know it's my hand?" she asked, now smiling triumphantly. "How can you be sure it's really here?"

"Well, I can feel it," Ewan answered, also feeling his gut tighten. "Can't you?"

She gave his hand a squeeze. "Yes, I can. That feeling is a combination of sensations: the warmth in your hand, the rough calluses on your palm. My skin perceives it and sends electric signals, like lightning, to my brain."

"Um...okay?"

"Now, imagine what would happen if someone built a machine to mimic those sensations. If your eyes were closed, could you tell the difference between my hand and the machine?"

"Yes," Ewan said, churlishly. "I could tell."

"But what if you'd never opened your eyes? What if you didn't know what else to associate with my hand?"

"But I do open my eyes; they're open now! And why would anyone build a machine like that?" The deep, primal anger stirred in him again; the suspicions he'd sidestepped for weeks reasserted themselves, sensing their time was finally at hand. "You make it sound like someone is trying to trick me."

Tree hesitated, but she took a deep breath and continued, determined to see it through. "Not trick. Simulate. Suppose that you didn't have any..." She glanced around. "I don't know—any trees in your world. You could still satisfy your desire to see them by simulating an image of them. If you built the right kind of machine, you could also simulate their touch, and other properties besides."

"Why not just plant a tree?" Ewan asked warily. "Wouldn't that be simpler?"

"Not if there aren't any more trees," she answered, chilling Ewan's blood as she looked across the waves, white-capped now as the winds picked up. "But suppose you had a memory, a detailed record, of them. If you knew how to make the mind perceive a tree, then you wouldn't strictly need to have one."

She turned to him again, worry etched in her face to reflect his own, and something else as well. Was it pain? Regret? Bitterness, even?

With a jolt, Ewan recognized that expression as the one she'd worn when looking at the natural sights around Whitehaven. The one she'd worn mere minutes ago, when looking back over the fields. All the clues he'd gleaned, the snatches of conversations and observations over the past months, drummed themselves into his mind like a rising tide, relentless and unforgiving now as he looked out beyond his world's boundaries.

The Gems claimed they'd created Veridor; she claimed her people sent his ancestors to live in it. In her rage, she'd treated the other Veridians like they were less human, just like the Diamond Lord had done in Whitehaven. Max said the Gems had thrived on interfering with Veridor, but the connection went deeper than that. People who logged out of his world went to hers. Veridor would die in a day without her world's support —and there was no respawning there. She had magic, somehow bypassing all of the Church's rules and power, as though they didn't apply to her. She'd even been unmoved by the grime in that inn, saying it wasn't real!

In a rush of dread genius, an explanation materialized in Ewan's mind as all the bits and pieces reassembled themselves into a terrifying pattern, the implications of it shaking him to his core.

*All of our history, and everyone in it...is it even possible? Who could do such a thing? And why? What is it that we give back to this other world? And has she come to collect?*

Ewan's jaw clenched as he stared out at the ocean and its waves. They continued to drive up the shore, each one governed by its own rules and physics. Like a beautiful, complex machine.

"Treanna." He started to shake as the rage told him he was dead right. "Why is your favorite color green?"

He could hear the tears in her voice, but he kept his eyes on the ocean. "I...it's not just that. It's also because it reminds me of you."

"I have to know." His heart was hammering now, joining with his anger against the truth as it settled like a shroud over his soul. His dad was right after all, but Ewan had chosen the path of knowledge over happiness. "I have to hear you say it."

"I like green the best because there is so precious little of it in my world." She cupped his chin, but he clamped his eyes shut, unable to face her, to face what she was saying.

"There are no trees anymore, my love."

For a second, he couldn't breathe, couldn't move into the next moment. A world without trees...what could have possibly happened to it?

*What did they do?*

"So what you're telling me is that your world is broken," he said, struggling to speak in anything less than a snarl. "And what, that my world isn't real? It's some kind of simulation, some kind of game?" He spat the word out, thrusting his free hand at the beach around him.

"Yes," she whispered.

Time lurched forward again, and his fury broke through at long last as he opened his eyes and flung all of his anger, all of his revulsion, at her. "Then what does that make the people, Tree? What am I, then?"

"Ewan, please!" She gripped his clenched fist. "You are my love! I'm bound to you; please remember that! The green in your eyes, it's the same as the green of your world to me. Healthy, beautiful, and full of life!"

By the way she recoiled from his glare, he didn't think his eyes looked especially beautiful right now. "Where are we, Tree?" he rasped, trying to regain control of himself. If he even had that power. "Really?"

"We are here, on this beach, but we are also in my world." Her eyes were wide, filling with the same terror he'd seen in them that day in Whitehaven.

*Gems of old...this was what she'd told the Church?*

"Where?" he exploded. "Where are you keeping us?"

"In the Centre!" she yelled back. "Your body is in a tube deep under the ground, with wires piercing your brain to connect you to Veridor!"

She collapsed to her knees, long hair tangling into the surf as her head slumped forward. "You've been there since you were an infant," she whispered, "just like everyone else in your world."

Ewan tried to jerk away from her, but she held tight, refusing to let him flee now that he knew her greatest, darkest secret.

"Why?" he screamed, channeling the fury of all Veridians, past and present, as he confronted their jailer. "My whole world, my whole life, it's all fake, and our real bodies are rotting away in some hole in the ground? You had no right; we never had a choice! What possible reason could you have for doing this, lying to us all for so long? Are we playthings to you?"

"No!" She yanked down on his hand, dropping him into the water in front of her, pinning him with a look of such wounded rage that he flinched back. "We did it because there was no other choice. My world was indeed broken by our ancestors, and the only way to save humankind was to go into hiding. Into simulations. You accuse me of playing, but your kind are the players! You get to live in a green fantasy world, while my people have endured the Wastes for millennia. Sacrificing our lives to preserve yours. Forever aware of how blissfully ignorant you are without us. And now it's time for you to return the favor. You've got to protect us, or we're all dead!"

She grabbed his face and tore into his soul with her withering glare, but he gave no resistance.

"Don't you dare accuse me of lying to you," she snarled. "Not when I've risked everything I hold dear to tell you!"

She shoved him hard, knocking him back into the surf as his rage disintegrated, swept away by hers. In its wake the bile rose, and he retched into the water, his simulated body trying to reject what the rest of him no longer could.

After he'd emptied himself, Ewan sat back, staring at her in fear and awe as her tears made salty tracks down her cheeks. Between that and the way her hair dropped into the surf, she looked especially like a willow. A weeping willow, doomed to soak up the mess his ancestors had made.

How much had her people suffered, living in a broken world with a thankless task? How much had she personally suffered, drawing the aggro of his world's leaders—and her world's, too—on a prayer that she could find someone to help her? She'd found him, but how had he answered her trust?

*By throwing a fit like a child*, he thought bitterly. *What happened to greeting the unfamiliar as a friend?*

"I'm sorry." His voice burned his throat. "I'm so sorry. I just… it's such a shock. I never imagined my world could be unreal, not even in my wildest dreams. Much less the reason why your people created it. I'm still angry about it all, I won't lie, but I shouldn't have taken it out on you. It's not your fault. The fact that you're here in spite of everything proves you're trying to make it better."

Tree watched him, her glare still in full aspect, but this time he met her eyes, opening himself up to her until she was finally satisfied.

"I forgive you," she said quietly, shuddering for a moment more as her own anger slowly bled away. "After what happened with the Church, I've been expecting you to react badly. I'm certain that if our places were reversed, I'd feel as upset as you do. Can you forgive me, for waiting this long to tell you?"

Ewan tried to laugh, but it came out as a cough. "Forgive you? Tree, I'm thanking you. For giving me the time to come to terms with everything...to fall in love with you."

"You still love me?" she asked, her voice shaking more than ever. "Even now?"

"Especially now." He leaned forward, wrapping her up in a tearful hug even as another thought occurred to him, stabbing his heart from a new angle. "But I'll understand if you don't love me back, seeing as how I'm not real."

Tree snuggled tighter against him, refusing to let go. "Of course I love you, you sweet fool! Perception is what matters, remember? Your world may be a simulation, but thanks to you, I've seen that it's far more alive than my own. And you are real, Ewan, by far more real to me than anyone I've met."

"The same to you," he said, sighing as the rest of his anger washed away with the waves. "And not just literally. You've brightened my life, given me a reason to improve. I'm still with you, all the way."

He leaned over and kissed the top of her head, then added, "For what it's worth, there's still one Tree in your world—and I think she's the bravest, most wonderful thing I've ever known."

She said nothing, but she shook as she cried into his simulated shoulder.

"But promise me something, okay?" he asked.

"Anything."

"No more secrets between us. In any world."

"No more secrets. I promise," she whispered.

They held each other tightly, listening to the crashing waves as the hidden sunlight faded behind the horizon.

## 15

## WORLD'S EDGE

THEY SAT UP A WHILE THAT NIGHT, TALKING AS THE WAVES
crashed ever higher with the rising tide. The brewing storm
passed them by, leaving a clear, starry sky in its wake. With the
initial shock and anger gone as well, Ewan's curiosity came
rushing back. And with the reassurance he would stick with
her, Tree was happy to answer his questions, finally explaining
everything she could.

And what a story she had.

"Approximately twenty-six hundred years ago," she said,
"my world suffered an ecological catastrophe."

"How bad?" Ewan asked.

Tree pulled her knees to her chest. "Bad enough to render it
uninhabitable."

"All of it?"

She nodded, looking out at the ocean.

"Gems of old," he murmured, trying without success to
picture Veridor just...dying. For good. "What happened?"

"We're not certain. A lot of information was lost, though
from the surviving records, I think humankind wasn't certain
when it happened, either. Whatever it was, though, everyone

believes it was our fault." She shivered as a gust of wind blew her hair back. "In the Centre, we like to think our labors help atone for the sins of our ancestors, to mollify the Mother."

"The Mother?"

"Mother Earth," she replied. "Most of us find it easier to cope by acting as if we work to appease a goddess, rather than an uncaring world. No one really believes in her, though." She sighed, hugging her knees again. "Not anymore."

Ewan wrapped his arm around her shoulder. "I can't imagine how hard that must be, for all of you."

"It helps us to think we never knew any differently," Tree replied sadly, with a touch of bitterness. "Our life is one of grim privilege, but we take comfort from being better than the players."

"Players?"

"Your kind. Ewan, you have to understand; the staff resent having to care for you, when you provide nothing in return. Some of us don't even consider you to be human."

Ewan remembered her fury at Dunbriar, the haughty rage finally unleashed after a lifetime of frustration. *Just like the Gems.* "Some?"

"Practically all of us," Tree amended, squeezing his hand as if to say she didn't think so. Not anymore. "It's a pity. If they could all see the game worlds as I have, then they would have a much better appreciation for our sacrifices."

"And why is that?"

"Because the players are our future. The Centre was founded to preserve humanity, its very best." She lifted her chin and looked right at Ewan. "So that one day, when the Mother is willing to forgive, her children can return, humbled by their punishment yet eager to rebuild. To do things properly, next time."

"No pressure, huh?" Ewan murmured. "So, this hole in the ground, it holds everyone in Veridor?"

"The game floors," she corrected, her tone slightly offended. "They hold far more than that. Veridor is but one of many game worlds we tend."

Ewan looked up at the stars, recalling what his dad had said that morning, when they'd last walked the Whitehaven road together. *I guess those scholars were right, after all.* "That's got to be something."

"It is," Tree said proudly. "The Centre's mission is unique, unparalleled in Earth's history. There are over a hundred virtual worlds, all existing in isolation from each other but managed in common by the Logos."

"So you do have the Logos, even there," Ewan said.

"Not like you do. The Logos is a kind of operating system, like a computer."

"A what?"

"Like one of Kate's machines. It weaves throughout the game worlds and ties everything together behind the scenes. We have an entire section, Programming, dedicated to supporting it."

Ewan laughed out loud. "I'd love to meet them. I'll bet they could answer every question I thought up in limbo!"

"Perhaps," Tree replied, hesitating. "But you'd have to log out for that."

The laughter vanished instantly, along with his stomach. "Oh...right. So, logging's the only way to get to Earth?"

"To transfer your consciousness, yes. Your body's already there," she reminded him, offering him a little smile. "During my first months here, before I obtained official support, I would sneak into one of the tubes on the game floors and log in with my credentials. Every night, after logging out..." Even in the dark, she was blushing. "I would stop by your tube, just to check on you."

Ewan leaned over and gave her a kiss, deciding to focus on

her sentiment instead of the creepiness. "Thanks. So logging isn't nearly as dangerous as we think?"

Tree shook her head. "It's not that simple. I can do it easily enough because my body is adjusted to the real world. But for a player, someone who's never left the tubes, I think logging out would be very dangerous, life-threatening, even."

"And there's no respawning?"

"Not in the real world. One life, that's all we get."

"That sucks." He sighed, looking at it from his Veridian—player's—perspective. "I guess that's why elders get logged most, isn't it? They're really dying in your world?"

"That's correct. One of my duties as caretaker was retrieving their bodies for recycling, making room on the floors for the next generation."

Ewan suppressed a shudder at the idea. "I guess your job's not for the faint of heart."

"The real world isn't for the faint of heart," she said.

With that comforting thought to haunt his dreams, Ewan slept badly. After a few hours of listening to Tree snore, he dug himself out from under her and walked down to the water, watching the moon sink into the unknown.

He could barely grasp the enormity of everything she'd told him, much less imagine how the past months had been, from her point of view. Her mission seemed more hopeless than ever. Even if they managed to talk the Church into helping—and that was a long shot at best, now that he knew the truth—how were his people supposed to do anything? And even if they survived logging, what kind of welcome awaited a player in a world of Gems made human, with all their resentment plain to see?

When the sun finally decided to join him, peeking warily over the dune's crest, he roused Tree for the last leg of their journey. After a quick bite to eat, they walked south along the beach. In almost no time, the walls and domes of World's Edge came back into view, regarding them stoically as if they still trusted in their strength to weather whatever storms Tree brought.

*If you only knew.*

They made for the smaller northern gate, but as soon as he saw his first World's Edgers out on morning business, with even the fair-skinned folk tanned to a rich bronze, Ewan knew that local gear or not, he and Tree had never stood a chance of blending in. Her narrowed eyes told him she'd noticed as well, so they made no attempt to disguise their approach as the whispers and curious stares started to add up.

The gate guards, all hulking tanks, glared impassively as the couple approached. Their leader, a man with a smart black pencil beard and pointed silver helmet around his onyx face, raised his massive battle axe in one hand and leveled it at them.

"You there. Halt!"

Tree stopped, then spoke calmly. "We are here to see the leaders of your Church. I believe they will know why."

The man returned a tight grin. "By fortune, they are eager to see you as well. Come, strangers. We will show you to the cathedral."

His soldiers shifted nervously. "Captain Al'Dashan," one said, "we can't leave the gate unguarded."

"And I will not leave these prisoners untended in my city for that arrogant Whitehavener to take. If the reports are true, these two are by far the greatest trouble we are likely to encounter today. Fall in!"

The other guards made a box surrounding Ewan and Tree, and together they began making their way down crooked, zigzagging streets toward the city center. A crowd gathered behind them, with children pointing and mothers hushing them as they peered intently at the prisoners. And around every corner, more Swords joined the escort, in case the outlaws had a change of heart.

*Or are they vying for the Diamond Lord's reward?* Ewan thought uneasily.

As the red dots continued to spill onto his local map, he glanced at Tree, but she kept her head high and equipped a satisfied smile, as though their captors were merely an honor guard.

[Tree, don't rely too much on your magic. These guys are seasoned veterans, not pushover cadets.]

[Trust me,] she answered, not breaking stride.

When they made it to the central square—more like a round arena than a proper rectangle—there were another forty or so Swords already there, just waiting for the trouble to begin. Ewan sighed at the rotten morning to come, but then he realized that this new batch had pale skin. Al'Dashan marched his prisoners right past the new group, his smile smug as they passed by a snarling Caleb Martin, but Ewan was already searching for the one Sword he actually wanted to see.

Paul was standing toward the back of his squadron, watching Ewan as suspiciously as the others, but when Ewan gave him a personal party invitation, the cadet accepted immediately and sent a silent message.

[What happened to you two?]

[It's a long story. Is my family okay?]

[Yeah, they're fine. The Church is monitoring your house, but they've taken no action against Kate or your parents.]

[Thanks,] Ewan sent back, letting that particular worry fall away. [Your buddy Caleb doesn't look happy to see us.]

[Watch out for him. The Diamond Lord gave him another buff before we came here.]

Ewan nearly tripped. [He came back? When, exactly?] he asked, trying to keep his eyes caged on the line of priests emerging from the main complex.

[Twenty-six days ago. He said he'd scried your location and purpose, then rewarded Caleb for trying to take you down before. We marched the next day. I barely talked my way into the party, after getting censured for failing to catch you in the woods. Why didn't you come back to Whitehaven?]

[We couldn't. A storm pinned us on the other side of the Spine, but we were going to have to come here anyway to unlock the Amulet.]

[The what?]

Ewan couldn't help smiling. [Old Max's secret weapon.]

[You found it? Thank the Logos!]

[We even had a good conversation with Max about it too—remind me to tell you later,] Ewan added, trying to split his attention as the Cardinal, a stooped old woman with soil-dark skin and snow-white hair, came forward and started talking at him and Tree, mostly accusing them of stuff.

He looked regretfully at his map. The quest marker was tantalizingly close, somewhere inside the cathedral. It may as well have been on Earth, for all he could reach it.

[Paul...Max cursed the Amulet. It won't be of any use until we go to every city.]

[How do you expect to manage that? You didn't even get two feet into this one before getting arrested.]

[Don't you think I know that? But you can do it.]

Paul's reply came back after a stunned moment. [You're returning an Epic quest?]

[It doesn't matter which of us does it, as long as it gets done! Make up some excuse to go on a tour, and get this thing unlocked!]

[I'll...sure.]

[Thanks.] Ewan turned casually, making a quick line-of-sight transfer of both the Amulet and the quest to his old friend. [Paul, things are a lot more serious than we thought. Tree's—]

"How dare you turn away from me, insolent boy!" came an

angry voice. Ewan spun back around to see the old Cardinal a foot away, glowering up at him.

"Sorry, ma'am," Ewan said, glancing at Tree. "I guess I just kind of tuned out. What else were you blaming on me, now?"

The Cardinal gave him a long, reproachful look, then spoke past him to Caleb. "Was he this rude to my counterparts in Whitehaven?"

"More so," the commander growled. "Mother, let me cut them down for you."

"For the hundredth time, no!" The white-robed woman rubbed her temples as she turned back to Ewan. "I asked you, boy, what your part in all this madness is."

"I'm with Tree—Treanna." Ewan glared down at the wizened face. "She's here in Veridor from the Gems' world, and she needs our help."

"And with what, precisely, does she need help?"

Ewan glanced at Tree, but she held her silence, her eyes asking him to do the explaining this time.

"Veridor is a part of something much larger," he said, casting about for the words to make the truth comprehensible —and palatable. "Something I didn't fully understand until only yesterday. My friend, and the Gems, they come from a dead world, but that world is our home as well. We're here in this dream we call Veridor, but we live there in the real world, too. And something's out there, right now, looking to kill us all in our sleep."

The Cardinal's brow furrowed. "Where did you hear such a preposterous story?"

"Treanna told me, and I trust her," Ewan answered simply.

"The boy is bewitched!" Caleb shouted, striding out toward them. Ewan went to block him, but the commander grabbed his arm and flung him aside, then advanced on Tree. "This creature from the Gems' realm will say anything to preserve her vile hide, but my merciful Lord has already told me her true aim. She seeks to usurp the Church's authority and unravel the foundations of our society. We must take her now and return her to the Diamond Lord, or face annihilation!"

"I've had enough of this," the Cardinal muttered. She shot Al'Dashan a pointed look.

The guard's lips curled up into a catlike smile. He nodded to one of his comrades, and they advanced on Tree, weapons materializing in their hands as they moved with deadly purpose.

And Tree just stood there, waiting, when for once she shouldn't have.

Out of patience as well, Ewan vaulted up, equipping his full combat gear and rushing them with a yell. Al'Dashan and his goon turned, but Ewan drove his blades home through their hearts—right as Tree shouted, "Ewan, wait!"

The men slumped to the ground, crimson blossoming out to stain the yew trees on their tunics, but instead of anger, their faces wore an expression of bewildered shock.

The Logos curtly informed Ewan it was tacking a double murder onto his criminal record, and that Paul had left his party.

"You see the madness she brings?" Caleb yelled, drawing his own greatsword. "They must be destroyed before it's too late!"

And then the square turned into an arena in truth as confused, angry Swords rushed in with weapons drawn. Tree skidded to a stop beside Ewan as he brought his blades up to meet the incoming soldiers.

"Are you blind? They were going to arrest Caleb!" she snapped as she flung up a shield to deflect the first volley of arrows.

"They—what? But they were moving toward you!"

"They were moving toward him; he was right next to me. I could see it in their eyes: they were all tired of the outsider telling them how to run their city." She snarled, venting her frustration by flinging a hail of icicles at the poor bastards in front of her. "I think the Cardinal might have listened after that!"

Ewan's stomach clenched as he actually looked at the battle. Some of the Swords, mostly Whitehaveners, were coming for them, but he could hear the Cardinal ordering a sizable contingent of World's Edgers to arrest Caleb, too.

"Nerfing hell," he muttered, bringing his sword up to block an attack that slid through the shield.

Ten feet away, the commander bellowed. He tossed his greatsword to one hand and equipped a shield as tall as Tree in the other, laying about and cleaving anyone fool enough to attack him, often two at a stroke.

Ewan started for him as well but was forced to parry a spear's thrust, chopping it in half with his spare blade before whirling about to engage a pair of soldiers attacking Tree's flank.

"Hey, guys, I'm sorry!" he shouted lamely. "It was an honest mistake, okay? Tree, disarm only! We don't want to make them madder," he added as she sent chain lightning arcing from helmet to helmet.

"Where was that clear thinking a moment ago?" she sniped back, but she laid off the headshots.

They fought on, but there were too many soldiers, too angry now. Tree's shield wavered as she lost her focus, and Ewan's health dropped as arrows began finding their marks.

But then Caleb came rampaging through, knocking people aside as he battled toward his quarry. "You're coming back with me, witch," he snarled, ignoring the arrows and raising his sword high. "The Diamond Lord's boon will be mine, and mine alone!"

Ewan leaped between them to deflect the blow. The force of

it knocked him to his knees, cracking the stone under his armor.

The commander roared, bashing Ewan with his shield and nearly taking his head off with the follow-up. "I have the Diamond Lord's blessing; you're no match for me now!"

"He's not alone," Tree called out, healing Ewan with one hand while flinging a fireball from the other to blast Caleb in the face. "But you are. Look around you, fool; you've killed your own men!"

In the moment she'd bought him, Ewan glanced at the map. Almost all of the red dots were gone now as the remaining soldiers fled, opting to let the madmen from Whitehaven kill each other and leave them out of it. Paul was conspicuously absent, too, as was the Cardinal.

Caleb swayed, smoking as he looked at the ring of corpses around them. "It doesn't matter. My Lord—"

Ewan rushed him and stabbed him in the shoulder. "You are the last person the Diamond Lord should give boons!"

Caleb ignored it, dealing him a savage kick that sent him tumbling across the bloodied stone. "My Lord values power, and the will to use it."

Ewan tried to sit up, but the commander threw his shield. The world went red, drowned in pain, and Ewan looked down at the metal wedged through his heart.

In an instant Tree was beside him, restoring his health, but neither of them could pull the shield free.

"It's okay!" Ewan was laughing hysterically, now. "It's not really there!"

She opened her mouth, but Caleb's gauntleted fist grabbed her hair and flung her aside. "Wait your turn," he snarled, yanking his shield out of Ewan and slamming it into her face.

She fell with a cry, then hit him with enough lightning to make Ewan's scalp buzz.

Caleb dropped to his knees, smoke and the stench of

charred flesh rising from the joints in his armor. But he laughed, throwing his head back. "I have them, my Lord!"

Ewan looked up through the death-haze, then swore in disbelief as a flaming sphere lit the sky, a great falling star from the other world.

"You see?" Caleb rasped. "He comes to collect his own, and to reward me. He'll take the witch back to his world to punish her. But for you, boy?" Caleb laughed again, leering over at him. "He wants us to make a nice example out of you, so no one would ever be fool enough to defy him again."

Ewan glanced at the oncoming fire, now a column, as it tore the sky. Its approach singed his face even from a distance, threatening to burn his eyes. "You're out of your frapping mind. We've slipped you before, and we'll do it again."

"Not anymore, you won't," the commander panted. "My Lord can find the witch from his realm, now. There is nowhere for you to run, nowhere in Veridor he cannot find you!"

"Then tell him we're leaving," Tree snapped. She blasted Caleb once more, just as the flaming column smashed down into the stone with enough force to blow them all back as it cooked their skin.

Tree crawled over and grabbed Ewan's head, then gave him a hard kiss, smearing her blood on his lips, and whispered fiercely. "Trust me, and keep fighting to stay alive no matter what!"

"Okay," he said automatically, only realizing what she was about to do right before the world vanished, leaving him with the searing afterimage of massive white wings flanking a tall, thin form as the Diamond Lord stepped into the square a moment too late.

# PART II

# THE CENTRE

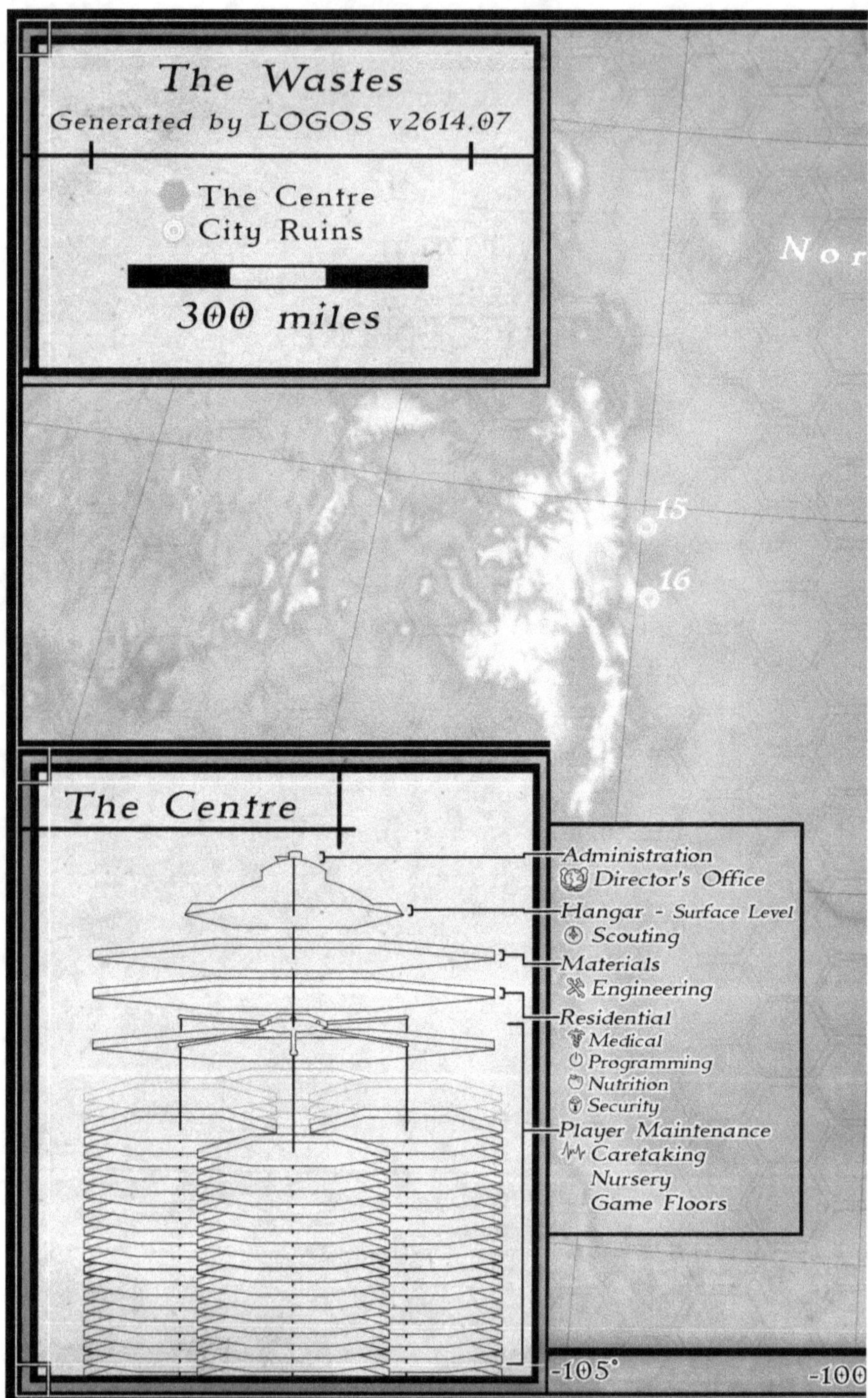
The Wastes
Generated by LOGOS v2614.07
The Centre
City Ruins
300 miles
Nor
15
16
The Centre
Administration
Director's Office
Hangar - Surface Level
Scouting
Materials
Engineering
Residential
Medical
Programming
Nutrition
Security
Player Maintenance
Caretaking
Nursery
Game Floors
-105°
-100

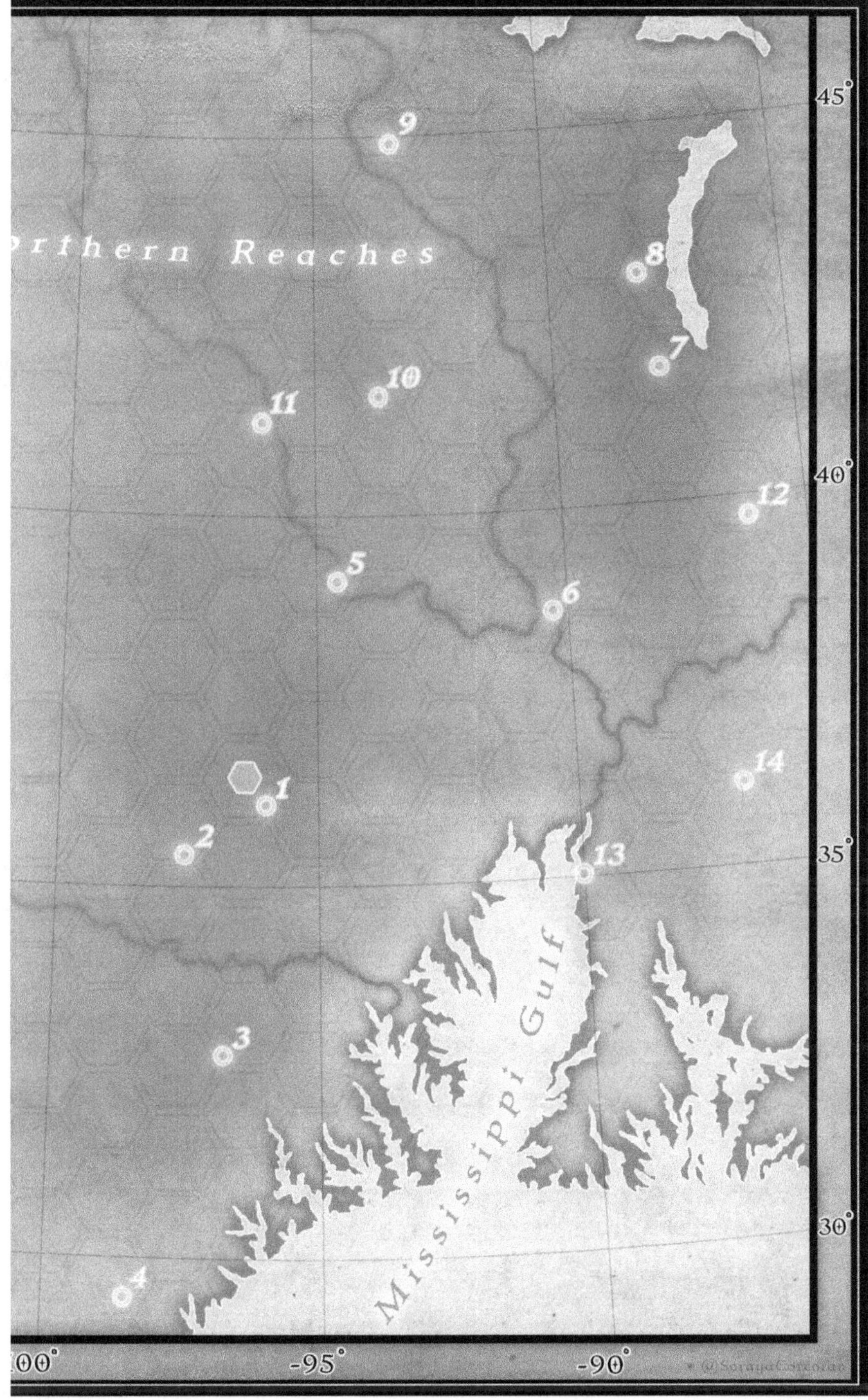

Northern Reaches
Mississippi Gulf
45°
40°
35°
30°
-100°
-95°
-90°
1
2
3
4
5
6
7
8
9
10
11
12
13
14

**16**

———

# THE OTHER SIDE

Darkness, utter and complete.

Ewan fought against the smothering blackness, willing his body to reform and take control, but it was no use. He tried desperately to open his eyes, to move, anything, but he might as well have been in limbo for all the reaction he got.

Pain suddenly erupted from everywhere at once, as though a dozen daggers had been pulled from him. He embraced it as proof he still had a form with which to take damage, used it to connect with that form. He recognized his neck and temples, throbbing and burning. His heart fluttered in panic against his ribs, but he reached out with his mind, following his blood as it raced to map the rest of his body: skin, wrapped tightly around sinews and bones; muscles, hard as rock but thin as paper.

Then, behind the pounding in his ears, he heard a hissing, thrumming noise from above his head. It whirred steadily, unrelenting, and with a thrill that was half elation, half terror, he realized that he could feel a soft breeze wafting over him—just like he had in limbo.

*I knew it!*

But as the seconds turned into minutes without any sign of a chime, Ewan started to worry.

*Menu*, he thought.

Nothing happened.

*Gems of old...I'm really here. I'm really logged out!*

He tried to open his eyes, but they were glued shut, as though they'd never been open. He tried to sit up, but he couldn't budge, as though he was pinned down by some invisible force. Was it a kind of magical shield?

He had a bad feeling it wasn't.

Fearing he really was as weak as Tree had warned, Ewan began counting his breaths, trying to steady them as his heart kicked into overdrive. He couldn't pass out now, or he might never wake again.

She was coming for him. She'd said to trust her and keep fighting to stay alive, so that's what he'd do.

He tried to remember what had happened only moments ago, in World's Edge. How Caleb had called the Diamond Lord, how the Gem had responded. Ewan shuddered in his mind, picturing the great white wings. Tree had saved his life, getting him out of Veridor like this.

*If it doesn't kill me first.* He prayed for her to hurry. *How big is this place? I never thought to ask!*

His breathing was coming too fast now, too shallow despite his best efforts. He felt light-headed, dizzy. He kept his attention on his unresponsive body, on the blood still hurtling through his veins as it thinned, but it was a losing battle. He began to go numb in a way even the Spine hadn't caused, a sensation of both heaviness and lightness, as if he was sinking into an abyss while at the same time cutting free of the dead weight. Whether the feeling came from lack of air or from dying, really dying, he didn't know.

A deafening crack resounded through space, and light—dazzling, formless light—stabbed his closed eyes.

He cried out in pain and surprise, but no sound escaped his lips.

Another pain, this one crushing, tore through the side of his neck. He nearly passed out right then, but it vanished again.

Then he heard Tree's terrified voice, loud enough to rattle his entire body.

"Ewan! Thank the Mother, you're alive. I'm here, love. Hang on!"

"We need to move him," boomed another voice. Male, older. "His breathing's dangerously erratic; he'll go into shock if we can't stabilize it."

More pain, through Ewan's sides and the back of his head, as though his rescuers had placed a series of red-hot irons beneath him. With a scream that remained trapped in his mind, Ewan felt his whole body stretch and crease around them, folding back in agony, but just as suddenly he was dunked in an icy lake, cold as the Argentine falls. It was shallow, only touching his back, but the shock knocked what little breath he'd had right out of him.

"We're losing him. Get the respirator!" ordered the male voice.

A crushing weight settled down around his face, blasting a jet of icy wind against his lips and forcing it into his nose, inflating his body as surely as if Kate's bellows had been shoved into him.

Something crushed his hand, grinding his bones.

"You're doing great, love," Tree's thundering voice assured him. "You're here now; we've got you, but you have to stay with me, all the way."

The ordeal that followed was the hardest and most terrifying Ewan had ever faced. The fight to stay conscious, to stay alive and not give in to the pain and darkness, became his entire existence. His body shuddered from hammer blows ringing up through the icy bed at intervals, and his closed eyes continued to be assaulted by more lights, passing by in time to the shaking. His ears were filled with a shrill screech from behind his head, hounding him like a banshee, while at his feet something yanked him deeper with a relentless heavy pounding, the drums of death calling him as he fell.

When at last it stopped, he was treated to another scorching, crushing attack on his back and head, then partly immersed in another frigid pool. As he lay there in a near-disembodied panic, the weight settled back onto his hand.

He could hear more voices, distorted and distant but still far too loud. There was light too, right above him and burning so badly that he yearned for the blackness of limbo. Had it not been for Tree's voice urging him to stay with her and telling him how much she loved him, how brave he was being, he would gladly have let himself die to be free of the pain, to respawn back home and forget all about this nightmare.

*But you can't respawn, not here*, he reminded himself. *The Diamond Lord would have put you through even worse if you'd stayed.*

His left arm screamed in protest as something cold stabbed into it, but then fire surged into his veins through the wound.

"It's okay, love. You can sleep now," Tree's voice reassured him, as though the torture was supposed to help him get there.

Did he dare? What if he never woke up?

The burning turned into a drowsiness that tugged at his soul, prying loose his tenuous grip on his body.

*No!*

He fought it as long as he could, but eventually he slipped away, cursing his failure as the darkness reclaimed him.

Ewan stumbled through a swirling chaos of fire and ice, where stinging winds buffeted him and the ground shook and splintered under his feet. Lightning flashed, rendering the tumbling landscape in harsh white light, and he threw up his hands. They were skeletal, emaciated, but before his aching eyes their skin darkened, giving his fingers a more solid form when the next bolt surged through the air around him. Then needle-like spires of rock flung themselves into him from every angle, piercing his new skin and stabbing through to his bones as he cried out in bewildered terror.

No one answered but his own voice, echoing throughout the madness.

He wandered through it, with no sense of time's passage or whether he was getting anywhere. When he couldn't keep moving, he would pass out and dream of the bright room and the pressure on his hand, not quite as crushing as it had been. It was always there, warm and somehow familiar, his one anchor in a world that had died and respawned around him more times than he could remember. He took heart from it, and when he inevitably woke once more into the madness, he searched for the feeling that pressure had instilled in him.

Then one day, lying there in the bright room, he heard a voice: one he'd forgotten in the storms' thrall.

*Tree!*

He tried to reach her, to call her name, but his mouth wouldn't move. He tried and tried again, feeling like his heart would burst from the effort of it, but the best he could do was crack his lips just enough to feel cold air sinking into them.

Panting in his mind, Ewan listened for her voice again. It sounded distant, not nearly as harsh as it had when he'd first logged out, and now he strained his ears to catch her words.

"...responding well to the treatments. His condition isn't critical anymore, but there is still no sign of motor activity beyond life-supporting functions."

That wasn't her; it was a male voice. The same as before?

"Then he's through the worst of it?" There she was, hopeful and questioning.

The man chuckled darkly. "Hardly. He may be alive and stable, but without basic functional strength, he'll be bedridden for life."

Footsteps approached, and the voice spoke again, much louder.

"Personally, I think he's lucky to have survived the initial UV strobe and hormone therapies. Melanin production has reached normal levels. Bone reconstruction has been stimulated, and most of his smooth muscle is healthy, but skeletal muscle is practically nil, and that's where the issue lies."

"I can help him with that," Tree said. "I've been studying rehabilitation since I returned."

"Treanna, you're not a therapist," the voice stated, a flat denial.

"You're right, Robert. I'm not. But he knows me. Trusts me."

"More than that, from what I've heard you telling him," Robert said, his voice edged with a mix of revulsion and curiosity.

Tree's voice had neither. "Yes, more than that. When the time comes, I want to be the one. I owe him that much for staying with me."

The pressure returned to Ewan's hand—*her hand, clasping mine!* He tried to squeeze back, but his strength failed him again.

The man, Robert, sighed. "If that time comes, then I'll inform the Director of your request."

There were some chirping sounds near his head, and another round of liquid fire rushed into his body. Soon after, Ewan descended back into the chaotic world, convinced now he'd had it wrong about which had been the dream.

The next time Ewan woke, the strange room was relatively quiet. The light above still made his eyes ache behind their lids, but it no longer burned him, and the pool he lay in felt more solid, almost spongy. The pressure on his hand was still there, along with another one that crushed his shoulder, making it easy for him to picture Tree snuggling against him, like they had in Veridor.

Silently thanking her, Ewan used the contact to check his status as best he could. His heartbeat felt strong and steady, and he decided that he was lying in a reclined position. His back ached, needing to pop like never before. The air felt dry on his face, somehow still wafting over him from behind. His breathing was still automatic, but now his nose could smell the air as it pushed its way into his body. It was foul, reminding him vaguely of the acrid stench of Kate's tanning rack.

Then a sound like a gust of wind came from the distance, followed by echoing footsteps. Their maker gave a sigh; then Tree's body shook, pressing into him.

"Annie, we need to talk," said a new voice. Male again, deep. Older and weary, but not unkind.

Her head lifted from Ewan's shoulder, but her hand remained. "Grandfather," she murmured. Then her voice turned crisp, alert. "Is there a problem?"

"Chief Nichols has informed me that our young ward has successfully completed his initial therapies," the man—her grandfather—said.

"That's wonderful news," Tree replied with a challenging edge that plainly said the opposite.

There was a pause. "He also informed me that there has been no indication that this player has responded to external stimuli. That for the past three weeks, he has been as in a coma."

Ewan blinked in his mind. *Three weeks?*

"He needs time." Tree's voice was heated now, her hand clamping down hard enough to make Ewan gasp inside his bodily prison. "His experience is unprecedented; we need to see it through."

"For how long, Annie? He's consuming resources."

"Not significantly more than he had been on the floors!"

"Consuming resources, including the exclusive use of this section of the ward. The medical staff have spent hundreds of man-hours on this player."

"But they were willing." Now Tree sounded afraid. She crushed Ewan's hand even tighter, but her trembling was vibrating his arm. "No one objected!"

"They wouldn't have, not to you," the man said, gently. "But as the Centre's director, I am privy to somewhat more information than you are."

*Director?* Ewan thought, startled. *Tree's grandpa's in charge of this place? She never told me that!*

"The consensus among the chiefs is that the player—"

"Ewan." Tree interrupted. "His name is Ewan O'Meara."

The man—the Director—sighed again. "Young Master O'Meara has reached the limit of his recovery. They have decided that he should be restored to his dive device and reintegrated into the Veridor simulation."

"No!" Tree cried, her voice punching Ewan's ears as the man's meaning sank home.

*They want to send me back.*

The old man continued, maddeningly reasonable. "It would be a mercy to him, a chance to live the life he was born to have, instead of languishing where he simply hasn't been able to function."

"But Grandfather—"

"Annie, you gave this project of yours the very best effort.

We all recognize that. None of the chiefs blame you or consider your investment a mistake."

The implication hung in the air. *Thus far.*

The Director cleared his throat. "Indeed, Chief Reid has listed your actions as being the inspiration for a proposal he submitted, one that would utilize the most potent military technology of the game worlds to address our security concerns more effectively."

Tree made an exasperated sound. "Gabriel? If he'd supported me in the first place instead of maneuvering—"

"The defense of the Centre must be my primary concern!" the Director snapped. He took a deep breath. "My personal preferences cannot override that priority. The idea of drawing on players for our current manpower needs was worth testing, but at this point we have other options, to say nothing of conclusive evidence that one so deeply integrated into the simulations simply cannot be rehabilitated into the Centre."

"No! You can't give up on him!"

Tree started to sob, breaking Ewan's heart and sending him into a tailspin. He'd promised to stay with her and help, but he'd failed, apparently doing nothing but landing her in even more trouble by sitting here uselessly. Now her grandpa would send him back home, back to the waiting Church and Gem. They'd never let him see the light of day again, he'd never see Tree again, and her quest would end in worlds-breaking failure.

He swore in his mind, enraged that the oath wasn't audible in the room. How could he be so alert and still not communicate with them?

"Treanna," the voice warned, the Director's patience clearly thinning. "If there was even one iota of evidence that this boy's mind is connected to his body, then I would grant you permission to keep him here. As it is—"

*I've got your evidence!* Ewan roared in desperation, the words rebounding impotently within his consciousness. *I've got to do something to get their attention. Anything!*

Knowing he only had time for one chance, Ewan tried to open his eyes.

At first, he couldn't even feel his eyelids. Just a blank, leaden curtain smothering his visage. But as he strained, he met unreal resistance, a near mountain of flesh and blood to lift.

How could they be so heavy?

He put everything he had into the effort. Tree's hand still clenched his, refusing to give up on him even now, and he took heart from her contact as she shouted at the man who threatened to end it all for them. He heard the Director turn and walk away, leaving to consign them to separation, and he threw the last of his strength into seeing this world—seeing her—one more time.

There was a tearing sensation, ripping and cracking, and then light, blue and harsh but oh so sweet, seared through the gap.

*More!*

He kept up the attack, forcing his eyes open a hair at a time. With agonizing slowness, the gap broadened until he felt his eyelids slide over the top, coming to rest in the open position.

Now he could make out the light's source: a strange blue rectangle, somehow trapped in a collection of little dark squares. He tried moving his eyes and was elated to discover they worked perfectly well. He darted them wildly around, taking in as much as he could of the surroundings before someone came to put him away like a broken toy.

He saw a form on his left, blurry but unmistakably Tree's face. He stared at her, cursing the lack of messaging, praying she would look his way.

She did.

Tree gasped, then screamed. "Grandfather! Grandfather, come back, please! He's here!"

Footsteps sounded from a far corner, and Ewan turned his eyes to see the fuzzy-edged figure of a man rapidly approaching.

"Mother of all," the man muttered, leaning over Ewan to peer at him with eyes even darker than Tree's.

Ewan sent a challenge through his own, a defiant and triumphant shout.

"Did he just…?"

"Yes, he did!" Tree's hand crushed Ewan's as she laughed, but he didn't care. "You told him to give you evidence, and he did!"

Ewan looked back to the Director as the other man's face slowly resolved into a bald brownish head and gray-white beard.

"Son, can you hear me?"

Ewan tried to nod but it was no good, so he moved his eyes frantically in response.

"Look up and down for yes, side to side for no," Tree ordered. "Do you understand us?"

Ewan vehemently rolled up and down, hooting in his mind as the Director drew a sharp breath.

"Impressive." He gave Ewan a long, deep stare, almost exactly like Tree's, then turned to his granddaughter. "Very well. The player—"

"Ewan!"

The Director sighed. "Ewan may continue rehabilitation. How do you want to proceed?"

Ewan looked at Tree, feeling his heart race for much better reasons as her features resolved before his eyes. Her hair was bound up in a tight bun, and her face was a bit drawn, but otherwise it was the same one he knew from Veridor: determined, intelligent, and easily the most beautiful thing he'd ever seen.

Her hand continued to shake as she spoke. "I want full

responsibility for him. I want him moved to my room so I can oversee every moment of his recovery, and I request a continuation of my leave of absence from my duties."

"As you wish," the Director said, his voice a mix of resignation and pride. "You have full custody and care of the player O'Meara, but it will be your duty to update the chiefs with weekly status reports regarding his recovery and resource consumption. You will also transport him to Medical every week and permit Chief Nichols to provide an independent assessment of the player's rehabilitation."

He turned to go, but then he quietly added, "Well done."

Ewan whooped for joy in his head. *We're still in this together!*

After the Director left with another whooshing sound, Tree threw herself at Ewan. Her body crushed him as she sobbed and kissed his face, each touch a hammer blow to his weak form, but now he reveled in them as confirmation of his own existence—in her world.

"Thank you," she whispered, tears splashing down onto his cheeks. "Thank you for holding on for me."

Ewan decided that the next thing he needed to work out was how to squeeze her hand.

## 17

### GROWING PAINS

Within the hour, Ewan found himself being rolled down a corridor on a special bed, furiously practicing his blinking as more of the harsh ceiling lights passed overhead. Tree was with him, as was the first man he'd heard, Robert Nichols, who had pale ivory skin, wore strange pieces of glass in front of his dark eyes, and had apparently been in charge of keeping him alive the past weeks.

The bumps and squeaks from the bed's wheels weren't too bad, and before long, Tree rolled him through another door. They passed into a darkened room, and Tree took a moment to thank Nichols for helping her transfer Ewan. The older man showed no offense at the clear tone of dismissal in her voice; instead, he simply remarked that he'd see them in a few days.

Once the door shut, Tree stepped over to Ewan, smiling sadly. "Welcome to my home. Now it's yours, too."

She lifted him carefully and settled him onto a bed, so soft after the months of outlaw living, he thought he could sink into it and drown. She climbed in beside him, sighing as she reached over and tilted his face to hers.

"I'm sorry," she whispered. "It's selfish, but I'm so glad to have you here. Rest with me, now? We can start your rehabilitation after that."

Ewan looked back at her, trying to message that he was glad to be with her too. She passed a hand over his face, stroking his eyes closed, then folded him up in a crushing hug until he fell asleep.

The blurred days that followed were far more pleasant than Ewan's previous stint in the medical ward, despite being much harder. After working out a basic system of blinks and eye rolls for communication, Tree put him through endless rounds of what she called physical therapy, which apparently meant hardcore strength and agility leveling. She pushed him hard, always dangling near-impossible goals just in front of him but constantly checking to make sure he wasn't getting discouraged.

Even when he was, Ewan kept pushing right back. They both knew he was here on borrowed time, and he refused to lose whatever toehold he'd achieved so far. Whenever Tree left him to rest while she updated the Director and his chiefs, Ewan would lie in bed, using the fear of separation and the questions burning in his mind to fuel bonus sets of his exercises—until she found out and reprimanded him for overtraining.

As he regained control of his neck, Ewan took stock of their room. His favorite part by far was the strange moving painting on the wall opposite the bed. Somehow, it had pictures of their forest hideout on it, every few seconds switching to a different image. When she caught him staring at it, Tree explained that she'd used her tablet to take them during her own training months. She blushed furiously when images of him sleeping and smiling came up.

Ewan would have kissed her, both for preserving a piece of his home and for loving him, even then.

There was also an alarm clock in the wall, the only way to

tell when morning came, given the lack of windows in the room —or much else, for that matter. Tree had no furniture, explaining that she only needed a bed and a closet for her gear, in addition to the perplexing "bathroom" beyond the door on the far side. At first, Ewan hadn't understood the point of the cold steel chair in there, but its purpose became embarrassingly clear shortly after he'd progressed from needles in the arm to sucking his food through a straw. Veridor had nothing like it, but the shame of sitting by while Tree patiently cleaned up his messes was more than enough to drive Ewan to master the toilet's use as soon as possible.

As part of their new daily routine, Tree also scrubbed him head to toe with a coarse sponge in the glass-walled alcove she used for cleaning herself. He'd been mortified the first time she stripped him down, between his nakedness and his scrawny frame, but she commanded him to relax and washed him anyway, as though he was a stray dog. The scouring did feel great, and Ewan imagined it as sloughing away his weakness, a layer at a time. To her credit, she did it with as much dignity as he could hope for, never once complaining or acting repulsed.

He swore in his mind that he'd recover his old body, before she did.

Every week, she put him back on the rolling bed and carted him out to Medical for inspection. There were plenty of revolted looks to go around there as the doctor and his assistants poked and prodded him, took blood for Gems-knew-what reasons, and proclaimed him as healthy as anyone could expect a mere player to be.

Outside of these torture sessions, Tree kept Ewan securely hidden in her room. On the rare times she had to leave, she made a point of telling him she'd locked the door. When he tried to ask why, she ignored him and encouraged him to practice visualizing the exercises while he rested, or pressed more and more food at him when it got delivered to their room.

Sometimes, when he couldn't muster the energy to move another inch, she would pull him back to bed, lay his head in her lap, and read to him from the tablet she always carried. He loved the way she told stories of old Earth, how her eyes lit as she recounted the deeds of its legendary heroes and described the wonders it once held.

But every night, after she'd fallen asleep holding him, Ewan would lie there wondering about his own home world, wondering what he could do to help. Was the Diamond Lord still interfering, or had that threat logged out with him? Was Paul able to get moving on his quest? Was the Church harassing his family, trying to figure out what had happened? Or did they have enough on their minds, just coping with his disappearance? The thought of his mom crying at his funeral burned his heart. He had to make it up to them all.

Somehow.

About three weeks after moving to Tree's room, Ewan managed to lift his fingers, inspiring her to gift him with a tablet of his own. The device was nowhere near as convenient as the Logos, but miraculously its layout was almost exactly like the menus from home. She showed him how to use it, and in no time he was tapping constantly, both for the exercise and for the opportunity to communicate with her in real sentences again, even if his under-leveled coordination made his spelling atrocious.

In secret, after Tree cut the lights and started snoring, he would inchworm his hand over to prop the tablet up and spend hours calling up everything he could find to learn about the strange, cold world he'd landed himself in. The first thing he did was read up on common items and systems, so he wouldn't make a fool of himself when he did eventually get out to meet other people. Robert Nichols wore glasses on his face to help him see better, which begged the question of why everyone didn't wear them. The lights were diodes, whatever that meant.

The clock and picture album on the wall were really the active screen of a computer, apparently a larger form of tablet. Like almost everything else here it ran on electricity, some kind of controlled lightning.

The Centre was massive according to the diagrams, reaching miles into the ground. The bulk of its space was taken up by the six assemblages of game floors, each one a sequence of roughly hexagonal rings extending down its parent shaft, accessible both by elevators—whatever those were—and emergency stairs along the outer walls. There were thousands of floors, each one in turn containing thousands of tubes for the players.

So many people, all completely unaware of their real circumstance.

One thing Ewan didn't find, however, was any reference to the Gems. The Centre's non-player population was surprisingly small, considering their importance in keeping everyone alive: only a thousand people or so, barely taking up a fifth of the available space in the residential area. The working-age people were divvied up into sections such as Caretaking, Programming, and Nutrition, but there wasn't a Gem section. Nor was there any sign that there ever had been: according to the records, it was the Centre's policy to avoid interfering in the game worlds. Ever since the initial colonization, he couldn't find any evidence of direct contact between the players and the staff here on Earth.

The Earth...what a shock that continued to be. The first time Ewan pulled up a map of the planet, he was blown away by its sheer size: hundreds of times larger than Veridor by the land area alone. At its peak, it had once supported billions of people, a number so huge Ewan had to look it up and stare at it just to get a sense for it.

What had happened to them all?

Just as Tree had said, there weren't many records to explain what kind of disaster had befallen the place, just a scrapbooked collection of lines and images. Sifting through them, Ewan gathered that the forests and agricultural fields had all burned from a combination of drought and intense thunderstorms, eventually turning the entire surface into a vast desert now called the Wastes.

The scope of it was staggering. How could an entire world, especially one this huge, just break?

As the weeks turned into months, Ewan felt he was doing pretty well with his leveling, despite the countless bumps along the way. He made a game of getting Nichols to raise his eyebrows in shock every time he came in for his assessments, until the sour old man conceded that not only had Ewan stayed ahead of the recovery curve, he'd flat-out launched himself off it.

Tree also made games to challenge him, giving him tender kisses to reward him for moving his arms and legs, sitting upright...and speaking.

The first words out of his mouth were "I love you," spoken one night in late October as Tree was falling asleep, just to surprise her. She stared at him in wonder, then kissed him fiercely before returning the sentiment. The desire in her touch was more reassuring than she could have understood, a small proof she could still be attracted to him even after putting up with his humiliating weaknesses in real life.

Unfortunately, Ewan's growth also meant that he started to feel increasingly awkward when his girlfriend kept treating him like a baby. Once he'd gotten to where he could sit up on his own power, Ewan tried to take over washing himself for modesty's sake. Tree stubbornly insisted on being present, though, telling him bluntly she wasn't about to let a slip in the shower put an end to their months of hard work. He couldn't argue with that, but he did make an effort to cover himself better as his usual proportions reasserted themselves.

One day, on a visit to Medical in early November, Nichols presented Ewan with a new device: a chair with a large wheel on each side.

"What's this?" Ewan asked, still savoring the way his mouth formed the words.

"This is called a wheelchair, amazingly enough," the doctor replied dryly. "Given your muscular development, Treanna and I believe you now have the strength to operate it, though naturally you need to continue working toward being able to stand upright."

"Here," Tree said, pulling the chair over for Ewan to lever himself into. "You use your hands to turn the wheels, like this." She gripped the little metal rails ringing the wheels and rolled him back and forth a few times. "I can help you when you get tired, but now you should be able to—"

"This is awesome!" Ewan whooped as he flung himself forward, then crashed into the bed. "Oof! Wow, I barely have to use any force at all."

"Not for a small space like my ward, no." Nichols grabbed the chair's handles and extracted him from the furniture. "Treanna, why don't you help O'Meara find a place with a little more room to move about? The gym, perhaps?"

"I don't know," she said after a moment. "I don't think he's ready to see the staff."

"I want to go outside," Ewan said. "I've been cooped up in this place for months—years, really. I want to feel the sun on my skin again."

Nichols and Tree exchanged a look.

She sighed. "Ewan...the Wastes aren't like Veridor."

"I know that," he replied happily. "I've read about them on the tablet. Tree, it's the real world! I want to see it with my own eyes."

"The dust will wreak havoc on his respiratory system,"

Nichols warned, turning to Tree. "He could set his progress back weeks while recovering."

Ewan snorted. "Dust? Come on, Tree, I can handle a little dust. I survived the Sprouted Seed, didn't I?" He grinned at her. "If I'm wrong, I know you can get me back up to spec."

Tree opened her mouth to argue, but he gave her the big eyes. "Please. I need to feel the wind on my face."

She watched him, boring into his soul to measure him for herself. "All right, but only for a moment. And if you do start choking, I'm going to give you artificial respiration," she added, eyes glinting.

"Better you than me," Nichols muttered, already moving into the next room.

Tree led Ewan to an elevator, which turned out to be a little room with only one door. Once inside, she said "Observation Deck" to the wall. Apparently it heard her, because the door closed, and Ewan felt a pressure in his gut as the room moved, reminding him uncannily of the *Esperanza*.

"It's okay." She squeezed his shoulder. "I won't let you stay outside too long."

"Thanks," he replied, not bothering to correct her.

After a few seconds the elevator chimed again, and the door slid open to reveal a completely different room. The new chamber was dimly lit and roughly circular, reminding Ewan vaguely of the dungeon where they'd met Old Max.

"At least we didn't have to climb a million steps," he said as lightly as he could, making Tree smile as he wheeled himself out. "Why's it so dark?"

"Power conservation," she replied. "Leaving the lights at low doesn't have much of a practical effect, as electricity and water are the two things we have in abundance. But people only rarely come up here, so there's no sense in wasting the power to light it."

"Why doesn't anyone come here?"

"You'll see."

She led him to the room's outer wall and pressed a button beside a sealed door, which whisked itself open to admit them into another small space. Unlike the elevator, this room had a second door on the opposite side, only opening after the first door hissed shut again. Tree reached for his chair, but Ewan rolled himself forward into the brown light beyond.

His breath caught in his throat, burning and stinging as he tried to cough but found his lungs somehow frozen in place. Eyes instantly watering, he beat at his chest and managed to knock some of the air out, before pulling his shirt over his face to try again.

He felt Tree's hands grip the chair and start turning him, but he grabbed the wheels, locking them like his lungs.

"I need to see," he rasped, still gagging on the remnant dust in his system. "Please."

She sighed, coughing as well, but she released him to clumsily wheel himself forward, clutching his makeshift mask around his face with one hand. He squinted against the wind as it howled dully around him, stinging his skin with coarse sand that by all rights should have stayed on the ground. It was as if the beach at World's Edge had been carried here somehow, blown in from afar.

As if there was no anchor grass to hold it down.

When they reached the rail at the edge, Ewan mustered all of his courage and strength to push himself up, stumbling as his legs protested. Leaning on his arms to grip the weathered metal bar, he blinked until his eyes cleared enough to see the landscape.

It was indeed a wasteland...but it went far beyond anything he'd imagined, even in his worst fears.

There were dunes as far as his eyes could see. Scattered among them in the immediate area were some rock formations, etched and carved by the elements. A particularly tall pair of them stood off to the right, some five hundred yards distant. The sun and sky were nowhere to be seen: the blue he loved so much shrouded behind a frothing, writhing blanket of black-tinged clouds that only admitted a dim brownish light. Those clouds moved quickly, driven along by the same winds that flung the hissing sands over everything, but there was no end to them as they stretched from horizon to obscured horizon, smothering any chance of life on the surface below. As they must have done for ages.

Ewan stared at it, horrified but unable to tear his burning eyes away.

*No wonder she hated the storms*, he thought as Tree's hand rested on his shoulder, witnessing it all with him. Despair rose in his throat, wrestling with the dust for control. *But how? How did it get to be this bad?*

When she pressed, he gave no resistance, letting her guide him back to the chair and return him to the safety of the only shelter left on Earth. The door behind them closed, and only then did the sound of the trickling sands cease, making way at last for his own choked sobs.

"I know," Tree said, softly. "Most people don't want to see it any more than we must."

For the first time, Ewan truly understood why Tree had been so upset on the beach. Why the Central staff resented players like him, living in their perfect dream worlds while the people of Earth watched them from the midst of that lifeless sandstorm.

They were the ones in the prison. There was no doubt of that, now.

He was startled by how mangled his voice sounded. "What can I do to help?"

"I don't know."

"We can't let it stay like that!"

Tree steered him over to the elevator. "All we can do is hope that one day it will get better again. But in the meantime, we need to survive."

*Survival won't be enough to fix this place,* Ewan thought bitterly, but he didn't have the heart left to argue just then, as they rode back down to the rest of the Centre.

## 18

## MAKING A PLACE

Ewan slept horribly that night, between the lingering
burn in his lungs and dreams of white wings, beating the sands
outside into a storm that buried the Centre forever. Reading the
tablet wasn't any help, so for hours he'd lain in bed, staring at
the moss covering the ceiling. Designed to clean the air while
tolerating low light, it was the only plant life he'd found.

*We're still sleeping in a cave,* he thought. The wall buzzed,
and he thumped it. *It's just not nearly as nice as the one back home.*

"Was that the alarm?" Tree mumbled.

"Yeah. How else are we supposed to tell when it's morning
out here?"

She tensed, then rolled over and gave him a long kiss,
resting her hand against his chest. "Maybe we need a better
routine."

Ewan's breath caught, but he felt her fingers tracing his ribs:
assessing how much further he had to go. "I'm serious. I need to
do something!"

"I know." Tree sighed as she pulled back. "Would you like to
see the game floors? You could check on your family."

"Maybe not just yet," Ewan said. *The last thing I need right now is the chance to skulk back into a tube.* "I'd rather see yours."

For a moment, her face was blank. "Grandfather? He's very busy."

"Not him, then, but I want to meet some of the staff."

This time she hesitated a good ten seconds. "Ewan, I—"

"Please," he insisted, trying to keep the frustration out of his voice. "I can get around now—with your help."

"The staff won't want to see you like this." She looked carefully into his eyes. Away from his nerfed body.

Ewan suppressed a growl. "They might as well get used to it. You were going to bring all kinds of players out, weren't you? What were you planning to do? Hide us out of sight, so we don't—"

"Stop it! We knew your recovery would take time."

"*We* knew? Tree, I had no frapping clue! I didn't plan for any of this!"

She turned away and glowered at the far wall.

"Hey...I'm sorry," he said. "I'm just fed up, and cooped up. We've spent so much time working my physical stats, but hardly any on my personality."

"Clearly," she muttered. "Ewan, you're in a bad mood. It will be difficult enough to introduce you, even under good circumstances."

Ewan sighed and gave her hand a little squeeze, with more effort than he cared to admit. "Look, if I misbehave, you can bring me back. I just want to meet these Centrals."

"Oh?"

"Yeah. I'm...I want to thank them, for keeping me and everyone alive all this time."

She seemed to understand that *them* meant *you*, and after a moment, she looked back at him with a smile that turned into an evil grin. "All right—but not until you prove you're feeling better."

Ewan kind of hoped they'd go back to kissing, but Tree had

switched to trainer mode. She put him through a brutal series of squats: holding him up by the shoulders as he struggled with his increasing weight, then letting him go to see how long he could stand. He hit the floor so hard the first couple of times that she nearly called it off, but he gritted his teeth and pushed through the pain. Bumps and bruises would heal, and eventually they'd make him tougher.

After a little while, he was able to haul himself up to standing again and again, rising as high as his atrophied legs would take him before pulling up the rest of the way on her hands. With each successful lift she gave him a smile and a little kiss, and before too long, his spirits lifted as well.

They quit once he'd managed a few dozen, and after another awkward shower session, Ewan went out and dressed himself while she cleaned up. Pulling the shirt over his head still seemed strange compared to simply equipping it, but he managed it after a few tries.

He climbed into the wheelchair, feeling pretty good—then quickly turned away when Tree came out wearing nothing but a towel.

In recent days, she'd taken to changing without a care for whether he was in the room or not. But while the rustle of her clothing quickened his breathing, her newfound lack of concern was another mixed message. One moment, she was kissing him like they used to, or cuddling with him in bed. The next, she seemed to forget he was there, ignoring him like he was a piece of furniture. Clearly loved, but not quite human enough to be a lover. Vividly remembering her anger when talking about her not-boyfriend, Ewan was determined to avoid being pushy. But with every day, every new level he gained, it was getting harder to hide his own renewed attraction to her.

"Okay, I'm finished," she lilted. "How do I look?"

Ewan turned and was instantly grateful he'd been openly invited to stare, because there was no way he couldn't.

Her Central uniform still seemed a bit on the stark side, but it suited her. With a neatly pressed gray blouse sporting black buttons that matched the little ribbon under her collar and the snug skirt that ended just above her knees, she looked sharp: at once attractive and professional. As she did every time they left the room, she'd bound her hair up tightly into a bun. As usual, it drew his attention to her neck.

She tilted one foot up on its toes, angling her leg to show off. The way she clasped her hands behind her hips turned her figure slightly, making the little zigzag pin she wore on her breast flash like the lightning she'd wielded in Veridor.

"Wow," he breathed.

"I'll take that as a compliment." She leaned down to kiss him on the cheek, then headed for the door, looking every inch as impressive here as she did in Veridor.

Ewan followed, but not before sighing at his comparatively sloppy pajamas and wheelchair.

They went down the hall, turning left at the first crossing instead of their usual right, heading deeper into the residential section. Ewan had seen little bits of it before on the way to Medical, but he'd quickly noticed Tree always seemed to take him only when the traffic was light.

Now, though, as if in response to his new quest goal, the corridors were full of people, but they moved so automatically that only a few even noticed the player in their midst as they went about their business.

He grinned to himself. *Caught up in their own little worlds.*

"So, where are we going?" he asked, startling a few drones as he peered at a cracked and yellowed map on the wall. "What do the people here do for fun?"

Tree colored. "We have designated recreation areas, although most of the staff don't bother."

"Recreation? You mean like games?"

"Not in the sense you're thinking," she replied, her

demeanor stiffening as more passing Centrals began whispering about the player out on display. "Needless to say, the idea of playing a virtual game in our free time is sadly looked down upon," she said loudly. "But we have a gymnasium, where the staff can go to exercise their bodies. It has a collection of weights for resistance training, a couple of ball courts, and a swimming pool. If you like, we could try that first; I'm sure it would help your rehabilitation."

"Tree, we're working on my personality, remember?"

Another passerby gasped, but she flinched away from Tree's glare.

Ewan sighed and pictured a health bar flashing up for his good mood. "Do you have any taverns or inns?"

"No," she said, now watching for the next person to bother them. "But we have a dining hall."

"That works. I'm feeling hungry anyway."

Tree guided him through the maze of corridors and stares and whispers, and eventually they made the final turn through a set of doors into a room unlike any Ewan had seen yet.

He didn't know what he'd been expecting—maybe something like the Toasted Tank, or at worst the Sprouted Seed —but while there were tables and people, that was where the resemblance ended. Glinting slightly from the light of the ever-present blue diodes in the ceiling, the tables were flanked by benches long enough that four people could sit on one side if they packed in. The tables were lined up, end to end, in long rows that stretched across the room, leaving only a little space by the walls for getting in and out.

The patrons of this real-world tavern were mostly dressed in gray Central uniforms, with the occasional oddball wearing the kind of plain athletic clothes Ewan had gotten used to. No matter what color their skin was, they all had a similar wanness, a peakedness, that made them look paler than they should have. Most of them were clustered in little parties, talking quietly amongst themselves, but as Ewan entered they started looking up, nudging their companions until he could feel every last pair of eyes on himself and Tree.

For a moment Ewan returned their blank stares, until Tree grabbed his chair by the handles and steered him toward a small doorway in the back.

Immediately, the mutters and whispers broke out.

"Mother of all, Annie," called a young blond woman with porcelain skin from across the room. "You turn down every man here, then go and pick a runt like that? He can't even walk! What use is he in bed?"

Ewan blushed as the Centrals laughed, but when he turned to look at Tree, her face was downright purple.

Saying nothing but grinding her teeth hard enough to make him wince, she wheeled him into the back room, to a stack of plastic trays resting on a steel shelf. She grabbed a tray and slammed it down on a line of three pipes that tracked beside long counters of food in buckets, resembling feeding troughs.

"Let it go," Ewan murmured, looking down at his frail body.

She ignored him and snatched a couple of plates.

The variety was limited, of course, but given what he'd seen yesterday, it was a miracle the Central staff could produce this much. Tree put a mix of vegetables on their plates, along with some spongy blocks of something.

"Eat this; it will give you protein for your muscles. And some of this," she added, slapping down what looked like a cross between a chicken breast and a piece of fat.

"Yes, ma'am." Ewan sighed as his girlfriend was replaced by the mollycoddling healer again. "Who cooks all of this food?"

She indicated a door behind the counter. "We've got a small kitchen staff, part of Nutrition. They prepare the food our growers and harvesters bring in from the hydroponic rooms and the wormeries, with additional nutrients gleaned from the hydrolysis system."

"The hydro—we're eating players?!" He'd lost a night's sleep last month reading about the Centre's liquid cremation system, but it hadn't occurred to him that some of the outputs wound up in here as well.

"We don't exactly have a lot to pick from!" Tree snapped. "And it's not as if we kill the living ones. Life eats other life to survive on Earth, so you'd better choose now whether you want to be the diner or the dinner."

"Okay, okay! Gems of old, this place sucks."

"Tell me something I don't know," she growled as she grabbed their trays and stormed off.

By the time he'd scooted from his wheelchair onto the hard bench at the table's end, Ewan felt like he'd already spent all his personality points for the day on Tree—not that he was about to tell her that. Oddly reluctant to dig into his player-fortified meal just yet, he looked around the room. Some of the staff had gone back to their food, but most were still watching him with open revulsion. The blond woman from before caught his eye from her nearby seat and made an extremely lewd gesture with her fork, provoking a blush from him and another growl from Tree, beside him.

He tried to take his girlfriend's hand, but she jerked it away when another round of whispers and laughs followed.

"I knew this was a bad idea," she snarled.

"Of course you did," Ewan said, his own anger rising to match. "But I didn't think you'd be so embarrassed to be seen with me."

Tree froze. "What? Oh love, I'm so sorry!" She snatched his hand back, crushing his bones to show him she meant it. "You don't embarrass me; they do!"

The room fell silent as everyone turned to her, but she matched their stares, her eyes shooting the lightning her hands couldn't. "That's right, you heard me. This man—"

"He's a player!" a voice shouted, rough and arrogant. "A

vegetable. I just had his grandpa for breakfast."

Laughter rebounded around the room, and Ewan's last bit of patience for the day dissolved.

"Who said that?" he called.

A man stood, halfway down the row across from Ewan's. He was tall, with cropped hair above small, simmering eyes, and birch-skinned arms bulging out of his shirt sleeves. "I did, veggie. What are you going to do about it?"

"Ewan, stay out of this," Tree whispered. "That's Jeff Harper, from Security. He's too big."

"He's no bigger than Caleb was in the cathedral, and I don't recall you minding my help then," Ewan countered, trying to keep his voice calm even as his nerfed muscles rallied to a battle's overture.

He pushed hard on the table, raising himself shakily to standing, then turned back to the man. "My grandpa was as tough as I am. You'd better be careful, or you just might bite off more than you can chew."

The hall went absolutely still.

Harper gaped at him, but then he laughed and dragged the back of his hand across his mouth. "I saved some room, baby carrot. Out of my way!" he snarled, knocking aside anyone too slow to clear out as he advanced down the long row.

Ewan leaned on his arms, letting the blood rush drown out Tree's arguments. Shifting his weight to his left hand, his right reached back, stealthily feeling about for his chair's handle.

Harper closed to within a few feet, cracking his knuckles, arms, and neck. "I'm gonna hit you so hard they'll have to put you back in the tubes," he growled. "Back in your place."

"You can try," Ewan said, a lot more confidently than he felt. *I was wrong: up close, this guy's definitely bigger than Caleb!*

Harper guffawed, then shot Tree a leering grin. "How about you come to my room after I drop this worm?"

Tree gave him a glare that would've had Greasy Tom

running for cover. "Not a chance." She stood and reached for Ewan's arm. "Ewan, let's go."

"No." He had to act soon; his legs literally wouldn't stand for much longer. Looking at Harper as his right hand finally found the handle, he said, "I don't care who you think you are, but you'd better apologize to Tree. And to all of the players you just insulted."

Harper laughed, an arrogant bellow that was exactly what Ewan's muscles needed. The big man lunged across the table with one hand outstretched, the other curling back in a fist.

Drawing on a lifetime of combat experience, Ewan's body snapped into action, almost faster than he could think to direct it. His tired legs twisted into the concrete floor, anchoring him as his left hand swung around to grab the chair his right hand was already spinning up over the table's edge. Whipping about, he smashed it into Harper's face, toppling the real-world guard across the next table in a shower of blood.

The impact staggered Ewan, and he nearly fell as the chair skidded over the table and plowed through the trays. He could hear people screaming through the pounding in his head, see them scattering as his vision grayed out. Forcing his arms to keep holding him up, he took a deep, shaky breath, determined to finish his message before he passed out.

"My name is Ewan O'Meara," he said to the crowd, his voice shaking as much as the rest of him. "I may be a player, but I have the right to be here."

The room swayed dangerously as his legs told him they were done, but a pair of hands gripped him by the shoulders. Tree's hands. She settled him back onto his bench, then stared into his eyes like she still had aura reading.

"Are you okay?"

"I'll be fine...but I think I just became an outlaw again," he added ruefully as the doors opened to admit another party of guards, coming straight for them.

*Frap. I couldn't even get through a single meal.*

But as they closed the distance and got a look at Harper's body hanging over the table, they made no aggressive moves, if anything giving Ewan a wide berth.

"Miss Rothchild, the Director wants to see you immediately," one of them said. His eyes flicked over to Ewan while his cronies picked Harper up. "You'd better bring the player, too."

A few minutes and an elevator ride later, Ewan found himself in a round room, maybe thirty feet across. It was well-lit, and naturally so at that. A bank of short, wide windows reached around the top to ring the entire wall, providing a view of the surface world's dusty clouds as they whipped past.

The room's most striking feature, though, was a great wooden desk in the middle. Crescent-shaped and curving with the wall away from the elevator doors, it looked ancient, even older than Whitehaven's yews, with a polished surface crisscrossed with dark scars and gouges.

*Probably the only wood left on Earth*, Ewan thought grimly.

The Director, Carmine Rothchild, sat in a high-backed chair behind the desk. He was flanked on either side by a group of men and women that Ewan didn't recognize, aside from Robert Nichols. Each one wore little black patches on their shoulders, with golden insignia embroidered on.

Each one was staring at Ewan. None of them were smiling.

"The chiefs are all here?" Tree whispered nervously, clutching Ewan's chair handles. "Grandfather, I can explain—"

"No." The Director held up a hand, silencing her as Ewan had never seen anyone do. "I've already heard from numerous eyewitnesses in the dining hall. Their reports agree unanimously, and so I trust them."

"But they all hate him! Let me—"

"I said no!" Rothchild's eyes bored into his granddaughter's until she bowed her head, seething quietly as he continued.

"The player from the Veridor simulation, Ewan O'Meara, violently engaged with a member of Security in the middle of the dining hall. Chief Nichols, what is Master Harper's status?"

Nichols looked down at his tablet, then straightened his glasses and glanced significantly in Ewan's direction. "Angela reports multiple fractures to the jaw, possibly to the skull as well. Three teeth missing, a moderate concussion. Harper's under supervision, but his injuries appear to be minor, considering the circumstances."

Ewan thought he saw the ghost of a smile cross the doctor's lips.

The Director looked at Ewan again, his bearded face offering no such ghosts. "Young player, have you anything to say for yourself?"

"With all due respect, sir, he made the first aggressive move. He was the hostile." *Not that that matters here*, Ewan thought. "He was rude to Treanna, not to mention myself, and all of the players in the Centre. When I asked him to apologize, he made to strike at me. So, I dealt with him."

"Do you regret your choice?" Rothchild asked, boring into Ewan's eyes now.

"Only because it might cause trouble for Tree. I'd fight that man again in a heartbeat, or anyone like him."

The chiefs started murmuring.

A gray-haired woman with mahogany skin, whose shoulders bore the same zigzag that Tree wore whispered, "Are they all like that?"

"He wasted our food!" added a middle-aged blond woman with maple skin and a sour face.

"I won't tolerate disorder," a large, hazel-skinned man with short hair warned, glaring at the Director. "My man was doing his duty."

"Harper was starting trouble, not ending it," Nichols countered. "A player did his job for him."

"But he is, nevertheless, a player," said a tall young man with fawn skin and sandy brown hair, drawing everyone's attention. Offering a thin smile to the doctor, he turned to fix Ewan with sharp blue eyes. "Ignorant, reckless, and fundamentally unsuited for real life. He should be returned to the simulations before he can bring anyone else to harm."

Tree snarled behind Ewan. "He's only just—"

"Enough." Rothchild waved a hand, at once acknowledging and ignoring them all. Still watching Ewan, he asked, "And what is it about Master Harper that would provoke you to fight with him again, pray tell?"

"He abused the trust of the people he's here to protect," Ewan answered carefully, painfully aware how tenuous his foothold on Earth had become. "Whether you consider those to be the players he obviously hates, or the staff—including your granddaughter—that he endangered by attacking a guy in a wheelchair."

Tree shook behind him; a moment later, her tears splashed onto his shoulders. His own little insignia.

He reached back and gave her hand a squeeze.

After a long minute, Director Rothchild turned to the chiefs again. "There, you see? His story matches that of the eyewitnesses."

Ewan blinked as Tree inhaled sharply. "What?"

"Master Harper provoked the fight, but this young player, after a lifetime of physical inactivity, rose up to defend one of our own." The Director caught Tree's eye and smiled. "And with chair-based combat techniques never before seen, at that. It seems to me that this is precisely the sort of behavior that Treanna sought to cultivate in a player-based defense force."

He stood and looked directly at Ewan. "You have my thanks, both as the Centre's director and Annie's grandfather, for taking right action at great risk."

"It's my pleasure," Ewan replied, hardly daring to breathe.

"Young man, you continue to impress upon me the resiliency and potential usefulness of your people. Accordingly, I am creating a new section of Emissary. I offer it to both Treanna and yourself, so that with the Centre's full support, you both may continue your efforts to recruit players to defend it—and its charges—from threat."

Ewan scanned the chiefs, now looking as dumbstruck as he felt. A few of them, including Nichols, nodded in approval, but most of them remained still. Some gave him murderous glares.

He'd thought for sure he was doomed, but now he'd been given an official profession? Here? A profession that meant he got to log more players out, showing them the truth and setting them free?

*I get to stay with Tree.*

He glanced back at her; she nodded, shaking now with silent, triumphant laugher.

Struggling to keep his voice even, Ewan said, "I accept."

"Excellent." Rothchild seated himself again and steepled his hands on the ancient desk as he looked at Tree. "We'll need to address the many logistical challenges of introducing players into a life in the Centre, of course, and we'll also need to discuss your timetables, but that can wait until after you've had a chance to prepare yourselves. For now, continue focusing on this player's rehabilitation." His beard twitched. "Our enemies may not have a steady supply of wheelchairs available. You are dismissed, Emissaries."

Ewan heard Tree's heels click together in acknowledgment, and he bowed his head.

*What on Earth have I gotten myself into?*

He turned his chair around before the Director could change his mind, then followed Tree to the elevator while trying to ignore the way the chiefs were still watching them.

## 19

## MANY HAPPY RETURNS

LATER THAT AFTERNOON, A MIDDLE-AGED WOMAN STOPPED BY Tree's room. She took Ewan's measurements as he lay on the bed, but the whole time, she talked with Tree as if he wasn't there: discussing how much he might be expected to fill out, the insignia for their new section, and so on. When she left with a promise to have the gear ready in a few weeks, Ewan scrubbed his face with a groan.

Tree came over and placed a hand on his forehead. "It's been an exhausting day; maybe we should call it an early night."

"I'm fine," he grumbled, pulling away. "It's just...how am I supposed to convince my people to log out if I can't make any friends here?"

"You earned their respect today," she said after a long moment. She snuggled up, resting her head onto his shoulder. "Some of them, at least."

"Maybe. But I don't think I can just keep bludgeoning people until they're all happy to see me. Don't you have any friends?"

She stiffened. "I've told you before: I don't get along well with the other staff. I didn't before I met you, and I certainly don't have the inclination to make friends with them after the treatment you've received."

Ewan sighed. *Tree, it's a miracle you opened up to me in the first place.* "Fine, not a friend. What I really need is to meet one good person to practice on, someone who won't flip out to see me up and about."

"Well...there is Michael."

Something about her tone raised Ewan's hackles, or maybe it was the way her eyes became distant. "He's not the guy who kissed—"

"Of course not!" Tree's fingers twisted his shirt, along with his skin underneath. "Michael is a caretaker, like I am, or used to be. Most of the caretakers revile the players, since they work the gaming floors. It's lonely, even compared to the rest of the staff positions."

"I guess we're not a lively bunch on the outside," Ewan said.

"No. But Michael always seemed to treat them well, even talking with them while we worked. I didn't feel as depressed when we had shifts together."

"Well...if he's what you've got, then I'll give it my best."

As it turned out, Michael wasn't the first other Central Ewan got to say hello to, without a chair. He and Tree went to breakfast in the dining hall the next morning, after arguing about whether he was holding his gains or inviting more trouble. Ignoring the whispers and stares, Ewan rolled himself back to the food room, grabbed a tray, and filled his plate himself—although he did let Tree tell him what to put on it.

As he wheeled for the doorway, a girl about his age came racing in, strawberry-blond hair trailing behind her as she ran.

"Chief Spencer, I'm sorry I'm late—aah!"

She careened into Ewan and knocked him sideways out of his chair, then tripped over the wheel and landed on top of him with a squeak.

"Watch where you're going!" Tree snapped, her voice muffled by the girl's chest smushing his face.

There was a grunt and a yelp, and the girl lifted free as Tree scruffed her by the collar.

"Miss Rothchild!" she gasped.

Tree ignored her, instead kneeling beside Ewan with wide, worried eyes. "Ewan, can you hear me? Are you hurt?"

"No, I'm okay," he said, still a little dazed by the encounter but not about to elaborate. He let Tree help him back into the chair as the girl straightened it out for him, her white face now blushing redder than her hair.

"I'm sorry I tripped you up," Ewan said with a friendly smile.

"Oh no, I'm the one who should apologize! You were getting breakfast after all, which normally I'd have been preparing, only I somehow slept in through my alarm for the third time this week, but next time I'll be here on time and can make you something good to eat to make it up, and—" She finally took a breath, blushing even more as Ewan's smile broadened. "I'm Lisa, by the way. Lisa Deering. I work in the dining hall, but I guess you can guess that already."

"Nice to meet you, Lisa. My name's Ewan," he replied, extending a hand. She looked at it curiously, then stuck out her own and gave an excited little bounce when he shook it. The movement drew Ewan's eye to the insignia on her breast, an apple instead of the zigzag Tree wore.

"I like your pin," he said, glad to see someone knew about apples here.

Tree made a disgusted noise and hauled Ewan by the chair handles, back to the front of the line. "If you don't mind cleaning up the mess you made," she told the girl, "we'll try getting our breakfast again."

Lisa wilted. "Yes, miss Rothchild. It was nice to meet you, Ewan."

"The same to you, Lisa." Ewan shot Tree a reproachful glance. "It's good to make a friend."

"Ridiculous girl," Tree muttered a moment later, as they moved to a table as far away from the other Centrals as possible.

"At least she didn't attack me," Ewan pointed out. "Not on purpose, anyway. Besides, it's kind of funny."

Tree slammed her tray down, making him jump. "Funny?"

"Um, yeah? Seeing that there are tavern maids, even out here and all."

Tree scoffed and pulled out her tablet. "Michael says he'll be here in a few minutes. You should eat now, before anyone else disrupts us."

The food tasted about as good as Ewan could expect, but he ate quickly, trusting it to help him get his legs back to spec. When he'd finished, he looked around the room, congratulating himself on completing a meal without a brawl; then he saw a teenage boy approaching, maybe a year younger than him, with close-cropped dark hair and an odd smattering of red bumps on his pale face.

"Hello, Treanna," the boy said softly as he arrived, nodding to her and then to Ewan. "And you must be Master O'Meara."

"Please, call me Ewan."

"Okay, Ewan," the boy replied, a pleased little smile reaching through the splotches. "I'm Michael Patton, but you can call me Michael."

"Nice to meet you, Michael." Ewan offered his hand to the boy and shook, after another confused pause. "So, how do you know Tree?" he asked as the boy sat down at his left.

Michael frowned. "Tree? What's a tree?"

"It's what Ewan calls me," Tree replied.

"It's what all her friends call her," Ewan said firmly. "My sister came up with it."

Michael thought about it, then gave his little smile again. "Tree...I like it. Your sister must be creative."

"Oh, she is that," Ewan agreed. He took a sip of his water, then looked at it in surprise: it tasted like oranges. "I'll have to introduce you to her one day."

"I would like that."

Ewan smiled. "You know, you're the first Central I've met who thinks of the players as people."

Michael hesitated, glancing over at Tree. "They are people. We may have been given a different set of circumstances, but we're really all the same."

"Yeah...I guess we are," Ewan said. "I'm only just getting how hard it must be for you, stuck here in the real world and all. I wish—I'm sorry."

Michael smiled again, but his brown eyes took on a sad cast. "It's okay. The game floors can be very quiet; a lot of caretakers feel very lonely down there. But when I walk the floors, I know I'm surrounded by people, people who would welcome me, love me, if only they could see me. Even if I can't be there with them, I like to think I can still share in a small part of their joy, just by attending to them."

Ewan listened, stunned, until the boy stopped to take a bite of his meal. "Well, I see you now," he said, as softly as his new friend. "And I do thank you. I promise to help you get your fair share."

Over the next week, Ewan kept speaking with Michael, and his admiration grew for the young man's quiet strength and his ability to deal with the hard world he'd found himself in. He also talked to Lisa, when he could get a word in. She seemed determined to make up for her clumsy first impression by keeping him optimally fed. Although Tree never quite relaxed around the exuberant girl, she did at least let her help plan his nutritional needs down to the meal as his recovery continued.

It did continue, and well at that. By mid-November, Ewan proudly traded his wheelchair in for a set of crutches. It felt great to be on his own feet again, and it was a relief to finally look the increasingly disgruntled Centrals in the eye as he worked his way through the halls. Tree always kept an arm around his waist, catching him when he stumbled—which happened often, thanks to her arm around his waist—but he pretended she wanted to hug-walk him the way she'd done in Veridor.

After that, they spent a lot of time in the swimming pool, letting the water boost his carry to practice walking on his own power. The Central swimmers looked at him askance, but after a few days they seemed to either resign themselves to his presence there or leave whenever he showed up. No one gave him trouble, not overtly at least, but Tree was constantly on alert—especially when Lucia Howe, the rude woman from the first day in the dining hall, came near. Equipping a swimsuit that left almost nothing to the imagination, Lucia took to swimming beside them and needling Tree, asking if her pet tube worm had firmed up enough to be any fun, before diving away with a flash and a laugh.

"Don't let her get to you," Ewan advised Tree, back in the safety of their darkened room after one such session.

Tree growled and twisted her hair dry. "It's not me she's trying to get to! Lucia's extreme, even for the staff. There's probably not a man in the Centre that she hasn't—you know."

"I'd kind of guessed as much. Well, don't worry. I don't think I'm a man to her."

He flinched and looked away when Tree yanked her own swimsuit off.

"Evidently not yet," she grumbled, before stalking off to the shower alone.

Things got worse the next morning. Ewan woke to the alarm as usual, sitting up and staring at the date. November 16. He cast about in his bleary mind for why that seemed important, but then Tree rolled over in her sleep, smacking him in the leg—and brushing her hand over his hip.

To his horror, his body eagerly answered her with a good morning of its own.

Face on fire, Ewan quickly extracted himself and retreated to the shower, leaning on his crutches under the stream of hot water, scowling at the reflection of his mostly-healed body in the polished wall.

*Thanks to you,* he thought at it, *she's gone and turned into our frapping nursemaid! How are we going to make her see us as a boyfriend again?*

It scowled back at him, showing enough of his old self to prove he wasn't a scrawny noob anymore. Far from it. He couldn't keep denying how he felt much longer.

What he still couldn't work out was how she felt.

It was obvious that she had a grudge against the Central dating culture, probably thanks to that jerky guy from before, but the problem wasn't her attitude.

Mostly.

The Veridian Church discouraged playing around outside of courtship and marriage, and Ewan had never really had a reason to dispute them on that point. The Lucias of either world made him uncomfortable, like they'd tricked him into some game without asking him, much less explaining what the rules were.

No, the problem was that Tree was acting as flagrantly as Lucia, even while squashing any response he could make. They'd slept together plenty of times in Veridor, camping under the stars by the river or huddling up in the mountains, but they'd always worn armor then, not soft, yielding pajamas that let him feel every—

He thumped his head against the wall.

Didn't she notice the difference? How much longer would it be before he couldn't hide it? And then what would happen? What would she say to him? What would she do? Would she kick him out? Would he have to move out, anyway? She'd told him before that Centrals were considered to be "of age" when they were seventeen years old, although she'd added irritably that the custom wasn't strictly enforced.

Suddenly it clicked—today was her birthday!

But instead of relief at solving his little puzzle, more questions came. Why hadn't she mentioned it to him? Had she forgotten? Didn't she care? Or did she think she could squeak by without having a celebration?

*Well, she won't get away with that.* Ewan chuckled to himself as he dried off and dressed again. He could show her how much of a boyfriend he was by finally getting her something nice.

Tree was still asleep. He sneaked around the bed as carefully as a teenager on crutches could, then leaned over and kissed her cheek.

"Mmm," she murmured, stretching like a cat and turning to look up at him. "What was that for?"

He smiled. "Happy birthday."

"Birthday?"

"That's right. November 16, remember?"

She rolled over to see the clock and stared at it as blankly as he had. "You're right."

Tossing his crutches aside, Ewan flopped back into bed and tickled her. The sneak attack bonus didn't cancel out his nerfed legs, though, and within a few seconds she'd pinned him under her, jabbing her fingers into his sides hard enough to make the room spin.

"Okay, you got me!" he panted. "But seriously, what can I get you?"

"I don't understand."

"You know, for a present?"

Silence.

Ewan sighed. "In Veridor, we give people something for their birthdays, to let them know how special they are. So, what can I get you?"

"Why would you get me something?"

"You're kidding, right?" he asked, convinced more than ever he needed to do this. "I love you, Tree, in case you've forgotten."

"I love you too," she said automatically, shaking herself a little as though she really had forgotten. Climbing off his back so he could turn over, she said, "But I don't deserve anything from you. You gave me so much in Veridor already, and I pulled you here."

"Tree, I want to be here, with you," he insisted, half truthfully. "Now are you going to tell me what you'd like, or do I get to guess?"

She leaned down and kissed his ear, then sighed as she sagged onto his chest. "Anything you get me would be wonderful, but I still don't understand what you expect to find here."

"That could be tricky on such short notice," he admitted. "I could ask Lisa to make you a cake, but I don't think Michael's got a forge or a shop."

"No, he doesn't. But the moles might."

"The who?"

"The moles," Tree said. "That's what we call the people in Engineering. I don't know any of them personally, though."

*That's because your social circle's more of a dot,* Ewan thought with an inward sigh. "We'll just have to go and meet them after breakfast."

Things started off well enough, with Lisa joining them to hear Ewan's plan. Michael's smile got quite a bit bigger as he made room for her, but she didn't seem to notice him at all, instead listening as Ewan explained about birthday parties and cakes and gifts. At first she was baffled, but her face brightened until her head was bobbing as much as Greasy Tom's, making her strawberry bangs jiggle.

"That's so cute," she said brightly. "Now I want a thoughtful player boy!"

Ewan jumped when her leg rubbed up between his under the table. "Um," he said, blushing furiously but afraid to move.

"We have recipes for sweetbreads," Lisa continued, as if nothing was happening. "That might do. What kind of cake do you want?"

Ewan hesitated but cupped his hands and leaned forward to whisper in the girl's ear, trying to ignore her busy foot—and the way the others were watching him.

Lisa ignored them easily. "Yes, I think I can do that. When do you want it?"

"We don't have our presents ready yet. Would it be okay if I messaged you the morning of the party?"

"Definitely! I can make it now and keep it in the refrigerator." She extracted her leg, then stood up and bounced off for the kitchen. "This will be so much fun!"

Unfortunately, she seemed to take all the fun with her.

"I should go too," Michael mumbled, not quite meeting Ewan's eyes. "Can I still come to the party?"

Ewan sighed as Tree glared after the kitchen girl. "Please."

Tree hardly spoke through the rest of breakfast, leaving Ewan to eat in a silence that was quickly broken by the barrage of messages Lisa started sending, updating him with every last detail about her preparations. When the chime announced the third image of a bowl of flour—this time with a spice mixed in —Ewan turned off his tablet.

"So, how do we meet the moles?" he asked.

"They're stationed just under the surface level," Tree

replied, picking at her meal. "Ewan…you really don't have to do this."

"I want to." He took her hand. "I haven't gotten to do anything nice for you out here yet. And besides, I'm having fun."

Lisa emerged from the serving room to wave at Ewan.

Tree shot him a dark look. "As much fun as her?"

Ewan surreptitiously smoothed out his pant leg. "Just trust me, okay?"

Tree sighed and pushed herself up to go. "Fine."

When the elevator doors opened a few minutes later, Ewan found himself squinting into a room so filled with red light, it made his eyes water. He blinked as a gust of hot air dried them again, giving him a view of a forge that Kate would've killed to see.

It was a massive chamber, at least as big as Whitehaven's square, with high ceilings supported by broad columns and smaller rooms walled off randomly around the space. A good four hundred yards out, great foundries poured orange-hot steel into molds. A constant din of clanging and buzzing filled the air, as if a hundred people were all steadily hammering away, making anything the Centre wanted.

Tree reluctantly led him over to a short, bronze-skinned older man with a short beard in crafting smocks. When he turned around, Ewan recognized him as a chief from the Director's office, one of those who'd supported him.

"Ewan," Tree said, "this is Karl Taylor, Chief of Engineering. Karl, this is—"

"The player boy," the man said in a scratchy voice. He grinned up at them both before giving Ewan's crutches an appraising shake. "What brings you to the hole?"

Ewan leaned on his other crutch, just in case. "I was hoping to make a birthday present?"

The chief's brow crinkled, and he looked around and

shouted. "Hey, Draper!"

An aurochs of a young man came jogging up, setting down a chunk of metal that looked to weigh more than Ewan did, before wiping black grease from his umber face onto his sleeves.

"These two want a birthday whatsit." Karl said. "Can you get them all set?"

"Sure," the boy replied with an easy smile. "Though you'll have to tell me how to make one. I'm Sam."

"Ewan." Ewan offered his hand for Sam to eventually shake, as the chief wandered off. "And this is Tree, Treanna Rothchild."

"Rothchild? Like the Director?" Sam wiped his big hands again before offering one to her. "It's nice to meet you, ma'am. What section do you work in?"

"We're part of a new section," Tree replied, lifting her chin. "Ewan is actually a player, but we're here on unofficial business."

"A player? No kidding!" Sam regarded Ewan bemusedly as he scratched the little curls on his head. "I didn't know you people could walk around."

"We can, given the chance," Ewan said civilly. "Now, about that present?"

Sam was very friendly, if not the sharpest blade on the rack. After giving them a quick tour of facilities that would have left Kate drooling, he took them to a little workshop of a room. Once he'd gotten a sense for the mole's skillset, Ewan asked for a set of earrings, as close as possible to the ones Kate had given Tree back home. Explaining this without letting Tree hear was no small task; he had to tell her that presents were supposed to be a surprise just to get her to give him some space. It didn't help that Sam kept repeating his whispers in a booming voice to confirm what he'd heard, but eventually he seemed to get the idea.

If anything, though, another new friend and the promise of a gift sank Tree's mood even more, to the point where she was obviously trying to avoid him—only she couldn't, since Ewan lived with her.

She said five words the rest of the day. The next morning, she told him she had to give her weekly update to the chiefs and headed straight for the door without him. He offered to come along, but she told him he needed to work on walking without crutches before she dared to demonstrate his recovery.

Irritated and worried, Ewan tried burning off his frustration in the pool, but in no time, Lucia came to tease him. When she began cutting him off to make him bump into her, he gave it up and retreated to Tree's room again.

Ewan waited there until lunchtime, but Tree never returned, so he went on his own and chatted with Lisa instead. The girl gleefully reported that she'd finished the cake, then offered to come hang out in Ewan's room until Tree returned. When she put her foot between his again, he refused as politely as he could.

So he sat alone in Tree's bed, waiting for her, alternately feeling lonely and put out. When five o'clock came and went, he pulled out his tablet to search for messages, then flipped through it, looking up everything he could find on Veridor before learning that most of it was restricted.

Around eight thirty, Sam messaged him to let him know the earrings were ready. Ewan replied with an invitation to the party next morning, copying Lisa and Michael—and Tree, figuring it would be like her if she didn't show up.

She came home after eleven and crashed into bed, with nothing more than an acknowledgment of his invite and a curt apology about the meeting running long. Then she curled up and fell asleep.

All told, Ewan was shocked when he woke the next morning to find her already up and about.

"Hey," he said, blinking.

"We'll need chairs," she replied. "Can you go find some?"

"Um, yeah. Sure."

Not knowing where to look, it took him took a while. Thankfully, he ran into Michael, and between the two of them, they made it back to Tree's room with furniture looted from an empty residence. When they arrived, Sam and Lisa were already there, with the mole positioning a table while Lisa held the covered cake.

"There he is," Sam said cheerfully. "I was starting to think you'd need help with those."

"Nope," Ewan lied, handing one over before sagging onto the other. "Did you bring the present?"

"Both of them," Sam answered. He gave Tree a sly smile. "Should Ewan get his first?"

"Wait—what?"

"Definitely," Tree replied, grinning wickedly.

Ewan rounded on her. "But it's not my birthday!"

"It will be, soon enough. My gift to you is really a gift for me, although I expect you to use it well to keep training yourself."

"Oh...what is it?"

"This!" Sam said proudly, and he pulled out something that caught Ewan completely off guard.

"No way," he whispered as he reached out to take a metallic guitar, made of steel and silver, from the big guy. He looked at Tree. "How?"

Sam cleared his throat. "Miss Rothchild, um, Tree, came by yesterday with schematics and everything from the archives. She said it's supposed to be made from something called wood, but we didn't have any of that on hand. It took all day to make, but she wouldn't let me quit until I'd gotten it right. I hope it works," he added, almost fearfully.

Ewan barely heard him. "This is why you ditched me yesterday?"

"Surprise, love," Tree said, smiling in a way that warned him she'd do it again in a heartbeat.

*Maybe her secrets aren't always bad*, Ewan admitted to himself as he returned the smile, ten times over. He cradled the guitar, pressing his fingers down over the frets. The strings bit into his flesh, but he played a few experimental chords.

"It's perfect," he said, figuring they'd get to know each other. Turning to Sam, he asked, "Now will you give me the other present?"

He took the box and cracked it open to make sure everything was up to spec—it was, more or less—before giving it to Tree. "Happy birthday."

She made a show of being surprised, but she had a joyful, knowing smile as she lifted the earrings out.

"Thank you," she whispered.

"You're welcome," Ewan replied, heart swelling as she equipped them. "Oh, um, Lisa. Can you light that cake now?"

Lisa came forward and placed her creation gently onto the table. She removed the cover, and at once the room filled with the scent of the orange geraniums Ewan had specifically requested.

"How does it look?" she asked anxiously.

"It looks perfect." Just like he'd asked, she'd made it in the shape of a willow, with eighteen candles on the ends of the branches. "Thanks for making it."

Tree placed a hand on his shoulder. "So, what happens now, Master O'Meara?" she asked as Lisa lit the candles and Michael dimmed the lights.

"We'd sing the birthday song," Ewan said, "and then you make a wish—don't tell us what, or it won't come true. Then you blow out the candles."

"What's a song?" Michael asked.

Ewan's grin faltered, but he decided to make good on his promise to bring some joy out from the game floors. "Maybe it would be easier to just show you."

He began playing, closing his eyes, remembering year after year of his own birthdays, celebrating with family while the early winter snows floated down from the mountains. Ignoring the pain from his noob fingers, he sang.

> *The passage of the sun across the sky*
> *And the turning of the seasons tried and true*
> *Remind us just how quickly time can fly,*
> *We age while the world around us is renewed.*
>
> *And though another year has come and gone,*
> *With laughter, light, and love to see you through,*
> *We gather 'round and gladly sing along*
> *To wish a happy birthday to you.*

When he'd finished, letting the last hopeful chord hover in the air, Ewan opened his eyes and returned to the present. Sam, Michael, and Lisa were staring at him with jaws hanging open, but Tree was beaming, tears openly rolling down her cheeks now.

"Did you make a wish?" he asked her.

She nodded, then took a deep breath and blew out every candle. Safe in the relative darkness again, she leaned forward and gave him a long, gentle kiss. "You are so precious."

"You too. Thanks for trusting me."

"Can you play the song again?" Lisa asked.

"Sure," Ewan said, smiling at his new friends when Michael turned the lights back on. "But only if you sing along, this time."

**20**

---

# BREAKING POINTS

Word about the party spread like wildfire. Over the following morning, Ewan got half a dozen messages from Lisa, each one a forwarded request from some Central or other for a repeat performance.

"They're all asking for cakes!" Lisa chirped as Ewan and Tree collected their lunch. "But it won't be as fun without the song. Tree, can I borrow Ewan? I'll make sure he has fun."

Tree's eyes flashed as though she'd also noticed the kitchen girl's happy foot the other day, but Ewan cut her off. "I'd be happy to. The more Centrals I can make friends with, the better. Right?" he asked, giving Tree a pointed look.

"If that's what you want," she said stiffly.

Unfortunately, playing music for Lisa and the others wasn't nearly as fun as he'd hoped. The strawberry-haired girl talked so much with the partygoers that Ewan couldn't get a word in edgewise, much less befriend anyone. By the third performance, he'd resigned himself to dutifully strumming out the chords, singing at people who stared back with an uncanny resemblance to the citizens of Dunbriar, while Lisa rambled about how great it was to have a player around to show them new and curious things.

By far, though, the worst parties were adult-only, where invariably Lisa would get invited to stay after for "extra" celebration. The kitchen girl eagerly agreed every time, regardless of who was asking, whether they were married, or how many other guests were also there. And when she invited Ewan to join in to be social—which was as often as she could—all Ewan could do was bail as quickly and politely as possible, juggling his crutches and guitar as he retreated to Tree's room.

Tree never asked what happened, and Ewan was too embarrassed to say, but her disappointed, disgusted expression drove home what she thought of her people's dating culture. Which only convinced Ewan even more that whatever Jerk Guy had done before, Ewan was locked into doing the opposite now. He had to show Tree he was different, or he'd never have the chance to get her back.

Even so, he kept risking her aggro by working at getting to know the Centrals in less dangerous settings, trusting that the more goodwill he could put in place now, the easier it would be for the Veridians who logged out afterward. And he smiled to hear tuneless snatches of the birthday song drifting through the halls as he walked—walked!—with Tree to Medical in early December.

"You've gone from thirty-five pounds at recovery to a full one hundred forty in only four and a half months, trending toward one hundred sixty," Nichols told him, looking at his chart in astonishment. "At this point, the only barrier to your continued progress is your own inherent laziness."

"Yeah, I'll have to watch that." Ewan gave Tree a grin. "Hey, at least you don't have to fuss over me anymore."

She glared at him and stalked away.

Ewan sighed inwardly. "Tree—"

"Don't let *me* get in the way of your social life!" she snapped, sweeping through the door with all the feeling of slamming it.

Ewan sat up to follow, but his tablet beeped. With another invite from Lisa.

Nichols sniffed beside him. "Might I offer you an old man's advice?"

This time, Ewan's sigh was outward. "Please."

"See that you don't fit in too well. She didn't put me to all this trouble so you could make merry for the staff's entertainment."

"I know." Ewan looked down at the invite. "But what else am I supposed to do?"

Nichols drew out his tablet, tapped for a moment, and gave him a thin smile. "Your job, now that you're fit to do it."

Another moment later, Lisa's message was replaced by a new one, to Tree and Ewan.

---

*Chief Emissary Rothchild:*

*Chief Nichols has informed me that the player, Ewan O'Meara, has been successfully rehabilitated to the point of normal operation. With congratulations to you on a job well done, you are ordered to report to my office immediately with Emissary O'Meara for a mission-critical briefing.*

*—Carmine Rothchild, Director of the Centre for the Preservation of the Human Legacy*

---

Ewan read it a couple times to be sure, then declined Lisa's offer. "Thanks," he said to the doctor.

Nichols answered with a tiny smile.

Ewan met Tree on the way to the elevator.

"Hey," he said, not quite meeting her eye. "Any idea what this is about?"

"I don't know," she replied tersely after telling it to take them up. "But since Grandfather asked you to come with me instead of the tavern wench, I would think it's for something important."

They rode the rest of the way in an uncomfortable silence and stepped into the Director's office. Tree walked ahead of Ewan and sat opposite the bald man.

"My, my. Up and about, I see," Rothchild said genially as Ewan took a seat beside her.

"Yes, sir," Ewan replied, grabbing at Tree's hand under the desk and missing. "I couldn't have done it without Tree's help—and her love," he added pointedly.

The Director harrumphed politely. "Yes, well, whatever your motivation was, it's past time for you to begin working. Master O'Meara, did Treanna ever explain to you what prompted her to log into your simulation in the first place?"

Ewan's stomach clenched like it hadn't for months, as birthday parties fell out of his head entirely. "Only that someone had attacked the Centre."

"In a manner of speaking," Rothchild replied. "We routinely send scouts into the Wastes in search of raw materials for our use. It is an inhospitable environment, to say the least. We occasionally lose transports to accidents, but this past April something, shall we say, out of the ordinary occurred."

He tapped his own tablet behind the desk, producing an image that leaped out and floated over the ancient wood. An image of what might have been a great metal carriage, now twisted and smoking as if it had run afoul of an epic mob.

Or a Gem.

Ewan leaned forward, cautiously poking a finger through it. "What happened?"

"We don't know," the Director answered simply. "From the engineers' assessment of the damage patterns, we believe an explosive destroyed the transport from inside."

"Explosive?"

"Like magical fire," Tree explained, "only there's no such thing as magic in the real world."

Rothchild nodded. "Our transports stock basic explosives for clearing areas, and the fuel is flammable. However, the initial detonation appears to have occurred in the control room. Some of the chiefs of staff—Treanna, for example—felt that the destruction was therefore the work of a hostile faction, henceforth unknown to us."

Ewan blinked. "You mean someone else. Out there?"

"The notion is difficult to accept," Rothchild agreed. "We have no record of anyone surviving an extended stay in the Wastes. Unfortunately, though, we now have conclusive proof that such a group exists."

He tapped again, and the smoking transport shifted over to make way for another. It was twisted as well, but this time, there were several corpses tied to the wreckage.

Tree drew a sharp breath. "Where?"

"Approximately two hundred miles west of the first incident," the Director replied grimly. "Clearly, someone was present in the aftermath to arrange the bodies. It seems you were right, Annie."

"I regret that I am," she whispered, now taking Ewan's hand.

Rothchild gave her a sympathetic smile. "The scouts who took these images returned quickly, needless to say."

Ewan leaned forward, acutely aware the corpses hadn't dematerialized. "When did this happen?"

"Approximately two months ago."

"Two months?" Tree nearly shouted. "Why wasn't I informed?"

"Because your project was under testing for proof of

concept," the Director answered bluntly. "We couldn't expect a player to fight such an enemy when he couldn't even walk."

"But still—"

"Now that this has changed, I saw fit to inform you both. Per Chief Reid's contributions, I have Engineering working on countermeasures and defenses for the transports. For the time being, we've taken the precaution of avoiding the disputed area, but it seems a conflict with this surface faction is inevitable."

He leaned forward, banishing the images to look intently at them both. "Our security forces aren't trained for combat; they were only intended to ensure that the staff were orderly. But the two of you, particularly O'Meara, have extensive experience in life-or-death situations."

Ewan's stomach twisted like the mangled transports. "Yeah...but this is completely different."

Rothchild's eyes flicked to Tree. "I have it on good information that you were able to escort a VIP through some of the most hostile terrain your world has to offer. Between your experience and our new weapons, we have a chance to defend ourselves. However, the timetable requires an adjustment to our original plan."

"What kind of adjustment?" Tree asked.

The Director steepled his fingers, watching Ewan. "As an emissary, your purpose is to recruit more players to the defense of the Centre. However, despite your extraordinary recovery, it has taken you over four months before you could walk on your own power, to say nothing of practicing your skills in combat. I expect your fellow players would have a similar recovery?"

"Probably, sir," Ewan admitted. "I'd say a good half year before they'd be up to spec, even if they logged out today."

Rothchild nodded. "Agreed. Which means this hostile faction has months to escalate its attacks before we can mount a response from that quarter."

"What do you need us to do?" Tree asked.

"I want you to train the staff for battle."

Ewan blinked. "The staff? You mean goons like Jeff Harper?"

"I mean anyone who is willing," the Director said. "Preferably everyone, at some point. I understand your feelings, Master O'Meara. I suppose I cannot blame you, given the circumstances. But like it or not, we are all in this together—and we will live or die that way."

*That's easy for you to say*, Ewan thought. *If I train them to do the fighting for themselves, my people will stay on the game floors. They won't ever learn the truth!*

But he could still picture that smoking wreckage.

"Okay...I'll do it. But I'll need weapons. Swords, if at all possible."

The Director tapped on his tablet, then leaned back with a satisfied smile. "Consider it done. You'll receive a request for specifications, shortly."

"Thank you, Grandfather," Tree said.

"Thank you, Annie," he replied earnestly. "Now, there is one more matter to discuss with you both. With all this new activity, we can expect the nutritional requirements of the staff to rise. I've conferred with Chief Spencer, and she believes we will reach the population limit soon."

"Population limit?" Ewan asked.

"The Centre has a limit to the number of non-player people it can support," Tree explained. "We've only got so much room, and so many resources."

"Precisely," Rothchild said. "Only so many meals. And if the mouths we feed get hungrier, then we'll need to have fewer mouths. This issue will only worsen as your efforts, shall we say, bear fruit."

Tree pursed her lips. "What should we do?"

"I don't know." He let out a long exhale, blowing through his mustache. "We're in this position in the first place because resources are scarce. Short of changing the planet itself, I don't see how we can do much about it. It's not anything you need to worry about yet," he added. "But given your likely recruitment goals, I felt it prudent to bring the matter to your attention now."

Ewan listened, chest tightening as he imagined extra people just disappearing. "How, exactly, does the Centre limit its population?"

"That's simple enough," the Director replied. "We reclaim fewer babies."

The tight feeling shifted into a numb, knowing dread as Ewan turned to Tree and found her already looking away. "From where?"

She sighed. "Everyone in the Centre...we were conceived by players."

Ewan glanced at Rothchild. The Director wore a stoic expression, but behind it, Ewan sensed a weariness. A resignation to the situation that aged him, enough to be a grandfather.

"You don't have parents," he whispered.

"None that wanted me," Tree said bitterly. "But it's just as well for the Centre. No one here has been able to successfully reproduce for nearly two thousand years."

"So...each of you was supposed to be born into a game world?"

"Yes," the Director said. "We raise the reclaimed babies as our own, explaining their parentage as they grow older and can come to grips with the truth."

Ewan slumped into his chair, his mind spinning the way it did every time he learned another one of Earth's lousy secrets. Every player unknowingly depended on the very people who'd been rejected from their worlds? Rejected, to live in the Wastes?

*No wonder they hate us.*

Rothchild coughed politely. "In any event, see about

attracting interest among the staff for combat training. I leave the how and where up to you."

"Yes, sir," Ewan said.

Once the elevator doors closed, he pulled Tree into a hug. "I'm sorry. I had no idea."

"It's not your fault...but thank you for caring," she murmured, hugging him back. "For what it's worth, I'm grateful that my parents discarded me, that I grew up here in this place. I'd never have known you, otherwise."

He kissed her head. How she could be so forceful one minute, so fragile the next? "We'll make it better somehow. I promise."

The following morning, Ewan was sitting in bed, flipping through his tablet and worrying about his family while Tree showered.

"I've been wondering what I could do for your birthday next week," she said after she'd finished. "To celebrate your coming of age. Is there anything you would like from me?" she asked, walking softly over to him and tilting the tablet down.

He looked up, then instantly forgot whatever he'd been thinking as he found himself face to face—in a manner of speaking—with her bare form, only a foot away and still glistening with little water droplets all over her—

*Stop staring, you fool!*

"Um, nope, nothing at all!" he yelped. He half dove, half fell to the floor, then scrambled to the safety of the chairs they'd kept from the party. "You don't have to do anything for me!"

For a moment Tree stood there, leaving him with a dizzying view of her back, but when she turned, her face was streaked in tears.

"I suppose I don't," she snarled as she snatched a shirt and stabbed her arms through it. "I expect the wench keeps you satisfied!"

"At least Lisa doesn't treat me like I'm blind," Ewan shot back. "At least she doesn't strut around frapping naked without expecting me to notice!"

Tree froze, her glare turning incredulous. "Don't you realize I'm not—"

"Like the others. You won't let me forget it! But how am I supposed to act, when you're as brazen as they are?"

Ewan charged out the door, racing blindly through the halls and swearing enough to make Kate blush. When he stopped, he found himself at the double doors to the gym. Yet another place he wasn't allowed to go, for fear of the Centrals' precious frapping sensibilities.

"Nerf your sensibilities," he growled. He shoved the doors open and stalked in, ignoring the inevitable head-turning that followed him. Snatching up a pair of short rods from a floor stand, he went over to a bag hanging from a chain and swung as hard as he could.

"That frapping woman!"

The bag thumped into the wall and came back at him.

On impulse, Ewan pretended it was Jerk Guy. "This is all your fault for making her so paranoid!"

He tore into it with everything he had, muscles re-specking all the mollycoddling and rehabilitation into the stances and forms he knew so well, as he vented his bottled-up fury with each strike.

Why did Tree keep treating him like an invalid, now that he was back to his old self? Couldn't she see how much he wanted her? How much she was tempting him, torturing him?

He yelled, running the bag through. The world around him yelled back in sympathy.

Why couldn't she see him as her boyfriend instead of her pet?

Then it hit home, like one of her lightning bolts.

*She's been telling me she wants me,* he thought, staring at the tattered remnant of the bag as it bled little pebbles out onto the floor. *The way everyone here does, but I've been running away every time! Does she think I'm the one who doesn't want her? That I've been running off with Lisa?*

"Oh, Gems," he panted as the bag wobbled a lopsided yes. "I'm such a fool."

"You got that right, you effing tuber," came a harsh voice from his right.

Ewan turned just in time to see Jeff Harper's fist connect with his face. He staggered backward as the world swam; then a hard kick in the ribs put him on the floor.

"You come out here where you don't belong," Harper growled. "Breaking my stuff. Eating my food. Poaching my girls. Stinking my halls up with your stupid song."

Ewan gasped for air, but his grip tightened around the rods he still held. He pushed himself up to standing and wiped the blood from his lip. "Music doesn't have a smell, you idiot."

"Yours does!"

Harper tore off his gray shirt in some harebrained attempt at intimidation, but the sight of yet another randomly half-naked Central only fueled Ewan's anger even more.

"I was done with that bag anyway." Spinning a rod in his hand, Ewan stepped out into the suddenly-cleared space as several dozen Centrals formed a ring around him. "I'll warn you: Veridians don't pull their hits."

Harper laughed, slow and quiet as he licked Ewan's blood from his knuckles. "Who wants to help me send this drip feeder to hydro?"

Three men emerged from the crowd with murder in their eyes, but unlike the Swords in World's Edge, they weren't coming to arrest one of their own. One man grabbed a metal plate from a nearby rack, hefting it like a golem with a boulder.

Ewan shifted, positioning himself at the center of the X they were making, while praying that his body would be up for this.

"Kill 'im!" Harper roared.

As he and his cronies rushed forward, Ewan couldn't help smiling at their noob mistake. Letting them all come to him, he dodged back and to the side just as the weight sailed through the center. It bashed one man in the head, laying him out hard as Harper leaped away with a curse.

Ewan swung his bars together as he rolled back to standing, buckling the knees of the second man with a satisfying crack and sending him to the floor as well. Imagining he had his behemoth-horn blades instead of nerfed little bars, Ewan whirled around and threw his right-hand rod as hard as he could. It took the weight thrower out with a strike to the forehead, then spun away through the stunned crowd.

Grinning savagely, Ewan turned to Harper. "Well?"

The older man spat at him and charged, leaning well off balance. Ewan sidestepped, tripping the brute and cracking his head with the rod. Harper hit the floor with a heavy thump, but Ewan was on him in a heartbeat, delivering a few good whacks to the face before the bigger man knocked him off with another vision-blanking punch.

Harper snarled, licking his lips as both fighters picked themselves up again. "You're dinner, worm."

"And you're just another mob."

Ewan took a swing at the guy's ribs, but Harper threw up a meaty arm to block. He grabbed Ewan by the shirt and slung him half out of it onto the floor, then stomped at Ewan's head, just missing as Ewan rolled away and pivoted into a hard kick that snapped the Central's knee from the side. Harper dropped with a bellow, and Ewan spun up with a vicious swing to the man's neck that would have decapitated him if he'd had a real blade.

Harper fell onto his back and didn't move.

Ewan stumbled over to deliver the final blow, but then someone screamed. The blatantly un-Veridian terror in the voice shocked him back to his senses—and he suddenly remembered how different Earth's rules were.

"Gems of old," he panted, wiping the mixed blood and sweat from his eyes as he swayed. *I almost murdered him!*

Letting the bar fall as he dropped to his knees, Ewan checked Harper's neck for a pulse. It was there: faint, but there. He scrambled over to the other men and jammed his fingers against their necks to make sure they had at least a little health. To his relief, they all did.

He heard movement in the crowd and whirled around, grabbing for the rod as he hauled himself back to standing.

A light-skinned boy about Kate's age stepped out, holding the other rod with something akin to reverence. "Can...can you show me?"

Ewan stared at him. "What?"

"How to do that," the boy said, glancing anxiously down at the bodies—*not corpses!*—before looking up again with wide, gray-green eyes.

A befuddled second later, Ewan's brain kicked back on. "What's your name?"

"Nathan Sanderson. From Scouting. Will you help us protect ourselves from...you know?"

*No wonder you're keen to learn*, Ewan thought grimly, but he split his lip with a smile. "Yeah, I can. In fact," he said, looking around the wary crowd, "the Director personally asked me to instruct anyone who's interested."

Most of them flinched back at that, but a tall man, a few years older than Ewan, strode past the boy. Ewan looked at him, then swallowed as he recognized the sandy-haired chief who'd wanted him put back in the tubes.

"O'Meara, wasn't it?" the man said, regarding Ewan without blinking.

"Yeah. But you can call me Ewan."

The man looked at Harper's prone form and shook his head, slowly. "I don't think the Director would approve of your recruiting method, O'Meara."

Another nervous ripple passed through the Centrals.

"Maybe not," Ewan admitted, lowering his bar. "But Harper started it—again."

"Is that so?" the chief said coolly. His blue eyes flicked to the mangled punching bag. "Wanton destruction of Central property notwithstanding, I suppose there's no permanent harm done, provided you haven't killed anyone. You are aware that real humans don't respawn, are you not?"

Ewan winced under the older man's gaze. "Very."

But then the chief gave a slight bow, his eyes now glittering with amusement. "In that case, I'll learn whatever you can teach. In return, I'll show you how to manage in this world."

"I'd like that very much," Ewan said, sighing gratefully as another ten Centrals joined the chief. "You just had your first lesson, all of you. Think on what you saw, what these men did wrong, and meet me here tomorrow at one o'clock. The rest of you are welcome to come, and join in if you like," he added to the crowd, noticing more than a few still watching the downed men. "Oh, and I'll make sure we get some safety gear soon. Chief, um—"

"Call me Gabe."

"Okay, Gabe. I've got to run, but could you please help these guys get medical attention? I, uh, may have overdone it."

"I'll see to it personally."

Thanking his lucky stars, Ewan stumbled out to the halls to find Tree and apologize.

He hadn't even gone two dozen yards when he heard footsteps running up behind him. He turned hopefully, but it was Lucia Howe instead, straining her athletic clothing as she bounded toward him. He stared, momentarily stunned, but then she grabbed his hand with startling force.

"That was some display," she purred, her voice deep and husky. "To think I called you a runt."

"Um, thanks," Ewan said, swaying again as he tried to pull free.

"I know just how big and strong each of those men is," Lucia continued, ignoring his escape attempt and pressing in closer, backing him toward the wall. "They're some of the best the Centre has, but you made them look like a gang of little boys." Her breath was hot and quick on his chest, now, but her tone suddenly became hushed. Desperate. "Maybe you have what I've been wanting all this time?"

"I—"

She slammed him into the wall, smashing her lips onto his with something between a giggle and a moan. Ewan tried to fight her off, but the woman was everywhere at once, a dozen hands all ripping the rest of his shirt away and holding him firmly in place, grabbing his hips—

"No, please!" he gasped.

She shut his mouth with her own, sucking on his blood.

Somehow, he managed to wedge his arms between their chests and push. "Tree—"

"What about Tree?" a familiar voice snarled—from only a few feet away.

Lucia laughed, then pulled back so suddenly, Ewan stumbled into her like he was the one grabbing for her. She gave him one more indecent pinch, then skipped off down the hall. "Next time, honey. Message me!"

Ewan faced Tree, but her eyes narrowed to slits as they traced down his body.

Cursing, she turned and raced down the hall.

Ewan ran after her, reaching her door just before she could

lock him out, but that didn't stop her from closing it on his arm as he threw it forward.

"Gah! Come on, Tree, let me in!"

"Now you want in?" she shouted as he forced his way through, slipping between the metal plates on his own blood. "I swear to the Mother, Ewan, I've been patient. More patient than I can stand. I wanted you to be able to focus on adjusting to life here, without stressing about pleasing me. But the stronger you got, the more you rejected me. Using me to heal. Leaving me for the wench. And then, just when I think I finally understand why? I get a message from Grandfather saying you've caused a disturbance, and when I come to rescue you I find you with Lucia?!"

She slapped him, hard enough to put him on the floor. "How dare you ditch me for her!"

"Me?" Ewan shouted back as he pushed up onto his knees. "What about you? I've been walking on eggshells trying not to be a jerk for fear of freaking you out, but you just get angrier by the day! How am I supposed to show you how much I want you without ticking you off?"

Tree stared down at him for a long moment. She moved her hand again...but this time, it cupped his bruised cheek.

"You want me?" she asked, softly now. Slowly, she knelt down to face him. "Still?"

"Of course I do," Ewan answered, ignoring the pain rebounding through his skull. "I've been going out of my mind for the want of you. The real you, the one I knew from Veridor. You can't seriously think I'd pick someone like Lucia instead."

Her hand shook against his face. "Not even once?"

He gripped it, held it steady as he tried to take a deep breath. "How could I? You're my best friend, my fiercest ally, sharing and saving my life every day since I met you. You're the only one I want, Tree. I love you."

"Likewise," Tree murmured. "Oh love, I'm so sorry. I've had it all planned out for weeks now."

Slowly, cautiously, she withdrew a steel ring from her pocket and held it up. "You told me your Church prefers lovers to be married. And I wanted you to know I was serious."

*And to know that I was,* Ewan thought, reeling, as she bit her lip. *By offering me another Epic quest. One that I'd be crazy to accept, and even crazier to refuse.*

"I had Sam make this for you, after my birthday," Tree whispered, the fire in her eyes dancing now, just like it had in the Argenones. "As part of my wish...I know you're not of age for another week..."

"But it's not strictly enforced," Ewan finished breathlessly, as his heart threatened to burst.

*Okay, Kate. You called it.*

Returning Tree's gaze, he slipped his finger through her ring, then pulled her into his embrace. The woman he'd just promised to marry.

# 21

## SHOW OF FORCE

Ewan slept in with Tree the next morning, reveling in the alternating passion and tenderness he'd come to expect and love from her. Finally reassured they were synced up again, she was careful to mind his injuries from the day before, but she made a point not to baby him.

When shower time came, he didn't protest her following him in.

They did split up afterward. She went to the Director's office to smooth over yesterday's brawl without Ewan's help. Grateful for the escape, he used the time to visit the hole. Ordering practice weapons took only a minute, but before he left, he stopped by Sam's workshop.

The mole was hunched over a bench, somehow threading a pendant onto a fine necklace chain with his big fingers.

"We've been getting lots of requests for jewelry," he said when he was done. "I'm not sure how I got roped into making it all, but it's kind of fun. Oh good, you're wearing yours now," he added, sighing in relief. "Tree warned me to keep my mouth shut or there'd be, um..."

"Consequences?"

Sam's forehead crinkled. "I think so?"

"Well, I'm glad you've been practicing," Ewan said with a grin, "because now you're going to make one for her."

After a little searching, Ewan settled on a band of gold, with a piece of diamond scavenged from the great saws in the workshops. He watched, from a safe distance, as Sam used a laser to carve it into a heart.

"Diamonds are tricky," Sam explained cheerfully as the chips flew. "They're the hardest thing on Earth and won't take a scratch, but they can get deep flaws. Hit one from the wrong angle, and it goes to pieces. Easy to lose an eye that way," he chuckled, tapping his safety goggles.

*Tell me about it*, Ewan thought, picturing his Diamond Lady. "I'll be careful."

Once the ring was finished, Ewan stopped by Medical, where Nichols chastised him for not coming in the day before.

"You've certainly made my work more interesting," the doctor said dryly, dabbing a salve on Ewan's wounds before inspecting his arm. "What did Harper do, bite you?"

"Actually, that was Tree."

Nichols just shook his head.

"How's Harper doing?" Ewan asked, wincing as Nichols began stitching his arm.

"Hoping to finish him off?"

"No!"

The doctor sighed. "He'll recover. Eventually, as will the others, but please try to restrain yourself next time. The Director hired you to protect the staff, as you may recall."

When noon came and Tree met him without Security following her, Ewan was in high spirits. After helping her equip her ring, they walked hand in hand to the gym. Ewan scouted around, and with Tree's help he dragged mats over to the ball courts to set up his makeshift arena. When Sam showed up later, they hauled a dozen punching bags in too, along with whatever random bars he could scrounge.

They were just finishing when the doors opened and Gabe walked in. He returned Ewan's friendly wave, then froze when Tree came back into view.

"Ah. Annie. What a pleasure to see you again, and so soon. Here to keep O'Meara out of trouble this time?"

"What are you doing here?" she snarled in reply.

Gabe spread his hands. "I'm here to learn, naturally."

"You? You called Security on Ewan!"

The chief—the other chief—sighed. "I've already explained myself to your grandfather. You were there. I merely took appropriate action in response to O'Meara's violent behavior." His eyes flicked down to Tree's hand, before shooting Ewan a sympathetic look. "What were you so angry about?"

"Nothing important," Ewan lied, though his face heated. "No worries about yesterday, then?"

"None here," the tall chief replied. "In fact, I'd like to offer my services, to assist your efforts."

Tree's eyes widened. "You can't be serious."

"When have I ever been less?"

"You tried to scuttle my section!"

Gabe gave a little shrug. "That was before I saw what the player could do. I'm a big enough man to admit when I'm wrong."

Tree's fists clenched, but she closed her eyes and sighed. "Fine. But your help had better be worth something."

"So," Ewan said, glancing between them before extending a hand to Gabe. "What section do you work for?"

Gabe hesitated, then shook it. "Programming."

"Really? That's great! I've been wanting to talk with a programmer for a while about a problem in Veridor."

"Nothing I couldn't fix, I'm sure. But perhaps now is not the time," the tall chief replied as Nathan and some of the other volunteers came through the double doors.

After a quick round of introductions and a few more fetched bags, Ewan stood before his original dozen, plus Sam and another new guy: Tim, from Security, of all places.

"Okay," Ewan said, hefting a bar and making most of them flinch back. "So you're all here to learn to fight the way you saw me do yesterday, right? We'll get to that, but first I'd like to get a sense for your current levels. How about each of you take a target bag and try striking it, as hard as you can."

The cadets obediently stepped up to their cylindrical foes—and started yelling and swinging like lunatics. Thomas, a bald older man from Caretaking, attacked so wildly that he slipped and landed on his bottom. A young dark-skinned scout named Amy smacked her bag once and danced back, looking like she couldn't decide whether to cheer or apologize to it. Tim jumped into the air as he swung, getting a nice uppercut for his trouble. Gabe jabbed bemusedly, as though wondering why his bag wasn't splitting open like Ewan's had the day before. Nathan gave his target a solid thwack, hooting with delight as it wobbled away on its chain, but he didn't get out of the way in time to avoid its slow counterattack.

"Okay, that's a good start," Ewan called, before anyone could really hurt themselves. "I'm glad to see you're all enthusiastic about this. Now, um, let's try and learn a few basics about stance and balance."

He took position in the center, one foot slightly in front of the other at an angle, then waved Nathan forward. "Okay. I want you to push me."

"Are you sure?"

"Yeah, go ahead."

The scout shoved Ewan in the chest hard enough to knock him back, but he moved with it, reassuming his stance as he landed.

"How did you do that?" Amy asked as Nathan's eyes widened.

"Well, the trick is to stand in such a way that your center of balance is about here," Ewan said, tapping his belly. "You want to keep your knees soft so they can react to whatever force your opponent dishes out. Keeping your feet out of line," he added, stamping his feet lightly, "will take away an obvious pivot point for your foe."

Gabe frowned. "So, no matter how many times you're hit, you recover?"

"Just like respawning," Ewan replied with a smile.

They spent the next hour working on stances. Once the group had the idea down, Ewan had them divide into roughly matched pairs to practice shoving each other, shrieking and laughing. When they'd gotten the hang of that, he challenged them to try and knock him down. Only Tree managed it, by tickling him unfairly.

The next few weeks flew as Ewan devoted all his energy to his new corps, having much more fun than he'd expected. He'd stuck to the solo route in Veridor, but there was a certain joy in devising new games, little quests for the cadets to complete. They were depending on him, trusting him to get them up to spec for whatever their world had in store. Under the weight of that trust, he worked to come up with new and greater challenges, and his chest swelled with pride whenever his charges rose to meet them.

Sometimes, he had them working in the increasingly converted ball court, using a good mix of dummy weapons to bash at the quintains the moles forged. On other days, he led them on runs around the residential section, hauling weighted packs in addition to their chosen gear to level their strength and endurance along with his own.

As word spread and more people signed up for lessons, Ewan found himself managing nearly four dozen Centrals.

They came from all sections, though most of them were scouts —or moles like Sam, eager to try out the items they'd been making. Michael signed up, though his heart didn't seem to be in it. Lisa joined in too, learning dagger work from Tree as a peace offering between them.

With his usual sparring partner occupied, Ewan turned his attention to Nathan, but to his surprise, it was Gabe who engaged him most. As bold as a Veridian, the chief programmer took on every challenge Ewan threw at him, grasping the principle of almost every move on the first try and refusing to quit until he'd mastered the day's lessons.

When Ewan announced in mid-December that he'd gotten permission to hold a Veridian-styled tournament on the new year—minus the killing parts—Michael immediately requested a private word.

"Is there any way I can sit out?" the caretaker asked, once they'd stepped away from the main group.

"I guess so," Ewan said, "but why?"

"I don't like fighting."

"Why'd you sign up, then?"

"Because I need to do my part." Michael sighed as he looked at the others. "I know there's something hunting transports in the Wastes. We all do. But...even so, I don't want to hurt anyone."

"There's no shame in that." Ewan patted his friend on the shoulder. "In fact, I'd say supporting the fighters is even more important. I know better than ever that I wouldn't be here if I hadn't gotten tons of help. I'll tell you what: we'll need referees for the tournament. Someone's got to make sure we're all fighting fairly, right?"

"Right," Michael said, smiling gratefully. "I think I can do that."

At nine o'clock on New Year's Day, a good four hundred Centrals assembled in the gym, a small ridge of gray shirts in the newly installed stands. The combatants worked in their new padded armor on four large mats spaced across the floor. Nichols and one of the nurses, a dark-haired woman named Angela, stood at the side with a stretcher, first aid kits, and grim expressions.

*Gems of old*, Ewan thought gleefully as he looked around the real-world arena. *I wish Kate and Paul could see this.*

Director Rothchild stepped up to a podium in front of the stands. He tapped on the microphone bolted into the top, and the room fell silent.

"My friends," he announced jovially, his deep voice echoing off the walls. "Thank you for consenting to come and bear witness to this violent spectacle from the simulations! Doubtless, it will inspire us all with confidence and provide us rich entertainment. Emissary O'Meara, would you explain the rules for the day?"

Ewan climbed up beside the Director, his enthusiasm flickering as he recognized a few unfriendly faces in the audience. A heavily bandaged Harper glowered from the corner. Lucia Howe caught his eye with a wave, but when her hands moved to her over-encumbered shirt, Ewan quickly looked away with a blush.

"Okay," he said into the microphone. "We'll start off with four sets of matched pairs. Each pair will fight with their choice of weapons, which are blunted and fairly safe. The referees will observe the fights and call for fouls, like striking the head. They'll also declare winners, but the basic idea is this: if a fighter gets knocked off of his or her mat, they lose. If they get pinned to the ground, they lose. If they yield, they lose.

"When all four fights in the set are over, the next set will begin, with the winners moving on to the next round against each other. When we get down to the last four players," he said, drawing instant mutters, "we'll push the mats together so the semifinalists will have more room to impress you."

He stepped back, not really knowing what else to say.

The Director clapped politely, prompting a trickle of imitation applause as he returned to the microphone. "In that case, let this tournament begin."

Ewan jogged back down to the floor and gave Tree a quick kiss. "Good luck, love."

"You'll need it," she replied before drawing her dagger and stepping out onto the mats to face her first opponent.

When all eight fighters were out and ready, Ewan raised his hand, and Sam struck a crude gong with the oversized hammer he'd taken to. The combatants rushed at each other as the sound reverberated throughout the room, and the crowd finally seemed to understand what was happening, making some noise as the fighting started.

Tree had little trouble defeating her opponent, using her experience to dodge his swing and gut-punch him with the dagger while he was off balance. When he keeled over, she brought her fists down into his back, then pressed her knee into the poor guy's throat until he signaled surrender, to the crowd's delight.

Ewan cheered too, rubbing his own neck in sympathy.

The other matches took longer but were no less entertaining, and the crowd cheered with increasing confidence as the cadets knocked each other about.

When the second round began, Ewan took his place on the mats, facing off against Thomas. The old caretaker grinned broadly, hefting a mace in salute.

Ewan lifted his swords, straight up in front of him. "Just do your best, and have fun."

The gong rang and Thomas rushed Ewan, holding his shield like a battering ram. Moving quickly enough to avoid

Ewan's counterattack, he ran most of the way to the far corner before turning about.

Ewan took his turn, blades whirling through the air and making a wall of fluid steel. Thomas shied away and Ewan pressed forward, driving him back an inch at a time as sparks flew from the clashing of sword with shield. When the older man ran out of room, Ewan spun, swatting the shield aside with both swords and delivering a back kick to topple the caretaker out of bounds.

The crowd applauded as Ewan helped Thomas up and slapped his back. "You did really well," he said, breathing hard. "Just remember that every part of a warrior's body is a weapon."

"I will," Thomas replied, wincing as they cleared the mat and headed to Nichols for a once-over.

As the day wore on, Ewan watched with increasing pride and surprise at how well his star pupils were doing. Tree dispatched her second- and third-round opponents with ease, despite her handicap of not having any magic. Gabe showed a calculated focus with his rapier and buckler, keeping the best positions and toying with his opponents. Sam's fights were short, but only because one hit from his massive hammer was enough to send people stumbling out of bounds. And Nathan swung his paired swords with a desperation that tugged at Ewan's heart, a reminder of why they were there.

At the end of the third round, the kitchen staff came through and delivered lunch to the increasingly festive—and definitely larger—throng.

Lisa bounced up to Ewan with a bean wrap and water bottle. "Hey, Master Hero," she said. "I'm having so much fun!"

Ewan took a grateful swig. "Glad to hear it. I missed your fight; how did it go?"

"Oh, I got knocked out in the first round. Gabe smacked me really hard," she lamented, rubbing her backside. "I couldn't get in close enough to get him back."

"Maybe next time," Ewan offered, but she'd already skipped off to pass out more food.

"They really have come a long way," Tree said quietly from behind him. "I realize they're not much compared to the Swords, but I think they could handle some low-level mobs now."

"Yeah," he said, letting her take his water. "So, who's your next victim?"

Her eyes flashed as she smiled at him. "You are."

When the quarterfinal round began after lunch, the crowd roared as Ewan and Tree walked out to their mat together and faced off. "Oh, my," came the Director's voice. "We may need to postpone the other matches for this!"

"Want me to take it easy on you?" Ewan asked her. "I don't want to be in trouble later."

She thumbed her dagger's blunted edge. "If you hold back at all, you'll pay for it tonight!"

The gong sounded and Ewan leaped back as Tree rushed him at full sprint, a lot faster than he'd expected. He parried her first strike, but she'd already closed in so much that he couldn't land a good hit on her. With every step he took back, she pressed forward, keeping close and pounding him in the belly with the dagger.

He grunted as she knocked his breath out, then spun aside to avoid getting stiff-armed off the mat altogether. "I'm glad you can't use magic right now," he panted.

She punched him again, her eyes gleeful and flirtatious. "I wouldn't want it to be unfair, love."

She lunged again, but this time Ewan was prepared. Dropping his blades, he grabbed her arm and twisted, spinning her around and driving her to the mat with his weight. She flailed and kicked, but he sat on her back and pinned her wrists with his hands, ignoring her attacks until Michael declared him the winner.

"That's what I get for feeding you," she huffed as he helped her up, but she gave him a hard kiss that inspired even more noise from the crowd. Face crimson, she took his hand and walked back to the sidelines with him to watch the other quarterfinal matches.

Gabe was there, squaring off against a mole wielding a massive approximation of a battle axe. On the next mat, Nathan saluted Tim, each with a pair of swords in imitation of Ewan. Sam hefted his hammer playfully at Amy on the third mat, though he eyed her sword and dagger cautiously.

When the gong rang out again, they all launched into each other with such ferocity that Ewan jumped.

"Where did they learn to do that?" he asked Tree as the spectators yelled.

She smiled. "You taught them."

"Yeah, but still," he muttered, passing a hand through his hair. *These aren't the same feckless Centrals I met a month ago.*

Gabe took his time with the mole, letting him wear himself down by stepping aside and deflecting the axe strikes with the buckler. When he stumbled, the chief rushed in and delivered a series of precise strikes to the throat—thankfully armored— that left the burly man on his knees, gasping for breath and signaling surrender.

Sam was hard pressed to deflect Amy's blades as she rushed inside his reach like Tree had done to Ewan. She landed a nice sequence of hits, punishing him with the longsword as he retreated from the dagger, but when Michael declared Gabe the winner of his round, she automatically glanced over. Sam gave her a quick thwack to send her out of bounds, then flopped over in relief to more laughter from the crowd.

But it was Nathan's fight that interested Ewan most. Both he and Tim had worked hard to master the basics of dual-wielding, and Ewan watched with pride as they fought.

*He would have made a fine adventurer in Veridor,* Ewan

thought as Nathan finally drove Tim out of bounds with a flurry of attacks. *I suppose that's what he is, out here. How can I make him feel like one?*

In answer, a fun, reckless idea popped into his head.

Ewan jogged up to the podium, leaning to the microphone as the Director made way. "If the other three semifinalists are game, I'd like to change the plan a little."

Sam and Gabe looked up, and Nathan stopped drinking his water.

"I think I'll challenge you, the best the Centre has, to fight me three on one."

Their eyes gleamed as his meaning sank in, and Gabe beckoned the other two over to strategize.

"Challenge given, and challenge accepted." Ewan laughed as the crowd cheered in anticipation. "Show me what you've learned, guys."

Tree met him on the floor and grabbed him arm. "Are you insane?" she whispered. "You just told me how much better they've gotten!"

"I know. If they beat me, it will give everyone here confidence. But don't worry," he added quickly, "I'm not going to just throw the match."

She pulled him to her for a kiss. "Be careful, okay? If you need to, surrender. I won't think any less of you."

Ewan nodded, then trotted over to the combined mat where the others were already waiting. He raised his swords in salute, watching them do similarly with a hungry zeal that nerfed his own somewhat.

*Well...time to see if I'm back to spec.*

The gong sounded once more, and Ewan backpedaled to the nearest corner, hoping to maybe cheap-shot one of them out of bounds before things got too intense.

It didn't go that way.

Gabe got there first on his long legs, slashing at Ewan's face in defiance of the rules. Ewan ducked, jabbing his right blade into his opponent's belly, but then the chief spun away to reveal Nathan rushing in from behind him, blades whirling. Ewan deflected the strikes and rolled aside, trying to work his way in from the edge—but the instant he got to standing, Sam's hammer connected full-on in his gut.

Faintly surprised he wasn't vomiting as he literally flew off the floor, Ewan barely managed to jam his blades into the mat to brake himself. He landed hard on his knees, and the crowd roared like the blood in his ears as he looked up to see all three opponents rushing him.

He gave them a sore, proud grin and stood, willing his body to ignore the throbbing in his middle as he met their combined attack.

Seconds dragged into minutes. The Centrals fell into a pattern of tag-teaming, corralling him into a small area and wearing him down while they stayed fresh. Every time he went for Gabe, Nathan was there to harry him. Every time he tried for Nathan, Gabe was right in his face. And Sam just kept laying about with the frapping hammer, threatening to take them all out.

He finally caught a break when Nathan overreached with a lunge. Ducking aside, Ewan swatted him on the back, then got his foot between the boy's legs and tripped him out of bounds.

Sighing in relief, Ewan turned around—just in time to see Gabe's rapier once again slicing through the air at his face.

He spun away and smacked the chief in the shoulder, hard enough to make him stumble, but Sam jumped in and clubbed Ewan back.

"Oh no you don't," he panted. "I don't want to go one on one with you!"

Ewan couldn't help laughing as Sam charged at him like a panicked cave troll. He backed up, luring Sam away from Gabe while the programmer nursed his shoulder; then he sprang forward. Sam flinched at the sudden change, giving Ewan time to rap both his hands and make him drop the hammer with a yell.

Reminding himself not to get carried away, Ewan pressed his blade tips into his friend's throat. "Do you yield?"

Sam chuckled nervously, then looked back at Gabe. "He's all yours!" he called, raising his hands in surrender and leaving the mat to wild cheers as Michael slipped in to drag the hammer off.

But as he turned to face his final opponent, Ewan realized that a good number of the spectators were chanting his name instead of Gabe's. The programmer seemed to notice it too, glancing back and scratching his stubbled chin with a frown.

"Shall we?" Ewan asked, grinning.

Gabe's eyes glittered as he lifted his blade and pointed it at Ewan's heart. "Let's go, O'Meara."

He rushed at Ewan, once again slashing high—*nerf it all, doesn't he know that's illegal?* Ewan ducked, then realized too late that Gabe was expecting him to.

Ewan screamed as the chief kicked him hard enough to crack his ribs, and fire lanced through him as he rolled back from Gabe's follow-through. He took a ragged breath, tasting blood. Through the crowd's now-distant roar, he thought he could dimly hear Tree calling his name.

Offering him the chance to spend another four months, being useless.

*Not happening*, he thought with a grim wince as he forced himself to standing and saw Gabe arguing with the refs and Nichols. *And nerfed well not for a cheap shot.*

"I'm not done yet," he croaked, trying not to clutch his chest.

Nichols grabbed Gabe's arm, but the programmer snarled something and wrenched himself free. He came for Ewan, stabbing in and parrying Ewan's counterstrikes with the buckler. Ewan retreated, trying not to rotate too much, but Gabe saw the change in his stance. Smiling triumphantly, he started harrying Ewan, striking in from the sides and dancing around him to make him turn.

Ewan stayed with him as best he could, but it was no good. He imagined his health bar shrinking as the world grayed out. Gabe patiently continued the attack, until at last Ewan was locked in a corner with nowhere to go.

"Well, O'Meara?" he asked, breathing hard as he dug the rapier's tip into Ewan's chest, ready to shove. "Will you bow to the inevitable?"

Ewan's heart hammered, punching his ribs more as it tried to beat the blade away. Behind Gabe, Nichols and Angela were running across the mat, stretcher at the ready. Now would be the best time to surrender. He'd bitten off more than he could chew, taking on all three at once. The Centrals had their confidence now, knew they could win in a fight.

But wasn't it even more important to show them never to give up, even when things went wrong? Even when the world cheated?

"Not on your life," he panted.

Gabe's eyes widened, but his jaw clenched. He stabbed forward, but Ewan twisted away, rolling the blade off his chest as he ducked to the right and jammed his feet into the mat. His ribs snapped, making him scream inside and out, but somehow he managed to keep his arms moving. His left blade slammed into Gabe's shins while his right struck the chief across the shoulders from behind, keeping Ewan upright a moment longer.

Caught off balance in the middle of his thrust, Gabe toppled forward, then landed on his face—just out of bounds.

The crowd roared.

Ewan fell too, but in an instant Nichols was looking down at him, shouting something he couldn't understand. Then Tree was there, and Angela, and Michael, all levering him onto the stretcher.

As his head flopped over, Ewan saw Gabe. The programmer was still lying on the floor, butt in the air and face frozen in stunned disbelief.

"Good fight, Gabe," Ewan rasped, coughing up blood. "Way to go all out."

Gabe's face colored, but he nodded stiffly.

Ewan gave him a vague thumbs-up, then finally relaxed and let the world get fuzzy as the doctor and caretakers carried him off to Medical again.

## 22

## DUTY CALLS

The worst thing about dislocated ribs was having them put back in.

Nichols wasn't particularly gentle about it, either. "It's a miracle no one was killed, the way you and Gabriel were bludgeoning each other," he said caustically. "What is the point of safety equipment and rules if neither of you bothers to use them?"

Ewan grunted as the doctor trimmed his armor off. "I guess we got caught up in the moment."

"You're lucky you're not caught up in a wheelchair again. Don't move."

Ewan didn't, but the world exploded around him anyway as the older man grabbed a rib and shoved it back into place with a pop.

"Couldn't you have given him something for the pain?" Tree asked anxiously.

"You're asking me that?" Nichols countered, jamming another rib home. "In this case, quick treatment is the best remedy."

"How long will I be in here this time?" Ewan asked, once he could breathe again.

The doctor sniffed. "You can go now. Try not to overexert yourself for at least a week, and check back in before attempting any more idiocy."

Tree took Nichols's instructions to the extreme, but despite her efforts to keep him in bed, Ewan was going stir-crazy by the end of the next day.

"Really, I'm feeling much better. Ow!" he yelped when she traced a finger over the purple-and-yellow swirls covering his chest.

She smiled, grimly. "Until your artwork fades, I'm keeping you here."

"Fine, but can't I at least sit up?"

"Oh, all right." She pulled her tablet over and turned it on, smiling as he levered himself up beside her. "Here. Grandfather's released the tournament footage. I'll let you watch it, if you promise to learn something from it."

*Good thing you don't know how I used limbo,* he thought wryly before saying, "Yes, ma'am."

Watching the duels on the tablet's little screen wasn't nearly as exciting as being on the mats, but it was nice to go back and look at some of the fights Ewan had missed. It was also fun to fiddle with the video controls, pausing and replaying the interesting moments. Before long, he'd grabbed his own tablet and started taking notes for his cadets, offering tips and thoughts on how they'd done.

His own bouts were a different matter altogether. It was odd enough seeing himself from a distance—he'd never realized how wiry he was—but that wasn't the reason he had a hard time believing what he saw.

"Gems, Tree, was I that fast in Veridor?" he asked, slowing the playback down to see his own moves better.

"Actually, you were faster." She snuggled carefully against his shoulder. "The mountains really honed our stats."

"I'll say," he murmured, staring at the finals match as it played out. How on Earth had he stayed in the ring when Sam whacked him? "But seriously, six months ago, I couldn't even move. How did I get so fast? And strong?" he added, watching himself flip Gabe out of bounds to win the tournament.

Tree giggled at the image of the chief on his face, then turned the screen off and gave him a playful kiss. "It's because you're wonderful."

A few bed-ridden days later, Ewan got a message from Nathan.

[Ewan? When will we start practice again? It's been a week.]

Ewan glanced at Tree, beside him. In reply, she jabbed a finger into his chest, hard enough to make him gasp.

[I'm still recovering,] he messaged back. [Tell you what. How about you take charge?]

[Me? But what about Gabe? Or Sam?]

[Gabe's already got a section to manage, and Sam's probably tied up.]

[I don't know...]

Ewan smiled at the typed hesitation, a plea for reassurance from the boy who had the most pressing reasons of all to keep practicing. [You'll be fine. You were a finalist too, you know. Would you ask Amy to help as well?]

[I'll do my best. And I'll keep you informed of our progress!]

As another week drifted by, Ewan found himself thinking more and more about home, unable to ignore a growing conviction he'd been away too long. Maybe it was because the tournament had fired his blood, waking his spirit along with the Centrals'. Maybe it was because he'd finally rebuilt himself and gotten adjusted to the real world, with nothing worse than the usual combat injuries to deal with.

Or maybe it was because Nathan's daily reports said the corps was doing just fine without him.

"Tree, what are we going to do?" he asked one evening as she dimmed the lights.

"About what?"

"About Veridor. It's been over half a year since the Diamond Lord came back. For all I know, he's run roughshod over the whole world by now."

Tree curled into him. "Your friend had the Amulet. I'm sure he's taking care of it."

"We don't know that. Isn't there some way to check in on everyone?"

"You...want to return? To the simulation?"

"Well, yeah," he replied, hackles rising at her tone. The one that said she'd already thought about it too—and come to her own conclusion, without bothering to tell him. "Wasn't that the plan all along? Go back in and get an army?"

"It was, yes."

The *but* fairly shouted in the silence that followed.

Ewan sighed, bracing himself. "What changed?"

"Love, we have an army now. One that the greatest adventurer in your simulation—"

"World."

"—personally trained. Given the hostile stance your Church took with me, Grandfather believes that forcing the issue with a return journey would be counterproductive."

"Counterproductive? Tree, what about my family? They've got to be worried sick by now, thinking I got logged!"

"They'd be correct," she said irritably. "And you're hardly the first person to vanish from his world to support it. You're doing more to protect them by training the corps."

"I don't want to work in the shadows. And it's not right that the rest of my world—or any of the worlds—doesn't know the truth. We need to bring out as many players as we can! Isn't that the whole point of our section?"

She twisted to face him, eyes hard. "And how would you feed them? You've seen what Earth is like, how limited our resources are. Even if the Church offered us ten thousand Swords, we couldn't bring them out."

He glowered right back. "That's your grandpa talking."

"No. It's the reality of the situation."

"But you were the one who logged in, in the first place! What were you going to do if the Church agreed to help?"

"I wouldn't have spent precious months as an outlaw instead of preparing our defense forces."

Ewan bit his tongue, barely. "Fine. But even if we don't go back to recruit, I want to check on everyone. Besides, the Diamond Lord admitted he was from Earth, too. Maybe we can deal with him out here."

"Ewan," Tree said with strained patience, "the 'Diamond Lord' is part of the simulation. It couldn't possibly have meant what it said."

"But Old Max—"

"Died centuries ago. What we saw was the Logos's creation."

That brought him up short, but only for a second. "But you've got the Logos on Earth too," he argued, holding up his tablet. "What if it knew something we don't, about the Gem?"

"In case you haven't noticed, we're not exactly overflowing with all-powerful beings in the Centre. If there were, we wouldn't be in such dire straits in the first place."

"I'm telling you, it doesn't add up!"

"And I'm telling you: it's not real and doesn't have to add up!"

"It's real to them! And it was real enough to you while you were logged in, in case you forgot."

Tree started to counter, but she sighed. "We're tired, love.

Let's discuss it more in the morning. I'm sure we can think of a way to contact your family."

Ewan flopped onto his back and winced. "Fine."

But once she started to snore, he pulled out his tablet and dug up everything he could on Veridor—again. As usual, he could find descriptions of the geography and culture, but there was nothing like a quest board, nothing to give him the latest news.

*Nerf it all...I just need to be able to send a message to Kate, or Paul.*

Then, at the bottom of one page, he spotted a little note directing further inquiries to Programming.

Chiding himself for not doing it sooner, he tapped out a message to Gabe.

The chief replied soon after. [O'Meara? What are you doing online this late?]

[I couldn't sleep. You?]

[Catching up on work from a week of medical leave, so if you don't mind, I'll speak with you at practice.]

[Wait! Gabe, is there a way to see what's going on in Veridor?]

The question hung in the tablet's miniature limbo, but eventually a response came. [Feeling homesick, are we?]

[A little, but it's not just that. When I left last year, I was involved in an Epic quest to hunt a Gem that came after Tree.]

[Come again?]

[A Gem. Basically an overpowered mob who should've been logged ages ago. He came back, and I was working to keep him from hurting my people.]

No reply came, leaving Ewan to stare at his own words and realize how crazy they must look to the programmer. [He claimed he was from Tree's world,] he added. [This world.]

Another moment passed. [That was no doubt harrowing, but rest assured there are no such things in reality.]

Ewan sighed. [Even so, I want to check on things in there.]

[What do you intend to do? Log back in?]

[I can't,] he typed, frowning. [Tree said her grandpa won't go for it, and she's with him.]

[How disappointing. What do you expect me to do?]

[Isn't there some way you could just hook my tablet up to message my family?]

He had to wait a few minutes for the next reply.

[After the Founding, the Centre had facilities designed to monitor conditions in the simulations, with an entire section dedicated to ensuring the original colonists adjusted to their new situations. The section was dissolved once it became obsolete, but the facilities were abandoned and left intact. I could refurbish one, with the Director's approval, of course. Even Annie wouldn't argue, then.]

[That sounds perfect! I'll see Rothchild as soon as I can.]

[Don't trouble yourself. I can do it later this month, during the general chiefs' meeting. If you like, I can even be discreet about your involvement, so as not to ruffle Annie's feathers.]

*A month?* Ewan sighed, glancing over at Tree's sleeping form. *It's still better than never.* [That would be great. Thanks, Gabe.]

[Don't mention it.]

Ewan finally got out and about in late January, but when he returned to the gym he found that another hundred Centrals had signed up for the corps, eager to feel the rush of combat for themselves. Nathan and Amy were leading them with such confidence and skill that when the scouts saw him and called him over, he merely smiled and waved before walking back out to the halls, more determined than ever to do his own job, once it got the Director's support.

And it did. After the chiefs' meeting, Tree came back with the happy news that Rothchild had approved Gabe's plan to refit one of the old monitoring stations.

"I seconded the motion," she told Ewan, face coloring a little. "We still need to keep our options open, since we can't anticipate what our manpower needs will really be...but the most important thing is that you'll have a way to contact your home." She looked away, watching the images of their Veridian forest glade on the far wall. "I'm sorry. Sometimes I forget you have a family that loves you."

He kissed her gently. "It's okay. Thanks."

It took until the second week of February, but eventually Ewan found himself putting in long hours on what everyone started calling the bridge, helping Sam and Michael install new equipment while Gabe worked on the computers.

"What's the point of bringing the tubes in here again?" Sam grunted as he strong-armed a large steel-and-glass cylinder into place alongside several others, all reclining at an angle on their new stand.

"Convenience," Gabe replied from under the bank of screens on the long wall opposite the doors. "If the Director determines that O'Meara should go back into the simulations, it would be more efficient to connect him from here instead of hunting around on the game floors for him."

"Exactly," Michael added, running a line of cables to the tube's back. The movement made his new pin flash: a sword and olive branch crossed over a shield, to match the ones Ewan and Tree wore as emissaries. "It will be easier for me to help Ewan up here. Or Tree as well, if she goes too. Where is she, anyway?"

"Tree?" Ewan asked as he held the tube steady for Sam to bolt in. "Um, she had a meeting."

"More likely, she's avoiding me," Gabe said, chuckling

under the spitting of his welder. "She never liked dealing with people she couldn't order around."

Ewan waited for Sam or Michael to argue, but they didn't. "But you're both chiefs, now."

"I'm aware of that," Gabe said dryly. "But I'm still her senior, regardless of how much she thinks she can invoke her grandfather to have her way."

"I guess you've known her a while," Ewan said, all too easily imagining little-girl Tree giving the chiefs orders from Rothchild's lap.

"It's a small Centre," Gabe replied after a moment. "We all know each other to some extent, but suffice it to say, Annie wasn't the most sociable person." Chuckling again, he added, "She's actually a lot more tolerable now, with you to act as a lightning rod for the rest of us, O'Meara."

Ewan grinned, despite himself. "Glad to help."

A week later, Ewan and Tree were trying to enjoy a sleep-in when her tablet chimed.

"It's Grandfather," she said, deflecting Ewan's attempts to pry the device out of her hands and haul her back to bed. "He says to meet him immediately."

"Want me to wait for you here?" Ewan asked hopefully.

She shook her head. "You're coming, too."

They headed for the elevators a few minutes later, running into Nathan on the way. "You too?" the boy asked anxiously. "I've never been to the Director's office before."

"Just let Tree do the talking," Ewan advised, giving his fiancée a wink.

When the doors opened onto the office, they opened onto a crowd. Amy and Gabe were seated at the ancient desk across from Rothchild, along with Karl Taylor and another chief with a compass insignia on his shoulders and graying, short-cropped hair over his weatherbeaten face.

"Please, take a seat," the Director said without preamble as the newcomers entered. "Master O'Meara, this is Chief Root of Scouting."

"Call me Ben," the chief replied, nodding to Ewan. "I saw your fight, O'Meara. Very impressive stuff you're doing."

"Um, thanks," Ewan said, glancing over at Nathan. "But I'm not the one doing it now."

"Which is precisely why Master Sanderson is present," Rothchild agreed. "I've called you all here as representatives of your sections and the Central corps, because we have a unique opportunity. Chief Reid, would you begin?"

"Certainly, sir." Gabe stood, smiling thinly as everyone turned to him. "We're due for a scheduled heavy maintenance of the mainframe computers in the coming months, replacing worn components and exchanging the coolant fluids. Unfortunately, we're short on materials, which Engineering tells me cannot be fabricated without a great deal of trouble."

He glanced at Karl, but the short man merely nodded, and the programmer resumed his seat.

"This maintenance comes up every ten years or so," Ben explained as he called up what Ewan assumed was a glowing map of the Wastes, floating over the desk. "Normally, we hit up Ruin 7, here," he said, spinning the map so he could point at a dot near what appeared to be a massive lake. "But it's currently in the restricted zone."

Ewan peered at the dot. "Restricted zone?"

"The area where the other transports went missing," Tree said. "Is there anywhere else we can find the materials?"

"The other usual source is out here, at Ruin 16," Ben said, spinning the map again to reach. "But that's rugged terrain out west, a lot harder to get our camels into."

Rothchild nodded. "If it was only a matter of getting the materials, then I would suggest that course. But there is more to consider. We cannot continue avoiding the northern reaches indefinitely, and at this point we have the means to reassert our presence in that area. How are the defensive modifications to the transports proceeding?" he asked Karl.

"We've outfitted one of the camels per Gabe's specs," the engineer answered. "Field testing was successful yesterday, although we went sparingly on the ammo."

"Excellent. And after last month's tournament, I know we have skilled fighters. What say you, Master O'Meara?" the Director asked.

"I'm sure we can handle whatever we find," Ewan said half to himself, mouth drying a little as everyone turned to him. "Besides, I want to see what's out there, so I can tell the Church back home and get their support."

"Aside from that," Tree added, "we need to know the nature of our enemy. I would rather we meet them far from the Centre."

"Agreed." Rothchild banished the map, then looked at each of them in turn. "This is a fact-finding mission as well as a scavenging operation, but I will be blunt. I want you to engage this surface faction. Show them we are not to be trifled with. Mother willing, you will neutralize them and resolve the issue then and there." He looked at each person in turn, dark eyes unblinking. "While Chief Reid will advise on the salvaging and Chief Rothchild will direct our player's actions, I'm assigning young Master Sanderson to lead the mission."

"Me?" Nathan asked, his voice cracking.

The Director gave him a reassuring smile. "As a scout and a tournament finalist, I have full confidence in your efforts. You will have support, of course, from all sections and corps members. Aside from Miss Black, who will be tasked with continued training in the event of a problem," he said, glancing over to a disappointed-looking Amy.

Nathan sat up in his seat. "Yes, sir!"

"Very well," the Director said. "I expect a mission plan this evening. You are dismissed."

"Wow," Nathan whispered as they all packed into the elevator. "I never imagined I'd be leading something like this. I've got so much to do!"

Ewan patted the boy on the shoulder, wondering if he'd looked so bright-eyed the first time his dad had taken him out adventuring. "Don't worry. It'll be fun."

## 23

## INTO THE WASTES

When the emissaries met Nathan and Sam in the dining hall early next morning, it was anyone's guess whether Tree or Chief Alice Spencer looked grumpier about the hour.

"I swear to the Mother, if Deering misses another early shift this week, I'll have her scrubbing the hydrolysis feeds for a month," the older woman muttered, tucking a strand of gray-blond hair back with its disheveled friends behind her peach-colored ear. She scowled around the room, counting heads a few times before looking down at the stack of boxes beside her. "Probably with Gabriel again, since he's missing too. You! Player!" she barked, glaring at Ewan. "Use that hard-fed strength of yours to carry his share, but remember that it's not yours to eat."

Ewan glanced at Tree, but she was also glowering at nothing in particular and didn't seem to hear. "Yes, ma'am," he said, taking Tree's box as well.

Unfortunately, the boxes' weight was a lot more than he'd bargained for. "What's in these things?" he grunted, lurching sideways across the hall when something in them shifted randomly.

"Food," Sam said obviously as he carried his own lightly under one arm.

"Probably flatbreads and dehydrated protein pastes," Nathan clarified without enthusiasm. "Plus the water to mix them in. They taste like sand, but they keep well. Don't worry. Once we get them to the galley, you can pull out the parts you want."

Ewan's arms were yelling in protest by the time they reached the elevators, but he forgot to be tired when the doors opened onto the biggest chamber he'd yet seen.

The room was round, more or less, easily a good five hundred yards across at the base. The walls curved in as they rose, meeting in a small circular ceiling about a hundred feet above the elevator shaft, where some sort of watchtower was built into it. The broad ring around the center was mostly empty, aside from a lot more foot traffic than Ewan had expected this early. Dozens of Centrals moved between the hulking metal carriages that crowded against the walls. Each person wore the same rugged brown armor as Ewan's party, some kind of padded real-world fake leather.

"Wow," he breathed, doing little dizzy turns as he tried to take it all in.

Nathan smiled. "Welcome to the hangar."

"How far down, or up, are we?"

"Ground floor," Nathan replied. He angled them to the left. "Just under the surface, just above the hole."

"It makes for easier transfer of materials from the ruins," Sam explained.

"How many of these things do you have?" Ewan asked, gesturing at the carriages and stumbling when a box tried to make a break for it.

"The transports? Several dozen, if you group all the different classes," Nathan said. He stood taller as he pointed. "You see those little ones over there? Those are 'roos—

kangaroo rats—to search out new sites. When they come back with a find, we send out the camels, like old Gertrude, here. We'll be taking her today."

It took Ewan a moment to realize that the building they were walking toward was actually a massive transport. The camel's wheels, six on a side, were encompassed by a belt almost half as thick as he was tall. Its body resembled a giant insect, with a small head in front of a bloated abdomen that looked big enough to hold his family's house, and Kate's workshop to boot.

"You're going to drive that?"

"That's right," Nathan replied with a smile. "Gertrude's a tough lady, one of the oldest in the fleet. More to the point, she's been modified to hold up in combat."

"How so?" Tree asked from right behind Ewan, making him jump.

Sam pointed with his free hand at a pair of bubbles on the top. "We added four gun turrets, based on the plans Gabe found. They're really fun to use."

Ewan shifted his boxes unsteadily to peer up at them. "Turrets? Like archery?"

"Like what?" Sam asked.

"It's something like that," Tree said quietly.

"Okay," Sam said, shrugging. "We also reinforced the exterior plating to offer better protection, just in case. See?" he asked, tapping a piece once they reached the transport.

Ewan looked at it, then frowned. "It's already got scratch marks."

"That's just normal wear and tear from the sand," Nathan said. Using his elbow, he pressed a button on a panel between two of the huge wheels. In reply, a small platform descended from above, near the beast's neck. "Okay, let's load up."

They stepped onto the lift and placed the boxes down—

Ewan and Nathan did, at least. Nathan pressed another button, and the whole thing lurched upward.

"Gems!" Ewan yelped, caught off balance while rubbing his arms. He stumbled, and for a horrible moment it was like he was back at the edge of the Argentine falls, but then Tree's hands gripped his waist.

"Easy, love. It's just like an elevator."

His skin crawled when something big and metal popped below him. "Elevators have walls."

Luckily, no one fell off. Once they reached the top, Ewan followed the others through an open hatch, hauling the boxes down a narrow corridor and into a small kitchen off to the left.

"We can unpack once we're on the move," Nathan said, looking as glad as Ewan felt to be rid of the frapping things. "Let's go see if the rest of the group is on board."

They made their way to a small room filled with seats, several of which were already occupied. A collection of screens covered the front wall, vaguely similar to how the bridge was taking shape, but below this was a bewildering array of dials and levers.

"Welcome to the cockpit," Nathan said proudly. "Everyone, this is Ewan, the player. He and Chief Rothchild are here as both emissaries and escorts."

Two women turned back and smiled, but a stern-faced, stone-skinned ponytailed man off to the side merely grunted.

Nathan cleared his throat. "Let's see...you all know Sam."

"Hey," Sam said, waving to the room in general.

"Ewan, this is Jennifer Tilley," Nathan continued, indicating the woman in the front. She looked to be in her thirties, with limestone skin and dark hair hanging loosely above her shoulders. "She'll be supervising the run."

"How's that?" Ewan asked.

Jennifer's head tilted as she regarded Ewan. "Nathan may be a great fighter these days, but he's still only apprenticing as a scout. I'm here to assess his performance, and give him a hand if he needs it," she added with a mischievous smile.

Sam laughed as Nathan colored. "You didn't think they'd let kids drive something this big alone, did you?"

"Anyway," Nathan mumbled, turning to a pretty brown-haired, almond-skinned young woman, maybe in her early twenties. "This is Maria Harris."

Ewan offered his hand. "Nice to meet you."

She took it gladly, but instead of shaking it she stroked it. "Such soft skin," she murmured. "We'll get you broken in yet."

Tree opened her mouth, but the ponytailed man beat her to it.

"Knock it off, Harris. I've only just eaten."

"And this is Vincent Coley," Nathan said, his smile fading. "He's been our liaison with the moles for the new weapons."

"I remember seeing you at corps training last month," Ewan said amicably. "Greatsword specialty, right?"

Vincent scowled at Ewan's outstretched hand without moving. "That's right. Once I heard a human was in charge instead of a player, I decided it was worth my time."

There was an awkward pause.

"This player is the reason we have a corps at all," Tree snarled.

"Just stay out of my way," Vincent growled in turn, at Ewan. "We're not here to play, worm."

"Yeah, sure." Ewan sighed. "Come on, Tree, let's go find—"

The doors slid open and Gabe strode in briskly, coming to a quick stop when he saw Tree still glaring murder at Vincent.

"Making friends so early in the morning, Annie?" he said pleasantly.

"And where were you?" Tree snapped, rounding on him. "You were supposed to help us carry the supplies up here!"

Gabe's eyes glittered in amusement at her clenched fists, oblivious to the spell she was no doubt imagining. "My apologies; I didn't realize the Director had also placed you in charge of package-hauling. If you must know, I was preoccupied with an urgent personal matter but waited for several minutes in the kitchen under the assumption I'd arrived first instead of last. I do hope O'Meara didn't mind carrying my portion, in addition to yours?"

Tree made an unflattering noise and stalked to the back row of seats.

"Take it easy," Ewan said quietly as he sat down beside her. "These are the people on our side, remember?"

"Hands to yourselves, children!" Gabe called.

Tree instantly released Ewan's leg, blushing at the snickers and another revolted curse from Vincent. "This trip is going to be a disaster," she muttered.

"Whenever you're ready, Nathan," Jennifer said as Gabe sat behind her.

A moment later, Gertrude rumbled to life.

Alarms blared outside. On the shaking monitors up front, Ewan saw people on the floor below, scattering to make room. Nathan hauled back on a large wheel mounted onto a pole, and Gertrude trundled backward, turning as the boy angled the wheel while using one of the screens to guide him.

He took them forward around the ring, turning again to face the outer wall before leaning aside to a microphone. "Camel I, requesting clearance from gate control."

Chief Root's voice responded over a speaker, crackling with static. "Clearance granted. Good hunting, Nathan."

The wall cracked, revealing a slit of yellowed daylight that slowly expanded into a massive, sandy opening. Nathan pushed forward on his control wheel, and Gertrude rumbled outside, vibrating steadily as she went—then lurched ahead, nearly throwing Ewan from the seat as Nathan let out a whoop.

As they banked around, Ewan saw the Centre out the right-

hand monitor: squat and rounded, like a steel version of the
domes of World's Edge.

"Wow," he breathed, straining his eyes to see the
observation deck where he'd stood months ago. "It looks so
small."

Tree took his hand. "It's all we have left."

The sun struggled to punch through the endless sandstorm,
but the best it could manage was a feeble backlight for the
scouting party as Gertrude ambled north at her steady pace.
Most of the others left the cockpit soon, eager to catch some
sleep while they could. Tree quickly passed out on Ewan's
shoulder, the camel's shaking be nerfed, but he kept staring at
the monitors out of a sense of duty, watching for signs of green
life.

There weren't any. Nothing but sand, and the occasional
blurry chunk of something.

After a while, Ewan gently scooted Tree's head to her seat
and undid the buckle keeping him in his own. He walked
unsteadily to the front, where Nathan and Jennifer were
discussing their best course while the camel somehow drove
herself.

"Hey, Ewan. What do you think of the Wastes?" Nathan
asked.

"It's very different from Veridor," Ewan said diplomatically.
"How do you navigate without the monitors?"

"We use old satellite data," Jennifer answered, indicating a
map almost exactly like the ones Ewan knew from home, on a
small screen between the scouts.

"Satellite?" Ewan asked, half expecting to see a quest
marker.

"Yes," Jennifer said. "Essentially, cameras that the people of old Earth launched into space."

"Space?"

She nodded. "You know, up above the sky?"

"There's something *above* the sky?"

"Well, yes." She gave him a curious, pitying look. "We lost contact with the satellites shortly after the Founding, so our base maps are out of date. We make updates from the transport telemetry after each run."

"A line-of-sight feed," Ewan said, feeling his way back to more familiar ground. "That's how the Logos does it in Veridor. Can you show me where we're headed?"

Nathan leaned over to point at a dot toward the top of the map. "This is Ruin 7, here. This is us," he added, tapping a blue dot in the lower part of the screen, "and that gray hexagon right next to us is the Centre. We should reach the ruin sometime tomorrow morning."

Ewan blinked. "Tomorrow morning? But the map says it's five hundred miles away."

"It is."

"That would take you across all of Veridor. In one day!"

Nathan grinned. "I guess you didn't have camels in your game."

"Not exactly."

Ewan heard footsteps approach, and he looked back to see Gabe. "Oh, hey."

The chief ignored him, instead turning a smile on Jennifer. "Tilley. If you're not busy, would you mind giving me the tour?"

"It would be my pleasure," she answered with a smile of her own. She rose quickly from her seat and patted Nathan on the shoulder. "Nathan, choose whichever route you think is best, but keep in mind, the gorge gets steeper as you go north."

"Can I come too?" Ewan asked.

Gabe stiffened, but Jennifer's smile broadened. "I don't see why not."

Ewan caught the programmer's glower, then realized what he'd interrupted—and accidentally invited himself along to. "Great!" he said quickly. "Um, let me go get Tree, too."

Gabe's expression turned incredulous.

Once Tree was awake, the four of them stepped out into the corridor, squeezing against the wall to let Jennifer pass through.

"Okay," she said brightly. "First time on a camel, all of you? You've already seen the galley and the cockpit. The cargo bay's through this door," she said, pressing a nearby button to reveal the camel's monstrous back room, largely empty. "Obviously, there's not much in there now, aside from tools and spare parts, but that'll change soon enough. There's a loading door in the back, so don't worry about squeezing the big stuff in."

Ewan nodded. "Where do we sleep?"

"General quarters are through here," Jennifer replied, guiding them farther along the hall. "Males on this side, females on that. Don't worry, we're not strict about it," she added with another coy grin.

"That's a relief—ow!"

Tree's hand smashed Ewan's fingers. "Perhaps we should practice using the weapon systems before a fight begins," she said firmly.

"A prudent idea, Annie," Gabe added. "Time enough for sleep later."

Jennifer looked between them, frowning as she tilted her head again. "Sure, if you'd prefer." She shrugged, then turned and passed the doors to reach a simple ladder, more like a series of rungs bolted into the wall. It led to a wire-frame walkway that branched out in four directions, two on each side. "Each of you can take a different turret."

"With pleasure," Gabe said, shouldering past Ewan to follow her up.

*Lay off it,* Ewan thought irritably. *Weren't you already busy this morning?*

Ewan climbed as instructed and soon found himself crawling up a second, smaller ladder into a glass bubble that immediately reminded him of Tree's shields, aside from the scratches the sand had already etched into its surface. The small space was dominated by a chair in the middle, seated to face a bundle of metal tubes, each about as big around as his arm. They protruded out from the glass, sealed by a rubber joint to keep most of the bitter air outside, but the side near the chair ended in a small box with handles and buttons.

Ewan sat, then stood again when he realized he'd sat on a funny little item made of three foamy circles connected by metal bands. He looked at it curiously, then jumped half out of his skin when Gabe's voice, slightly distorted, leaped out of it.

"Headsets work better over your ears than under your bottom, O'Meara."

Jennifer's laughter came from the thing, along with Tree muttering something. Ewan looked out across the camel's top and saw Gabe lifting his own headset off, then reequipping it with exaggerated slowness.

"Um, right," Ewan said, face burning as he tucked the item over his ears. *Sure, make me look stupid to impress your new girl.* "You Centrals do some goofy things to make up for not having a Logos."

"We make do. Tilley, please continue, now that we're all listening."

"Right," Jennifer said. "As I was saying, the moles had no problems installing these Gatling guns from the games, and they seem to work as intended. Do you see the pedals on the floor? Pressing those will rotate your turret side to side."

Her bubble spun, swinging the gun around. "Notice how the guns track up as you turn in toward the center, to avoid issues with friendly fire."

"I feel better already," Gabe said wryly, as Tree immediately turned in his direction.

"Aside from that, you'll find you can rotate your weapon anywhere in your field of view. Go ahead and face out, then try pulling the triggers to fire."

Ewan dutifully pressed on the left pedal, clutching his seat as it yanked him about. He squinted into the sand to hunt out a target, but there wasn't a lot to choose from, aside from the occasional boulder. He took aim at a pair of horse-sized rocks about a hundred yards off, then squeezed the little buttons.

The gun rattled and spun, belching a spray of metal and fire that pulverized the rocks in a flash.

"Frapping Gems!" he yelled as he dropped the handles.

"Do you have a feel?" Jennifer asked. "Good. Don't waste ammo, though. The moles went over budget building these things, but Ben will be sending 'roos out to search for materials to make more. Turn to face me, please."

Ewan turned back around, but the scout's turret—gun— was still pointed out, lining up on what took him a second to realize was a huge grain silo, half as tall as the Church's spire.

A ball of fire burst forth from the gun's tip, trailing smoke as it flew. It streaked toward the silo's base and exploded on impact, kicking up a shockwave of sand as the whole building toppled over and smashed into the ground beyond.

"We only have a few of these rockets so far," Jennifer said matter-of-factly. "So don't use them unless there's a need. Any questions?"

*None that I want to ask*, Ewan thought, staring at the smoke until it vanished into the dust behind them.

When his feet hit the corridor floor again, he caught Tree's eye. She gave him a sympathetic smile that told him he looked as ill as he suddenly felt. "Will you be okay?" she asked.

"Yeah...I just need to lie down for a bit."

Not waiting for a reply, he stumbled over to the men's quarters, which contained a series of cots arrayed in two layers.

Choosing one as far away from Vincent as he could, Ewan flung himself down with an anxious sigh.

*Those guns are totally overpowered,* he thought as he rubbed his face. *Gem-like. All you'd have to do is press a button and boom— the whole frapping world goes up in smoke.*

*Is that what broke this planet?*

Ewan eventually got to a troubled sleep, but it seemed like he'd only just closed his eyes when he woke to the sound of thumping overhead. Momentarily forgetting where he was, he sat up and reached for his swords, but then he heard Gabe grunting as he shifted in the cot above. A couple bunks over, Sam was splayed out, snoring like a behemoth. Below him, Nathan was curled up, facing the wall with a pillow clamped down over his ear.

Ewan lay down again, still breathing hard, but then the thumping picked up—and he heard Jennifer give an excited squeal.

*Oh, come on!* Ewan spun out of bed and angrily made for the door, then stumbled when he heard Maria's voice as well.

"Jen, the player's up! He's kind of cute. And shy, too. Come back; we'll make room—Gabe, don't pinch so hard!"

Face burning, Ewan ducked out and raced to the galley. Tree was there, looking exhausted and gnawing dispiritedly on a bean-and-bread sandwich.

He took one as well and sat beside her, slowing his breathing and counting his blessings he hadn't turned around. "Couldn't sleep?"

"I didn't want to. I don't trust my roommates not to bring someone else in there while I'm unconscious and defenseless."

"Yeah, well, I think you're safe enough," he muttered. "They're busy having a party with Gabe in my room." *That frapper had to get back at me for screwing up his date.*

Tree took a savage bite, then washed it down with a cup of water. "I can't stand these people!"

Ewan chuckled, despite himself. "You should tell them. They'd never suspect it."

She smacked him, but she did smile a little. "Now do you understand why I preferred to deal with the players in Dunbriar?"

*Like lighting them on fire?* he thought. "Yeah, I can see it." He took a bite of his own sandwich, deciding after a moment that it tasted more like clay than sand. "Sometimes I wish we could go back. To Veridor, that is. Things made sense there. No rockets, for starters."

"I thought you might not like that."

"Not like it? Tree, I don't like archers. Those things are more like a Gem's gear. What are they even doing here?"

"They're necessary," Tree said carefully. "If our enemy used something similar to destroy the other transports, then we must be prepared to use them as well."

"I guess," Ewan admitted, not liking the implications at all. "What did you think?"

"I found them comforting." She took another bite. "They remind me of my magic."

"Oh? How so?"

"They both require a force of will to use. The knowledge that the balance between life and death is a matter of targeting and focus."

Ewan recalled the silo toppling, for no better reason than Jennifer had noticed it. "It doesn't take a lot of will to push a button."

"It does if you care about the consequences." She sighed and put her food down, then snuggled up against his shoulder. "Love, would you take the first watch?"

Ewan sighed. *I guess we're still two against the world. Any world.* "Sure."

In no time Tree was asleep, leaving Ewan to wait and wonder if he'd been right about real-world Gems after all.

## 24

# THE MEMORIAL

Ewan woke feeling stiff, despite Gertrude's constant rattling massage. Trying not to disturb Tree, he stretched as best he could, wishing that real-world sleep would grant the automatic perks of a good Veridian rest.

Tree was still, almost as much as she'd been the first time he'd seen her sleep in Veridor. Back when she'd been logged out, leaving him a copy of her body for his own peace of mind.

*Not that I've had an overabundance of that,* he thought grimly. *Not since before that day.*

He sighed and slid his arm free, then rested her face on the vibrating table. Checking the stark pantry on the wall didn't give him any miraculous new food options, so he picked up his half-eaten sandwich again and started for the door.

It opened before he got there, revealing Vincent Coley. The scout froze, eyes locked on Ewan in a bemused glare for a moment—before seeing Tree.

"Don't you little shits have the decency to sleep in a bed?"

Ewan planted his feet. "Why should we, when the rest of you don't?"

Coley took a step toward him, but then Gabe appeared in

the hall. His eyes flicked from Ewan to the ponytailed man, and he reached out and gripped Vincent's shoulder.

"Is there a problem?" he asked neutrally.

"Yeah," Vincent growled. "We've got roaches in the galley."

He stepped aside, and Gabe stifled a chuckle at seeing Tree still face-down on the table. "Ah. I'm sure O'Meara will intervene for you, if you ask him nicely."

Vincent swore again and pushed out past the programmer. "I've lost my appetite."

"Don't mind Coley," Gabe said as he stepped in, edging around Tree to get breakfast. "He's surly to everyone without his coffee, or so I hear. I hope we didn't bother you last night?"

"I couldn't sleep anyway," Ewan replied, half truthfully.

Gertrude lurched sideways, causing the chief to stumble into Tree. Both he and Ewan flinched, but she only muttered incoherently.

Gabe carefully extracted himself, offering Ewan a sympathetic smile. "A lot on your mind?"

"Yeah. It's all so different from anything I knew. I never—it's hard to picture the other players getting the Church's blessing to log out, much less what they'd think when they got here."

Gabe's smile faded. "Yes...I warned the Director it wouldn't be as simple as recovering the nursery's refuse."

Ewan sighed, seeing the now-familiar Central pain in the programmer's face. "I guess we're all pretty split, huh?"

"For good reason. The staff barely has enough food, as it is."

"I know, but...we've got a lot to offer." Ewan closed his eyes, picturing the way Kate's lit up when she had an idea for crafting. "Maybe we can help change things, somehow."

"Perhaps you could, but what might you create in the process? Mistakes have a way of lasting here in the real world, as you may have noticed."

Ewan scoffed. "It'd have to be better than all this."

The programmer gave him a long, pitying look. "Would it?"

"Love?" Tree murmured.

Gabe silently excused himself, and after reading and rereading a little instruction label while Tree rubbed her face, Ewan managed to brew some instant coffee for his fiancée. He tried some, then quickly decided that if he could change things, the bitter drink would be the first to go.

After choking down his sandwich, he followed Tree to the cockpit, where Sam was humming tunelessly to himself while looking out the side monitor.

Maria turned around in the pilot's seat. "Where did you go last night?" she asked Ewan. "Jen thought we scared you."

"I wanted to stick with Tree," Ewan said quickly.

"She could've come, too," Maria said. She gave them a puzzled frown, then returned to the controls.

"Did everyone hang out or something?" Sam asked. "I guess I slept right through it."

Ewan shook his head. *Yeah, well, you weren't the one drawing Gabe's aggro by cutting in.* "So, what's our status?"

"We're almost there," Sam said, pausing to give a friendly nod to Nathan as the boy drifted in, looking like he hadn't slept through the fun but very much wished he had. "We've got plenty of fuel, since we're not hauling anything yet."

Ewan gave the young scout a sympathetic smile as he passed by to take a turn driving. "What does this thing eat, anyway?"

"Gertrude?" Sam asked. "She runs on oils distilled from the hydrolysis effluent, but we recapture as much as we can from the exhaust to route back in."

Ewan sighed, wondering why he was even surprised anymore. "Figures."

The mole shrugged. "It's a closed system. We all eat something's waste. They say the Mother did it that way too, but I guess she had a lot more to work with."

He turned around, leaving Ewan to fume to himself as the

rest of the party shuffled in—and as Tree pretended to fall asleep again, to avoid conversation.

After a while, the forward monitors revealed a low, gray splotch peeking through the dust.

"Is that our destination?" Gabe asked, reclining in his chair.

"That's it," Nathan said. "Welcome to Ruin 7."

"What kind of a frapping name is that?" Ewan grumbled.

Jennifer glanced at him. "A descriptive one?"

"It just sounds so—I don't know—dead."

"Then it fits well," Maria replied, trying another smile on him. "No one's been here for thousands of years, not since our ancestors left it for the Centre."

"You mean to become players," Ewan corrected, cutting her smile off. "Well, I'm giving it a better name. Let's call it the Memorial."

"Whatever you say," Sam said cheerfully. "It won't care, either way."

A few minutes later, Nathan sent Gertrude crashing through the outlying ruins with a lack of respect that sank Ewan's mood even further. When the camel finally shuddered to a stop, Ewan followed the others into the cargo bay to pick up their weapons and equip masks to keep the dust from clogging their lungs.

"Okay," Nathan said, his voice muffled and full of static over the mask's built-in headset. "We'll be here all week, so there's no need to rush out and do everything at once. Since we're on alert, I want two people on watch from the turrets. Anyone volunteer for the first shift?"

Ewan half expected Tree to sign up—alone in a bubble with a gun sounded just like her—but she saw his own hands hiding behind his back and pressed lightly against him, leaving Maria and Jennifer to tend the camel.

"All right, the rest of us will go in teams of three," Nathan said. "Sam, Gabe, you need to coordinate to get the best materials for the overhauls, so how about you go together, and I'm guessing you two want to stick together," he added to Ewan and Tree. "Vincent, who would you rather go with?"

Coley spat on the floor, then equipped his mask and joined Gabe and Sam.

"That works for me," Nathan replied with a touch of relief. He handed Coley a device that resembled a tablet's big brother. "In the event of contact with hostiles, call it in immediately and regroup at the camel. Any questions?"

No one spoke, so the young scout pressed a large yellow button by the door. A moment later, Gertrude's back side unfolded, making a ramp for the parties to follow to the surface.

The other party wasted no time splitting off, and before long, Ewan was stumbling down a broken street with Tree and Nathan, its surface pitted and cracked into a ghastly parody of Whitehaven's cobblestones under the dusty sky. Sand trickled across it, ushered on by the stiff winds; it stung Ewan's cheeks where the mask didn't cover.

They kept an eye out for anyone else in the ruins, but it was painfully obvious to Ewan that there wasn't anything alive in this place. Hadn't been, for centuries.

The sand crunched underfoot as they made their way, but more trickled past to pool up against the husks of hundreds if not thousands of small metal carriages lined up along the crumbled sidewalks, apparently abandoned long ago. Most of them had frames so pitted and rusted through that Kate wouldn't have bothered with them, and their broken wheels held only scraps of some mix of metal and rubber, an older and less durable version of Gertrude's treads.

Overhead, the dull sunlight cast its usual yellowed tinge on the skeletons of buildings, taller by far than anything Veridor had to offer. Their steel bones, also stained red with rust, swayed ominously in the winds, threatening to join their less fortunate brothers, already toppled across the ground to block the party's way here and there. Half-emptied window frames groaned as the wind blew through them, a haunted echo of what must have been a city bursting with activity before everyone left and the sands came in to patiently bury it all, an inch at a time.

"How many people do you think lived here?" Tree asked, peering up as well.

"I'm not sure," Nathan said. "We've probably got a figure in the archives, but judging by the number of buildings I'd say maybe ten, twenty million?"

"Gems of old," Ewan murmured. "Everyone in Veridor could fit in a place like this."

"Everyone in Veridor does fit in such a place," Tree pointed out. "They simply don't realize it."

Ewan ignored this. "Are all the ruins this big?" he asked Nathan.

"A lot of them are, yes. Though Ruin 7's one of the biggest."

They kept on, the emissaries mostly following Nathan around while he scoped out the buildings for raw materials. His scanning tablet apparently had the skill to peer through walls, but Ewan noticed the scout also looking about with the alert tension of someone expecting to get jumped any minute.

After a while, they arrived in what seemed to be the Memorial's version of a city square, lined with the remnants of buildings whose towering bulk made those on the outskirts look tiny. Statues ringed a broad swath of stone in the center, their features so weather-beaten and eroded that they were only just recognizable as being human. *Just like the Centrals,* Ewan thought darkly as he walked up to one, about the size of Old Max's statue in Whitehaven. Who had they been? What had the champions of Earth needed to do to earn such recognition, when there had been so many people?

"I wonder what it looked like, before everything broke," he said aloud.

Nathan shrugged and headed toward one of the more intact buildings, but Tree hesitated. "We have some images...and there are two simulations designed to mimic Earth as it was before the Rapture, to as fine a detail as possible."

"But this place is huge. How could you fit so many players into the Centre?"

"We don't. We use the Logos to simulate the remaining population, similar to how it simulated Maximilian's spirit in Veridor."

Ewan looked around the windows, trying to do the math. "But you're talking about billions of people."

"Not people," she said gently. "Simulations. They're not real."

*Who's not real?* Ewan thought, looking up at the worn figure once more, before following her into the building where Nathan had gone.

They spent the next few hours poking through it, splitting up and pulling chunks of wall apart to grab at the wiring inside, per Nathan's directions. It was depressing work, tearing up what little remained of the place—and somehow Tree's consolations, that it wasn't any different than eating the bodies of the dead, completely failed to lift Ewan's spirits.

It didn't help that now and then, he'd come across the skeleton of some small animal or another, preserved from the sands, for now at least. Most of them were curled up, as though they'd simply given up on living when their food sources withered away.

As he stooped to lift the remains of a small cat, no bigger than the one he'd had as a child, Ewan realized he was shaking. It wasn't just the humans who'd been driven off the face of the Earth. It was just the humans who'd gotten away, fleeing the consequences of whatever madness they'd inflicted on the planet.

*This whole world's one big frapping consequence. Any change would be for the better!*

But what could he do? He barely understood how the real world worked, and the more he learned, the more he hated it. His mom's gardening skills were good, but even she couldn't grow vegetables without sunlight, even if by some miracle there were still seeds to plant. But the sandstorms were impossibly huge, and they'd been around as long as Veridor had. He didn't have anything like Tree's shields to block them, much less a Gem's power to get rid of them altogether.

Tree was right: if the Gems lived here, surely they'd have fixed it by now.

Then Maria's voice tore through his headset.

"Enemies spotted on the ground! Four—no, six. No, dear Mother, where did they come from? We need help—"

Shots rang out, punching Ewan's ears. Maria cut off with a terrified scream, leaving only static.

25

## LOCUSTS

Ewan hadn't realized how far into the city they'd gone, but it took way too long to get back to the camel. He raced with Tree and Nathan under the darkening brown sky, hurdling debris while hiding his eyes from the stinging sand, wishing for one of Tree's shields as the stale air cut through the mask to burn his throat. The sand on the ground deepened as they moved toward the outskirts, concealing pits along with Gems knew what else, but they kept going as hard as they could.

All Ewan could think about, as Maria's scream echoed between his gasping breaths, was how there was no respawning in the real world.

"Don't overdo it," he warned as Nathan pulled ahead. "We can't fight them if we're tanked out."

Nathan sprinted on. "If we're too slow, there won't be anything left to defend!"

Ewan turned the corner to join him, then tripped into a hole and fell on his hands. "Nerf it all! Where did he learn to be so reckless?" he panted as Tree helped him up.

Her worried eyes answered him more than her words. "Go on. I'll catch up."

Ewan sprinted after Nathan, praying to the Mother when he remembered that the Logos couldn't hear him anymore. The boy knew what was out here, better than Ewan did. Surely he'd be careful. Surely he knew better than to just run up to whoever he encountered and start swinging.

*But that's exactly what you trained him to do*, he told himself. *You made it into a game for him.*

Swearing again, Ewan picked up his pace.

When the camel finally came into view, turrets smoking but silent, Nathan was already halfway to the lift. And when a robed person leaped up from hiding in the sand to block his way, the boy ran straight for them.

"Nathan!" Ewan shouted, coughing. "Wait!"

The scout gave a fearless yell, swords out. But the person raised their hand; light flashed out—gunfire—and Nathan fell with a cry.

The surprise in the boy's voice boiled Ewan's blood. Yelling, he charged the shooter, only to dive behind a piece of rubble as they trained their fire on him.

"Everyone, watch out!" he called into his headset as a swarm of bullets punched into the cover. "They've got little guns!"

"We know," came Gabe's terse reply. "Coley's been hit; I'm going to help him. Draper's on his way."

The shooting stopped.

Dearly wishing he had a map with red dots, Ewan peeked his head out. The enemy was advancing toward him, only twenty feet away now. They fired again, driving Ewan back, but Ewan spun around the rubble's other side and hurled his right blade. The robed person ducked aside, but the distraction was enough for Ewan to close and run the bastard through with his other sword.

A man's voice gurgled as the body sagged on Ewan's blade,

but Ewan slung him off and ran to Nathan. The scout's face was pale under the mask, and his eyes were distant, dazed.

"Hang in there!" He felt about, finding a hole blown through the boy's shoulder. He automatically called for his menu to grab a healing potion, but all he got was a bubble of panic, and bile in his throat.

Nathan's eyes glazed over. "I...tried."

"But you're not going to die," Ewan finished, a lot more firmly than he felt.

Tree came running to meet them, still darting glances around her. She dropped to her knees on Nathan's other side, but her eyes narrowed when Ewan revealed the wound. "We need a first aid kit."

"There's one in the galley," said Sam, puffing as he joined them from the other direction. "At least the Gatling guns work, right?"

Ewan looked up in confusion, but then he followed the mole's gaze. A good dozen corpses littered the ground, already half covered between their robes and the sand, but some were torn into bloody pieces by the camel's weapons.

Tree took a quick look around, then tapped her headset. "Harris. Tilley. Report."

A moment later, Jennifer's terrified voice whispered back. "They're here."

Tree's eyes narrowed even more. "How many?"

"I don't know. Three or four?" The headset crackled with her shaking sob. "They came up the side...got Maria."

Ewan's heart froze, but if Tree felt anything, she didn't let on. "Where are you?"

"In the turret. I...I closed the hatch before they found me. Help me. Please."

Tree broke contact, then looked at the others. "I'm taking command. Samuel, move Nathan to cover by the lift. Put his feet up, and keep pressure on that wound. We'll throw down a kit once we can."

Sam hesitated but nodded, then knelt to scoop Nathan up.

"Love," Tree said, locking hard, frightened eyes on Ewan. "You're with me. Loot the corpses. We'll disguise ourselves, then retake the camel and retreat."

"What about Gabe and Vincent?"

"They'll escape with us, if they're quick enough."

Ewan swallowed. "Yes, ma'am."

She darted off to one of the bodies, and he stepped over to the robed figure he'd impaled, thinking a bloody gash in his outfit might be less of a giveaway than a giant frapping hole. But when he pulled the robes free, he knew with a sickened jolt that blood was the least of the differences in appearance.

The man's copper-skinned face was scarred all over in what was obviously a deliberate, artistic pattern, as though he'd mistaken a knife for a pen. His nose and ears were pierced through with bits of metal, with hair and beard braided and bound in wire that could have come from the ruin's walls. His muscles were lean and hard, far better fed than should have been possible for someone from the Wastes. Even in death he had a feral air about him, a lingering lethal intent that had Ewan half expecting him to leap out of the sands again.

His hand still clutched a gun, hardly bigger than a tablet. Ewan reached for it, hesitated, and left it to retrieve his thrown sword.

He went back to Sam, waiting now near the bottom of the lift, and soon Tree joined them. She drew a gun of her own, inspecting it for a moment before yanking bank on its top.

It clicked.

"Careful," Ewan warned. "We don't know how they work."

In reply, she pointed it at the sand and fired, making him leap back with a yelp.

"Trigger's here," she said, indicating a little curled piece near the handgrip. "Pull back to arm."

"But how—"

"I told you, it's like magic." She scanned him, then huffed when she saw his empty belt. "Honestly, there are only so many ways it could work."

With that, she began scaling the camel's side, hoisting herself up on the wheels, grabbing handholds as if she was back in the Argenones. Ewan sighed, then hauled himself up behind her.

When he joined her on the lift platform by the now-open door, she gave him an unreadable look. "I want to know who they are," she whispered, "and why they're here. Make sure we take one alive."

"What if there are more?"

She ignored him, spinning to the door with the gun raised in both hands. "The hall's clear."

They checked the galley first, moving as swiftly and silently as they could, but aside from some ransacked containers, no one was there. Tree grabbed a white box with a red cross from the wall, then ducked back out to throw it down to Sam.

Ewan moved on to check the turrets, but then he heard movement in the cockpit. He glanced back at Tree and she nodded, eyes hard like they'd been when she was warding off storms in Veridor.

When Ewan peeked in, he found another cloaked person at the controls. He crouched, duck-walking forward—and his boots made a horrible crunching sound. He just had time to look down and see a patch of sand scattered across the doorway before the robed figure whirled around, gun coming up.

Ewan dove for the chairs, but the shot rang out from behind him with ear-splitting force. Cringing, he looked up to see Tree, smoke trailing from the gun's tube as she kicked the sand aside.

They exchanged a look, and Ewan scrambled to the man—

woman, he realized as he pulled her hood back to reveal black hair pulled back in a severe ponytail. Tree's bullet had punched her in the leg, but she didn't cry out or give any sign of being hurt. Or of being afraid.

"Take her gun," Tree ordered, still in the doorway.

Ewan pried it from the woman's fingers, trying to ignore the murder in her fierce dark eyes, the way her face was also done up in scars. Tucking the weapon into his belt, he drew a sword and held it at her throat.

"Do you understand me?" Tree asked, her voice a hard-edged threat.

The woman laughed, hoarse and bruised. "I understand you, hunt-maiden."

"Then you will surrender and be bound, for the attacks on our transports."

The woman's eyes burned. "Your transports are not welcome here."

"We've used these ruins for centuries," Tree countered. "You're trespassing."

"No. We claim the right of habitation. You are the trespassers."

"Habitation?" Ewan asked, shocked. "You mean you actually live here?"

"You do not?"

"No!"

The woman's face was confused for a second, but then she smiled. A hungry, triumphant smile. "Then the whispers are true."

"Whispers?" Ewan's blood chilled. "Who are you?"

"I am Ikrela, hunt-maiden of the Wolf Clan." Ikrela looked up at him, the scars lining her chestnut face indeed giving her an eerily wolfish appearance. "But who are you? Where do you live, you who take without possessing?"

"Don't tell her anything!" Tree snapped.

Ikrela huffed, but her eyes were locked onto Ewan. "Is this female your alpha, pup?"

Ewan decided not to answer that. Glancing back at Tree, he said, "If we want to know who they are, we need to be willing to trade."

"She is a prisoner!"

"She's a human being!" he shot back, half to convince himself. "Living in the Wastes, where no one else can. Doesn't that make you wonder how?"

"No one?" Ikrela said. She laughed again, her voice a soft growl. "No, pup. We are many."

*Many?* Ewan's stomach clenched. "But how can you survive out here?"

The wolf-woman continued to watch him, assessing. Waiting. "We take what we need, and we move on."

Ewan looked down at her, and for a moment he saw an image reflected in her eyes. An image from his nightmares: waves of people moving across the land, consuming everything in sight as they went.

Leaving a dead world behind.

"You're locusts," he whispered, tracing a drunken cut across her neck as his arm shook.

"No. We are the Twice-Forsaken."

"How many clans are there?" Tree asked, voice tightening.

Ikrela said nothing.

Tree shot the woman's other leg. "Answer me!"

But Ikrela barely moved, only showing the pain in her eyes. "As many as the Great Mother's children were; we are born to fill their place. Wolf. Lynx. Lion. Eagle. And many tens more, all answering the call. The whispers are true!"

"Call?" Tree asked warily. "What call?"

Ikrela laughed, leaning against Ewan's sword as she shifted. "Your own transports call us, hunt-maiden. We have caught the scent of the promised land at last, and we will come."

Tree pointed the gun at her head. "Not if I can help it."

"Tree, no!"

Ewan automatically moved between them—and the next thing he knew, Ikrela had hauled him down and had her pointed nails digging into his throat.

Using him as a meat shield.

"Foolish pup," she rasped, her musk strong enough that he would have reeled if he could have moved. "You are soft and weak, and foolish, protecting the hunter from her prey. Will your Alpha make the same mistake?"

Ewan looked at Tree's hard eyes and had a sudden, horrible certainty that she wouldn't. "We're not your prey!"

"You are from the promised land. I feel the fat in your flesh, the water in your skin." Ikrela dug her fingers into his throat, making him gasp. "Tell me where it is, and I may let you live as my pet."

Had Ewan not already been watching Tree's face, he wouldn't have gotten out of the way in time. He wrenched hard just before the gunshot rang out, flinging a bullet that disintegrated Ikrela's head right behind where his own had been.

"Gems of old!" He scrambled back from the corpse before staring up at Tree in shock, half imagining a bounty in his vision. "You murdered her!"

"I had to," Tree snarled, pushing past him and offering an oath of her own as she looked at the controls. "She's activated the distress call...there'll be more coming." She turned, looking like she might yet point the gun at him too. "We need to secure the camel and escape. Now!"

Ewan shivered, cursing himself for a fool as she kicked the corpse aside. What was he thinking, trying to save the locust woman when she was trying to kill them? What was Tree thinking, shooting at her without trying to talk more, when she'd been the one who wanted a prisoner in the first place?

What did Ikrela mean by *we will come*?

They moved back out to the hall, Tree checking both ways before stepping into the open. "Get Tilley. Tell her to start the engines."

"What about you?"

She spared him another dark glare before turning to the cargo bay. "I'm going to try to capture one, without your help."

Ewan sighed and climbed the ladder, quickly finding the locked hatch. Quietly, he rapped on the metal. "Jennifer?"

"Ewan? Is that you?" A moment later, she opened the hatch and fell into his arms. "Thank the Mother...is it safe?"

"Not yet. We killed one in the cockpit, but not before she signaled her friends. We've got to get out of here."

Jennifer nodded and eased her way past him, pressing up closely in a way that just the day before would have had him panicking for totally different reasons. Totally stupid reasons, given everything happening now.

He caught her shoulder. "Where's Maria?"

"Up there," Jennifer answered, pointing with her eyes toward the turret opposite her. "Be careful. I don't know who's with her."

Trying to stifle his breath as his pulse raced, Ewan crept to the open hatch. Soft wind greeted him, tinged with the Wastes' acrid foulness and the scent of blood. He poked his head through and saw Maria: slumped on the floor against the bubble with a dagger clutched in her hand, a series of bloody trails connecting her to as many holes in the glass above.

The chair turned.

Ewan hurled himself through the hatch and drove a sword to the hilt in the robed man's shoulder. The locust wrenched forward against the pin, grabbing for his gun, but Ewan spun his other blade in his hand and struck him across the face, hard enough to knock him out.

Heart hammering, Ewan shoved his second blade into the

man's other shoulder, then knelt beside Maria. The scout's eyelids fluttered as his fingers pressed into her neck, and he moved where she could see him.

"Player boy?" she asked, eyes glassy in a way he knew well but had never taken seriously.

Until now.

"You've got to hang on, okay?" he whispered, fighting the burning tears as he counted six wounds in her chest and belly. "Do it for me?"

Her pale lips lifted into a weak smile, but her eyes clouded over. "Too...late. Can't...now. But it...doesn't...matter."

A small, cold puff followed the words; then she lay still.

Ewan sat there for a moment, unable to move as the image —the picture of real death—burned into his heart. Gently, he closed Maria's eyes and activated his headset. "Tree, I've got one."

There was a loud crash and the sound of another gunshot, followed by Tree's yell.

Swearing again, Ewan dove back down the ladder, leaping off as soon as he was clear. He landed hard on the floor, then looked up to see yet another locust standing over Tree's downed form—with a gun pointed at her heart.

Ewan rushed forward, tackling him in a wild, desperate dive. They hit the floor, but Ewan stayed on top. The man tried to point his gun up, but Ewan grabbed his hand and twisted hard, breaking his wrist. The man tried to bite him, but Ewan grabbed his face and slammed his head into the floor, enough to crack his skull.

"Why?" Ewan screamed, smashing his enemy's head again and again. "What gives you the right to treat us like prey?!"

The only answer was the man's lifeblood, spilling out across the floor to coat both steel and sand.

The heat of it brought Ewan to his senses again, and with them came sudden, revolted horror. In Veridor, he'd always gone for quick kills. Partly for the cool factor, but also to show some respect for the quarry.

*But now*, he thought as he pulled his fingers from the corpse's throat, *now I'm showing as little as these bastards. There's nothing cool about any of this!*

Fighting the urge to retch, he crawled over to Tree. For a second his heart iced over, gripped by a cold wolf's teeth, but then her chest rose, and fell. There was no bleeding, not outside at least, but she had a nasty bruise on her face from where she'd been hit.

Thanking the Mother, Ewan forced himself to standing— just as Sam's panicked voice came over the headset. "Hey, I need help!"

Wondering if anything would go their way, Ewan staggered back out to the dusty lift platform.

On the ground below, Sam was swinging his hammer at another locust, a giant of a man coming toward him and Nathan. "Get away! You can't have him!"

The man reached out a massive white hand to catch the hammer's head. Grunting from the force of the impact, he twisted the weapon with incredible speed, and Ewan watched in stunned terror as Sam—big, hulking Sam—sailed through the air like a leaf on the wind to strike a piece of rubble, full-on.

"A cute toy," the brute rumbled, effortlessly tossing the hammer to flip it before advancing on the mole. "I will give it to my son, and he will decorate it with the bowl of your skull."

Ewan shouted, but the giant didn't hear him. He was out of range. Even if he jumped and somehow didn't break his legs, he'd never make it in time. And even then, he'd spent his swords. All he had was—

*The gun!*

Cursing his slowness, Ewan pulled the weapon free. His right hand wrapped around the grip, and his left yanked back on the top, like he'd seen Tree do. It clicked, and he took aim, stilling his shaking limbs to line up the little pegs on the tube's tips over the man's chest, exposed as the hammer rose.

He pulled the trigger.

The gun almost leaped out of his hand as his ears nearly burst, but the locust turned at the noise. His blow went wide, and instead of crushing Sam's head, the hammer crunched into his leg, provoking a scream of pain that tore straight into Ewan's heart.

Ewan lined up again and fired.

The man's robes burst red and he staggered back, looking up and roaring as he raised Sam's hammer again.

Ewan fired again, pulling the trigger over and over until the gun clicked and spat no more and he realized he'd destroyed the man, along with a piece of himself. Chest heaving, he threw the frapping thing away and slumped back against the wall. Just like Maria.

*What's wrong with you?* he shouted at himself as he crushed his eyes closed. *You know how to fight! How to kill! It's the reason you came out here!*

*No. It's the reason they brought me out.*

Another shot rang out from the ground. Cursing as the bullet pinged off the camel, Ewan dove forward and peeked over—and saw a pair of scouts shooting at him.

"Gabe! Vincent! It's me, Ewan!"

They fired again and he rolled away, wrenching off the filthy robes. "Guys, quit shooting! See?"

One of them took another potshot—*frapping Vincent!*—but the other pointed at Nathan and Sam. A moment later, Gabe's voice came in over the headset. "O'Meara, what happened?"

"We got jumped, but I captured one of them. Everyone's hurt, though."

*Or worse.*

Gertrude's engines roared to life.

"Wait!" Ewan shouted when the camel lurched forward. "The others are here; give me a second!"

Jennifer's voice crackled over the camel's speakers in reply. "Radar's reading three transports approaching at high speed from the east. We've got two minutes, tops."

"I'm not letting anyone else die today!" Ewan snapped as he jammed the lift button.

Gertrude stopped again, and a second later, Ewan was running out to meet the others. "Help me get Sam and Nathan on board—Vincent, what happened to you?"

"Just a love tap," the scout growled, pressing a locust robe to his face while holding a gun with his other hand.

Ewan's heart hammered out the seconds as the lift strained its way back up, but as soon as he was inside, he tapped his headset again. "We're on. Go!"

The camel plowed through buildings, making a wide turn to the south. Ewan and the others stumbled, but after a few harried seconds, they managed to tie Tree, Sam, and Nathan in place in the galley.

"They're giving chase," Jennifer warned over the speakers. "Everyone who can, get in the turrets."

Ewan looked at the people on the floor and table...his friends. He didn't deserve their friendship, not when he'd stupidly led them into—

"O'Meara!" Gabe snapped. "Move, or the rest of us will die too!"

Ewan shook himself, using his guilt as a focus. "Yeah, okay."

"I'm coming too," Vincent growled, strapping a bandage to hold the robe in place on his left cheek. "I'm not done gutting these bastards."

A moment later, they were taking their seats.

"Couldn't you find a better way to stow your prisoner?" Gabe's voice came over the headset, followed by the thump of another body getting dumped on the floor.

Ignoring him, Ewan swiveled around to the back. The clouds were dark now, but he could make out three streams of sand, turning sharply as Gertrude made her escape. A moment later, the forms of three very non-camel transports resolved inside them.

"Enemy spotted," Vincent shouted. "Eat this, you bastards!"

The other rear turret spouted fire and metal; one of the locust transports swerved and flipped over.

"O'Meara, you're in my way!" Gabe's livid voice came as fire streaked over the back of Ewan's bubble. "Take a shot!"

Gritting his teeth, Ewan lined up the Gatling gun and fired, nailing the second transport. It spun and flipped on its side, then exploded in a burst of fire and light that made Ewan wince.

"Incoming," Vincent warned as the third transport launched a fireball of its own at them.

This time, Ewan didn't hesitate. He led the rocket, streaming bullets at it until it blew up only a few dozen feet from Gertrude's backside, flinging metal against his bubble, cracking it in half a dozen places.

The camel shuddered, but it kept going.

"My turn," Vincent rasped with savage glee.

A rocket flew from his turret, tearing through the sky, leaving a column of fire in its wake as it screamed toward the last transport. When it made contact, it detonated with such force that the ground shook and the sands lit up in the only kind of day left on Earth.

Then the sound of shattering glass tore through the headset.

"Prisoner escaped!" Gabe shouted. "Running across the roof!"

All three turrets swung in toward the center, where the man Ewan had pinned earlier was sprinting for all he was worth, right past them. Everyone opened fire—but the safeties prevented them from aiming low enough to score a hit.

Vincent roared in frustration, shooting wildly into the sand as the man dove over the rear side and vanished into the darkened dunes. "I'm out of rockets! Player, do something!"

Ewan tried to blast the ground, but his sweaty, shaking hands slipped on the controls. "We should search for him," he mumbled, fear and shame wrestling for his heart. "Jennifer, stop the camel."

"If we do, we're going to lose more of the injured," she answered. "As the acting mission leader, I can't condone that."

"But—"

"You let him get away, you useless worm!" Vincent shouted. "You should've killed him when you could!"

"Coley," Gabe said wearily, "O'Meara was no doubt following his chief's orders to capture the enemy. I'm certain he wouldn't have done anything so blindly compassionate as allowing one of them to live and report back with our improved combat capacity. Am I correct, O'Meara?"

"Improved capacity, my ass," Vincent grumbled as Ewan cringed. "We just got ourselves trashed."

**26**

———————

# WORN WELCOMES

Tree woke up a few hours into the long ride home.

"What happened?" she asked, her dazed eyes finding Ewan as he came to cut her free. "Did we survive?"

He looked at the bodies on either side of her. "More or less."

She saw them and stiffened. "Do we have any medical supplies left?"

In reply, he pointed to the gutted boxes he and Gabe had looted from the cargo bay. "We already did what we could."

"You're not a healer."

"Neither are you!" Ewan snapped, instantly regretting it when she flinched and bumped into Sam. "Look...I'm—"

She pushed past him and snatched the kit. "I have to try. This is all my fault!"

*Hardly,* Ewan thought as he slumped back against the wall. *Admit it, Tree. I'm the wrong player for the job.*

She spent the next long while tending to the others, using her under-leveled skills to improve on what he'd already tried to do. She cleaned and dressed Nathan's shoulder, but when she cut open the bandage Ewan had clumsily wrapped around the mangled mixture of flesh and bone where Sam's leg had been, she retched and came to sit beside him, sobbing quietly.

Ewan sighed and looked at Maria's body, only a foot in front of him. Still riddled with bloody holes, because they hadn't had a reason to clean her up, not when there were others who needed it more.

Who had she been? What kind of person was she, beneath all her Central weirdness? Could they have gotten to know each other, become friends, even? Trying and dying together was a surefire way to make friends in Veridor.

*But this isn't Veridor. Nowhere even close.*

He replayed the mission in his mind, coming up with ways he could have saved her, could have prevented disaster. Most of them were at the planning stage, but that didn't do her any good now. Eventually, he just sat there and stared at her corpse, waiting for it to dematerialize like all the mobs he'd killed in fair play.

It never did.

There were no fanfares, no celebrations to welcome the party home the next day. After the doors had opened and Gertrude rolled into her spot with a smugness at taking only minor injuries herself, Robert Nichols and a crew of nurses swept into the camel to collect their new charges.

Eying Nathan's wounds with the skill of an aura reader, the chief gave Tree a small nod. "Not bad."

She glanced at Sam, then looked down. "It wasn't enough."

The other scouts said nothing, but the hard looks in their eyes, the glares after seeing Maria's black-shrouded corpse being carried away, were all pointed at Ewan.

Chief Root met them at the elevator. "The Director wants to see everyone who's able. Now."

Ewan followed the others to Rothchild's office, hardly noticing the ride. The Director was already seated at his desk, flanked by most of the rest of the chiefs and looking more ominous than Ewan had ever seen.

"Report."

"We were ambushed while exploring the ruin," Gabe said, his voice distant. "The enemy was extremely stealthy, adept at disguise, and armed with handheld firearms."

The Director's eyes narrowed. "And how did our own weapons fare against them?"

"We had a critical disadvantage at range," Gabe answered. "We could manage once we'd closed with them, but we were vulnerable until then."

"The camel's weapon systems were decisive, sir," Jennifer added quickly. "We were pursued by three transports, but between the guns and the rockets, we were able to fend off their attacks and destroy them."

Rothchild's eyes flicked to Gabe, then to Tree. "And what did we learn about this enemy?"

"A little," she answered carefully, "but we lost the opportunity to learn more when Gabriel allowed our sole captive to escape."

Chief Spencer paled. "He did what?"

Gabe scoffed. "A wild exaggeration, considering that Chief Rothchild was unconscious at the time. O'Meara managed to incapacitate one of them, but he didn't secure the man."

"Because I was saving the rest of your hides!" Ewan snapped.

"Like Harris?" Gabe said cuttingly, shutting him up. "Suffice it to say that in the heat of battle, the man roused himself and escaped."

"Escaped," Rothchild repeated. "To where?"

"The Wastes," Tree said. She shot Gabe a dark look. "From our interrogation of another woman who was later killed, we learned that these people live in nomadic clans. They wander the Wastes, scavenging food and supplies from the ruins. Like… locusts?" she asked, turning to Ewan.

He nodded.

"Evidently," she continued, "this locust nation has moved within our operational range and staked a claim to that area. I believe they now know enough about us—and the direction in which we retreated—to pose a dire threat."

The Director's face was expressionless. "And how do you propose to counter it?"

"With the same methods as before," she answered. "Log players out; train them to defend the Centre."

"Gabriel just said this boy's weapons and strategies weren't enough out there," Spencer countered, glancing at Ewan. "What's the use of bringing out more of them and starving ourselves, if they can't even protect the staff?"

The Director held up a hand, then tapped his tablet. "Chief Nichols, what is the condition of the injured?"

"Harris was dead on arrival, due to coronary trauma," the doctor's tired voice replied over the device. "Sanderson has a broken shoulder blade but should recover with near full mobility. Which is better than I can say for Draper; his left leg will need to be amputated. Coley's face sustained significant damage, and he is now deaf on his left side. I've not seen the others, but if they are with you, I'm sure there's nothing that serious."

"Thank you, Robert. Do you have any further comments?"

"Considering the fate of their predecessors, this group fared quite well, albeit not without losses. I believe Chief Rothchild is on the right track with her section goals. Now, if you don't mind, I have work to do down here."

The Director cut the line, then looked solemnly around the room. "You all know Chief Nichols administers his praise sparingly, but his remarks further highlight the question at the crux of our situation. Is it in the Centre's interest to continue recruiting players?"

"Of course it is!" Tree said, eyes widening. "Without Ewan, we'd have lost the transport and everyone on it."

The big chief of Security, Shane Powell, snorted. "It was the player's overconfidence that led you out there in the first place."

"Players aren't conditioned to Earth's limits and needs," added the gray-haired woman, Chief Maura Pell of Caretaking. "It's unrealistic for us to expect them to take real life any more seriously than the games they live in."

All eyes turned to Ewan.

"I take it seriously," he whispered.

"We've suffered a setback," Tree said. "But the players' resiliency is their greatest strength." She drew her gun and placed it on the desk. "With the right training and equipment, they can defend the rest of us."

Karl Taylor reached out and took it, gnarled fingers probing. "This is what they used?"

"Yes," Gabe said, sliding another gun to him before turning to the Director. "I'll cross-check the design with simulation data. Perhaps we can find a feasible improvement."

"We could also turn our attention to the southern ruins," Ben added. "There are dozens of military installations we've ignored, having never needed to use them."

The Director frowned. "All this is helpful, but it leaves open the question of who will wield the new weapons, especially in light of our defense corps and its performance today. Treanna, what argument can you give for continuing to recruit players, now that we have the technology and people to defend ourselves?"

"But we don't," she argued, voice heating. "There are only a few hundred of us, each one here to serve a specific purpose! We may be able to bring in more advanced weaponry, but no one here is trained to use it."

"No one in O'Meara's medieval world is, either," Pell countered.

"I grant that, but their warriors are experienced in combat, able to handle the kind of violence we saw out there. And...they are numerous. Thousands, even millions at great need, if only we can convince them to help. Isn't it in our interest to use them for combat, rather than risk sacrificing more of ourselves?"

Ewan glared at her as everyone fell silent, but she kept her gaze locked on the other chiefs.

At length, Ben Root coughed into his hand. "I've already lost people to these Locusts. People I can't replace. If Chief Rothchild and her section can get players to protect my scouts, I'm willing to tighten my belt to make room at the table for them."

"We're not just weapons," Ewan growled. "Players are people too, with loads of talent and ideas you'd never think of. The more of us you bring out, the better!"

Spencer scowled at him. "The Centre couldn't support that kind of indulgence, even if we were so inclined to try."

"He has a valid point," the Director said. "The players are in the simulations precisely to preserve the human spirit and ingenuity we will need to counter this threat. One player brought a scouting party home, and with our first real information about these Locusts."

Spencer turned her scowl on the Director. "Carmine, you can't be serious!"

"Things have changed, Alice. We must change with them. If swallowing our pride to replace our lunches is what it takes to ensure the Centre's survival, then that is what we will do." Turning to Tree and Ewan, he said, "Use whatever resources you can to expedite the recruitment and installation of player forces, and any justifiable support personnel. War is upon us, and we must be equal to it."

When they were dismissed to the elevator and she had no

chiefs to impress, Tree pulled close against Ewan. "I'm sorry," she murmured. "I said what I had to, or we'd never have had a chance."

"It's okay," Ewan lied, heart sinking as they returned safely underground.

When the emissaries reported to Medical the next morning, the ward was partitioned into a labyrinth of rooms by a series of thin curtains hanging from the ceiling. They heard Nichols in the back—in the middle of a quiet, heated argument with the Director.

"I'm telling you, the test results strongly suggest a connection!"

"Impossible," Rothchild said flatly. "For centuries there hasn't been any record—"

"Why would there be? I was lucky to find a template at all, between the data purges and clearance locks—oh, there you are!" he said loudly as he saw Ewan and Tree approach. "Can't you keep an appointment?"

"Is everything all right?" Tree asked.

Rothchild's face was grave as he indicated a pair of corpses on the beds beside them: the Locusts Ewan and Tree had killed, one apiece. Both missing heads. "Under the circumstances, yes," Rothchild said. "Chief Nichols kindly undertook the initiative to perform an autopsy in order to learn more about our mysterious enemy."

"Any luck?" Ewan asked.

The doctor exchanged a glance with the Director. "No."

"Whoever these people are, they are clearly adapted to the Wastes," Rothchild said. "It is possible, however unlikely, that they are the descendants of people who never registered during the Founding."

Tree frowned. "But why would they come now, after all this time?"

"I don't know. What matters now is ensuring they are kept at bay."

"Yes, Grandfather."

"Very well. If you'll excuse me, Master O'Meara?" the Director said curtly, exiting once Ewan got out of the way.

Nichols led them to a different room, where he examined them with an even more caustic attitude than usual.

"You have an infection," he groused as he probed the claw marks in Ewan's neck. "Didn't you think to use any of the antiseptic on yourself?"

"Don't mind him," Sam called through the curtain. "He's just disappointed that he couldn't mend my leg."

Ewan winced, but it had nothing to do with the stinging ointment Nichols smeared onto him. Once the doctor shifted his focus to Tree, he escaped to see the mole, laid up in bed with a bandage wrapped around the stump where his left leg had been.

"Sam...I'm so sorry."

"It's okay," Sam said, almost managing to make his smile look natural. "I'm just glad you saved the rest of me."

"I know, but still, if I'd only been faster..."

"Is that Ewan?" came Nathan's voice from the next room.

"Yeah," Ewan said. He gave Sam a pat on the shoulder before moving on to find Nathan and Vincent in a pair of beds. The older man grumbled and rolled away, leaving Ewan with a stark view of his bandaged head, but Nathan was sitting up, looking happy if anything.

"The Director came by earlier, and you won't believe what he asked me to do," he said.

"What's that?"

"He's just made the defense corps into a full section, and he wants me to be the chief!"

Ewan blinked. "He did? He does?"

Nathan's smile faltered, as it dawned on both of them that Ewan had just gotten fired. "Uh...sorry."

Ewan sighed as he looked around, at the results of his leadership. Nathan's shoulder was done up in a sling, and Vincent's ear wouldn't grow back. Sam's stump was still visible through the gap in the curtains. And in the room beyond, Ewan could just see Maria's body, no doubt marked for liquid cremation in a world where people were reduced to eating their own.

*And just like that, the Centre's down another scout, and an engineer is crippled. What would've happened if we'd lost a chief?*

Tree was right; they needed players. People who knew what they were about in a fight, people who could adjust to the new weapons. People who were expendable, because no one here thought of them as being people.

"I'm the one who's sorry," Ewan murmured. "It wasn't really my profession to begin with. Can I give you some advice, though?"

Nathan nodded, almost desperately. "Anything, please."

"Those guns are totally overpowered, but they'll run out of ammo. I think you should keep training people in melee weapons as well—and get onto Karl to make you some better armor."

The young chief's face fell as his new responsibility sank in. "I will."

Ewan sighed again and started toward Maria's room to complete his tour, but he froze when he saw a man already inside, with his back turned to the opening. He was leaning over Maria's body, shoulders hunched, but in the sudden silence Ewan could hear his anguished, choked sobs.

His own heart breaking anew, Ewan went to offer his condolences, but a firm hand gripped his arm.

"Best to give Master Frasier some privacy, O'Meara," said Nichols.

Ewan hesitated. "I got her killed. The least I can do is apologize."

"He knows; I assure you. I make a point of giving spouses a full report when someone dies."

"Spouses?" Ewan's heart twisted as the man, Frasier, bent to kiss Maria's shrouded face. "But she and Gabe—I mean, I didn't think you people, um—"

"Love each other?" The doctor gently turned Ewan away with a sad smile. "Some of us do, in our own way."

"I...sorry."

Nichols gave the barest nod as Tree stepped in, a second tablet in her hand.

"Robert's agreed to train me as a field medic," she said, her eyes also taking in the injured. "We'll need all the healers we can get."

"Good idea. Should I join you?"

She shook her head. "I want you to keep working on the bridge. Coordinate with Gabriel. Don't let him procrastinate."

"Yes, ma'am." Ewan moved to give her a kiss, but she was already walking away. Working to develop her skillset, without him.

When Ewan arrived at the bridge that afternoon, Gabe was there with two other people. One, a slender woman with mahogany skin, greeted him with a smile that was more predatory than friendly. The other, a shorter, ash-skinned man, turned, and Ewan winced in guilty recognition.

Gabe glanced back from a console. "O'Meara? What brings you here?"

"My duties," Ewan replied warily, suddenly feeling he'd walked into the wrong room. "Who are your friends?"

"These are my programmers. Alex Johansen," Gabe said, indicating the woman, "a systems manager. She specializes in heads-up displays and player-menu interfaces. And this is James Frasier, one of our game masters. They're here for the finer work, now that the hardware installation is complete."

*Frapping hell*, Ewan thought, his face coloring. *Maria's last lover was her husband's boss, but the aggro's all on me.* "It's nice to meet you," he lied, first extending a hand pointlessly to Frasier. "What does a game master do?"

Frasier's jaw clenched, making a vein twitch on his forehead. He pushed past Ewan—or tried to, but he bounced off. He glared up with a look of such raw grief and hate that Ewan stepped back, letting him storm past to the hall.

"Sorry, O'Meara," Gabe said. "I'm afraid Frasier doesn't much care for your kind. Frankly, I was surprised when he volunteered for bridge duty."

Ewan sighed. "I'm sure he has his reasons."

The chief gave him a sympathetic smile. "You understand that most of us try not to think about the simulations; as a game master, he spends his days constantly staring into them, debugging glitches as they occur."

"Debugging?"

"To ensure the players have as pleasurable an experience as possible," Gabe replied lightly. "Adjust a parameter here, and that stormy day clears up. Adjust another there, and you'll get 'bonus experience' in combat when you wear some trinket or other, so all your effort doesn't feel completely wasted." He chuckled to himself. "It really is mind-numbing work."

But Ewan's blood chilled as he imagined how *debugging* would look from inside the game. "Does he go there in person?"

"What, log in?" Gabe's smile turned mischievous. "Aside from Annie, no one's that much of a masochist. Frasier wouldn't stoop to it, even if all the women in the world lined up for him."

"He'd never get us to, anyway," Alex said, coming to hand

her chief a tablet as her dark eyes lingered on Ewan. "Even the player is built better than him."

"Thanks to Nichols's efforts," Gabe pointed out.

"Nice to meet you too, Alex." Ewan offered his hand, but he wished he hadn't when she grabbed it and pried up a fingernail. "Ow!"

She gasped. "It can feel pain here."

Ewan wrenched his hand back. "Of course I can!"

"Fascinating," she said happily, then reached out to squeeze his chest before he could dodge out of the way.

It went downhill from there: before long, Ewan couldn't believe he'd ever wanted to meet the programmers. He was totally useless as Gabe and Alex moved about the room, connecting wires and tapping on the consoles quicker than he could follow. And when Frasier eventually returned, the game master found his voice and used it to fling threats.

"Get out of my way, or I'll disable your respawning algorithm the next time you log in," he snarled when Ewan stood in the wrong place yet again.

"Can he do that?" Ewan asked Gabe as he quickly made room for the widower.

Gabe's smile was anything but reassuring. "In theory, yes. But we try to discourage such petty behavior."

Alex was friendlier, but if anything, that made it worse. She hounded Ewan with a barrage of questions about life in the game worlds as she worked, ranging from *Is it true that players don't remember Earth?* to *What does dying in your game feel like?*

"What about reproduction?" she cheerfully pressed. "I know the caretakers help you along, but can sexual interaction bring any pleasure to you? And now that you're out here, do you feel physically stunted from years in the tubes? Has anyone been twisted enough to have you?" she asked with a wicked gleam in her eyes.

"Please, Johansen, we're about to go to dinner," Gabe said.

He glanced up as the doors slid open to admit Tree. "But if you insist, there's the woman to ask."

"Ask me what?" Tree said.

"About how the player measures up to the men you've had," Alex said with a smile.

At once, the room felt colder than the Argenones.

"Not that it's any of your business, but he's worlds beyond the Central men!" Tree snapped, glaring at Gabe like Alex's rudeness was her chief's fault. Taking Ewan's arm, Tree muttered, "Come on, love. Let's go get something to eat."

Dinner wasn't any better. Tree ignored him completely, eyes on her medical texts, but plenty of people at the surrounding tables were happy to tell him to go back to the tubes and quit eating their food.

Like he wanted worms and corpse water, anyway.

The following days blended into a dismal haze, with Tree trying to comfort him by night, only to disappear by day to work with Nichols or confer with the Director, while Ewan resigned himself to fresh torture by the programmers. Wondering more and more why he was there when no one wanted him around, he started bringing his tablet with him to look up everything he could on Veridor—which was still next to nothing, even after Gabe hacked him into Whitehaven's quest boards.

Then one evening, while he was sitting on the bed, staring at the computer's forest images and trying to feel the late spring breeze on his face again, Tree placed her hand over his.

"Come with me," she said quietly.

She led him straight to the elevators. "Caretaking," she ordered as the doors closed, and the box took them down, opening onto a darkened office Ewan hadn't seen before. A broad hexagonal desk with a high counter dominated the center, but each of the outer wall's six faces opened onto a long tunnel with scrolling walkways, moving like a camel's treads.

Without pausing to explain herself to him or the few caretakers who glanced up at her from behind the desk, Tree led Ewan into one of the tunnels. A long, assisted walk later, they reached a cluster of elevators with glass doors and walls, arranged around a common shaft.

"Floor 823," Tree told the one they entered.

Ewan's stomach lurched when this elevator dropped like a stone, plunging them into near-total darkness, but as his vision adjusted, he saw they were descending past row after row of levels, each with tiny lights arranged neatly around the edges, as if the starry sky itself had been captured and put on low power.

Which it had, he realized.

"Tree," he asked slowly as he recalled the schematics from months ago. "Are we where I think we are?"

"The game floors," she confirmed. Her hand trembled in his. "This was where I came, every day. After I met you, I would come every night after logging out, to check on you."

"There are so many of us," Ewan whispered, staring almost against his will at the millions of lights sailing up past them.

"Yes...and we need their strength more than ever."

Eventually the elevator slowed, then stopped. With a chime, its doors opened onto a small platform ringing the shaft, connected to the floors proper by a number of bridges across an abyssal chasm. Tree took his hand and led him across, turning right and passing dozens of tubes under the hanging moss before arriving at one labeled 1742.

Her voice was hollow. "Here we are."

Ewan glanced at her, but her eyes were fixed on the tube. He let go of her hand and stepped forward to see what player lived here, still thinking all was well with the world. But the tube was empty, its small ventilation fan disengaged and the thin wire filaments hanging limply by the sides.

Staring at the pad, Ewan's spine tingled uncomfortably. Nostalgically.

"Tree, is this...?"

"Your tube," she finished, taking his hand again. Guiding him.

At once his heart started thundering, as he understood what she was doing. Did she really think he'd given up? Had he really been that down?

*Yes*, he realized with a horrible, guilty thrill.

"Tree—"

She silenced him with a kiss, then pulled back to lock teary eyes onto his. "I've been selfish, forcing you into the real world without asking your permission. Trying to make you fit into my life because I wanted you here with me, even though I've subjected you to the vilest abuses."

Ewan opened his mouth to protest, but no words came to mind.

Her hand released his and slid, shaking, to the tube's—his tube's—latch. With a practiced movement, she opened it, popping seals as the lid lifted away. The floor seemed to tilt in response, threatening to trip him onto the pad and right out of the real world.

His face burned when he realized he was leaning forward.

"What about you?" he asked, barely hearing his own voice over the heartbeat echoing in his ears. Just like it had, the day he'd been logged with only the barest warning. "What will you do?"

"Whatever I must." Her voice came from behind him: distant, bitter. Alone. "I have no place in your world, even less than you do in mine. But I swear to you, I'll protect you as long as I can. No matter the cost. I...I want you to be happy," she whispered miserably.

The pain of a thousand small cuts threatened to split Ewan's heart open, searing its every beat as he realized that she really meant it. That as much as she loved him, she was prepared to send him away.

That as much as he loved her, he was tempted to leave.

He took a step, leaning against the tube's sides, panting as he inhaled the faint antiseptic odor that lingered from a lifetime of use. Lifetimes, reaching back through the centuries.

"Forget about us," Tree whispered. "Live your life, the way you were meant to."

The fan above the headrest activated, calling him with the comfort of limbo, bringing with it the promise of all the simulated spring breezes and clear skies he could ever wish for.

Starry skies. And for the rest of his life, however long that would be, the shame of knowing he hadn't been equal to what lay beyond them.

"No," he said, and the floor righted itself, letting him see the myriad tiny lights with perfect clarity.

Tree's voice broke. "Why not?"

"I've got every reason." He turned and gripped her hand. "First of all, I love you. I'll never ditch you, or stick you with fighting battles that I was afraid to."

"But—"

Ewan shook his head. "All my life, I've looked for the deeper meaning in things, no matter how many times it killed me or made me enemies. You've shown me what the world's really like...and in spite of everything, I refuse to believe I have to choose between knowing the truth and being happy."

She blinked away tears, but her hand crushed his. "Love... I'm only trying to help."

"I know," he said, grabbing at the thread of courage holding his resolve together. "You've been helping me all my life. You and so many others, both here and back home. And I've needed it," he said, laughing and crying as he thought of the caretakers. The priests. His family. "I've absolutely needed it! But there are some things I have to do for myself. Some things that are my choice to make, no matter how much others try to make it for me. Tree...I choose to stay. I choose to *want* to be here in this world, because broken or not, it's what we've got. And most of all, I choose to make it better. Even if I die—really die—trying."

She stared at him a few seconds more, then pressed into him for a kiss so hard and passionate he nearly fell into the tube anyway. But his body was strong now, thanks to her, and he kept his balance: planting his feet on the hard, dark floor, refusing to let go.

After a long moment she pulled away, looking up at him with shining eyes that reflected the tubes' lights as brightly as they'd reflected the starlight in the Argenone mountains. She waited, silently, as he gently closed his old tube for good, then took his arm to lead him back to their home.

**27**

———————

# THE BRIDGE

EWAN STAYED UP A LONG TIME THAT NIGHT, STARING AT THE mossy ceiling while Tree snuggled against him, breathing slowly and deeply the way she rarely did when awake.

It was peaceful, the darkness. Still, in a way that gave him a chance to see things how they really were.

Once his eyes had adjusted.

The more he thought, the more his spirit kindled, a bright flame shining in that dark. Even Old Max had never logged out or learned the truth. Living in the real world was the biggest challenge he'd ever faced, that any player had ever faced, and he was determined to meet it. He'd wanted a big break, needed one for years, and he'd gotten more than his dreams—or his nightmares—had ever imagined.

Just hours ago, he'd contemplated giving up and running back to Veridor. Now, lying in the real world's limbo, Ewan wanted to return more than ever, but it wasn't to hide. Far from it.

*I am here to fight,* he thought with a relieved grin. *But I'm fighting to bring out the others. We can fix this world, I'm sure of it!*

When the alarm rang to signal the start of another dreary

day outside, Ewan shrugged off his habitual dread and sat up, flipping the blankets off Tree and getting slapped for his enthusiasm. They shared breakfast, which Ewan ate with pointed gusto, and then he walked her to Medical before heading to the bridge.

The programmers were there already, caught up in their work.

"Morning!" Ewan said with determined cheerfulness.

All three turned back to him, their faces ranging from Frasier's glower to Gabe's arched eyebrow to Alex's toothy grin.

The chief's blue eyes fixed on Ewan's, seeming to ask if he really had the resolve to stay and work. "You're late, O'Meara."

Ewan returned the gaze, unblinking. "I'm here now. What can I do to help?"

Ewan's spirits continued to lift over the next few weeks as he hunted out and found little reminders of the good he'd already done. Lisa's cheerfulness, while not entirely his fault, was reassuring, and she eagerly picked his brain for his favorite Veridian meals. He gave her the Swords' favorites, too, imagining Paul's reaction to the Central dining hall. The birthday song still drifted around the corridors. And Tree wasn't the only one with jewelry anymore; even Alex was wearing a mole-crafted necklace.

And every time he saw Nathan, Sam, or Vincent, Ewan reminded himself that he'd saved more people than he'd lost.

It all gave him the endurance he needed to deal with the programmers, which did eventually get easier. On the bridge, he made a point of engaging Alex, putting up with her tactless probing in exchange for answering some questions of his own. And in fairness, she treated him more like a human the more he did.

"Logos?" she repeated one afternoon, smiling at his explanation of how the Church's lock fees scaled with player inventories to make corpse-running unprofitable. "We just call it that because it's easier than saying 'Long-term Ordinating General Operating System' all the time."

"I guess so," Ewan admitted. "Who built it?"

"Oh, that would've been the Founder...what was his name, Gabe?"

"Bellview," the chief replied without looking up. "Honestly, Johansen, don't you know your history?"

"Yes, I do! Anyway, Director Bellview was a brilliant programmer. He developed the Logos, literally creating your world and everything in it, players aside."

"That must have been an epic quest in its own right," Ewan replied, before shifting to what he really wanted to learn. "Does that mean he programmed the Gems?"

"The who?"

"Gems. You've never heard of them?"

Alex thought for a moment. "Sorry, I haven't. I mostly work on the menu systems, not agents and rosters. James, do you know any Gems?"

Ewan looked over, but the thin man was already watching them with a smirk that raised Ewan's hackles. "There's no such actor in that player's simulation."

*Liar*, Ewan thought. "No frapping way. Our whole culture's built on the legacy of a war we fought with them! The last time I was in there, the Diamond Lord himself was hunting Tree down."

Frasier's smirk deepened. "You are welcome to return and try to ask it yourself, but if you wish to do so from the comfort of the bridge, then let me work."

Ewan sighed and glanced to Gabe for some backup, but the chief was restraining a chuckle of his own. "Sorry, O'Meara. I'm sure it was another, ah, epic quest, by the sound of it."

The bridge situation improved even more in early March, when Sam clomped in from Medical on the strength of a metal leg. It was a no-frills kind of thing, pretty much a straight length of steel with a spade bit for a foot, but the big guy's return helped Ewan relax—and look smarter, by comparison.

Tree received her medic certification around the middle of the month, but she still avoided the bridge like it was a cursed item. Instead, she devoted her freed time to training with the new firearms, scavenged from the southern Wastes and refurbished by the moles. As the bridge work moved further from hardware into software and the programmers got less patient with his interruptions, Ewan started coming to the practice range with her.

"We're coming a long way," Nathan said one day, after the three of them had finished a round. "Ben sent another party just the other day to scope out the old military bases to the west."

"That's nice," Ewan said, as the target papers crept back toward them along their tracks. "How goes the training with melee weapons?"

Nathan's face fell. "Oh…it's still going. Amy's leading most of the drills now, since my shoulder's not fully recovered. So, how do you like these?" he asked, jiggling his gun in a way that made Ewan flinch.

"Just like magic," Tree said kindly. "I'm sure the other players will take to them naturally."

*Not like you did,* Ewan thought in wary awe as she retrieved her paper and traced a heart around the cluster of holes in the target's chest. *At least you're in a good mood again.* Ever since that day on the game floors, she'd thawed out slightly with the other Centrals. At least, with the ones who treated Ewan with respect.

"When will you have more players out?" Nathan asked.

"Soon," Tree replied. "Gabriel claimed at the last staff briefing that the bridge would be operational within the week.

Even so, it will be months before they're ready for combat. Can you manage until then?"

Nathan nodded, looking older than his fourteen years. "Sure. We'll just have to pick our battles wisely."

Gabe's estimate proved true: six days later, Ewan was half dragging Tree as he sprinted down the halls.

"Love, slow down!" she said. "The message said no one's logged in to test it."

"But that's where we come in," Ewan laughed. "Who better to tell them if it works than a player, right? I might even get to see home!"

They rounded the last corner and went through the doors —to a room as different from the bridge Ewan had worked on, as Veridor was to the Wastes.

The far wall's monitors were a blaze of colors and motion, each depicting a scene from at least two dozen games. The tubes on either side, while empty, reflected the overhead lighting with an eagerness that mirrored Ewan's. One of them was open, letting Michael adjust the wire bundles inside.

"Hello," the caretaker-turned-emissary said.

Gabe glanced over his shoulder. "Ah, Annie. Finally decided to see what we've built for you?" he said lightly, giving Tree an amused smile that she completely failed to return. "If you'll kindly approach the rail, we can get started with our walkthrough. You too, Patton. You'll need to know how to handle things when these two are in their little world together."

"But won't you and the other programmers be here?" Ewan asked.

"In all likelihood, yes," Gabe replied, giving him a wan grin. "But regrettably, my staff have other duties and cannot be given entirely to Annie's whims. It would be a shame to have to abort a mission simply because no qualified personnel were available."

"I won't let that happen," Michael said. He closed the tube

and came over to join the others as they gathered around Gabe and the broad screen he'd built into the rail.

"This is the operations center," the programmer said. "We have secondary consoles along the front wall for multitasking, but a single game master can control everything from this position."

"Game master?" Ewan's scalp prickled. "You mean Frasier?"

"Sometimes, but we'll extend the term to anyone operating the rail for convenience," Gabe said, before sweeping his hand in from the left and tapping on a spiral icon. "Now, behold: the virtual galaxy!"

The console screen swept out to several clusters of small dots, which did resemble stars coming out in the early night sky, but Ewan found himself watching Gabe instead. The chief's eyes flashed with pride, the master programmer at home in his element in a way that Ewan had never seen, even from a man who'd taken to sparring like a natural.

*These are his worlds*, Ewan thought, awestruck to see his friend in this new light. *The Centre's greatest treasure—us—and his life's work is making it shine.*

"It's incredible," he murmured.

Gabe stiffened, seeming to hear Ewan's sentiment. "That, it is. Now, in keeping with general procedures, the game worlds are clustered according to similarities in global parameters and rulesets. Over here," he said, tapping a particularly dense cluster, "we have simulations which hold elements of the fantastic to them, such as magic or monsters. You'd be right at home in these, O'Meara."

"There are so many of them," Ewan said, finding *Veridor* among names like *Ilvenbael* and *Sah'rassa* as the words faded up beside the dots.

Gabe nodded. "It's hardly surprising, given the circumstances, that most of the original players opted for such games. If it's realism you want, you should try here."

He pinched the screen, returning them to the big picture, then tapped a cluster with only two dots.

Ewan read the names uncertainly. "Terranova? Galaxia?"

"These are the Earth simulations I told you about," Tree said softly.

"Learning secrets from Grandfather, are we?" Gabe chuckled. "In fact, Terranova was my inspiration for the camel's weapons. Unfortunate, but clearly necessary in retrospect."

He tapped on Terranova's dot, and Ewan jumped as the monitor bank turned into a single huge screen, magnifying one of the many smaller images until it was as though they were looking into the simulated world from a great window…

Onto a nightmare.

On the other side of the glass, two armies of epic golems clashed over the heart of a city, stomping people underfoot, swatting trees and buildings aside as they flung fire and steel at each other. As though Gertrude's rockets would have been a mere tap on the shoulder for them.

Ewan stared, horrified, as one burst into flame and toppled into a neighborhood. "Gems of old…I thought you said this was realistic!"

"What's not realistic about people killing each other for territory?" Gabe asked, manipulating the console to zoom in on the downed golem.

Ewan watched it blankly, then paled in understanding when a warrior crawled out of the mob's belly, only to be cut down by more gunfire.

Gabe's voice drifted across the back of his mind. "As Annie mentioned, Terranova is a full-scale Earth simulation. The players there can be as human as they like, without the less pleasant repercussions to the environment."

Ewan kept staring, unable to look away as the monstrous machines tore each other apart, along with most of the town they'd been fighting over. "At least they respawn, right?"

An awkward silence followed, which Tree broke at length. "No, love, they wouldn't."

"What?" Ewan whirled around, shocked to see no one else was furious. "But there's no reason for them to really die!"

"Of course there is," Gabe said. "Everything about Earth was simulated, except for the destruction of the world's ecosystems. Surely by now you realize there's no respawning on Earth?"

"But—look at them!" Ewan argued, waving his hand at the killing splattered across the monitor.

"I have," Gabe countered without humor. "Why do you think I recommended against recruiting players?"

Ewan glared down at the console, but he didn't know how to banish the image. "You said there was another simulation, right?" He turned to his friend. "Of Earth. What's it like?"

Gabe's jaw clenched. "Worse."

"We've seen enough," Tree said. "May I?"

"By all means," Gabe replied, moving out of her way as she took the console.

She tapped on it, and Ewan sighed in relief; then his breath caught as the battle vanished and the giant screen refilled with a lush green landscape of forests and fields, patched with late-season snows.

"Is that your world, Ewan?" Michael asked.

"Yeah," Ewan breathed, heart soaring as Tree took his hand and guided it to the camera controls. "You see those peaks there? Those are the Argenone Mountains. I'm glad we didn't try to cross them this time of year," he added to Tree with a playful grin. "So, if I turn like this, we should see...Whitehaven!"

He brought them about, hurtling toward the gleaming city faster than any eagle, almost feeling the wind on his face. *Kate's right*, he thought giddily, whooping as they passed through the

Church's great banner on the central spire. *A flying machine would be amazing!*

"What is the player doing at the rail?" came a sharp voice from behind them.

Gabe tsked. "Now, Frasier, he may be called upon to operate, especially if Annie's section swells with newly logged players."

Frasier snarled in reply, sweeping past them to one of the front consoles. "I've finished checking the connection protocols; we're ready to test the diving interfaces. Player! Climb in the tube!"

Tree rounded on Frasier, but Ewan patted her hand and offered him a rakish smile. "I'd love to. Tree, what do you say? Want to meet Mom and Dad?"

She hesitated, but nodded. "All right. Gabriel, log us in at Ewan's house."

Ewan showed Gabe his house on the console's map, then hopped lightly into one of the tubes.

"Try to relax," Michael said as he guided the wires to Ewan's temples. "This may hurt a little."

Ewan felt a light prick as they pierced his body, but the feeling soon faded, along with the rest of the room, as they sent new information straight to his brain, bypassing his eyes and skin.

He heard Michael's faint voice wishing him luck, and then everything went black and still.

For a moment, nothing happened, but then eight words appeared in the darkness.

*Ewan O'Meara: Logging into Veridor, Please Stand By...*

And then, just like that, his old bedroom shimmered into being. A light breeze ruffled his hair and Tree materialized, lying there right beside him.

He gazed into her dark brown eyes, convinced she was even more beautiful here than on Earth, but then her face paled.

"Ewan, behind you!"

The world turned red as pain stabbed through his heart, flinging his health bar up just in time for him to watch it fall to near nothing.

He looked down to see a steel blade, sprouting from his chest into Tree's, before it slithered through him, drawn back by its wielder. A massive, gauntleted hand grabbed him by the shoulder and hauled him up to within a foot of an all-too-familiar face.

"Welcome back, ghost." Caleb Martin sneered. "We've been expecting you."

# 28

# THE HOME FRONT

For a horrible moment, all Ewan could do was stare at Caleb's triumphant leer as his life bled out. But then Tree's healing spell coursed through him, and his wounds closed as if they'd never been.

*Gems, I've missed that!*

"Duck!" she shouted.

He obeyed, but not quickly enough to avoid getting his hair singed as her lightning tore into Caleb's steel armor. The Sword dropped Ewan with a cry as he staggered back to the dresser against the far wall.

"Where's that great aim from the guns?" Ewan grumbled as he drew his behemoth-horn blades, their grips fitting his hands perfectly.

"I'm a little out of practice," she snapped, zapping Caleb again and igniting the dresser for good measure.

Ewan rushed the commander, but Caleb lunged at him with a speed Jeff Harper could only dream of, grabbing him by the throat and flinging him *through* the wall.

Ewan picked himself up, just in time to duck again as the greatsword arced through the timbers and plaster. Caleb kicked him in the head, sending him stumbling into the kitchen table. From the other room he heard Tree shout, but a heavy thud silenced her and triggered a warning in his vision that she'd been knocked out.

"There's no point in arresting us," Ewan half taunted, half panted as Caleb plowed through his makeshift door, dragging Tree's body behind him. "Tree can log out again, and so can I."

"I'm not after the witch this time," the Sword growled. "My Lord wants you."

Ewan blinked. "Me? Why?"

"Because you've drawn his aggro!" Caleb swung his greatsword, simultaneously equipping a massive shield and catching Ewan with an uppercut that flung him across the room.

Ewan grunted as his health went under half again, but Tree was still out. Stalling for time, he asked, "So, you've been sitting here, waiting for me this whole time?"

"No." The Sword's hands shook around his weapon, but his eyes—mad, burning, zealous—stayed locked on Ewan. "My Lord was most displeased when the witch slipped his net at World's Edge. He stripped my gifts and departed for his realm, and the frapping priests locked me in the dungeons to rot. But my faith never deserted me," he said, glancing up as if to prove it, right then. "And lo! my Lord appeared again in the cathedral only last night, foretelling your arrival."

Ewan's blood froze. "Last night? He knew I was coming?"

Caleb grinned. "He made them release me, and he rewarded my faith with even more power and the honor of helping him destroy your soul!"

The commander grabbed the table with one hand and flung it at Ewan, following with a downward strike from the greatsword that Ewan only saw coming thanks to his map.

Mind racing, Ewan rolled up through the ruins of his mom's

kitchen...and he suddenly realized no one had come out to join them.

"Where's my family?" he asked, as a new dread clutched at his heart.

"Whitehaven." The Sword chuckled darkly. "I took them myself. The old man never even put up a fight, but that girl, though. She's quite the screamer."

With a curse, Ewan rushed the bastard again, but it was no good. Caleb's ridiculous new stats just absorbed the blow, and in seconds his hands were around Ewan's throat, crushing his remaining health away.

Ewan dropped his swords and beat at them, but they held firm. "They were innocent!" he gasped.

"Not in my Lord's eyes. He told me last night he's going to —argh!"

He let go of Ewan and clutched at his chest, then dropped dead right there, in the splintered remains of the O'Mearas' kitchen.

Ewan grabbed a sword and prodded the corpse, trying to make sense of what had just happened, when a message flashed up in his vision.

[Mother of all, O'Meara. Can't you get along with anyone?]

"Gabe? Is that you?"

[Of course it is. Resetting Annie's parameters now.]

"What?" he said stupidly.

[A simple 'thank you' would suffice.]

A moment later, Tree picked herself up. She brushed debris off her shoulder, giving Caleb's corpse a hard stare. "Thank you, Gabriel. Please reset the local environment as well."

Ewan yelped as the rubble flickered and was replaced by the intact furniture in its correct place. "But—what just happened?"

[I set that man's health to zero,] Gabe explained.

"But—that's cheating! I didn't ask for your help."

[I have a section to lead, O'Meara. I have neither the luxury nor the inclination to watch your imaginary swordplay.]

"We need to see the Patriarch," Tree added gently. She placed her hand on Ewan's arm. "The mission comes first, love."

Ewan wrenched away and rounded on her, too. "The mission's going to be an epic failure if you just kill anyone who opposes us! We're here to get these guys on our side, remember? We can't do that if you two go around acting like Gems."

[Shall I revive the brute?]

"No!" Ewan and Tree both shouted.

Sighing, Ewan added, "But no more cheating. We've got to play by the rules here and convince the Church to help us for the right reasons, or it won't count for anything."

[As you like, O'Meara. We'll be watching; shout if you change your mind.]

"Fine," Ewan muttered as the message box vanished, leaving him to glare at nothing. He looked around at the kitchen. Seeing it suddenly fixed by a Gem's power was somehow even worse than seeing Caleb tear it apart. The whole situation was unnatural.

Why couldn't the Centrals understand? Was it because everyone here was mere players to them? Or had they gotten so run down by the real world that they didn't care whether they cheated, so long as they survived?

*What choice do they have, with the Locusts bearing down on them? What choice do any of us have?*

Tree slipped her arm around his, bringing him back to the moment. "What do you want to do?"

Ewan closed his eyes, trying to order his thoughts. The Diamond Lord knew they were here, had known in advance. There was only one way that could have happened in Ewan's mind, but after Gabe's display, the last thing he wanted was to ask for more help. No, he'd deal with the Gem as a Veridian, but he didn't stand a chance without the Amulet.

Which meant he needed to find Paul.

"Let's go meet up with an old friend." He led her out the front door to the path up the hill, praying his family wasn't suffering too much for his sense of fair play.

It was a beautiful spring day, with only a few clouds frolicking across an otherwise crystal-clear blue sky as a cool breeze swept in from the north to ruffle the fields' grasses. Just like old times, Ewan and Tree took the back roads, ducking behind bushes and diving into ditches whenever his map revealed a Sword patrol moving by.

His Veridian body felt odd, as though it had slightly different specs than the one he'd rebuilt in the Centre, but the ease with which it responded and the richness of the world around drove home how powerfully immersive the simulation was—and how hard it would be to convince any player of the truth.

They made their way to Whitehaven without incident, and Ewan reluctantly allowed Tree to change their player registrations back to Cormac and Alicia Mullen as they squeezed in with the crowds moving in through the city gate. Oddly, the guards didn't seem to be on alert, as if the Diamond Lord hadn't shown up again the night before. Ewan didn't complain, and the emissaries slipped through the gate with no trouble.

"I kind of get the feeling Caleb's still being a glory hog," Ewan muttered to Tree as he led her down the side streets. "I wonder if any of the other Swords are even looking for us?"

"If he is, then it only serves to help us," she replied.

Eventually, Ewan's destination presented itself, the sign with the fleeing adventurer as outrageous as always.

Tree peered at the dragon. "The Toasted Tank?"

"Yeah." Ewan pulled the door open with a wince as the raucous tavern noise spilled out onto the streets. "Hopefully Paul hasn't given us up for logged after all this time. Not that he'd have been wrong."

"Is it always this crowded?" Tree asked as they stepped through, pausing as a greasy-haired bard sang about the joys of warmer weather and what it meant for women's gear.

"Yeah," he admitted, having to shout over the din. "Although it does seem especially packed now."

Her expression hardened. "Because of us?"

Ewan checked his menus, then laughed when he caught the date. "No, it's because of the festival! You see, every year on the turn of spring—that's today—the Church stages a little re-enactment of the Great War. At the end, Old Max chases the Diamond Lord right out of town." He shook his head, embarrassed he'd lost track after over half a year in the Centre's perpetual blandness. "I'm surprised they're holding it this year, what with the Gem actually being here again."

He jumped when someone gripped his left arm, then nearly jumped again when he whirled around to find the same barmaid he'd seen the last time he'd been in here. Her bright blond hair was pulled up in a pair of bushy pigtails, still long enough to frame a low-cut blouse that made Lucia Howe's uniform look like the picture of modesty.

She scooted close with a playful grin. "Hey there, stranger."

"Um," Ewan said after a moment.

"Um?" Tree snapped from behind him.

"Tina!" he blurted, using his aura reading to remind himself. "Tina Mayberry! She works here."

"I can see that," Tree said acidly. "How do you know her?"

"I'd be happy to serve you in our private room," Tina said

sweetly, winking up at Ewan as the nearby patrons began staring. "Will your sister be staying out here?"

"I'm his fiancée," Tree growled as the Logos warned Ewan she'd just equipped her dagger. "Now, how do you know Ewan—Cormac?"

"Oh, he's a friend of a friend," Tina answered smoothly, but she gave Ewan a meaningful look. "Besides, I'd remember those green eyes no matter what cover name he's got."

Without waiting for an answer, the barmaid twirled with a flip of her tiny skirt and dove back into the sea of waving mugs and pinching fingers, giggling and squealing all the way.

Ewan watched her for a stunned second, then stumbled forward when Tree pushed him. Some fool mistook her for another barmaid, but he quickly yelled and plunged his smoking hand in his drink.

[Don't you ever tell me your people are any less ridiculous than the staff!] Tree messaged through her snarling. [How do you know her, really?]

[She's Paul's friend! Nothing more!]

Tina led them through a swinging door into a dimly lit back room Ewan had never seen, filled with high-backed benches around little tables and bearing none of the main tavern's liveliness. She made her way to a table by the far wall, but when she turned about, her demeanor was completely different. Professional.

"Have a seat. I'll fill you in on Paul's quest status."

"You can do that?" Ewan asked. "I thought you just, um—sorry," he added, blushing as his eyes dropped of their own accord.

Tree smacked him. "Honestly!"

Tina gave them an amused little smile as she leaned back. "Paul's good-looking enough, but the best thing about him is that he's sharp. When he realized most criminal business gets started in rooms like this one, he approached me and offered to party up to ferret out the bad guys. He gives my boss a Church waiver on property taxes, and in return I keep him well-supplied with information."

"Gems of old," Ewan said, looking at Tina like he hadn't seen her before. Which, he supposed guiltily, he hadn't. "And that actually works?"

"Oh, yes," Tina replied. "We've nipped several plots in the bud, but this Epic quest you have him running is something else." She narrowed her eyes for a moment. "He says hi, by the way, and asks if you're still helping the lady Gem. That would be you, I take it?" she asked Tree sweetly, obviously not as afraid as she should have been.

"Yes, that's right," Ewan answered quickly. "This is Treanna Rothchild, from Earth."

"Never heard of it. Is that where the Gems are from?"

"No!" Tree snapped.

"Yes," Ewan said at the same time. He caught Tree's eye before continuing. "I don't know if Paul told you much about World's Edge, but I logged out with Tree to escape the Diamond Lord."

Tina gave him another knowing smile. "He may have mentioned that. I take it you were 'out there' all this time?"

"Yeah. Tina, it's nothing like anything you'd imagine...Hey, Gabe, are you still there?"

"Who?" Tina asked.

[Alex here,] came the reply a moment later. [We started taking shifts when it looked like you'd be in there a while. What do you need?]

"Can you get me a virtual copy of my tablet?"

[Sure, hang on.]

Ewan waited, then gave the barmaid a grin of his own when she gasped at the tablet's sudden appearance on the table.

"Here." He pulled up a few images of the Centre and the Wastes, before passing it to her. "Let me explain."

She took it about as well as he could expect, staring at the screen in horrified wonder over the next few minutes as Ewan described the real world, Central life, the reason for the simulations, and the Locusts.

"So," he finished, "Tree came to ask for volunteers, people to log out like I did and fight to keep the Locusts away from the Centre."

"I think I understand," Tina said slowly, her eyes still locked onto the tablet. "At least, as much as anyone could. So right now, we're in a game of some kind?"

"That's right."

"And there are people—like us—who keep us alive because their world got wiped out?"

"Our world," Ewan corrected, sighing. "The real one, at any rate."

"And they're...watching us?" Her hand went to cover her chest. "Even now?"

"I'm afraid so; some of them, at least. But don't worry; I've got some ideas about protecting our privacy."

"Good. A girl's got to be off-duty some time. But if these locust people are the problem, then how does the Diamond Lord fit into all this?"

"He doesn't," Tree said.

"Actually," Ewan said, turning to her, "I think he's one of the Central staff, trying to disrupt your mission."

Tree groaned and jammed her face into her palms. "Love, we've been over this so many times. There aren't any all-powerful beings on Earth!"

"There don't have to be! You were there this morning. You saw what Gabe did to Caleb from the rail!"

"Well, yes, but—"

"There's no difference between that and what the Gem's been doing. I don't even know how many times Frasier's threatened to glitch me in the past month, but if it's that easy, then I bet you all it would take is one determined Central, and a little help from a jerky programmer to get the right kind of access."

Tree's face instantly turned crimson. She opened her mouth, but then she glanced over at Tina, still watching them with her dazzling smile.

"As you can see," Tree said carefully, "we're not entirely certain. The most likely explanation is that this 'Diamond Lord' is just part of your simulation and playing its role, nothing more."

"But Frasier said—"

A fanfare exploded through the room from everywhere, with horns so piercing and insistent that all three of them dove for cover under the table. After a second the sound faded, leaving only a thrumming that rattled Ewan's ears.

Then a chorus of voices spoke in unison, seemingly from inside his head.

"Denizens of all Veridor, your Diamond Lord addresses you."

Ewan glanced at the others; their faces said they'd heard it too.

"Nearly one year ago, I returned to this world, my dominion, after a long slumber. I sought to protect you from a great evil, and through my beneficence, permit you to continue with your wretched lives as though you did not depend every moment upon me and my realm for your very existence.

"But some of you, foolish even for your kind, have resisted my advent. There is one among you who has even gone so far as to ally himself with a traitor from my own realm, deliberately upsetting the delicate balance of the worlds and exceeding the limits of my patience. For his reckless audacity in walking among us, and for his unforgivable stupidity in inviting ruin to us all, I sentence Ewan O'Meara of Whitehaven to annihilation of the spirit, beginning with the obliteration of those he holds dear."

Bile surged in Ewan's throat, scalding his heart as an image of his family appeared in his vision. They were in shackles, herded by a squadron of disgruntled-looking Swords—with a respawned and elated Caleb ordering them along—to a makeshift stockade in the main square.

"No," he whispered, literally unable to look away as the commander clamped them into it.

The Gem continued speaking, apparently to everyone in the world. "Lest there be any remaining doubt in your puny, deficient minds, let me speak clearly. I am your god. To defy me is to court oblivion. To Ewan O'Meara and any insolent fools like him, I offer this challenge: stop me, if you think you can. Come at once, and together—I invite you!—so I can eradicate you all the more conveniently. Everyone else shall bear witness to your destruction and renew their devotion over your ashes, that I may once again be merciful."

The voices ceased abruptly, leaving only the pounding of blood in Ewan's ears as he stared into the afterimage.

Shaking with fury, he looked over at Tree. "Still think he's not real?"

For once, she didn't argue.

**29**

---

## THE DIAMOND LORD

Ewan raced back into the street, with Tree right behind him.

"Love, wait!" She grabbed his arm to stop him.

He turned and glared at her, his heart still running hot. "You heard him! You saw Kate and my parents! There's no telling what he'll do to them!"

"If it is someone from the Centre, you can't fight him in here! Johansen," she called, looking up at the clear sky. "Report!"

There was no answer.

Tree checked her menus. "She just ended her shift. Frasier should arrive shortly."

"Frasier?" Ewan yanked his hair. "He probably *is* the frapping Gem! We can't ask him for help!"

Tree locked eyes on him. "But we don't have the Amulet. You rushed out so quickly, that girl never had a chance to tell us whether Paul even got it prepared. We can't go rushing into things again like we did in the Wastes!"

Ewan's throat tightened, but he wrenched free. "I have to do something."

He took off again, equipping his combat gear. With a muttered curse, Tree did the same.

A huge crowd of people was already there, as many as usually showed for the spring festival, but now they jostled nervously against the ring of Swords maintaining a perimeter. Gritting his teeth, Ewan slowed and pushed his way through, drawing more than a few nervous whispers and glares, but the soldiers made no attempt to arrest him or Tree as they entered the square proper.

Even across the wide space, Ewan could see a charred hole in the main cathedral's roof, but whether it was from the Diamond Lord's first visit or from the previous night, he couldn't tell. On high, someone had taken the Church's banner down from the great spire, giving it a much creepier, alien appearance, but Old Max's statue still held its swords, unyielding, on the ground below.

*Keep him off me*, Ewan thought at it. *At least until I've got my family free.*

The stockades were midway between the statue and the broad steps, flanked by several rows of priests and Swords—and Caleb, standing beside the O'Meara family with arms crossed and a grim smile as Ewan approached.

"Hey!" Ewan shouted, marching right toward them. "Let them go!"

Caleb sneered at him. The other Swords looked to the priests, who looked at each other.

But Jack O'Meara lifted his head in surprise. "Ewan? Is that you, Son?"

"Yeah, Dad. It's me!" Ewan stopped about ten yards away, hesitating. It was a shock to see how gray his dad's hair had become. How tired and haunted the eyes looked. His mom's, too, as she fixed a stare on him that promised a warm meal and a long lecture.

"Sorry I took so long," Ewan added, offering her a chastised smile.

Jack's brow furrowed. "But where have you been? They told us you were logged out."

"I was, but it's not at all like we thought." Finding the Patriarch among the priests, he called, "I've seen the other side: the real world!"

The old man said nothing, but he turned and swept back up the steps. The other priests followed him, as did a fair few Swords, ignoring Caleb's orders to stay put.

"This is all your fault, Tree-elf," Kate growled, straining against her bonds while the commander shouted at his men. "I'll wreck you! Kidnapping Ewan and—"

"Kate, it's okay," Ewan said. "She didn't do anything wrong —and we're getting married!"

Tricia gave Tree a sharp look at that, but Jack laughed almost as much as Kate did. "Married?" he asked, his broad smile out of place in the stockade, but much more like the man Ewan remembered. "At your age?"

Ewan's face burned as Tree's hand crushed his fingers, but he grinned. "Yeah. We've been through tons together, and I love her. Can we get your blessing?"

Jack glanced at his own wife, and they both nodded. "Of course, Son. Gems of old, it's good to see you again."

"Be quiet!" Caleb barked. He turned and cuffed Jack across the face, then jumped down to the stone in front of Ewan, equipping his sword and shield. "Playtime's over."

"You got that right." His own legs ready again, Ewan drew his blades and rushed the commander, as Tree cast a slew of buffs to his strength.

Horn met steel again, but this time Ewan was stronger. He stabbed right through the shield, then yanked the commander around to make room for Tree as she sprinted past to the platform.

"You there," Caleb bellowed at the few Swords he'd retained. "Kill the witch!"

They stayed put, as still as the crowd. As still as Old Max's statue.

"They're not going to help you," Ewan taunted, trying to stab Caleb's arm. "Not without your master to make them."

Caleb unequipped the shield to free himself, but Ewan was ready. As soon as it vanished, he swung at Caleb's head, forcing the other man to duck—right into the kick he'd already started.

Caleb grunted under the blow, but his free hand lashed out and snatched Ewan's ankle. He spun, twisting hard, and Ewan felt a horrible wrenching pain in his leg as he flew. He landed on his back, but before he could stand, Caleb was there, reequipping the shield and slamming it into his face. Head spinning, Ewan looked up as Caleb raised his sword high.

"You stupid noob. It doesn't matter how strong you are. My Lord will always—"

He yelled in pain and dropped the blade as a pair of axes swung into his sides from behind.

"That's what you get," Kate huffed. She pulled an axe free, then clanged it into Caleb's helmet when he turned. "Frapping kidnapper!"

Snarling, Caleb equipped another sword and lunged for her, but an arc of lightning ripped through him, staggering him with another yell.

"Thanks," Ewan grunted as Tree healed him with her other hand. "You too, K."

Kate looked at him like she hadn't decided whether to belt him, hug him, or cry. A moment later, she did all three. "You owe me, big!"

"I know," he whispered, grunting when his back popped.

"Ewan," Tree warned.

He turned for Caleb's next attack, but the commander was standing a good two dozen yards away, arms upraised in prayer.

"My Lord!" he shouted. "The boy is here, just as I promised! Come to me now and grant me your divine power!"

At once the sky darkened, or perhaps it only seemed to, in contrast to the swirling helix of light and fire that appeared high above.

"Oh no," Ewan whispered. "Kate, quick! Take Mom and Dad and go!"

The flames tore down with unreal speed, slamming into the ground—right where Caleb was standing. The commander just had time to yell and he was gone, consumed by his master's fire as a shockwave of wind and dust erupted across the square, knocking everyone to the stone.

*Like a rocket*, Ewan thought with surging panic.

"Kate!" He pushed himself back up to standing. "Go!"

The dust flew away to reveal a being in the center. It was human-like in shape, but it was tall, at least seven feet high, with great feathered wings of sparkling white that stretched out languidly. Its hair was a gleaming platinum framing a snow-white face, and when it regarded Caleb's remains, its icy silver eyes glittered above an even colder smile.

It looked at Ewan.

"I am pleased you were foolish enough to accept my challenge," the Diamond Lord said in a chorus of voices: male and female, young and old, the malice in each one a frigid knife in Ewan's heart.

"He's not a fool," Kate sniped. "He's brave!"

The Gem's smile broadened as he raised a hand. Kate shot through the air, yelling and kicking, straight to him.

"Courage is the hallmark of the ignorant," he replied, holding her by the throat a yard off the ground.

Ewan stalked toward them. "Let her go!"

"No." The Gem's smile broadened even more. "Not unless you offer me something worthwhile."

"How about a blade in your chest?"

The Diamond Lord laughed, his voices the harsh braying of hunting horns as he tossed Kate onto the stone. The moment the other O'Mearas went to help her, he threw up a shield to hold them.

"You wish to test my power? By all means, then; do your worst, fool."

Muscles strengthening as another round of Tree's buffs kicked in, Ewan rushed the divine mob. The Diamond Lord merely stood there, smiling and opening his arms wide in invitation as Ewan closed the final steps, swinging with all his might—

And bounced off, as though he'd hit Gertrude with a stick. The behemoth-horn blades shot out of his hands, humming from the blow. They clattered across the stone, and Ewan fell onto his backside.

"Well?" the Gem asked.

Fuming, Ewan jumped back up and retrieved his swords. Aside from Tree's cursing as she tried to break the shield, the crowd around them had fallen absolutely still, a cage of terrified eyes and voices that dared not protest.

Ewan walked up and hacked again, but his attacks glanced harmlessly off the Diamond Lord's robes. He struck again and again, swords skittering off the Gem's body, wings, and infuriating face, but nothing he did had any effect.

The Diamond Lord laughed softly as Ewan gasped for breath. "Entertaining as your failure is, you'll have to offer me better than that."

"How's this?" Tree called, just before her lightning struck the Gem, square in the chest.

For a fleeting second Ewan thought she'd done it, but then the spell rebounded, arcing into him instead to turn his world into searing agony.

"Stop meddling where you don't belong," the Diamond

Lord told her. "You've done enough damage, as it is. This is now a matter between myself and the player."

"I knew it!" Ewan rasped, standing gingerly as Tree undid her own spell's damage. "You're a Central!"

"Obviously." The Diamond Lord smiled again, ice in his eyes. "Have you still not grasped what 'Gem' means? G-M. Game Master."

Ewan's limbs numbed, but his blood heated. "Game master...Frasier! Is that you?"

The smile turned into a smirk. "You need only know my name here, in this delusion where you belong."

Ewan charged him again, only to bounce off once more.

"What do you want?" he asked, pacing in a slow circle around the Gem in a vain search for a weak point.

The Diamond Lord folded his hands in mock consideration. "Firstly, I demand that you remain in this place, and never trouble the Centre again."

"Not happening," Ewan growled. "I was invited."

"Only by that woman." The Gem sneered at Tree. "Don't delude yourself; you were never welcome. The real world has no room for your kind."

"The real world's full of players," Ewan shot back. "Just because you got adopted—"

In an instant the Diamond Lord's arm was buried in his chest, up past the elbow, the Gem's hand gripping Ewan's head from behind. Too stunned to even cry out, Ewan looked up at the pure murder in the silver eyes, and the fingers crushed his skull, replacing the world with the familiar death message.

But then the square re-formed around him, filled with the now-panicking crowd as his health returned to full, while the Gem towered over him.

"I must remember my strength," the Diamond Lord mused. He raised his arms, and a series of shields rose to contain everyone before he turned back to Ewan. "You die so easily, but I won't allow you to escape like that."

He reached down and grabbed Ewan, hauling him up by the hair with a snarl. "Yes, I would have been a mere player like you. But life had a greater fate for me, far more to teach me than my useless family could. And I have learned well. The real world is a place without mercy or hope, quick to crush any who would pretend otherwise."

Ewan struggled, prying at the Gem's fingers. "It's not hopeless."

"It is!" The Diamond Lord whipped him into the ground and killed him again, only to reset his health and haul him back up. "You've seen it with your own eyes. The Mother is long gone; she rejected humanity the same way my own flesh and blood did to me! The best we can do is ride comfortably down into oblivion, to pick at the corpses left to us. To prolong the inevitable."

Ewan beat at the arms, but they might as well have been steel. [Tree, get a hold of the bridge! We've got to stop him!]

[I've been trying, but there's no response! I can't break his shields, either—]

"Quit speaking as if I couldn't hear you," the Gem snapped, lashing out at her with a wing. "Ridding Earth of this player is the only way to preserve the Centre!"

He flung Ewan into Old Max's statue, breaking his back against the stone. "You've done nothing but make wild promises of miracles and a vibrant life, insistently blind to the simple truth of the world and our tenuous place in it. Now we are all faced with the Locusts hunting us! How many more will suffer and die for your ignorant hope?"

Tree healed him again, but Ewan barely noticed. Maybe it was some trick of his ears, or the dizziness from dancing on death's edge, but he suddenly recognized distinct voices in the Gem's chorus. Alice Spencer, furious that the Centrals would have to go hungry to feed a player army. Vincent Coley, appalled at Ewan's hesitation in the Wastes. Jeff Harper, enraged because a bit of player culture showed everyone how bland Central life was. And Maria Harris, her dead eyes laying the blame at his feet, saying it was better to feel nothing than to feel joy for only a passing moment.

*Mother of all...what if they're right?*

"We can beat them," Ewan said, his voice as unsteady as his legs as he pulled himself up again.

"Not with players," the Gem spat. "I give you a choice. Remain here in your blissful little fantasy, or I will destroy your spirit so that it doesn't matter what world you infest."

"Never," Ewan growled, charging again as Tree topped his health off. "I'll destroy—"

His body wrenched to a sudden stop, frozen a few feet away from the white wings as a warning flashed up that his carrying ability had gone to zero.

"I tire of this game," the Diamond Lord said quietly. He raised his arm, and a crystalline scepter materialized in his hand. "I will start with the girl."

He turned to Kate and dispersed the shield, but Jack immediately stepped in front of her.

"I won't let you hurt Kate," he said, calmly looking up at the Gem of old. "I won't pretend to understand what problem you have with Ewan, but the two of you need to settle it yourselves."

The Gem's eyes flashed, but he laughed, softly as snow falling onto a grave. "So this is a parent's love: throwing your life away to buy your wretched spawn a few more seconds. But then," he asked, his voice freezing over, "why have you not come to your son's aid, when he so clearly needs it? Could it be that you've already cut him loose, as all parents do to their real-world progeny?"

"Not at all," Jack replied. He gave Ewan a reassuring smile, as though they were debating over dinner. "Ewan's growing up;

he doesn't need my protection anymore. He's followed his heart to your world and back. Even if he's bitten off a mouthful again, I'm proud of him for standing up to a bully like you. He's got the right of it, and I have faith he'll win out in the end."

The Diamond Lord stared at him in disbelief. For a moment he looked haunted, almost afraid, even. Then his eyes hardened back into ice, and his hand tightened around the scepter as he leveled it at Jack's heart.

"Delete player."

Frozen in place, Ewan could only watch in horror as a searing ray of light erupted from the scepter. It slammed into Jack's body, and then he was gone, wiped from the world.

Kate stared, pale and shaking, at the void where her dad had been, but Tricia screamed and grabbed her, shielding her in turn.

"Tree!" Ewan shouted, still seeing his dad's serene face. "Get to the game floors! Hurry!"

"I can't! Log-out is disabled, and I still can't reach the bridge!"

*Then no one's coming for him,* Ewan realized as his heart threatened to burst. *No one even knows!*

He swore at the Gem, fighting with all his strength—and going nowhere. "You nerfing, murdering, evil—"

"I offer mercy again, player. Remain in this world and I will leave it, along with what remains of your pitiful family."

"No!" Ewan yelled, praying that his dad had been right. "I was summoned to Earth to help, and that's what I'm going to do!"

The Diamond Lord raised his scepter again. "Delete player."

With another flash of light, Tricia vanished.

"Of course, I don't have to say the command out loud," the Gem added conspiratorially as Kate scrambled back, her face as white as his wings as she stared up at the scepter. "But it does make for dramatic effect, doesn't it?"

Finally, Tree got him moving again.

Ewan roared, racing to cut the scepter in half as the Diamond Lord turned to Kate, but it was pointless. His blades rebounded off the rod, and the Gem knocked him aside with a wing, forcing Tree to heal him again.

"Delete player."

Ewan looked up just in time to see Kate's terrified eyes meet his, and then she was gone.

Along with his heart.

He let out a primal, anguished scream as he fell to his knees, tears raining down onto his armored hands.

"Do you feel it now, player?" the Diamond Lord asked softly. "The keening cry of despair from deep within your soul? The knowledge that no matter how many times you try, you simply cannot make a difference?"

Ewan tried to stand, to rush the bastard again, but his muscles couldn't bring themselves to move, not anymore. What was the point? If this was how the Centrals really felt, what did he owe them? If this was how the world really worked, then why bother?

*Kate. Mom. Dad...I'm sorry.*

"Good." The Diamond Lord chuckled as he walked toward Ewan, swatting Tree away again. "Perhaps you are one of us now, broken enough to live in the real world. Allow me to speed you back to the Centre, where you will trade your resignation for these players' continued existence." He waved his rod at the crowd, drawing a wave of screams. "With luck, you may even see your family at tomorrow's breakfast."

Ewan closed his eyes, resigned to his fate as the blinding light burst forth to consume his virtual body for the last time.

But a shadow jumped in the way, followed by a familiar grunt. "Gems, this guy's strong!"

Ewan opened his eyes in wonder. "Paul?"

"Sorry I'm late," the Sword panted, digging his shield into the ground as the Gem tried again to delete them. A moment later, an item transfer menu appeared in Ewan's vision. "Go on, take it."

Ewan stared at it, half aware of the Gem's red dot sweeping toward them on his map. "You're giving it back?"

Paul shrugged and glanced over his shoulder. "I saw your family. You know this guy, right?"

"Yeah."

"Then take him down. I'll back you up."

Ewan accepted, equipping the Amulet as soon as it touched his inventory. The moment he did, a message flew up across his vision.

[The Amulet of Balance is a Priority 0 Artifact, capable of revoking system access privileges from all other local players. Do you wish such revocation?]

Ewan had to read it twice, but then he shouted in his mind. [Yes!]

His movement penalty vanished, replaced by a surge of renewed hope and righteous fury.

"Paul...thanks."

"You can buy me a drink later. Right now, you've still got to take this jerk out."

"We'll do it together," Ewan began, but Paul flew off to the side, beaten away by the Gem's mace. He landed a good thirty yards off, rolled to the crowd's edge, and lay still.

"Why can't I delete you?" the Diamond Lord snarled, eyes wide in shock as he swung at Ewan. "What on Earth have you done?"

"What in Veridor," Ewan corrected fiercely, dodging with Tree's buffs on top of his own agility. "Even game masters have to obey the Logos's rules!"

The Gem overreached as his blow missed, and Ewan brought his blades down onto the rod.

This time, it shattered.

The Diamond Lord dropped the handle and leaped back, but Ewan swung again, slicing through his wings and tearing them open in a spray of crimson.

The crowd roared, almost as loudly as the blood in Ewan's ears.

He pressed the attack, driving his enemy back toward the cathedral's steps, but the game master quickly recovered, lashing out with a broken wing to fling him through the air yet again.

"Love, he's still overpowered!" Tree warned pointlessly as she healed him.

"Then I'm on familiar ground." Ewan wiped the blood from his face and turned to the Diamond Lord. "I'll give you a choice, now. Leave Veridor and never return...or I'll make you anyway."

"That's not a choice, you fool!" The Gem's face contorted in fury as he raised his arms overhead. "Clearly, removing your family wasn't enough. Delete! Delete it all!"

Screams erupted from the crowd as people—and chunks of the square—started vanishing. One of the yew trees dissolved into nothing, and Max's statue followed it soon after.

Ewan rushed the game master again to draw his aggro. The moment he got within ten yards, the deletions stopped abruptly.

[Tree, the Amulet only works if I stay close to him!]

The Diamond Lord spun around, equipping a flaming sword at least six feet long. "You," he snarled, the chorus of voices somehow even more murderous now. "Get out of my way!"

He lunged at Ewan with absurd speed, nearly taking his

head off with the first blazing swipe and forcing him to roll away.

[Tree!] Ewan messaged, beating out the fire in his hair. [Log out! Try to save the people he deleted!]

[But he'll kill you!]

[It's just a game for me now, remember? If Frasier's at the rail, take him out!]

She cast another set of buffs and backed out of the Amulet's range; an instant later, the Logos informed him that Treanna Rothchild had logged out of Veridor.

Unfortunately, the Diamond Lord stayed right where he was. Gritting his teeth, Ewan flung himself back into the fight, but he couldn't get close enough without leaving himself open to that ridiculous sword.

They danced around the broken square, flames leaping from the swords' contact and setting everything ablaze. The ordeal dragged on into an unending nightmare of fire and screams: Ewan fought to stay alive while keeping the Gem preoccupied with him, and the Diamond Lord kept beating him away, deleting every piece of Veridor within reach with no sign of slowing down.

"You can't protect them all." He sneered, driving Ewan back again and deleting a few more people. "You're only one fool, fighting a hopeless battle!"

"But he's not alone," came a voice from the cathedral steps, clear and strong.

Ewan glanced up to see the Patriarch himself, dressed in white-caped armor, leading three dozen priests with twice as many Swords flanking. "Veridor has no need for you, not when the Logos has provided!"

"Idiot!" the game master snarled. "The Logos needs me!"

"No." The Patriarch raised his hands to Ewan. "It needs a good man."

The tingling sensation of a strength buff coursed through

Ewan's body, startling him so much that he almost got hit by the flaming sword when it came around for him. Then the other priests raised their hands as well, and a symphony of warmth and power surged through Ewan's muscles, as though a bolt of lightning danced inside him.

"Gems of old," he murmured, as the Logos informed him his strength had gone up by a factor of ten. "Thank you!"

The Diamond Lord lunged, but Ewan batted the fiery sword away with ease, then spun inside to stab him through the shoulder as the priests superbuffed his agility, too.

The Gem cursed, kicking Ewan back and racing toward the priests, but before Ewan could chase after him, he got a party invitation from Tina Mayberry. Then another one came from someone he didn't know, and then dozens—no, hundreds— poured in, smothering his line of sight.

[Accept all!] he ordered, and his stats surged even more from the combination of every potion and enhancement the Whitehaveners had to offer.

The rush of power was beyond anything he'd ever dreamed of. *It's like I'm a Gem. Unstoppable! Is this what Caleb was after?* he thought dizzily as the broken ground seemed to fly under him.

He tore into the Diamond Lord, hacking a wing off as a handful of priests vanished from the simulation. "Quit picking on them and fight me fairly!"

"Only a fool seeks a fair fight!" The Diamond Lord turned to defend himself, but he was hard-pressed now. His face went from rage to shock to alarm as Ewan's blows began raining through his defenses. His health started to drop noticeably under the onslaught, but just as Ewan's first wave of buffs expired, the Swords rushed in to harry the Gem while the priests renewed Ewan's health and stats. Even the civilians joined in, flinging bottles of poison, and some more aggressive priests cast fire and ice of their own.

The Diamond Lord turned on them all, killing and

deleting, but it was too late. Ewan leaped in between the Gem and the Veridians, fueled by his people's support and faith, and the game master crumpled under his assault.

Finally, Ewan struck the Diamond Lord across the face, tearing his cheek open. He staggered back and fell onto one hand as he raised the fiery sword in a last-ditch defense, but Ewan swatted it away with his left blade and thrust with his right, straight into the bastard's heart.

"I'm going to find you out there," he rasped, staring into silver eyes, burning with hate as the Gem's health dropped the rest of the way. "And I'm going to make you pay."

The Diamond Lord spat blood in his face. "You won't have magic and miracles to save you there, player. The real world is cruel and harsh, and it crushes anyone who pretends otherwise. You and your ideals have no place there."

"Then I'll make one," Ewan answered.

A message from the Amulet appeared, offering to delete the Gem's avatar and profile.

"See you soon," Ewan promised, affirming savagely as he twisted the blade.

The Gem's body disappeared, in a now-familiar rush of wind.

Ewan slumped to the cobblestones, feeling a staggering dizziness as the buffs and potions wore off, a piece at a time. His blades suddenly felt too heavy in his hands; as they dipped into the bloody pool around him, he sank with them, staring bemusedly at a message indicating that the duel had just gained him several levels' worth of experience.

But the crowd roared in triumph and rushed over to their champion. In a frenzied moment, they lifted his exhausted body and passed it across to the priests by the cathedral steps. They set him down gently, and someone replaced his behemoth-horn blades in their sheaths.

*Kate's masterpieces...Sis, they were perfect.*

The Patriarch stepped forward, his white armor and sand-colored face stained with soot and blood, and Ewan rose unsteadily to face him as his bounty helpfully displayed itself in his mind's eye.

"Ewan O'Meara of Whitehaven," the old man said solemnly. "You have caused our Church no end of trouble this past year. You drew censure for your heresy, aided a fugitive, assaulted countless holy warriors, and conspired with one in our service to risk—and ultimately succeed in—bringing the Gem's wrath down upon us all. And, most of all, you have defied our sacred teachings by returning from the world beyond logging. Have I missed anything?"

"The city square has been demolished, Father," a nearby priest offered.

The Patriarch nodded, then fixed his hard eyes on Ewan again. "Yet despite the danger to yourself and everyone around you, you ultimately aided the girl from the Gems' realm and defeated the Diamond Lord, when we believed this to be as impossible as returning from the world beyond. You have given us much to ponder."

He paused, but for once, Ewan didn't have anything to say.

"I offer you my thanks, along with the gratitude of every Veridian. With the power vested in me by the Logos, I absolve you of your crimes."

He narrowed his eyes slightly, then frowned before giving Ewan a wry grin. "You'll have to unequip that amulet, child, now that we're out of combat."

"Oh. Sorry, sir." Ewan hastily returned the Amulet to inventory; a moment later, his bounty dropped to zero, then faded out. "Thank you."

"Assembled citizens," the Patriarch called out, his face proud and grave as he looked around. "I present to you Ewan O'Meara, the Hero of Veridor!"

He grabbed Ewan's hand and thrust it into the air, but Ewan only swayed as the crowd thundered its approval.

"Sir...Father. I can't."

"And why not?" the Patriarch asked, a knowing gleam in his eyes. "Do you really want no recognition at all, after all these years of boasting in confession?"

The other priests chuckled.

"Thank you," Ewan breathed, awestruck, but as he looked out, all he could see was the devastation in the square—and the absence of the people he'd come for.

"I'm sorry, but I need to go now, to try and save everyone who got wiped out. There's a chance Tree and I can do something for them, but only if we act quickly."

The Patriarch rested his hands on Ewan's shoulders in blessing. "Then by all means, Hero, do your best."

"I promise," Ewan said, already accessing his menus and calling up the new icon to log out. *Tree was right. I'm not just a player anymore.*

"I'll return with news, as soon as I can. Will you hear Tree out, now?"

The Patriarch nodded. "You have earned our ear. We will await your return, emissary to the other world."

Ewan started at the title, but then he smiled and bowed, heartened that the worlds could at least agree on that point, as the square around him disappeared.

**30**

---

## FACING REALITY

The blackness only lasted a moment, then vanished abruptly with the tickling sensation of the contact wires retracting. Seconds later, Michael wrenched the tube open.

"Ewan, are you okay?"

"Yeah," Ewan lied. He looked past the caretaker. "Where is he?"

"Who?"

"Frasier! Did Tree already get him?"

The bridge's doors slid apart and Tree stormed in, followed by Carmine Rothchild. The Director regarded the monitor, still locked onto the devastated square. His face darkened; when he spoke, fury laced his words.

"Where are the programmers?"

"Coming," Gabe huffed as he raced in, wearing casual clothing with shaving cream half-covering his jaw. Still breathing hard, he pushed through to the rail, but his eyes narrowed as he read the output.

"Report!" the Director thundered.

"Give me a second!" Gabe dragged the back of his hand

across his face, then slammed the console. "Someone hacked into Veridor. What did he or she do in there, O'Meara?"

Ewan bristled. "He deleted my family! And others...I don't even know how many."

"One hundred sixty-seven," Gabe supplied, tapping furiously while Alex entered the room and took a seat at one of the front consoles. "Along with deletion of eight percent of the local environment. Johansen, salvage what you can from the buffers."

"Yes, sir," Alex replied. "I should have any residual player profiles within the hour."

"They won't last that long in the tubes," Ewan said anxiously. "We've got to save them. Have you started getting them out yet?" he asked Tree.

"We have not," the Director said.

Ewan whirled to face him. "What?"

"Need I remind you that we lack the resources to support that many players suddenly entering the real world?"

"Need I remind *you* that the Church isn't about to help a Centre that leaves its people stranded to die?"

"They need not know."

"I just told the Patriarch we're doing everything we can to save them!" Ewan jabbed a finger at the screen. "If I go back and tell them you didn't even try, that you let one of your own murder them? You can kiss your player army goodbye!"

The room went still, aside from the programmers' tapping.

The Director's voice was distant, a deadly storm on the horizon. "You had no authority to make such a promise."

"Even so, it has been made," Tree said quietly, watching Ewan with all the meaning of a private message. "And witnessed. Reneging now could set us back by months, while we negotiated with another simulation."

Ewan yanked his hair, to keep his hands off the Director's

throat. "People are dying, right now! Good people! Parents, and children! Saving them is the right thing to do—the human thing to do." He glared at Rothchild, racing heart counting down the seconds left for deleted players, struggling to move. His family, dying for no good reason. "Prove that you're as human as we are."

Even the tapping stopped.

Rothchild's eyes bored into him, seeming to quietly assess just how much trouble his pet player was going to be in the long run. Whether a player army was worth that trouble. Whether Shane Powell would be capable of simply knocking him out and dragging him back to the game floors.

Then he sighed, blowing through his beard. "Yes, you're right, of course. Treanna, report to Chief Pell with my orders to rescue the logged players with all due speed."

Tree spared a proud, worried glance at Ewan, then raced out of the room.

"See that your Church cooperates," the Director threatened as the programmers resumed their own rescue attempts.

Ewan offered a hand in truce. "I will, sir. Thank you."

But Rothchild ignored him. "Report," he repeated, to everyone.

"The Diamond Lord jumped us in Whitehaven," Ewan said. "The moment Tree and I logged in—"

"For a test," Gabe interrupted. "They encountered one of the player soldiers, from whom O'Meara learned his family had been arrested. They elected to stay in-simulation to deal with the problem, believing that making use of the rail would be, how did you say, O'Meara? Cheating?"

Ewan's throat tightened. "Yeah."

"Then this whole incident could have been avoided," the Director said.

"But Ewan did get his people to listen," Michael said, glancing down when all eyes turned to him. "They helped him fight off the Gem."

"You witnessed it?" Rothchild asked. "Master Patton, tell us what you saw."

"Well...Tree messaged me twenty minutes ago, saying there was an emergency. When I got here, she had logged out on her own, but Ewan was still inside, fighting in the square. Fighting with an angel."

Rothchild waved his hand dismissively. "But who was on duty, here?"

Alex exchanged an uneasy glance with Gabe.

"James was supposed to be," she replied, meekly.

The Director's face darkened again. "Supposed to?"

"When I finished my shift, the emissaries were talking to a player girl," Alex explained. "There wasn't any sign of immediate trouble. I had a date planned..."

"And you didn't wait for him to report in?" Rothchild roared.

She looked to Gabe, but if anything, his face was even angrier. "No, sir. I'm sorry."

"The rail log shows it was never locked," Gabe said slowly. "Anyone could have come in and used it."

"But no one was in here when Tree logged out," Ewan protested.

"Enabling remote control via a tablet is something even the likes of Lisa Deering could do," Gabe countered. "Whoever it was need only have been present long enough to establish the link."

A vein twitched on Rothchild's temple. "Can you track the culprit by the avatar used?"

Gabe tapped for a moment, then cursed softly. "No. It seems that O'Meara somehow effected a profile deletion—from within the game. All relevant data and metadata have been erased from the archives."

Just then, James Frasier came hobbling through the door on crutches.

Ewan rushed the man and punched him in the face. Frasier's hawk nose crumpled, and he fell to the floor with a cry.

"You bastard!" Ewan stomped at the man's head, but a pair of hands grabbed him from behind, followed by Gabe's voice in his ear.

"O'Meara!"

"Let me go!" He tried to break free, but his friend's arms hooked his own, pinning him. "It's him! He's the Diamond Lord! Look at him!"

"Bloodthirsty imbecile!" Frasier snapped, cradling his broken nose. "What is the meaning of this?"

"There has been an incident," Rothchild said. "Where were you?"

"Medical," Frasier answered, hauling himself back onto the crutches when no one helped him. "Being treated for a sprained ankle. Now I'll need to return for my nose."

"I'll return for your head!" Ewan snarled, struggling against Gabe's pin.

"Reid, get him out of here!" the Director ordered. "Expect a full inquiry into your section's procedures, first thing tomorrow morning."

"Yes, sir," Gabe growled, before wrestling Ewan through the doors.

Ewan kept trying to break free. "Gabe, listen—"

"No, you listen!" the chief hissed, shoving Ewan's face against the far wall. "We need proof before taking action. You won't last long enough out here to see the truth if you simply kill anyone who antagonizes you!"

"I don't care!"

Gabe's hand crushed him into the metal, threatening to break his own nose. "Damn you O'Meara, it's not about *you*! How many others have you endangered so far? How many more will you endanger, if you don't measure your actions?

Your purpose is to support the Centre, but you can't do that if you continue acting like a player!"

Ewan tried to push back, but he was exhausted...and Gabe was right. Scores of Veridians, deleted because he'd refused Gabe's help earlier that morning. His family, deleted because he'd treated the Gem as nothing worse than a behemoth. And now they were all paying for it.

*I've got to do better...I can't let the Diamond Lord be right.*

His tablet chimed.

"Fine," he growled. "Teach me about the real world."

Gabe released him, blue eyes hard as Ewan turned. "I will."

Ewan scanned the new message, and his heart froze. "Tree's got Kate," he breathed.

"Go," Gabe said.

Ewan ran.

He met Tree just outside the elevator, and the two of them pushed Kate's gurney to Medical as quickly as they dared. Ewan's gut twisted at seeing his sister, at once familiar and completely strange, with her red hair tangled up with the respirator pumping air into her body.

But Medical was filling with bodies, so many that the beds were already taken and the staff were tripping over more arrayed around the floor.

"Another one?" Nichols groused the moment they entered. "Angela, cardiac stimulant."

The nurse whistled and tossed Tree a syringe. "Just like the last one."

"Right." Tree uncapped the syringe, then slammed it down into Kate's chest. Ewan flinched in sympathy, but Kate was either too weak to react, or...

*No, she's got to pull through!*

"She's still alive," Tree said gently, reading his mind as she checked Kate's pulse. "But only just."

"If she's stable, bring her over here," Nichols ordered. He

threw them a blanket as a pair of nurses made a path through the less fortunate bodies. "Cover her; her skin's no protection."

Together, Ewan and Tree lifted Kate's form and transferred her to a space near the far corner.

The doctor knelt for a check of his own, then glanced at Tree. "Tell me this is the last of them."

Ewan glanced about, doing a quick head count. "Gabe said there were over a hundred fifty."

Nichols looked around his ward in despair, then set his jaw. "Treanna. Direct two thirds of the additional rescues to Hydroponics 2. Angela, take what you need and stand by there. I'll send Richard and Travis when they return."

"I'll help," Ewan said automatically, but as he stood, he caught sight of another familiar face coming through the doors. "Dad!"

Angela gave Jack O'Meara the stab treatment, but Ewan was already scanning the other faces until he found his mom on a bed by the wall. "Put him over there."

The nurse looked up. "There's no room."

"They're my parents! Please."

"They were the first to be deleted," Tree murmured, coming over to look at Jack's body with worried eyes.

After a moment of careful shuffling, they managed to wheel the gurney in beside Tricia's bed. Ewan stood behind the pair of them, heart thundering as if it could make up for theirs, as Tree and the others left him alone with Nichols and the players.

"Mom, Dad...hang in there," he whispered. "I'm here. Kate's here too; it's going to be okay."

But as the minutes passed and more players came in to demand the doctor's attention, Jack's skin paled even more. Nichols moved with frantic speed, but the stream of newly dying kept coming, even with most of them going to the spare ward in hydroponics. Ewan tried to help, but beyond stabbing the newcomers through the heart to welcome them to Earth, there was nothing he could do.

Eventually, the flow abated enough for Nichols to treat the O'Mearas. He checked them, then checked Jack a second time before looking up at Ewan with haunted, exhausted eyes behind the glasses: eyes that Ewan hadn't thought existed in the Centre.

The eyes of someone who knew the pain of watching a loved one slip away.

"No," Ewan whispered.

"I'm sorry," the doctor said quietly, making room for him. "Your mother received earlier treatment and stabilized, but..."

"No!" Ewan shouldered past him and looked down at their taut faces. A vein pulsed slowly and steadily in Tricia's neck, but Jack's showed only a tiny movement, weak and erratic.

"Dad! Mom," he called softly, pleading, as the doctor drew a paper curtain around them.

They didn't respond—couldn't respond.

"Dad!" The tears fell freely now onto his father's limp form. "Please, wake up. Don't go. I'm here, Dad. I got the Gem; he won't bother us anymore, okay? So you've got to hold on. You've got to see Tree and I get married! You said you wanted to!"

But the pulse only weakened.

Ewan took Jack's hand and placed Tricia's in it, clamping them together in his, willing them to recognize each other. "You've got to hold on for Mom!"

Neither of them showed any sign they'd heard. With a dread that hung from his heart, threatening to pull it out altogether, Ewan knew his father was in the last seconds of his life.

"I'm so sorry." He shook with grief and fury at his own impotence, at the cruel reality that Nichols hadn't had time to treat Jack properly, but most of all at his own recklessness, and

how the person he admired most in all the worlds had suffered
for it.

And now that person was going to die.

But even as his heart broke, Ewan could imagine hearing
his dad's calm, easy voice, offering him his own unhurried
thoughts. *I'm glad you could find it, Son. Truth and happiness, in
your own way. That's worth a death in my book.*

Ewan whispered, speaking aloud for both of them. "Thank
you...for showing me how beautiful the world is, for teaching
me to love it, mobs and all. I swear I'll keep on making you
proud...I love you."

He didn't know how long he sat there, holding his parents'
hands. Eventually, the pulse in Jack's neck stopped and did not
return.

But as Ewan wept, Tricia's pulse remained steady, offering a
mother's love and forgiveness with each beat. He continued to
hold her hand, squeezing it as hard as he dared, long after her
husband logged off into whatever next world was out there
waiting for him.

Eventually, Nichols slipped into the makeshift room and
placed his hand on Ewan's shoulder. "We've gotten everyone we
could," he murmured, before carefully draping the blanket over
Jack's face.

Ewan wanted to stop him, but he couldn't. "How many?"

"Sixty-five. We simply didn't have the resources."

Ewan's heart pumped out a few more tears, but behind
them came a hard determination that clenched his jaw.
"Promise me something: no one here gets liquefied. They get a
decent burial."

The doctor sighed. "That isn't—"

"Promise me!" Ewan snarled, whirling about to grab the
man's shirt and haul him close. "I know we all get eaten
eventually, but not like this! Not for these people! Let the

worms in the cages have them if you must, but bury them. They're human beings, and they deserve no less."

Nichols's eyes widened, but there was at least as much sympathy in them as fear. "I'll inform the Director of your 'request.' In your presence, so you'll know I made an honest effort. But right now, I need to attend to the survivors. Is that all right with you?" he added irritably, glancing down at Ewan's fist around his collar.

"Sure." Ewan released him, feeling suddenly hollowed out. "Thank you, Doctor."

"Call me Robert."

"Okay. Robert." Ewan offered him a weak smile, mollified by this more than everything else the chief had said. "Message me, though, will you? If anything comes up with my mom or sister?"

"I will."

Ewan made his way back out through the labyrinth, automatically counting the bodies, over half of which were covered by sheets. He didn't remember the walk back to his room, nor did he remember lying down in bed, but when Tree returned later, she snuggled up close against him without a word, just as she had in the mountains.

The staff was surprisingly lively the following week. A good number of Centrals came up to Ewan, asking for all the details. A few even thought to offer condolences, but he let Tree steer him away. He couldn't talk about it, not yet.

On Saturday, several hundred staffers assembled in the wormery adjacent to Hydroponics 2. Roughly twice as long as it was wide, the room's main feature was a massive tank, deep enough to take part of the floor below it. At the top, a five-foot wall in front blocked the view inside, but from his vantage point on the catwalk above, between the Director and Tree, Ewan could see the dirt fairly writhing, the animals within eager to consume anything the growers deposited in there.

*It's efficient, I'll grant that,* he thought grimly.

The moles had rigged up a second platform in front of them, on which rested one hundred two shrouded forms in a line, granted at least a modicum of privacy before the real world absorbed their corpses in its own way.

One hundred two names Ewan now had engraved onto his heart.

The Director tapped his tablet, connecting it to speakers brought in for the occasion, and a chime sounded—the same one players heard when respawning. Ewan looked at him in surprise, but the bald man only gave him the barest hint of a nod before turning to address the staff.

"Dear friends, we are gathered on this occasion to commemorate the lives of the players who perished as a result of an incident in the Veridor simulation. They may have been players," he said, glancing at Ewan, "but I have it on good information that they were no less human than we are. Indeed, it has been the work of our generations to preserve that quintessential spirit which they maintain in our Mother's exile. A moment of silence, if you please."

The Centrals bowed their heads as one.

After the moment had passed, Rothchild's amplified voice rang out again. "As you have no doubt heard by now, the incident was sparked by the intrusion of someone from the Centre, apparently with an agenda to prevent the players from coming to our aid." He paused for effect, giving the staff a chance to mutter amongst themselves. "It is our belief that this person used high-level system access to forcibly remove elements of that world. Chief Reid has kindly consented to lead the investigation. I ask you all to cooperate fully with him, so that the culprit may be apprehended."

Ewan's fists clenched. The inquiry had been a farce: Frasier smirking around his crooked nose as he explained that he'd hurt his ankle trying to exercise like the player and therefore had missed his shift, which Robert confirmed. Naturally, Frasier's tablet had no trace of Gem activity. In the end, lacking any conclusive proof but needing the game master's skillset, Rothchild had acquitted him of all charges—though he did issue a formal reprimand to Gabe for poor leadership.

In return, the chief immediately demoted Frasier to debugging the communications array.

Ewan shook himself back to the moment as the Director resumed speaking. "This incident illustrates precisely why the staff have been discouraged from involving themselves too directly with the simulations. But the genie is out of the bottle now, as the ancient saying goes. I ask that each of you consider temporarily sacrificing your mobility by going in-game, in order to allow the survivors a chance to recuperate before their eventual re-introduction."

A disgruntled murmur rippled through the crowd, but Ewan saw a few heads nod. Lisa, near the front, was hopping with her hand up.

"We are entering a new era," Rothchild continued, "one in which there will be traffic between the Centre and its charges. I expect each of you to behave with decorum and civility. I will hold the incoming players to the same standard," he added, giving Ewan a look. "Does our first emissary from the virtual worlds have anything to add?"

"Yes." Ewan leaned toward the tablet. "Thank you, all of you, for coming. I've walked among you now for the better part of a year, but I still can't begin to understand how hard it must be for you to stand vigil over the players." He hesitated, watching the crowd. "Especially since you were supposed to number among them."

There were mutters, but no one challenged it.

"On their behalf, I also want to thank all of you, from the deepest part of my soul, for giving us the chance to live happy lives. I promise to bring only the best of the virtual worlds to Earth, so we can share some of that happiness with you, who need it—deserve it—the most."

He turned his gaze to the row of bodies below, fighting to choke the words out while he could. "To my fellow Veridians. My friends, my family...I wish you a peaceful rest. May you respawn in a brighter place."

He stepped back, and the Director raised his hand. In response, Sam pulled a lever from his place at the tank's side. The platform swung down, allowing the shrouded bodies to slide gently into the waiting, famished earth.

Ewan looked at the corpse in front of him—his dad's corpse—and held up a small bouquet of flowers that Lisa had smuggled out of hydroponics for him. "Goodbye," he whispered as he tossed it down, unable to hold the tears back anymore.

Then, to his wonder, Lisa and Lucia each stepped up and threw their own flowers into the bin. Then more Centrals came, dozens of them, honoring the dead in a gesture that healed his broken heart even as he watered the new soil with his tears.

When it was over, Ewan and Tree headed to Medical, where Robert had rearranged the ward to better accommodate the remaining players. "O'Meara," he said briskly as the emissaries entered the now-darkened room. "Come here, please."

"Is something wrong?" Ewan asked anxiously, not sure he could do much more crying.

"Quite the contrary," the doctor replied. He ushered them into the back of the room, where he'd placed Kate beside her mother. "You come from good stock, it seems. They've already developed sufficient melanin to withstand normal lighting levels, but I've kept the lights low for now, to give them a rest."

He paused, stiffening as though embarrassed that he'd

shown empathy for a patient. "Anyway, look. Here," he said, gesturing Ewan to lean in close to Kate. "Tell me what you see."

"Hey, Sis." Ewan peered into her drawn face. The veins weren't quite as apparent, thanks to the radiation treatments, and her hair maybe looked a little fierier. "How are you feeling? We're here, Tree and I. Just wait till you see this place!"

The tendons in her neck twitched.

Ewan blinked, then looked up to see the doctor smiling. "No way—Kate, can you hear me?"

He watched her intently, hardly daring to breathe, then gave a cry of joy when her eyes very clearly moved behind their lids. "You're doing great! Even better than I did! Keep it up, okay? Once you're out of Medical, we can give you a tour!"

The emissaries stayed for a few minutes' visit, but as the conversation was one-sided, they eventually took their leave and headed home to spend the rest of the day together. As Ewan pulled off his Central grays, he caught the flash of his pin in the mirror and looked up, pausing to see a person he didn't quite remember from a year ago.

He was definitely leaner than his Veridian avatar, and maybe a little shorter, though it was hard to tell. But what got him most were the eyes: the brightness he'd had was now tempered, dimmed under the weight of experience.

*So much has changed.*

He smiled despite himself, recalling the flowers the others had thrown on the grave. He'd never have planned it like it turned out, but it was exciting to think of Veridians and Centrals going on a forced exchange tour. It could only help the two groups come to a better understanding.

Mutual respect, even.

And they needed to get there, as soon as possible. Only three days ago, Ben Root reported to the chiefs that one of the 'roos had stumbled across a Locust convoy moving in from the east. Thankfully they hadn't lost anyone, but the news was a grim reminder that time wasn't a luxury anymore.

In response, he and Tree had logged back into Veridor that afternoon to open negotiations, and true to his word, the Patriarch had heard her out. After a long discussion and a funeral service for the lost Veridians, he offered the Church's full support for the emissaries' mission. He even named Ewan the Central liaison of the newly formed Ether Corps, headed up by none other than Paul. When the Churchman also mentioned that Caleb had been arrested immediately upon respawning, Ewan gladly volunteered Gabe to nerf the disgraced commander's stats back to normal, once and for all.

"Hey," Tree said, coming over to rest her hand on his bare shoulder as she looked at him in the mirror. "What are you thinking about?"

"Oh...how much more we have to do."

"I know." She sighed. "It all seems impossible, sometimes."

Ewan smiled, catching a glimpse of that old brightness in his eyes after all. "Yeah. But I know we can do it."

She reached around to give him a hug from behind, and they stood there, holding each other in the small metal room, as images of the forest glade scrolled idly by on the computer's screen.

# EPILOGUE

Ewan stood at the edge of the square, awestruck by the crowd that filled it to bursting. The only way through was a narrow gauntlet of Swords, all wearing full armor, all watching him intently. He swallowed, offering the nearest one a nervous smile. As if in reply, a brilliant flame burst from the top of the cathedral's spire, bright and clear as the perfect summer sky above.

A fire that called him to his new home.

"They're ready, dear," Tricia murmured. She rested a hand on her son's armored shoulder.

Ewan swallowed again. "Um, yeah." He ran his fingers through his hair, but he'd already checked his appearance parameters a thousand times over with Alex that morning. "I wonder if she's nervous, too."

"I'm fine," Kate said from his other side, smirking. "Better than ever, actually, thanks to my Lil' Shockies."

Ewan winced. Even before she'd finished rehabilitation, Kate and Robert had worked out how to build some kind of electric iron maiden that zapped a recovering player's muscles into growing. Kate boasted they could take a player from comatose to combat-ready in three weeks, but Ewan only needed one look to be grateful he'd gotten the crutches-and-wheelchair treatment.

Not that they could afford to wait that long for the others. Not anymore.

He shook his head. "All right. Let's go."

The moment he stepped forward, the Swords nearest him drew their weapons. Gleaming steel swept up and out, forming an arched tunnel that rolled ahead, wavelike, across the square. Resisting the sudden impulse to turn and run, Ewan began marching, feeling the weight of every step. Every person present. Every person absent.

*Dad...you should be here.*

He cast back, thinking about the past month. Once the shockies were ready, he and Tree had logged in to visit each of Veridor's great cities, riding in Church carriages with Paul and a brigade of Swords in a strange mix of celebrity tour and Ether Corps recruiting, beginning in World's Edge. The coastal city extended a warm welcome to the former outlaws, and the guard captain, Al'Dashan, was the first to volunteer for Earth duty, previous murders and arrests forgiven at the prospect of glory to be shared in the real world.

He wasn't the only one.

After the Cardinal had shown them around, the emissaries set up in the square, pulled out their tablets, and regaled the Veridians with tales of Earth and the Battle of Whitehaven, as it was being called. And the people rallied, rushing to sign up and do their part to wreck the Locusts and take down the rogue Gem. Paul was happy to take their names, far more than Ewan would have guessed likely.

Far more than could fit in the Centre.

So it had gone, city after city, with the new recruits tagging along, so that by the time Ewan saw Whitehaven's spires again, he was leading an army in truth.

He glanced up as his current party passed the under the newly rebuilt statue—now depicting a pair of dual-wielding heroes, back to back. Somehow, the Whitehaveners had sculpted it during his tour without help from the bridge. He still couldn't quite believe it was real, simulation or not.

*How did you deal with it, Max? All the people's hopes, all their faith?* He sighed as he looked ahead to see a black stone wall behind the restored yew trees at the stairs' base. He'd been there when that went up, personally etching his father's name among the one hundred two Veridians who'd died for the Centre. So far.

*Did you feel like you didn't deserve it, either?*

He moved on, taking comfort from his remaining family as they walked with him. The Sword arch ended at the first step, with Paul and Al'Dashan doing the honors. The World's Edger watched him inscrutably, but Paul cracked a smile as he approached.

[Marrying a Gem...that's even scarier than getting logged.]

Ewan ignored him, already focused on climbing the steps. Ahead, the Patriarch waited in full regalia with the Amulet of Balance gleaming on his chest. As Ewan reached the top and Kate and Tricia moved to one side, the Churchman regarded Ewan stoically.

"Are you certain, child?"

Ewan swallowed. "Yes, Father."

The Patriarch nodded, and the Amulet vanished. Within seconds, dazzling light appeared, only three yards away. A gentle breeze flew from it, pushing the air aside to make room as the light formed into Tree. She wore a shoulderless gown of pure white, with her hair done up in a more elegant version of her usual bun. She took a deep breath, savoring the feel of her avatar's reappearance, then looked at Ewan with shining eyes.

He gave her his best rakish grin, sure her aura-reading had already tattled on his racing heart. [Hey.]

Director Rothchild appeared behind her, wearing full Central grays and a long wool coat that no sane Veridian would've worn this season. He blinked and stared up at the bright blue sky, eyes widening in wonder, before he turned to shake hands with the Patriarch. "It is an honor, your Holiness."

"The honor is mine, Director. On behalf of the Church of Veridor, I bid you welcome to our world."

[Gems of old,] Kate messaged as both men refused to let go first. [It's the Battle of the Pompous Old Guys!]

[Katrina!]

Ewan dared a glance back, but Tricia was covering her smile behind her hand.

"People of Whitehaven," the Director said, his voice magically amplified. "Your Patriarch informs me that he has already given the benediction but has kindly consented to allow me a few words. In the spirit of newfound cooperation between our respective peoples..."

Ewan tuned out the most powerful man on Earth, instead glancing over the crowd near the steps. Paul was still there, but now he had one arm linked with Tina—and the other around Lisa. Ewan blushed when both girls gave the new lieutenant a kiss on each cheek; then he jumped when Tree huffed beside him.

[They're like sisters,] he offered. They actually could be, for all he knew.

[Sisters don't share a boyfriend,] Tree countered, frowning as Lisa giggled at something Tina said. [Not in Veridor, at any rate.]

Ewan kept his mouth shut and searched out his other friends. Gabe wasn't there, called away on a scouting mission as part of his new second job heading up intelligence—a job he'd taken to get back into the Director's good graces. Sam was easy to find, seated on the step's edge and wearing a greasy apron. One of Kate's, Ewan realized with a frown. She'd made the mole a new leg as her first project in the real world, but how much time had they been spending together?

Sam noticed Ewan and shifted uneasily, then flinched when Kate snapped at him.

[What are you sitting for, Mule? You've got two good legs here, so use them.]

"Okay!" Sam said out loud, drawing puzzled looks from the people around. He stood quickly, bumping into Michael as he lined up his tablet for yet another picture.

[Smile,] the caretaker messaged, waving to get Tree's attention. [You're live on the bridge!]

She obliged him, trading a glance with Ewan. [I'm sorry. Grandfather doesn't know when to stop.]

[No worries,] Ewan replied. He glanced up at the sky, that perfect shade of blue he liked. [It's hard to believe we logged out a whole year ago.]

[It's been a busy one. Did you see this morning's war report?]

[Yeah.] He sighed, looking over white tunics in the crowd. His Swords, with no idea what they were getting into. [At least the shockies are up and running.]

[That's *Lil' Shockies*,] Kate sniped, jabbing him in the back. [Call them by their proper names.]

[I would, if you ever gave anything a proper name!]

[They've been invaluable,] Tree messaged. [Grandfather isn't likely to contest our choice of player recruits, after you.]

Tricia tsked. [I still don't like the idea of you living in that place, all alone.]

[Gems, Mom! Ewan's going to be right there!]

[I know, but he'll be busy with his marriage.] She placed a hand on Ewan's shoulder, turning him as if to check that he remembered the heart-to-heart she'd had with him on the topic just that morning.

[You're welcome to stay in the Centre, Madam O'Meara,] Tree offered.

Tricia's eyes flicked to her daughter-in-law-to-be, and her chin rose a hair. [No, thank you. My home is here, even if I'm the only one in it.]

Ewan's chest tightened. [I'll keep an eye on her, Mom. And we'll log in regularly,] he added when she didn't let go. [Promise.]

[If I might interject, our guest is nearing the end of his speech.]

Ewan blinked, then colored when he saw that the last message had come from the Patriarch. He quickly closed the window and did his best to look interested, but his eyes kept drifting back to Tree as Rothchild wound down.

The Patriarch clapped politely, then stepped forward as a priest herded the Director back behind Tree. "Dearly beloved, we are gathered here on this day in the presence of the Logos, to bear collective witness to the union of Ewan O'Meara of Veridor and Treanna Rothchild of Earth. Such union, esteemed and honored in all civilized realms, is not to be undertaken lightly." He glanced at Ewan one last time, a tiny smile playing at his lips. "But entered into with sobriety and a resolve to endure, no matter what the seasons of life and death bring. If any person can show why these two should not be wed, let them speak now or forever hold their peace."

Ewan automatically looked up, but no columns of fire were forthcoming.

"Very well," the Patriarch continued. "Who, then, will commit this young couple to their course?"

Tricia pressed Ewan's back, walking him to meet Tree as the Director did likewise. [I'm proud of you, dear,] she messaged, sniffing as she let go and stepped back to Kate. [Your father would be, too.]

Ewan choked back a tear of his own, but he couldn't dwell

on it, not with Tree standing only a foot away and smiling more than he'd ever seen her do. After a moment, he held out his hands. After a moment, she placed hers into them.

"Ewan," she said, softly at first until the Patriarch magically amplified her voice. "You've opened my eyes to wonders I never dreamed possible. You've nurtured hope in my heart, and love long forgotten in my world. Continue to be my hope, my conscience, my courage...and I will be forever yours."

*Frap*, Ewan thought as his mind raced to come up with a response. *She didn't tell me she was doing her own vows!* "Tree—Treanna...you've opened my eyes too. To wonders, in their own way." She stiffened, but he held tight. "You've nurtured me too, in more ways than I can count, but the most wonderful thing of all is that you looked at me and saw a real person to love. Um... keep seeing me like that, show me I can make a difference, and I swear to you I'll give you my best, no matter what life we're on or world we're in. I'm still with you, all the way."

The Patriarch stepped forward, resting his old hands across theirs. "Let all who have heard hold these two accountable. What they create together, let no one tear asunder."

He paused, turning to look at Ewan expectantly.

[E!] Kate messaged. [Here!]

Ewan glanced back, receiving a line-of-sight transfer, then smiled as he drew out a ring. Its center held a rich green bloodstone flanked by diamonds, above delicate bands of woven gold. Breathlessly, he lifted Tree's left hand and slipped the ring onto her finger, then let her do the same for him with a band of pure coresilver.

The Patriarch raised his hands. "By the powers and authority vested in me, I pronounce you husband and wife. You may kiss."

Ewan leaned forward and got bashed on the mouth as Tree flung herself at him, but the square erupted into roars and applause. The blood in his mouth vanished, replaced by the

cool tingle of her healing magic, and he kissed her back until
Kate messaged them to knock it off already.

Without a word, they walked hand in hand down the steps
as the Swords renewed their arch. In the morning, they'd
return to the Centre and deal with the escalating war, but it was
a new world out there. A world where players and Centrals
could coexist, sharing the best that each had to offer. A world
filled with promise, still buried miles under the Wastes, but
finally waking up again.

A world, Ewan knew, they would remake together.

## FIRST EDITION PROLOGUE:
## WAR'S END

MAXIMILIAN STRODE ACROSS THE MOONSPIRE'S DESOLATE
courtyard, with not even a ghost to waylay him. Ahead, the
great alabaster tower pierced the night sky a thousand feet
above. It was the center of the world, had always been, but now
it was also a tombstone for its creator's race. Would be.

Maximilian regarded it stoically. Resignedly. The only way
left was up; the only thing to do, make one last kill.

As if in reply, a silver flame blazed forth from the spire's
pinnacle, glittering brightly enough to rival the moon behind
him. A fire that had no place in this world, his world, anymore.

Maximilian's sole companion, a wizened light-skinned man
beside him, peered up as well. "The Diamond Lord expects us."

"Of course he does, Marcus." Maximilian grunted to cover a
sigh. He combed his fingers through his long, grizzled beard.
The gray he saw by daylight was gone, now. In the darkness he
trusted, darker than his own scarred skin, he was as young and
hale as ever.

On high, the flame pulsed and disappeared.

"Are you worried, old friend?" Maximilian murmured.

"Not for myself, no," Marcus replied. He gave Maximilian a

sideways glance. "After surviving five years of war, I can hold on for one more night. It is for you that I worry, Max."

"I'm fine." Maximilian lifted an amulet from his torn white tunic and ran a finger across its golden surface, tarnished in defiance of nature's will. Its etched lines depicted a map of the world, with precious stones inserted where the great Veridian cities were.

Where the Gems' palaces had been, before his Swords cast them down.

"The Diamond Lord won't fight," Maximilian said quietly as he tucked the amulet away. "Even if he tries, it won't do him any good. Not anymore. He knows it as well as I do."

The two men met no resistance as they reached the Moonspire's base. Maximilian led the way, climbing the great, seemingly endless stair, but each step carried him deeper into a catacomb of memories, all scorched by the fires of bitter war.

*How young was I, the first time I made this climb? How naïve?*

Like so many who grew up in the Moonspire's shadow, he'd chosen the adventuring path, braving the wild world and the perils it offered. Unlike the rest, he'd excelled at it, questing for the elite of Veridor and ultimately the Gems themselves as the Diamond Lord, chief deity of the Moonspire, took interest in his exploits.

In no time, they had become fast friends.

The toe of his bloodstained greave caught against the next step, tripping him, but he steadied himself.

It was far easier to remember the last time he'd climbed this stair. Maximilian had been at the height of his career. Everyone in Veridor knew of his prowess, bowed at his approach. The Diamond Lord welcomed him to the court, then dared him to cross the Argenones alone, promising armor to match the dark celestial steel of his swords, gifted years before, if he could reach the distant western coast within ten days.

Maximilian's fists clenched, bending the scorched, mundane steel of his gauntlets.

He should have seen the betrayal coming. The Sapphire Prince of the World's Edge had recently announced the construction of yet another monument to himself. Slavers had been hunting the area around the coastal fortress for weeks. That was normal, merely the consequence of the Gems flaunting their power. But they only harvested slaves from the peons within reach, never anyone who was anyone.

With a mere curse, the Sapphire Prince had reduced Maximilian to no one.

Pain shot up Maximilian's arm. He looked down to see his fist, implanted in the cracked stone wall on his right.

"Have faith," Marcus said gently, taking his arm to guide him. "The Logos will provide."

Maximilian nodded, but now he struggled to control his breathing, his heart. Unsure if the man beside him had spoken, here in the tower stair, or if the words were just another intruding memory. He felt rain, splattering his face and the bloody rags around his hands, as he and Marcus pushed a great stone slab through the mud. Heard the driver's whip crack, stumbled as the body of its victim fell against his back.

His lips trembled as he whispered prayer after prayer to the Logos, swearing with all his heart to put an end to his people's suffering, if only he could have his old strength back.

And the Logos answered.

The slaver's whip came for him next; in an instant, Maximilian was face-down in the mud. Already, feet were trampling him, rushing to fill the space, to forestall another mass execution. But there, half-covered in the muck, lying as though waiting for him to fall upon it, was the amulet. The moment he put it on, the Logos dispelled the Prince's curse. Then it granted him a vision of standing triumphantly over the Gems, with his swords at their throats.

With a fervent roar, Maximilian rose, knocking the other slaves aside. Wielding a strength he'd forgotten ever having, he strangled the driver with his own whip.

And the war had become his life.

"The Diamond Lord does have a nice view," Marcus observed, bringing Maximilian suddenly to the present as it was. The men had finally reached the Moonspire's top: a narrow landing, ringing a windowless central dome with a single door. "Perhaps we should leave this citadel intact, for a change?"

Maximilian shook himself to clear his thoughts, then gazed outward. The moon was sinking in the west, its bottom edge already clipped by the jagged mountain peaks beyond the farmlands. Much closer, his Swords' campfires burned in the fields, their orange lights a man-made reflection of the stars above.

"Do what you like, Marcus. There's only one thing I have left."

Marcus sighed and turned to the door. He knocked softly, then pressed it open when no response came. It pivoted soundlessly into the room, as though the air itself was made of silk, to reveal an unlit chamber within.

"Ah. Right on time," said a musical voice from the dark recesses beyond. Voices: a choir, speaking in unison. "Welcome. Patriarch, now, yes?"

"That is correct," Marcus replied warily. "Why do you wait in the darkness?"

"That, I fear, is the work of our champion."

Maximilian grunted, then removed the amulet from his neck as he stepped inside. At once, the room filled with soft light: hues of silver and blue, lazily intermingling in air that was suddenly permeated with mist. "There. Offer any resistance, and I'll kill you."

"Naturally...old friend." Seated in a throne of purest crystal, the only furnishing the room had, the voices' owner offered Maximilian a smile: a thin crease of the lips that seemed to lack the energy to touch his cool silver eyes or moon-pale face. The Diamond Lord stood slowly, spreading long fingers, unfurling the massive white wings anchored to his back as he towered over the mere humans.

"I have no weapon," he said softly.

"You are a weapon," Maximilian growled, "just like the rest of your kind. I've learned that well enough over the years."

The Diamond Lord's smile faded. "Yes, I suppose you have. But then, how do you view yourself? Maximilian 'the Great,' now wielding a power even greater than my own?"

Maximilian ignored the whispered answer from his heart. "Righteous."

"Righteous?" For an instant the Gem's face twisted, a visage of fury and torment that had Maximilian reaching for the amulet, but just as quickly, the face smoothed again. "Is that how you felt during the sack of Anthar?"

Maximilian glared at him. "They had it coming."

"I'm certain the women did, once your men broke through," the Diamond Lord said coldly. "An atrocity worthy of a Gem, was it not?"

"Don't liken me to your kind!"

"Then don't liken me to you!" The Diamond Lord's fists clenched, silver eyes now burning. "Will you still not recognize my support for your holy war, after five years? Your forces wouldn't have lasted the first winter, had I not granted them sanctuary in the Moonspire. Surely, even you can admit that much. Is it not the reason your people now call my home the White Haven?"

"It is," Marcus interjected, his voice cautious but respectful. "As the first Patriarch of the Church of Veridor, I speak for us both when I thank you for your help during this difficult transition."

Maximilian scoffed. "Call it what it was, Marcus: a years-long slaughter on both sides."

"That, it has been," the Diamond Lord agreed, feigning regret. "You cannot understand what has been lost."

"You should have brought the other Gems around," Maximilian growled.

The Gem leveled a glare at him. "And perhaps more of your people would have rallied to your cause, had your methods been gentler."

Marcus lifted his hand to still Maximilian's response. "We have returned with success from the jungles to the south," he said. "The Emerald Lady has fallen."

The Diamond Lord's voice became a soft requiem as the room dimmed. "I know. Did she die well?"

"Eventually." Maximilian pulled out the monster's snakelike fangs, then grinned at the Diamond Lord as he drew them down the slashes in his tunic. "Once she had nowhere to run."

Marcus shot him a chastising look. "You know why we are here, then, ancient one?"

"Of course," the Diamond Lord said. He took a slow breath, aware that he was approaching his last. "But after all that has transpired, I remain concerned for the fate of this green world."

"That's likely," Maximilian muttered.

"Believe what you will!" the Gem snapped. "Whatever else your histories will say of my race, know that we always labored to keep Veridor safe."

"You had an odd way of showing it," Maximilian countered, relishing the past tense of the statement.

The silver eyes dimmed. "I admit that. Nevertheless, it is the reason I insisted on your Church's creation, so that my authority would have a worthy successor."

Marcus bowed, slightly. "We have done our best to meet your requirements."

"Oh, you have, Patriarch. Your Church is all that I asked for. I simply pray it can withstand our absence."

"That's the idea," Maximilian said grimly.

The Gem regarded him, and Maximilian's chest tightened involuntarily at the exhaustion on that familiar face. The haunted eyes, searching for the future Maximilian had denied him. "I still care. From the moment my people first set your sun in motion, this world would have failed without our constant attention. But the situation has changed; now the time has come for us to withdraw to our own realm, for good or ill."

Addressing Marcus, the Diamond Lord said, "Before I depart, though, I give you this final warning. However independent you believe yourselves to be, you do not exist in a vacuum. You never have, and you never will. A day will eventually come when your kind must rise above themselves and make restitution, to we who sacrificed so much."

Maximilian's fists clenched. "It wasn't the Gems who've suffered!"

"We hear your warning and acknowledge the sacrifice you are making on behalf of our people," Marcus replied. "You have my assurance that we will rule this world well, and impart only our noblest traits onto our descendants."

"Then I must be satisfied and hope for the best." The Diamond Lord sighed, his eyes unfocusing as he gathered himself within. "Patriarch, I invest in you and your Church the powers and authority necessary to maintain this world, as it should be."

The room's ethereal light flickered, then stabilized.

"On behalf of the Church of Veridor, I receive them with our thanks," Marcus intoned, his own eyes unfocusing in turn as he processed the gift.

"Then my work here is finished, but for one thing." The Diamond Lord turned to Maximilian, looking as old and tired as the other felt as he stepped across the room to meet him.

"My friend. You who have seen and experienced the worst of gods and men. Your deeds have inflamed the imaginations of unnumbered souls, including many in my own realm. Know it or not, we are a formidable pair, you and I." He glanced over Maximilian's shoulder, at the swords strapped onto his back. The swords he'd awarded to Maximilian on the day they'd sworn friendship. "For years, you have battled for what you believe is right, tearing down the old so the farsighted can install the new."

Maximilian scowled up at him, bristling against his own heart's murmurs. "That battle's over, now. We've won."

"The battle is only beginning. You have no idea what you've started!" The Gem took another long breath and pressed his hands together, as though praying to some power even higher than he was. "Our Father has forsaken us in our arrogance. But perhaps the Mother will be forgiving for once, if only we can find the courage to face Her again. Courage, like yours."

The hairs on Maximilian's neck prickled. "What are you talking about?"

"You wouldn't believe me, Max, not unless you see it." A slow smile formed on the Gem's lips, easing some of the weariness. "And you need to see it. I need you, out there. Max... come with me. Please."

Maximilian blinked, but his stomach clenched. "What? To your realm?"

The Diamond Lord's silver eyes kindled. "Exactly! You don't belong here, any more than I do. You've proven that. Forget this world we've both outgrown, and help me create a new one, one that can support us all!"

Maximilian took a step back, caught off guard by the sudden desperation—the human desperation—in the voice. Since when had a Gem ever needed a human for anything?

Since when had a Gem ever said *please*?

Maximilian's battered heart stirred with a long-forgotten

curiosity. An eagerness, to explore the great unknown and wrestle it down. One last quest beyond the very pale of his world, with only the Gems knew what wonders and perils awaited.

But even as his blood flowed, it carried a bitter poison steeped in years of war. Years of betrayal and suffering laid at the Gems' feet, years filled with acts so vile, even his nightmares feared them.

Maximilian's fingers closed around the amulet. "I'm through running your errands."

The spark in the Diamond Lord's eyes flickered and died, leaving behind a defeated pity as he regarded the general. "I know...I know. In that case, I give you my body as the final casualty of this long conflict, along with a prayer that your descendants will one day be healed of your resentment."

Maximilian said nothing. There were no more words.

Returning the amulet to his neck and plunging the room back into darkness, he slowly drew his blades. Their black, meteoric steel flickered in Marcus's torchlight, as though they, too, had been scorched by the fires of war.

"Must you destroy me with my own gift to you?" the Gem asked sadly as he opened his arms wide.

Maximilian slammed the twinned weapons into the white chest: a final act of vengeance against the beings who had used him and his world as their playthings.

But the cry that echoed through the air was his own.

The Diamond Lord sank to his knees, pressed his brow to Maximilian's. Then he dissolved, lighting up the room one last time in a blinding flash.

Maximilian gasped and fell to his knees in turn. The wrath of years was finally expended, but it left him hollow, unable to ignore any longer the void it had spawned in his own heart.

*The world will know me forevermore as the hero who destroyed the Gems.*

Marcus walked to him and held his torch out, watching his companion's face. "That wasn't like the others," he said quietly.

Maximilian could only stare at the empty space where his friend had been.

"It's almost a pity he's gone," Marcus continued into the silence. "We owe him much."

Maximilian let out a slow, shaking breath. He took the amulet off and held it up, looking numbly at the fresh blood coating the diamond at its center. "He was right about one thing."

"Oh?"

"I've become a worse monster than the Gems ever were. I've got to get rid of the amulet."

Marcus was very still. "Are you certain?"

Maximilian held back his tears, forcing them instead into the emptiness in his chest. "More than anything. Veridor is better off without it." *Or me. I should have gone with him.*

"If that is what you believe is best," Marcus said.

He placed a comforting hand on the general's shoulder, but Maximilian ignored him and stood, feeling stiffer than he ever remembered. He needed to sleep. To sleep forever, though now, the Logos would deny him that for years to come.

*Gems above...my friend!* he prayed, crying out in his broken soul now that it was too late. *Can you hear me, even now? Can you take me with you?*

But no answer came. No answer could.

Without another word, the men returned down the long stair. In the morning, Marcus—the Patriarch—would announce the end of the war and the beginning of a new world. A world without divine masters or a fragmented, strife-driven society. A world without grand quests, in which adventurers would become a dying breed.

A world without Maximilian or the Gems, despite it being the world they'd made together.

# Evening Song

Ewan O'Meara

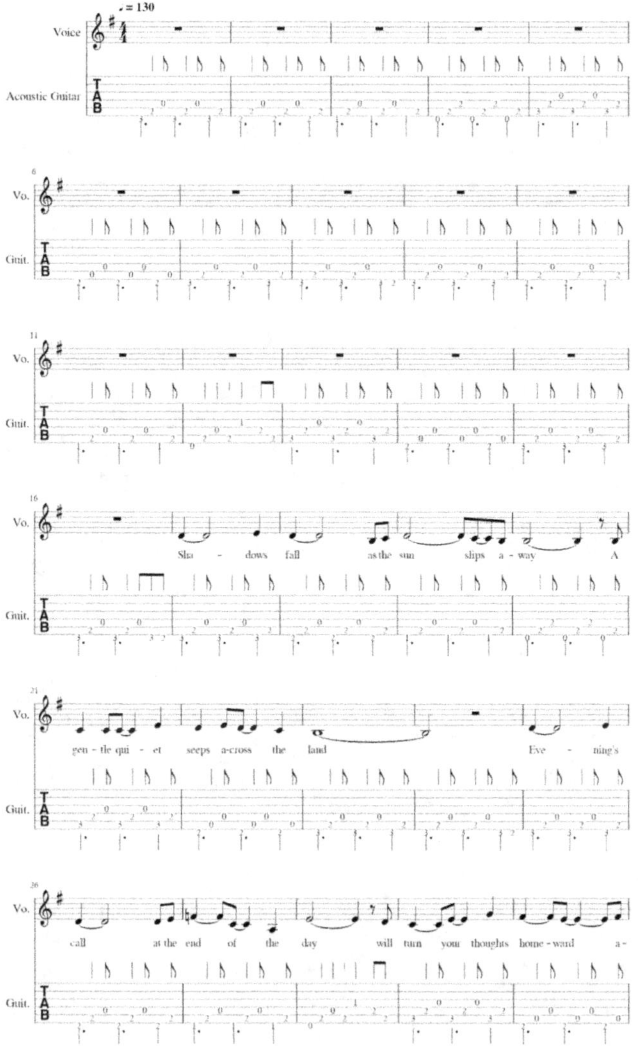

gain     The world     set-tles down     as the light     fades and
dies     and wear-i-ness     be - gins to bow     your     head
Drift-ing from     the     town     you can     hear the muf - fled     cries     of     child-ren be - ing
head - ed to     their     beds     But when the light     of     day is gone     the
stars     can tru - ly     shine     Their flick' ring light     made     of     the stuff     of
dreams     A hid - den world     re - veals     it-self     to

Vo.
Guit.
those who make the time It teach - es us the u - ni-verse runs
deep - er than it seems In - sects sing in the
air cool and clear Their mu - sic e - choes through the dark - ened
sky Bats - take wing as the birds dis - ap -
peat To ride the winds a - bove the branch - es high But
as more crea - tures stir si - lent phan - toms in the night You

real – ize that     the fam – il – iar world     is     long     since     dead     and     gone     Your
heart     is gripped     by     fear     and     it     beats     with all     its     might     Re –
mind – ing you     how     far     you are     from     home     But     when     the dark – ness
seeps in–to     your     soul     do not cry     Don't     give     it pow – er to     rob     you of     your
mirth     Al – low     the night     to     teach     you that     the
rea – son we     all     die     is     so     we can     ex – per – i – ence     the     won – der of     re –

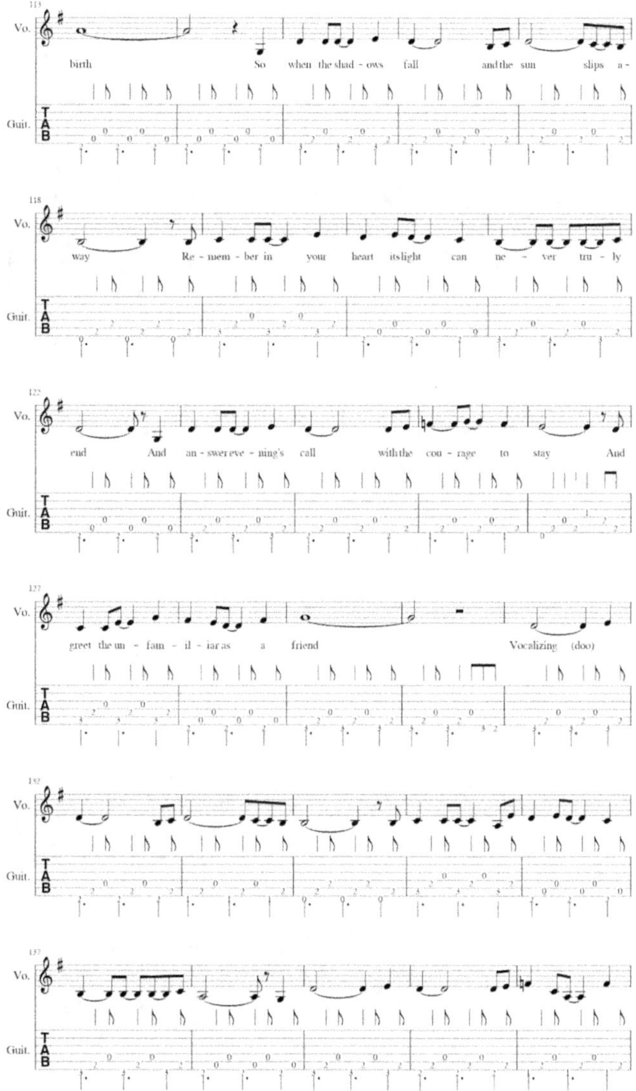
Vo.
Guit.
birth So when the shad - ows fall and the sun slips a -
way Re - mem - ber in your heart its light can ne - ver tru - ly
end And an - swer eve - ning's call with the cou - rage to stay And
greet the un - fam - il - iar as a friend Vocalizing (doo)

# Birthday Song

Traditional Veridian

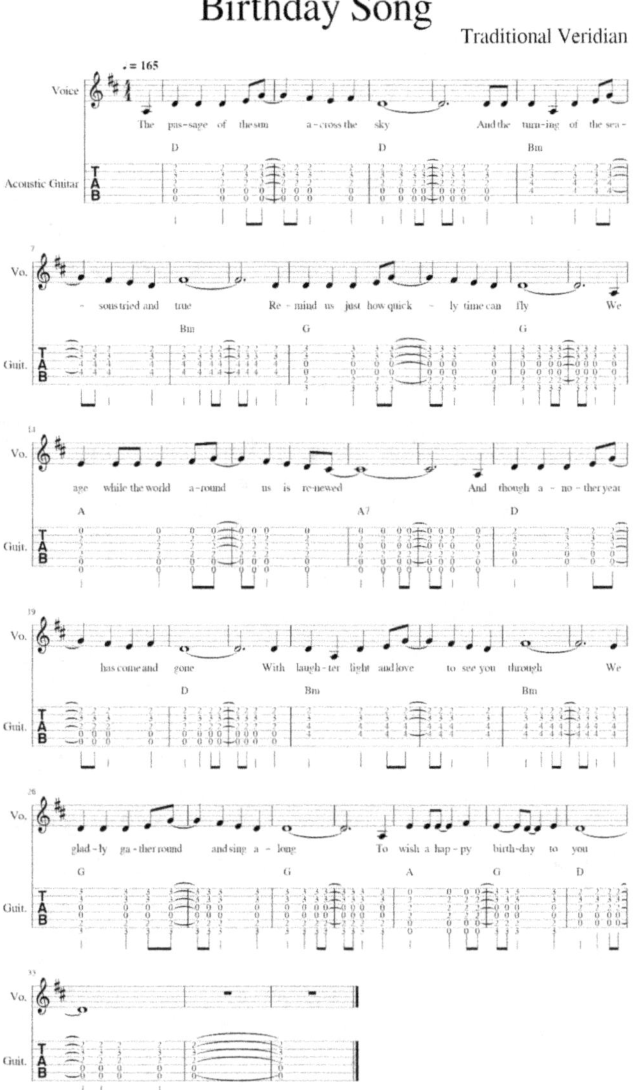

# ACKNOWLEDGMENTS
## (2ND EDITION)

As with the first edition...where do I begin? So much has changed both for the story and in the world at large, yet the core conflicts and themes remain constant and more relevant than ever. My own writing skillset has continued to grow, and feedback from the first edition pointed out some unintended issues that I'm grateful to have the chance to correct now.

I had several reasons for updating this novel: updating the cover art to reflect a series design; adding an epigram to match styles with the sequel, *Sandstorm*; correcting oversights in character descriptions to make them clearer and more inclusive; and showing the Central culture as being quietly more warm and caring than Ewan's perspective assumed. I couldn't resist the temptation to write an entirely new prologue, because just like for the main story, the second telling is best from Tree's perspective. The end result is a book that has changed slightly, so that it could change a great deal for the better.

*Emissary* has been a fixture in my life for almost a decade, now: the catalyst for my growth as an author, husband, father, and human being. I could easily say that anyone I've ever spoken with, anyone who's inspired me or revealed a piece of the world to me, deserves mention here. But that's a cop-out, as Ewan might say, so I'll try not to forget anyone obvious below.

First of all, I thank my children, Elanor and Bridget. The way their eyes lit up all those years ago, when I first read aloud the Duel of Ewan and the Behemoth, is fundamentally what inspired me to chase this story. Watching them grow up as my story matured has given me no end of joy and comfort. I wrote *Emissary* for them, to show them that one could always work to improve even the bleakest of worlds.

I thank my extended family: my sister Lauren and her husband, Ben; my stepsister Lily, who suffered through the early alpha drafts before I had a clue what I was doing; my mom and stepdad, who probably would have said they liked it no matter what nonsense I wrote (but it's good to hear, all the same!). I thank my sister Marian, who was too busy raising toddlers to finish the first edition but took the time for this current version. I thank my dad, who had the sense to say a book about video games wasn't his cup of tea, but whose constant admonitions to my childhood self that "life isn't a video game" certainly contributed to this book, somewhere.

I thank the writing community on Twitter for their warm welcome back in 2018, and the many online author friends who became invaluable beta readers, able to offer feedback from both a reader's and writer's perspective. In alphabetical order: Rebecca Fryar, Sarah Joy Green-Hart, C.D. Hanson, Laura "HippoCook" H., Sydney Kennedy, J.E. Klimov, and J.E. Reed. Thank you all, for helping me make this story shine! On the topic of colleagues, I also thank David Walker, for reading over my creative work on top of my scientific writing.

Likewise, I thank the freelancers who helped me bring the images in my mind to life. Soraya Corcoran, who patiently let me nitpick every last detail of her amazing maps of both Veridor and the Wastes. Anna Crews, who upgraded my pencil sketches of the various emblems and insignia into full and flexible line art. And, on the copyediting side, thanks to Tim Marquitz for his fresh set of eyes and thought-provoking feedback on the myriad capitalization conventions I'd created! Thanks to Kirk DouPonce for the cover art of the first edition, and Julisa Basak, who took that cover art concept and brought it to a new level in her own amazing style. Here's to amazing matching covers for the rest of the quintet!

Last and most important of all, though, I thank Kristina Brooks for being my wife, critique partner, and best friend. I fell in love with her stories, even as I fell in love with her. We've spent countless nights sitting together, writing drafts into the evening and sharing them in all their rough glory, and countless nights since, taking stories that we know backward and forward and reading them yet again to make them that much better. Kristina didn't just inspire me to write. She showed me how stories are the paths of the soul, and I remain forever grateful to her for getting to share each and every one we discover.

# ABOUT THE AUTHOR

E.B. Brooks started crafting his debut novel, *Emissary*, in 2014, while working as a scientist to monitor landscape changes and make projections into our world's likely futures. He lives in the southeastern United States, building his house and homestead with his wife, two children, and many pets.

You can find out about his other stories at EBBrooksFiction.com.